Pixie Dust

Pixie Dust

Henry Melton

Wire Rim Books
Hutto, Texas

Pixie Dust ©2010 by Henry Melton
All Rights Reserved

Printing History
First Edition: April 2010
•215

ISBN 978-0-9802253-8-9

Website of Henry Melton
http://www.HenryMelton.com

Cover art by Arthur Wang
ArthurWangArt.com

Printed in the United States of America

Wire Rim Books
http://www.WireRimBooks.com

Thanks for all the help in getting this tale through all its incarnations: Jim Dunn, Linda Elliott, Alan McConnell, Chris Meadows, Mary Ann Melton, and Mary Solomon.
Additional thanks to the Spanish Teachers at Hutto High School, the workers at Ledel Carnival Midways in Ft. Worth, and the friendly people of the many little towns and cities of West Texas.

Dedicated to my parents, Gene and Evelyn Melton, for their quiet wisdom, endless patience and unwavering support.

Contents

Issue 1: Origin Story

1

"Jase!" Jenny Quinn skidded off the two-lane county road onto the gravel, skidding to a halt with both little feet shoving hard on the brake pedal. Her Professor Williams staggered on the shifting wooden boards of the trailer, nearly missing his grip on a wide yellow strap. Like a giant stainless-steel ball-bearing, the shiny bright eight-foot tall tank was straining for the sky, only held back by the web of straps. *I was only gone fifteen minutes! It's already strongly negative!* Jase, wrench in his free hand, was working on the bolts that held the orange-slice sections of the zero-point chamber together.

She jumped out of the car, dragging the parachute behind her. It was bulky, hard for someone four-feet ten to carry.

"Get back!" He growled, glancing up from his task. His penetrating dark eyes chilled her. In the three years she had worked for him, he'd never appeared frightened before. She'd rented the parachute from the crop duster down the road as a joke. Now, she gripped the straps even tighter.

"What are you doing, Jase?" She stepped closer. She wasn't about to stand back and watch.

"If I can open the chamber, and let the stuff out, maybe I can save the chamber itself. Now keep clear. It's dangerous."

Jenny could see that the yellow straps were taut. He'd lashed ropes around the nearest trees to hold the trailer down. With every shift in position, they were stripping bark from the trunks. How had the chamber gained so much negative weight in the short time she was gone?

"I mean it Jenny. Stay clear."

"I can handle a wrench. And besides," she smiled, "I have a parachute. It looks like you just might need one."

She grabbed a strap and pulled herself onboard. The trailer bounced like the surface of a trampoline. Wheels were off the ground and every movement sent the platform rocking. She clipped the parachute around a low guardrail, and dug into the toolbox.

"You just sent me on a wild goose chase to get rid of me! The crop duster pilot said he didn't know anything about an FAA alert line."

He didn't answer, concentrating on freeing the bolts. Another one came free and dropped to the wooden bed of the trailer with a thud.

"I appreciate the effort to keep me out of harm's way, but I'm having too much fun!" Her socket wrench made quick work on the first bolt.

After a pause, he said tensely, "I broke the vacuum seal, hoping that it would act like a gas and escape. No luck."

"It's a solid inside?"

He shook his head, "No conjectures. Maybe the inside lining itself has been altered. I don't know."

Some kind of exotic matter is breeding inside, and you want to see it! You would risk being launched into space to do so. "Jase. You're crazy!"

"And who is riding this bucking horse with me?"

She felt a little dizzy, and gripped the strap a little harder. How many hours had she been at this? She had come on duty, monitoring the experiment, at ten PM last night. It was now well past noon. Once she had noticed the massive vacuum chamber getting lighter, her eyes had been jammed wide awake as if running a caffeine drip straight into her veins.

This was not at all what Professor William's experiment had predicted. The radiation detectors she had personally designed, lining the inside of the chamber, had still not detected a single event. This negative weight was new physics.

We should have asked for help. Jase never trusted anyone outside of his small circle of graduate students. He liked being a father figure. Jenny chaffed at the relationship. She risked another look at the intense concentration on his face. His dark hair was traced with new gray, but he wasn't old. Not really. This close, she could feel his presence.

The crack of abused wood was louder than a gunshot, and just as startling. Jenny dropped her wrench, and almost fell as one end of the trailer rose. The steel chamber, repelled from the earth, was trying hard to escape into space. One of the ropes had broken free. It was going to fly, and it was going to carry anything attached to it along. She dangled from a strap, the chamber now above her.

"Jenny! Jump free!" Jase held on with a death-grip of his own.

"I'm okay!"

But the rope on the other tree only took a couple of jerks before it snapped a secondary branch then ripped free. Her stomach told her first, and then the wind. They were climbing!

At first, all she could do was to hang on. They were tumbling like a leaf in a storm. Her end of the trailer, with the hitch and the fork, was the heaviest and for a heart-stopping moment, her legs dangled over nothing but air and the shrinking green landscape below. Speed increased. Ugly aerodynamics and shifting weight threw them into a spin.

The car below traced a circle in the green. If the spin got much faster, Jenny knew that she would be thrown clear.

The parachute!

She forced herself to focus on the trailer. The world outside was a nightmare of spinning blue and green.

There it is. Still clipped to the railing, she saw it flapping in the wind. *I need to get over there.*

She clamped her teeth together. *Do it step by step. Make no mistakes.*

Over the wind, she heard Jase cry, "Jenny!"

"I'm here!" she replied, but she didn't look for him. No time for that.

A steady hold took two hands. To get to the parachute would take hand over hand climbing through the web of straps. There was a scream, bubbling in her chest, waiting to break free. She tried to pull herself around the restraints. Fighting the wobbling spin, she hooked her leg over a strap.

A shoe came loose, falling away like a leaf in a hurricane. *Forget it!* She had to inch down to the railing. The sun had become a streak in the sky orbiting around them.

Just then, the tumble changed again. The trailer started flapping hard, in a one-second rhythm. Even over the wind, she should hear the chamber slam against the wooden bed. *It's going to break!*

The flat yellow strap in her hands tensed and relaxed under the stress. The trailer slammed hard again, and she was flung to the side.

Jase! She could see him now.

He too was crawling toward the parachute, but that last shock must have loosened his grip. He was hanging on to the railing by one arm, his other arm and legs sticking out into the air from the centrifugal force of the spin.

She froze up. Nothing she could do would make her hand loosen. She couldn't move to the next handhold.

Jase looped his arm around the railing. He pulled himself towards the parachute. When he got close enough to snag the flapping bundle, she realized she was holding her breath.

Move, she ordered herself, and turned her will to the task at hand—getting herself down to the railing.

She didn't make it.

The strap she held tightly went from taut to loose in an instant. CRACK!

The bed of the trailer slapped the sphere hard. Jenny could see the gap widen where they had removed the bolts. Brute force was shearing off the remaining ones.

The metal ball was opening up.

What was that? Sunlight reached inside the ball. Something—something indistinct, was blurring the light.

She turned to Jase. He had paused in his struggle for life with the parachute straps. With her, he stared at the mystery inside.

CRACK! CRUNCH! Snap!

In less than a second, the trailer bed slapped the chamber broadside, scattering fragments of lumber to the winds. Then, one of the yellow straps broke free of its mooring. Like a seed popping out of its pod, the chamber slipped free.

Time slowed by adrenaline, she watched the two halves of the sphere open up like an oyster.

The pearl, a ball of concentrated heat haze, the shimmering embodiment of mirage, hung before her for just an instant.

Then it exploded.

There was no noise, no flash, just a stinging throughout her body, instantly gone. She was flung free of her lifeline. The trailer went one way, the pieces of the chamber scattered off in other directions. Jase, with the parachute, went tumbling head over heels.

She was alone in the sky. Falling.

2

Wind-whipped hair stung her face. She was disoriented and lost. *Like when Joe died.*

The three of them, her mother, her father and she had been blasted apart by another kind of explosion from out of nowhere. Her stomach had been in freefall then as well and she'd never really recovered from her brother's death. She had felt like dying herself.

But this time it's for real.

"Jase!" she screamed in panic. The rest of her cry was wordless, mindless. Only the whistle brought her back.

The wind! It was slowing. The physicist in her latched on to the data. *Freefall, but I was falling up!*

The chamber had dragged her into the sky, still climbing.

Jase. Where is Jase?

The ground was that way. She could feel the moment of stillness come and go. She was falling for real now. Jase had the parachute. She had to find him.

She blinked her eyes hard. The wind would turn them blurry again soon enough.

There! That's the trailer. Seconds later, she saw a glint of light that could only be a piece of the chamber.

The wind was growing, and she fought her fear. *Is he above me, or below?* She was lighter—he was larger.

She'd never skydived before. *Learn fast.* She moved into a spread-eagle like they did on TV. Her spinning stopped. Movement caught her eye.

Jase was below her. If he hadn't been tumbling, she would never have spotted him.

How did James Bond do it? She couldn't remember which old movie, nor which Bond actor, nor which enemy, only the ridiculous handrails on the outside of the airplane for the actors. Bond had been in freefall without a parachute, just like her.

She held her arms in tight, and felt herself dropping faster. It was a start, but she quickly overshot his position. She tried to stop and threw herself into a spin.

How high am I? How much time do I have?

She fought the spin, knowing she had to get back under control. Jase's loose tumble had her worried. She turned in the air, and started back for another run at him. She missed again.

On the third pass, she snagged the shoulder strap on the parachute and tried to pull herself in closer, in spite of the spin it caused.

He was unconscious, with a bloody mark on his head. The explosion had thrown him against something on the trailer, or maybe a piece of the chamber had struck him.

Jase wake up! I'm not strong enough for this. She checked the straps and felt her insides twist when she realized that he hadn't managed to secure the straps. The chute could have slipped off his shoulder at any time.

They tumbled slowly together. Jenny couldn't spare the time or effort to do anything but find the buckles. With a click that she felt, rather than heard, she finished the job.

I have to hold on! There would be a strong jerk when the parachute opened, and there was no way she could get a strap around her.

A glance at the ground—everything was sharp, not hazy from distance—was clear warning. *No time.*

She twisted one arm through the shoulder straps. The other had to be free. She closed her eyes and pulled the big metal handle.

Jenny could see the fabric coming out, but her whole being was centered on holding Jase in a tight embrace, one that nothing in the world could pull apart.

Pop! The sheet blossomed overhead. Her free arm slipped. Pain in her other shoulder was the welcome sign that she had survived. She grabbed at his belt and pulled herself back into a bear hug.

For a long grateful moment, she relished the relative silence, the feel of the man in her arms, and the pull of gravity at her feet.

Jase moved his arm. "What?"

"Jase, you're alive!"

He thrashed arms and legs. She concentrated on holding on.

"Jase. Calm down. We're together on a parachute. Don't knock me off!"

"Parachute! What happened?" He put his arm around her.

"Can you remember? The chamber took us up."

"Yes. Dark matter explosion. Then...."

"It knocked you out. I learned to skydive. You've got to land us. I can't see anything but the button on your shirt pocket."

"My head hurts."

"It's bloody."

"But I can see a farm house. Metal roof."

"Can you steer these things?"

"Maybe." He moved his arms, and she was once again holding on to him by herself. He pulled on something, and the parachute turned slowly in the air.

She gripped tighter, stifling the irrational feeling of abandonment when he had removed his arm from around her.

Jase had been her anchor from the first year she had arrived at the university. In spite of the man's academic reputation, he still enjoyed teaching undergraduates, and that first year introductory course had caught her imagination like nothing else. After that, she managed to take as many classes as she could from him and to attend all the colloquiums where he was a presenter. When he took her into his circle of graduate students, she had never been happier.

He had been married—she had found out from the rumor mill—and he dated, but never his students. Jenny had absorbed that piece of information with stoic acceptance. He really was too old for her, and her interest in him wasn't romance, it was the exciting exchange of minds. It was just platonic.

But that didn't stop her occasional daydreams.

"The ground is coming up. I'm aiming for a flat open field, but it'll be rough."

She renewed her hug, laid her head flat against his chest, and closed her eyes. There was a shift in their momentum, almost as if they were climbing, and then they hit.

There an instant of pain in her shoulder, then a confusion of light.

Her first clear thought was of being flat on her back in a field of small sharp rocks, and grass so dry it snapped at the touch. Jase was standing over her, still trailing the parachute cords.

"Are you okay Jenny?"

She blinked at the sun. "Yes. I think I blacked out."

He sat down, a little too hard. "I need to get this thing off. The wind is trying to catch it."

She got slowly to her feet, conscious of her body. There was a new bruise on her leg, and her shoulder felt like it was sprained, but she was alive. One-handed, she helped him out of the harness.

They were going to need help. She reached for her cell phone in her jacket pocket, but somewhere in the craziness, it had slipped out. Air flipped a few yards of cloth over and she turned to chase it. Her shoulder protested.

"Do you think you can fold this up? I'm not going to be much help, and if I get it damaged, I'll never get my purse back."

While she had tried unsuccessfully to explain to the crop dusting pilot that she needed to send a warning to the FAA about an 'experimental rocket launch', she had noticed the parachute. What a cute joke on Jase, she thought! She would wear it while they struggled with their homegrown 'Cavorite'. The pilot had been reluctant to let her take it, not without collateral.

The parachute had been an excellent idea, but hardly a joke.

He was unsteady, but he nodded. "Don't worry. You saved my life. I won't let you lose a penny."

"I saved my own life."

"Don't argue. I was careless, and I would be dead now if you hadn't acted. That's good enough for me."

Neither of them were in any shape to take on the world. Under questioning, Jase admitted to double vision and dizziness. Her shoulder was swelling, and the spreading pain from it was threatening to take over. They were only half-done folding the chute when the pickup arrived.

"What're you doing here?" Asked the rancher, with a scowl.

Jase spoke, "We've had an accident."

The rancher looked them over again. "What happened here? I thought you were skydivers, but they all wear those jumpsuits. Was there a plane crash?"

Jase shook his head, "No, it was a science experiment."

The scowl deepened. "I don't understand this. Did you jump out of a plane?"

"It's a complicated story, an accident."

He crossed his arms. "You tell me, or tell the sheriff. You're trespassing on my land."

Jase sat back down in the dirt. He shook his head. "We're from the government. It's all secret. There won't be a thing in the papers about a crashed airplane. It will all be covered up."

The rancher laughed, after a few seconds. "Aliens, right? And people who dress in black suits with sunglasses will come by and flash lights at me? I saw that movie. It was a hoot."

Jase smiled. "No, not quite. Businessmen with lawyers."

The rancher twisted his face into a grimace. "I'd rather have the aliens." He looked at Jenny. "You're hurt. Come on, get in."

They rode back to their car in the bed of the rancher's pickup.

"Why did you make it sound like a spy story?"

He shrugged. "I can't think straight. I had to tell him something. Sometimes reality can't be believed." He smiled. "The scariest part was the punch line."

Jenny didn't pursue it. Her father was a corporate lawyer, and she had mixed feelings about that.

"The important thing," Jase added, "is that we keep this absolutely secret. There are many players in this game. If we lose control, we could find ourselves on the outside, locked away from our own discovery."

The rancher stopped the pickup and they climbed out, he followed, looking high and low over the wide place next the road. His eyes latched on to the destroyed trees, their freshly skinned trunks and the smashed branches scattered widely over the ground. He gave them a wide-eyed look, and then without a word, got back into his truck and drove off.

When they returned to the campus health clinic, Jase's story mutated into a mountain-bike spill. He was much better by then, and he blustered past their concern that he had a concussion, although the knot on his head had swollen to quite a bump.

Jenny let him do the talking and spin the lies. Her own pain sapped all the energy out of her. She was ordered home for bed rest. Jase drove her. Taking her pain pills, she crashed fully dressed onto her bed.

There was a test in Spanish class, and she hadn't studied. It was a semester test, and it would destroy her class standings. She grabbed for her texts, but there was nothing in the pile but her comic books. She thumbed through page after page of superhero action, but all the text balloons were in Spanish and she couldn't understand a word. The class bell was ringing and ringing and ringing.

Jenny tried to reach for the alarm clock, but the pain in her shoulder was too intense. She blinked her eyes free of sleep.

The phone. She reached across with her good right arm and picked it up. "'Lo?"

"Jenny! Where is Professor Williams? The lab is locked up." It was Ben Mitchell.

Jenny looked over at the clock. *Had it only been just this morning?*

But what was she to tell Ben? Jase had been firm. Keep the incident just between the two of them. Ben didn't know the chamber was lost, not yet at least, but there was no way he wouldn't find out. Tell him that much of it.

"I was there this morning. Jase loaded up the chamber and relocated it."

"What? He can't do that!"

"He can. He did. It's his project."

"That's crazy! I needed to be there to shut down the vacuum properly. It could wreck my whole Master's project. Were you there when he did that? Did he follow the steps in my notebook?"

"I don't think so, Ben. It was just—close the valve and turn off the power switch."

"Oh no! The getter chamber is probably ruined. Did he...."

"Ben, I'm in bed, tranked out on pain pills from a wrenched shoulder. I can barely talk. You'll have to ask Jase."

He grumbled on the phone and hung up. She was so grateful to be free of the questions that she was willing to overlook his distinct lack of interest in her injury.

Ben had never been sociable, for which she was thankful. He just wasn't her type. Geeks with a one-track mind, focused on the problem of the day, were valuable people to have in your team, but they made poor conversationalists. When they did have something to say, they were so intent on making their point that they often didn't notice whether you were agreeing with them or not.

I miss Gary. She hadn't met anyone like Gary Russel here at the university. Gary had been the closest thing to a real boyfriend back in high school. They had common interests. They could talk on for hours about any subject in the world. Yet, when the final day of their senior year passed, they never met again.

Jenny felt her own failure to call was reasonable, given the trauma her family was going through, but why had he never called her? Did they just outgrow each other?

Or maybe he was never interested. Comic books had brought them together, and when that faded, there was nothing else. *Maybe no one has ever been interested in me.*

Jenny turned off the alarm clock and changed her luke warm ice bag for an electric heating pad. She took a double-dose of ibuprofen and went back to sleep.

R ing! *I thought I turned that off.*

If Jenny had been dreaming, it vanished in the noise.

Phone. She fumbled for the receiver. *If it is Ben again....*

"Hello."

"Is this Jennifer Quinn?" A lady's voice.

"Yes. What is it?"

"This is the Dean's office. I'm afraid there is some bad news."

She fumbled for the light switch on the nightstand.

"What is the problem?"

"There has been an accident. I am afraid Professor Williams has been killed."

3

Jase? Dead?

"I think there has to be a mistake. He was in a bicycle accident."

"No. I am sorry to say that there is no mistake."

Oh no. He did have a concussion. There was a brain hemorrhage. It is all my fault.

But the lady from the Dean's office wasn't finished. "I have been told it was an accident at the Plasma Confinement Lab. He fell from a high scaffolding."

Jenny's mind was a blur. "Are you sure?"

"Yes, my dear. There were several witnesses. He was talking to Professor Hausman at the time. The police were called. There is no question."

Jase? Dead?

Jenny was able to mumble "Thank you."

"Is there anything we can do for you?"

"No. Bye." She hung up the phone.

Jase, what were you doing? She felt a burst of anger. He had no right to leave right now.

Where does that leave me? What do I do now?

She checked the clock. Ten AM She had dark window shades to help her sleep during the day, since she had the nighttime shift on Jase's project.

Jase's project! There is no project, not now. Jase is dead. I don't even have a job now. Angrily, she reached for the alarm clock and reset the alarm from 10 PM to 6 AM *No more night shifts for me!*

She slammed the clock down on the nightstand. The glowing digits flickered and died. She had broken the clock.

Jenny picked up the rebellious piece of plastic and heard the rattle of something loose inside. *So, you abandon me too.* She threw it as hard as she could. The power cord snagged on the stand and threatened to knock it over. The clock made a splintering noise as it hit the floor.

Her sore shoulder twinged at the exertion.

Jenny collapsed with her face in her pillow, and cried.

Ding-Dong. Ding-Dong. Ding-Dong.

Jenny opened the door. The beginning of a greeting froze on Rae Bellamy's dark expressive face. "I see you've heard the news."

Jenny nodded. She ached too much to make either a smile or a frown. "They called a couple of hours ago. Come on in."

Rae made an effort to support and comfort, but it was clear the death was an exciting event on campus. Rumors were flying fast. "And I heard," she smiled slyly, "one version that said he committed suicide over one of his female grad students."

Jenny barked a harsh, short laugh. *And I bet you would love to hear me confess that it's all true.*

She shook her head sadly. "Jase wasn't that type."

"Which type?"

"The type to commit suicide."

"Oh. But what about the other part? Did he show any interest?"

"Rae, you are shameless. But the answer is 'no'." Jenny took in a breath, "Oh, he was charming enough. He was nice to be around. But it was always … business." She could barely speak the sentence through.

"No student-teacher relationships?"

"Rae, the subject never came up! If he had any deep feelings for me, he hid them well. He hid them very well."

For once, Rae caught her meaning. "Oh."

Jenny nodded. "Now if you really came over to help me out, I need to fix my hair, and with this shoulder, I can barely move."

As she walked the distance from the parking lot to the lab, Jenny could hear little fragments of conversations.

'Murder' was a thread, as part of some unknown conspiracy. 'Accident' was the common sense favorite. 'Suicide' was a distant third.

Jenny paused at the entrance to the lab. Had it just been yesterday that she and Jase had struggled together here, waiting to see if the negative weight matter would explode when they turned off the power?

"Jenny! There you are. Do you have a key to the lab?"

It was Ben Mitchell, together with two men. One was a campus cop. The other was a policeman in a rumpled suit.

"Hello, Ben. Yes, I have a key."

"Good," said the man with his badge dangling from the breast pocket. There was a name—Davis. "We need to check the room."

"Why?" Jenny said, digging in her purse. She produced the key, and they started down the corridor.

"We just need to check. There has been some speculation about a suicide, and in such cases, we need to check for notes. His home and office have been searched, but we needed to look in the lab as well."

Jenny shook her head. "Suicide doesn't make sense—not for Professor Williams."

"The witness reports agree with you, but we have to make these little checks, just to be complete, you understand."

"What witness reports? I have yet to hear what happened."

The policemen exchanged looks. "I don't think there is anything much to report. Professor Williams arrived at the plasma lab to speak with Professor Hausman, who was up on the top of the scaffolding, making the last minute changes before starting an experiment. It appears that Professor Williams slipped, and fell off the catwalk. He hit his head when he landed. Death was instantaneous. All the witnesses report that he cried out when he fell. No one was close to him when it happened. It sounds like a simple accident."

Jenny shuddered. So much for saving his life. At best, she had extended it a few hours.

The door lock clicked open.

"What has happened here?" Ben charged in. He headed straight for his vacuum system.

At first, Jenny thought it looked exactly like they had left it when she and Jase had removed the chamber, but then she noticed some changes.

"Mr. Mitchell reports," said Davis, holding a pen and notepad, "that the experiment here was shut down for no known reason."

Jenny frowned, "Professor Williams wasn't a man to put the project at risk for no good reason. I was here when he shut it down and loaded the chamber onto a trailer. He was very clear that he was moving it to a cave to give it better shielding from cosmic rays. He said that he had done this before on a previous experiment."

The deception came rattling out without any thought. The real reason for trying to get the chamber to the cave wasn't likely to be believed, now that the dark matter was lost to the world.

In the first hour after she had discovered the chamber was losing weight, it had lightened by ten kilograms. In the next hour, more than thirty. The growth rate of the negative weight substance was exponential. If they had waited a day, the stainless-steel chamber would have irresistibly gone negative to the tune of many tons. It would have destroyed the lab. Jase was concerned that it might explode.

He'd been right.

It occurred to her that Jase's reasons for secrecy were probably gone with his death. She was just a grad student. Jase would probably get the credit for the discovery, but the research would be in the hands of others.

"Do you know where this cave is?" Officer Davis wrote on his pad.

She tried to collect her thoughts. It was hard.

"No. Somewhere in Blanco county is all he said."

Davis made more notes. "Thank you. I must ask you to leave everything where it is for the time being. We should have the investigation completed shortly."

Ben protested that he needed to begin repair work on his system, but Jenny didn't bother to back him up. What use was the vacuum system without the chamber?

The police re-locked the lab room and went off on their business. Ben ranted on for another ten minutes about his vacuum system, but she tuned it all out.

Why did I lie to the police? What is there to hide anymore? If they try to re-trace our movements of yesterday, they will find out soon enough that I was with him every step of the way. There are lots of witnesses. He left records in the credit card system when we rented the trailer. Even the project logs will catch me up.

But what will they think if I tell them about the dark matter and the anti-gravity? How long would it take them to find a motive for murder? How long before I get held for questioning?

She managed to escape Ben's company when he snagged an on-looker to listen to his tale of woe. She needed to think, and it was impossible with Ben talking.

The park bench was available so she sat, staring vacantly across the campus.

Why was Jase talking to Professor Hausman? And what has he done with all the logs, and the computer? It was clear he had come back to the lab after dropping her off yesterday and removed all records. There was nothing left in the lab but the equipment. *If the real story does come out, how will I be able to document what really happened?*

And what if it wasn't an accident? What if someone had pushed him off the catwalk? Who was there with him? Was Professor Hausman the only one on the scaffolding with him? There were 'witnesses', but what did they actually see?

If Jase was killed for the dark matter discovery, am I in danger?

She looked around at the students moving from one place to the next. Even on a Sunday, there were so many innocent looking faces.

Don't be silly. The policeman said it was an accident. He should know, shouldn't he?

She looked at her hands, twisting her handkerchief into a tight looping knot. *Jase, what should I do?*

Jenny stood up, angry with herself. Jase was gone, and anyway, what did he have to do with it? She left home and came five hundred miles to be on her own, to make her own decisions and to stand on her own two feet. *What makes you think,* she told herself firmly, *that he would make the right decisions for you? You are a scientist. You can think for yourself!*

She headed for the parking lot. *I can't sit here all day crying over something that never would have worked out anyway.*

How would a scientist solve a murder? Jenny mumbled, "Collect data, make a hypothesis, test it."

4

Data. What kind of data? The logs, of course. The videotapes of the experiment. Jase had removed it all. Where had he put it? Did the police have it? The university, Professor Hausman? Or was it still where Jase had left it?

There was other data too—the police reports of Jase's 'accident'.

That will be hard to get. Maybe I can duplicate it. Who was there? That should be fairly easy. Find out who was working on Hausman's project and ask them.

My motive for asking? Well, Professor Williams was her friend. *If I don't do it right, it will just reinforce the idea that I was his girlfriend. I can't have that.*

She coaxed her aging Honda Civic back to life. The first order of business was to collect every scrap of data she had in her possession about the project.

"Hello?"

"Hi, Mom."

"Jen! It's so good to hear from you. I've been looking for a letter every day."

"Did you get the email I sent?"

"Oh, did you send one? I haven't checked lately."

"Now, Mom, I told you. You have to log-on regularly."

"Okay," she sounded contrite. "I'll do it right after we talk."

Jenny waved in the air, "Oh, you don't have to rush. Everything I said is out of date. Something has happened."

She could hear her mother sit down in her chair. She could imagine every worry line on her mother's face.

"Now don't worry Mom. It wasn't something that happened to me. My professor has died."

"Oh!"

"Yes, it was a lab accident. Not my lab, not the one I work in! It was another lab he was visiting. He fell off a walkway and hit his head on the concrete floor."

There was silence on the other end, then "Are you okay, Jen?"

She sighed, and then almost lost it. She had been doing okay for the entire day, taking it easy, sleeping late. Several people had called, and she had kept her cool. *Yes, wasn't it terrible? No, she had no idea what she was going to do now. Yes, she was fine.*

But this was Mom. They had cried their eyes dry in each other's arms after Joe had borrowed the family car and spread it all over a cow pasture in an attempt to see how fast it would go.

It had been the fourth or fifth time he had done it. Daddy had confiscated his mint-fresh driver's license and his key, but apparently, Joe had made a duplicate. He had waited until everyone had gone to sleep and then managed to get the car out of the driveway and away without waking anyone. The county sheriff had arrived with the news before anyone had noticed that Joe wasn't there. Weeks went by in a blur. Daddy handled everything, the funeral arrangements, the rental car, and the endless visitors. Mom and she—cried.

"Mom...Mom, I had a crush on him."

"I know Jenny. I know."

"But...It was just a one-way thing. He never noticed me. We worked together, but...."

"He seemed to be a nice man."

Jenny remembered her graduation, when she, like hundreds like her, brought her parents around to shake hands with friends and professors. She had also chosen that time to tell them that she was staying on, to seek her advanced degree. They had not been happy about it.

"He was wonderful. He always helped me...." Once started, she couldn't stop. Her feelings for Jase came spilling out in a torrent. Her mother said nothing more than comforting words for more than an hour.

When the call ended, she was a wreck. There was nothing her mother could do to help, not this time.

"Tuesday: This is Journal One of my investigation into the death of Professor Jason Williams."

She looked at the words. Putting it down in a fresh lab book made it real somehow. Her chosen profession was making its impressions. Everything had to go into a lab book. They were for sale in all the campus bookstores, little blue or gray books, blank except for the ruled paper inside. The pages were hardbound, and numbered. No one was ever supposed to tear out a page. Everything was supposed to be written in ink, dated and initialed. Never erase anything. 'X' out or draw a line though the offending paragraph, but the original should always be readable.

Even in this day of automated data collection, lab books were the heart and soul of patent claims. This was a proof of which researcher thought of the idea first. In a high tech world where a file could be erased undetectably, and where computer records could have their date stamps altered with a few easy keystrokes, her instructors drilled old-fashioned lab book habits.

She added a few more lines, outlining what she intended to do. This was not at all like the notebooks full of numbers and experimental notes from the vacuum decay project, but it comforted her to follow the procedures.

I have to do this. It was what she had told Mom, after she had been invited back home. Yes, her academic plans had been shattered. She was in the same boat as Bob. Her Masters project was now in limbo. Without the professor's project, there was no more funding. With the notes and data about her radiation detection array missing, there was no way to write her paper. Yes, she had even lost her job. Although she hadn't formally received a notice she had been fired, her teaching assistant job surely vanished the instant he died.

If I go home, what is there to do but cry? I've done that for Joe, I don't need to do that anymore.

Joe's death had destroyed her family. Yes, she still loved both her parents, but somehow Joe had been the glue that made them a unit. Her mother was now timid and afraid of everything. Her father was...remote.

It was not at all like they had been before. They were all broken.

I came here to start a new life. I had one. Now it's broken too.

There was a loud noise, from outside, and it startled her.

Jenny jumped up and went to the window. Nothing was visible out on the tree lined residential street.

I'm jumping at shadows. It was just a car's backfire.
I am not going to be my mother!

Angrily, she picked up her lab book and stuffed it in her backpack. She picked up her car keys and headed for the door. *I am not going to stay here and wither. I am a scientist, and I have a puzzle to solve.*

Yellow police tape had been removed from the plasma lab, and it looked as if nothing had ever happened.

"Can I help you?" asked a man she didn't know.

"Sorry. I was working with Professor Williams and I just had to see..."

"That's okay, I guess. Sorry I didn't recognize you."

She shrugged. Particle physics and plasma physics were sometimes two different worlds. "I was wondering what he was doing here. Our project had nothing to do with fusion."

"Can't help you there. He was excited about something, but he only wanted to talk to Frank."

"Frank?"

"Professor Hausman. They seemed to be on first name basis."

"You were here when it happened?"

The man winced. "Yes. Not something I ever want to see again. We were preparing for another test run, charging up the capacitors, and Frank was up on the top. Professor Williams couldn't wait and climbed up there with him. I was working at my station when Williams went sailing off the catwalk, screaming the whole way down. I'll never get that sound out of my head."

She shuddered. "What happened to him?"

The man rubbed his temple. "Everybody has been asking that. The police, the OSHA inspectors, even Professor Hausman, and he was standing a couple of dozen feet away him when it happened. OSHA is already all over the place, asking lots of questions no one has answers for."

Jenny was a little shaken, and hesitated to act like the police with her questions. The man tried to be helpful, but he really didn't know much more.

"Come back Thursday. By then, we will be starting the experiments again, and Hausman will be here. He might know more what Williams was doing."

"Thank you. I will."

*S*o *it was likely just what the police said—an accident.* Jase must have been excited and anxious to confer with his friend, and got careless.

Jenny hated to think that of him, but she didn't like the idea that someone would murder him either. Good people were sometimes careless. *Just a stupid accident. No one was close enough push him.*

She reached the parking lot, and stopped dead.

There was Jase's car.

She walked over to it. Yes, there was the trailer hitch, and fresh scrape marks from when the trailer started swinging free. She hadn't memorized the license plate, but she was sure this was the right one.

She looked in the window. Down on the floorboard was a canvas bag. Beside it was a stack of removable hard disks; just like those they used to back up the lab computer.

The doors were locked, but she had to get that data. It was too important. The car might be stolen; the sun might warp the disks. The police might find it—would find it eventually—and lock the data in a dusty file cabinet forever.

If anyone has a right to it, it's me. I am the only one who understands what's happened. I discovered it.

A shock went through her, and her whole body started to shake. *I discovered the effect. Everything happened after that. I am responsible for Jase's death.*

She tried to shake that thought away. It had been the same with Joe. She had fought with her brother over who had more right to use the car just that week, and she was sure he had taken it out for a joyride just because of her. It had taken a long time for her to shake that conviction.

I am not responsible for Jase's death! She forced herself to believe it.

She walked around the car a second time, and just as she went past the left rear tire, she sensed ... something.

On impulse, she reached up under the fender and there it was—a key hideaway. She slid the compartment open, her fingers tingling all the while, and removed the key. She put the little metal box back and glanced around to see if anyone was looking at her.

The door lock popped up. *I should call the police.* But the thought vanished as quickly as it had come. The data was important.

The funeral was bad. The services were crowded; much of the physics department was there, as well as many students. Jason Williams had been a very popular instructor, and with all the publicity of his strange death, many who normally would have avoided funerals came anyway.

Jenny didn't have a black dress, but rummaged and found a dark blue that would do. She packed her purse with tissues, just in case, and steeled herself for the ordeal.

It was a closed coffin ceremony, for which she was grateful. Surprisingly, Professor Hausman appeared to be the man in charge, and the one who gave the eulogy.

She found herself smiling as Frank Hausman, his voice breaking at times, told tales of his friend of forty years, and the simple examples of his kindness.

He did know Jase. She shook herself of any final doubts about the man who had been closest to him when he fell.

Later on, when the long caravan of cars wound its way to the cemetery, and the small clumps of people drifted off after the short internment ceremony, she wandered alone among the people who had stayed to talk.

She caught a stray sentence or two, "... Hausman paid for it. He had no family and didn't leave a will. The courts will probably reimburse him, but it was a nice gesture."

Okay. Jase trusted him. They were friends. I'll give the data to him. He should be the one to make that decision.

She looked around the crowd for him, but he must have left earlier. *Tomorrow. He will be at his lab. I'll bring the data then.*

Just then, a different face caught her eye. *Davis, the policeman. What is he doing here?*

She could think of two answers. She didn't like either of them. *Either he doesn't buy the accident theory, or he is looking for clues to the missing lab notes.*

Either way, avoid him.

5

She laid out the lab books on the table, one by one, sorted by date. *Somewhere in here, magic happened.* She frowned at the stack of disks. There was more, the raw data captured from the chamber itself, but her personal computer, bought while she was in high school, didn't have a good enough statistics package to crunch it all and writing spreadsheet macros wasn't the way she wanted to kill the time. The videotapes were missing, but that didn't matter, the numbers were here.

I have one night to review this. It all goes to Hausman tomorrow, come rain or shine. She remembered the low level scowl that seemed to be Officer Davis's permanent face. She couldn't afford to hang on to the data. Maybe they would give it back to her, but that wasn't likely.

It was also the key to her degree, and Ben Mitchell's as well.

She picked up the first one, and started reading.

Lights were already flashing when she arrived at the plasma lab. There was a fat zebra-stripped line on the floor, walls and ceiling, and the large sign: *Warning! High intensity magnetic field beyond this point. Remove all metal objects.*

There was a wooden shelf with plastic tubs against the outside wall. Jenny stopped and surveyed her pockets, and was surprised to find a pen with a metal pocket clip. She had paid particular attention this morning, dressing in clothes with nothing but cloth and plastic in their construction. No wristwatch, no jewelry—she brought nothing that would be in the least magnetic with her, and in spite of it all, here was this pen.

Jase had been excited by the discovery. I planned ahead and still made a mistake. Could he have been shoved off the catwalk by a magnetic pulse? No one said anything about that. Surely they would have checked his pockets.

She put the pen in one of the plastic tubs, and flipped through the lab notebooks once again. The computer disks were still back in her car. There was no way she was going to bring them close to these magnets.

Waa! Waa! Waa! It was the warning alarm. *They are starting.* She put the lab books back in the canvas bag and hurried down the hall towards the main confinement lab, the huge three story tall room that just barely housed the behemoth of plasma chambers and superconducting magnets. She shifted the bag to the other arm. Her shoulder still ached.

The building creaked, as the magnetic field affected everything iron in its construction. It also affected Jenny.

Her foot slipped, and she fell. "Ahh!"

Her arms went wide, ready to hit the ground.

But she hit the ceiling first.

Down below her, the lab books scattered across the floor. Her arm hit the edge of a sprinkler fixture, scraping a red weal on her skin.

Then, she fell. It was ten feet from the ceiling to the floor and she hit hard. The breath was knocked out of her. For several long seconds, she tried to breathe, but could not.

Gasp! Gratefully, she pulled in the air.

What happened? Dazed, she looked around at the rectangles of blue on the tile floor.

The dark matter! She remembered, in a vivid flashback, the shimmering transparent ball spilling out of the chamber, high in the sky. It exploded. There was a sting, all through her body.

It's in me! I'm contaminated with dark matter.

It was quiet, except for the panicky huff and puff of her breath. *The alarm, it's off.* Somehow, the magnetic field activated the anti-gravity aspect of the dark matter. *That's what killed Jase! That's what threw him off the catwalk.*

She looked around at the lab books in the deserted hallway. The lights were still flashing. They could pulse the magnets again at any time. *I've got to get away from here!*

In spite of the pain—new bruises, maybe a re-injury to her arm—she gathered the books back into the canvas bag. No time to organize them. Just grab and go!

She got to her feet, and ran.

Waa! Waa! Waa! As the alarm started up, she put on more speed, dashing past the plastic boxes. No time to recover the pen.

Her foot slipped, and she grabbed for the brass handle on the door. The world tumbled. She held tight with one hand while up and down reversed themselves.

It was milder. She was in a less intense magnetic field, but it was enough to lift her.

As abruptly as it started, she fell to the floor. The alarm stopped. Her hand was still tight on the handle.

Jenny's eyes were wide with fright, and her breath fast and ragged.

Get out! She opened the door, and dragged herself and the bag of books out into the sunshine. She limped, but nothing was going to stop her from getting as far away from those magnets as she could.

S he got into her car and turned the key. As the starter cranked, she could feel her body shake in time with the noise.

I can feel the starter motor. I felt it before, but I didn't notice.

She drove all the way home with every sense alert. She feel the magnetic tugs all around her!

I am contaminated. I'm just like Bruce Banner. Any instant I'll turn into a freak.

She glanced in the mirror. At least she wasn't turning green like the Incredible Hulk. *Not yet.*

J enny dropped the bag onto the couch.

I feel normal. Beat up, but normal. She walked into the kitchen. She waved her hand past a refrigerator magnet. There was a faint, but noticeable flicker of sensation. *That's how I noticed the keyholder on Jase's car.*

She started the little desk fan. Yes. There was a vibration from the electric motor. It wasn't enough to send her flying, but some part of her was reacting to the magnetism.

Jenny sat at the table and stared at the books.

If she didn't turn them in, eventually Davis, or the university, or even Ben Mitchell would discover them, and she would be in a lot of trouble.

But if she turned them in, as is, the discovery would come out. Her contamination would be discovered. She would be a freak, and a lab rat. There was no doubt what her future would be. She was a walking container, somehow, of dark matter—antigravity dark matter at that. It was the only sample left. She would be very valuable to a lot of very sinister organizations. *Kiss my future goodbye.*

I need the data. Jenny shivered. How many times had she daydreamed of being one of the super-heroes of her comic books? The wish had come true, and it was likely kill her.

But I'm the only person who knows enough to find the solution. I have to keep the data.

She pawed through the lab books again. She had been up to three AM the night before reading through them, looking for precursor signs. There had been nothing, not until that final day, her final readings.

The last book—she flipped it open. It started tamely enough. Routine measurements filled the page, initialed by her.

She thumbed through the pages, empty except for the ruled lines. It was only partly used.

Eight pages. Most of them are my entries.

On her desk were several empty lab books, fresh from the bookstore.

Why don't I? I would just be copying myself. It's not like I am forging anything. Just duplicate the entries up to the last minute—before I accidentally pushed the chamber and noticed that it moved.

She collected several pens, and got to work, duplicating the last of the lab books, line-by-line, number-by-number. She initialed the first set. *This isn't so hard.*

On the third page, she stopped cold. Angular numbers, in Ben's hand-writing, stared back at her.

No help for it. She changed to a blue ink pen and started duplicating his entries. At the bottom of the page, she paused, and then inked her initials. Ben wouldn't likely remember any individual set of numbers, but Davis just might have an eye for people's handwriting styles. If it was her handwriting, the initials had better be hers as well.

A little later, with a cramped hand, and a worry that wouldn't go away, she finished. *Let someone else guess why Jase moved the chamber.* They certainly wouldn't find the reason in the lab books. She set the new final book with the others, and hid the original among all the other schoolbooks and old school notes she had accumulated over the years.

Jenny debated whether to photocopy the lab books before turning them over to Hausman. *No. I would be seen. It would look suspicious.*

"Thanks for seeing me, Dr. Hausman."

"Not at all. Have a seat."

Jenny sat in the comfortable chair, and set the bag of notes and tapes next to her. There were pictures on all the walls. Most of them had Hausman in it, but one caught her eye. A very young Jase Williams and a young Hausman stood arm-in-arm posed before something large and metallic.

She forced herself back to the present. She didn't wait for him to talk.

"First off, I want to thank you for what you did for Jase... Dr. Williams. I didn't realize that he didn't have any family left."

He waved it off. "Jase and I were old friends. I'm sure the university would have handled it, but I have always been a bit pushy. I owed him a few favors."

"I'm not sure how much he had told you about his last project..."

"Vacuum decay, wasn't it? I remember him talking about it at length at a party, oh, about six months back. The last I heard, there was nothing much to report, but that was the whole point, wasn't it?"

She smiled. "Nothing to report about nothing. We joked about it a lot."

"And I am sorry everything fell apart for your team. I hear the experiment has been taken down?"

"Yes, it appears so. He was going to move the chamber to a cave underground, but no one knows where it is now."

"Sad. And hard for you, I am sure. I have asked around, and I know that there were at least two grad students on the project."

"Yes. That is part of why I wanted to talk to you." She reached for the bag and set it on his desk. "These are the project lab notes."

His eyes widened and he smiled.

"Ah! The missing notes! You have just saved the university from a big stink. Jase got his funding almost entirely from the Texas Energy Consortium and they have already been asking some rather pointed questions about why the equipment and data have both managed to disappear."

"They were in Jase's car. I noticed it in the parking lot. Jase had a hidden key, and I didn't want the disks to warp in the sun so I took it. And now, if it wouldn't be too much trouble, could you handle it for the university? I have no idea who owns this stuff now."

He nodded. "Oh, the TEC has already made that clear. Their contract with Jase was a model of covering the details." He had another thought. "Oh. You probably have data for your Masters project in there as well."

"Yes. Ben Mitchell looked particularly upset when he found that these were missing. He designed the vacuum pumps for the project."

Hausman shook his head. "You kids sure got the short end of the stick on this one. I know plasma physics isn't in your area, but I probably can make room for one more teaching assistant. I doubt that there are any openings elsewhere at this time in the year."

Jenny was startled at the offer. "That's very nice of you. To be honest, though, I am not really sure what my plans are. Could I think about it?"

"Of course."

What will I do? she asked herself on the way home. She depended on her TA income to help pay the bills. She should have taken the offer right then.

But what if he wanted me to help in the lab? She shuddered. She could sense tiny magnetic fields everywhere. Going back into that lab might be fatal.

And I need time to understand the data.

I can't ask my parents for any more money. They had gone into debt to send her here in the first place. They weren't a poor family, but her original education plans had been centered around the local Junior college, where there was no dorm expense and tuition was low. If she wanted to go beyond the two-year associate's degree, they had talked about sending her to the school in the next town, only twenty miles away, where she could still commute and live at home.

But when Joe had died, and there was only one child to put through college, Mom and Daddy had agreed to her sudden change of plans with little argument.

Her desire to go on for an advanced degree had upset their budget a little, but with a student loan and the money she made as a TA, she had been able to find an apartment without taking on a roommate.

And how much have I cost them because I fell in love with my professor?
She shook her head angrily.
None of that! I am a scientist. I wanted to be a scientist, and I am good at it.
I'll have to be, or I'm dead.

Issue 2: I Can Fly!

6

The phone rang as Jenny lugged the large plastic trashcan in through the front door. She let it drop, and raced to answer it.

"Hello?"

"You told Hausman to hire me."

"Ah, hello Ben. How are you doing?"

"Why?"

Jenny was flustered. Ben had a one-track mind. He was smart enough, but nothing, including social pleasantries, could knock him off course.

"Yes, Ben. He only had a TA position for one of us. Your work would be valuable to him. My detector works best on single isolated events, not the bulk radiation that comes from his fusion trials. It only makes sense for you to get the job."

Of course, there was more to it than that, but her explanation stopped him for a moment, but just a moment.

"You didn't get an offer from Lin's group?"

Jenny sighed. There was not a chance that Professor Lin's high-profile Higgs particle group would reach out for more help. They probably had barricades up to keep out eager grad students aching to get their names on as co-authors to that paper.

"No, Ben. I have no other offers. TA's just aren't that valuable. There was only one job, and you got it."

"What will you do?"

"I don't know, Ben. I'm still thinking about it."

"Oh. Well thanks for the recommendation. Do you want to go out sometime?"

Two shocks—one that he bothered to thank her, two that he asked her out. He had never seemed interested in girls, nor boys either. He had struck her as geek-neuter.

"Maybe sometime. I'm not feeling very well right now."

"Yes, your bike accident. Well, I'll talk to you later." Click.

Jenny set the phone down.

Will wonders never cease? He remembered. Maybe she had misjudged Ben from the beginning.

J enny winced as the new car battery scraped on the concrete, but she couldn't carry it. It was hard enough to lift it out of the car. It cost more than she liked to think about, but a car battery was the best power supply she could manage on her dwindling bank account.

Up the steps and into the apartment. She set it on an old copy of *Nature* magazine and pushed it. No sense in scraping the wooden floor. The store clerk said it came charged, she hoped he was right. She needed to hold off on buying the battery charger until she found a job.

She moved it next to the 35-gallon plastic trash barrel. It was now covered with gray duct tape, where she had taped coils of wire around it. The wire had been expensive too. She had opted for 4-strand telephone wire from the hardware store. With four wires in the same cable, she could wire all four together to carry more current, or link them in series for more turns of wire in her large homemade electromagnet.

A few more components from Radio Shack completed her experimental apparatus. She checked her circuit diagram against the sketch she had made in her private lab book

I need another meter to measure the true voltage across the coil. Unfortunately, even at $15, the cost of another meter was too much for her checking account. There was the unbearable urge to charge it to her card, but with no job, and her final check from the university still another two weeks away, she had to stick to her priority list. Rent had to come first. The electricity bill was due in a week. Food could be cut, but not totally. She couldn't live on fat like some of her peers. She had resolved to make do on the half tank of gas that she had left in the car. With no all night sessions on campus, she could exist on the bus runs.

I have to get a job—soon.

She ran her finger over the circuit, double-checking the meter to make sure it was in the right mode. She dialed the potentiometer to the highest resistance, for the lowest current, and flipped the switch.

She felt her heart skip a beat. *What was that?*

Her feet were still on the floor. She looked at the meter. Just a few milliamps. Practically nothing was going through the coil. The pot was blocking almost all of it.

She turned the dial and let in more current. There was something different. She could feel it.

She waved her hand in the air, next to the mouth of the barrel. *It is much stronger inside.* It almost felt like a gentle breeze was flowing out, although she was sure that there was no airflow at all.

Her fingers flipped the switch. *I felt that.* Her whole body was reacting to the magnetic field.

She picked up the pen and noted down current, her observations, and the date and time. She initialed the paragraph.

What now? She glanced at her list, although she already knew what she had planned. It was just a little frightening. Her bruises weren't going away fast enough. She didn't want any more of them.

She set down the pen and walked around the house, going to the bathroom, gathering her resolve.

No more delays. The stepladder was already propped next to the barrel. She unfolded it, and climbed the three steps and eased herself down into the barrel. The new plastic smell added to the tension.

She reached for the switch, and then paused. *No.* She unclipped the wire instead, and tapped the bare metal lightly to the other side of the switch.

Jenny was launched out of the mouth of the barrel like a jack-in-the-box. The alligator clip ripped free of the circuit, still clasped in her fingers. She hit the ceiling, slapping her back up against the plaster, knocking white powder loose.

With the circuit broken, and no magnetic field, she fell the eight feet from ceiling to floor and landed with a *whoof.* Plaster dust rained down on her.

She blinked her eyes, and saw the oval dent she had made on the ceiling. She giggled.

At least it started as a giggle, but as she struggled to her feet, it grew to a laugh. She danced up the steps again and from inside the barrel, still laughing as if she couldn't stop, she dialed the current to half and clipped the circuit active again.

Whoo! She popped up and hit the ceiling again, only this time it was no more than a pat. The wire had come loose again, and she dropped, but she was ready for it, and almost landed on her feet.

She sat on the floor, struggling to breathe, and trying to control the laughing jag.

It works! Simple magnetic field. Inside the coil works so much better. She pushed herself back up to her feet. She took a deep breath, then another, until she could breathe without the *ha-ha-ha* shudders.

Take notes. She picked up the pen, and in quick strokes, noted down the currents and the effects. She looked up again. *How am I going to explain that to the landlord?*

A grin took hold of her face and she raced back inside the barrel for another jump.

Jenny had mixed feelings about gray duct tape. It was so very versatile. The straps she had rigged from the trash barrel handles, up over her shoulders were all duct tape. Unfortunately, it was also sticky. Her efforts to double the tape over and keep the sticky sides together hadn't worked perfectly and she'd have glue to wash off.

But at least her idea worked.

She turned the knob slowly, and felt the straps press against her shoulders. The wiring was now inside the barrel with her, and she was kicking herself at the sight of the heavy car battery sitting uncoupled and forlorn down on the floor. A few AA batteries provided all the current necessary.

I feel like Dick Tracy. "The nation that controls magnetism controls the world." Her high school comic book store had some coffee table books of vintage newspaper comic strips, including Superman, Flash Gordon, and Dick Tracy. For a detective story, Dick Tracy had been surprisingly steeped in science fiction, with everything from the wristwatch TV communicator to a hidden race of aliens on the far side of the moon. For part of the series, he sailed around the city in a magnetic flying contraption that looked like a flying bucket.

Just like me. She adjusted the current again, and stopped her rise before she bumped her head against the ceiling. Carrying the coil around her, she drifted like a balloon in the faint air currents inside her apartment.

"Uh, Oh." Her makeshift flying craft was drifting towards a floor standing lamp. She bounced off it, and down it went with a crash. She fumbled with the knob with one hand and pushed off the wall with the other. Seconds later, as she skimmed over the table, her limited visibility caused her to knock over a glass. It shattered on the floor.

The laughter threatened to come bubbling out again, and she clamped her lips tight. She adjusted the knob, settling with no more than a couple of bumps against the furniture, safely on the floor. She felt gravity reclaim her as the magnetism died.

Sticky. She shed the straps and got out of the barrel, although she had to tip it over to get free.

Where is the broom? Flying was fun, but it was murder on the furniture. *But I'm not going outside dressed in a barrel, like a cartoon destitute person.*

I need a costume. Her mind's eye flashed through thousands of pages of comic book super-heroes, in their colorful, skin-tight suits.

I wish Joe were here.

Joe Quinn had been an artist. He had sketched cartoons since he could hold a crayon. Back at home, in the room that contained the last posses- sions of her brother, was a steamer trunk that contained art tablets, his old pens, charcoals and pastels.

But the bulk of the artwork was several bundles of notebooks, school binders usually, that contained his drawings. A lot of them were single panel cartoons. He had a quirky sense of humor, and whenever life handed him a giggle, he turned it into a black and white line drawing.

Many were lost, down in the trash, or on the back of an assignment that had to be turned in. Hundreds had been given away to friends. However, as he got older, he started to keep his work in little collections, sometimes he even composed complete comic books. Almost all of them were in the trunk.

Almost all. She smiled. There was one she had personally burned.

Some time after Jenny had started her multi-year infatuation with comic books, Joe had started drawing some super-hero comics of his own. She had been embarrassed when some of the female characters, in capes and high boots and deep cleavage costumes, started looking a lot like her.

He was unrepentant; merely pointing at the characters in the books she was spending big money for. She had to admit that he was just following the commercial tradition.

But one day, she was looking for some school supplies while working on her homework, and wandered into his room. Barely hidden in a stack of notebooks was a full nude that looked exactly like her. She pulled out the notebook—a dozen pages, many panels, and an illustrated story line that had her in and out of clothes every time she turned the page, and had several explicit scenes in full copulation with various beefcake males, one of which looked something like Gary Russel, and another that just might be Joe himself.

With her face feeling redder by the second, she was stopped cold by one scene, with her naked, lounging in the tub. She stomped quickly down the hall and entered the bathroom. Looking around, comparing the drawing with the room, she positioned herself where the angles of the walls and tub matched exactly. She was standing directly in front of the laundry hamper. She opened it.

A small person—and Joe was small too—could hide inside and look out the three, wide air ventilation slits in the hamper door. She looked again at the drawing, showing the bottle of her bubblebath, and the floral towel she had used, if memory was correct, just a week before.

That was enough. She tore back to his room and started looking through every drawing he had. It took a while, but she located three other nude drawings of her, disturbingly realistic in detail. They went immediately into her locked hope chest.

She tracked him down, returning from a bike ride to the nearby convenience store.

"I found them."

"What?" asked Joe, but the look on his face showed he knew exactly what she had found.

"One comic book, three drawings, and one hiding place in the bathroom hamper." He wilted under her words.

She poked her index finger right in his face. "If you EVER, draw me like that again, or even THINK of spying on me, they go straight to Daddy! Understand me?"

He only nodded, and he was uncharacteristically timid for a month after that.

Of course, Jenny had burned the pictures the very next day, but he never knew that. They never talked about the incident again.

She thought that was the end of it, until one day, several months later, when she saw Joe hand Gary one of his black and white, full size comic books. Gary looked up at her and grinned.

She had blood in her eye and zeroed in on the two of them. Joe shrank a little at her approach, but Gary didn't seem to have a guilty conscience. She demanded the book and he handed it over.

Yes, it was her, and it was Gary too, but they were typically dressed superheroes, and the story line had nothing more salacious than a kiss among the clouds. That was embarrassing enough, with Gary standing there reading over her shoulder, but it was nothing she would murder Joe for.

After that, there were other comic books, with her in costume, flying the skies, destroying the monsters or villains. She started asking to read them. Perhaps her brother enjoyed drawing her figure more than he should, but he also came up with a number of very nice costume designs.

And I could use some good ideas now.

"May I help you?" asked the woman behind the counter.

Jenny held up her sack. "Can I rent the use of one of your computers?"

The gray-haired lady frowned, "You have a graphic you need to print?"

"No, I just need to read these disks and make a spreadsheet from the results."

"I don't know. We lost our computer person last week, and I only know how to print from the photo programs."

"Oh, I know how to do the work. I've already checked. You have the right disk drive and the software."

"If you say so." She handed Jenny the key disk that let her logon to the computer.

She went right to work. It had been surprisingly easy for her to borrow the data disks, if 'borrow' was the right word, and she had only a limited time to extract the data she needed before the real secretary noticed that they were missing. It had been a rude surprise to discover that the computer labs had the wrong kind of removable hard disk and that she couldn't read the project disks there on campus.

I should have taken care of this before giving them to Hausman in the first place.

A few anxious questions later, she had been pointed to this copy shop. In addition to the rows of photocopy machines, this place did high quality color printing from computer masters. They were set up with Macs and Windows computers preloaded with the most popular graphics and document layout software, and they supported all the popular removable disk formats.

Now all she had to do was to insert her handcrafted macro program that would read the disks, extract the power supply readings and load it into a spreadsheet. She had a puzzle to solve, and this was the only data she had.

Her calculations on the jack-in-the-box experiment in her apartment had produced impossible results.

Lifting her from the floor to the ceiling took about 870 joules of energy. The energy she drained from the battery during that moment was less than 20 joules, and most of that was probably spent heating the wires.

Something for nothing. Impossible.

Not that the impossible is all that remarkable.

She inserted the first disk, and hit the RETURN key.

Still, the energy had to come from somewhere. That was a religious article of faith. It wasn't from the batteries—that had just been a catalyst for the real process, she was sure.

It had to come from the dark matter. But where had the dark matter gotten the energy? Indeed, where had the dark matter come from?

She hoped to get some answers from the data. If she could spot a change in the power supply current in the days before the chamber started losing weight, then that would give her some direction.

She looked up from the rhythmic click-click of the disk drive. It would take time to feed in all the disks.

A high school girl whimpered softly nearby. Jenny turned.

"Problems?" Jenny asked.

The girl looked at her with fear at the edge of her eyes.

"I think it ate my file, and the project is due in the morning!"

Jenny looked at the progress bar on her own screen, then went over to help. "Show me."

After a bit of research, Jenny discovered that indeed, the computer had eaten the file, but from her own long, painful experiences with computers, she knew where the software kept its scratch copy of the file, and was able to restore it.

The girl got her large-format color printout, and Jenny suffered the abject gratitude.

"I'm happy to help. I'm restoring a project of my own."

After that, the highlight of the evening was finding where the solitaire game was hidden. Finally, the last disk was processed, and she went to the counter to pay her fee.

"Thanks for helping that girl. You are good at computers?"

Jenny smiled, "Sometimes. You can't get through school these days without them."

"You wouldn't want to work here would you? The manager is finally convinced that we need a replacement."

Jenny paused at the thought. *I don't really want a job. It takes too much time. I just want the money.*

But her only other choice was to call home.

"Sounds good. I need the work."

8

The world had a surrealistic quality to it, Jenny decided, as she walked from the bus stop to the administration building to return the data the next day. Not only did the disks tickle her leg as the bag swung at her side, but the whole campus area was alive with magnetic hot spots.

I am getting better at this. She held her hand out over a grill in the ground, normally hidden behind the bushes. She had always thought that the university was an island of greenery in a city that had succumbed to blacktop and concrete. There were trees and grass everywhere, and the buildings popped up out of the green like square-edged mushrooms.

But it's really a façade. The earth beneath the grass had to be a maze of tunnels, and wiring conduits, and machinery. She could sense passages like invisible ley lines, and the quivering magnetic nimbus of electric motors at work.

The entrance steps led from the green to the tile and plaster world of administration. She walked the corridor, her eyes to the electric outlets and light switches. *I can tell where the active wire runs are.* She ran her hand along the wall, the tips of her fingers trailing on the texturing of the plaster, but her hand sensitive to little magnetic fluctuations below the surface. *I'm a stud finder, too.* Her face was in a permanent pixie grin.

The girl at the desk was her age. As Jenny watched her fumble with her files, she revised the estimate a couple of years younger.

"Oh, here it is." The girl squinted at the handwriting. "'Put disks in the file room, log it with date and time, and call Davis.'"

"Davis?"

The girl looked up. "Oh, are you the one who is supposed to call him?"

"What is the number?"

The girl puzzled it out and repeated the string of digits.

Jenny's heart had gone into staccato mode. *So, the cops are still watching. What do they suspect?*

"No," she mumbled, "I wouldn't be the one to call." *But I need to remember that number.*

Jenny signed the logbook and left the disks. She headed back across campus, angry with herself for feeling like every tree and bush hid police spies, watching her every move.

The comic book store was a dark warren of twisty little passageways among shelves and shelves of long boxes. It was practically deserted, as was typical in comic stores most of the time. Only on delivery day was there much life, when the regulars tried to be in place when the weekly shipments from the comic book companies arrived. So many of the issues no longer made sense on their own. People didn't buy single comic books. They followed a storyline. A single issue was like one episode of a TV soap opera, full of strife and fury, but impossible to take seriously unless you had been following the lives of the characters.

Local comic book stores managed a balancing act, trying to buy just enough of a given title to keep their regulars happy, without stocking too many that would rapidly loose shelf value and end up in the quarter bins. Many places kept 'pull lists'. A customer would leave a list of titles. The store would use the totals from the pull lists to order, and then the store would pull pristine, untouched issues out of the shipment for their regulars.

Jenny missed the excitement of delivery day, with the welcome masked faces and spandexed bodies on the covers promising another monthly—or weekly for big names like Superman—installment in their lives.

But she only let herself linger over the new issues for a few minutes, resisting the urge to dig in and try to pick up the threads of the story she had abandoned so long ago. She was not here for new revelations, new heroes, and new villains. She had come to dig in the back issues.

A long-box held about a hundred copies, fewer if they were bagged, like the ones she now pawed through. Collectors kept their issues individually bagged in plastic, or the more expensive Mylar, to keep the air from decaying the paper. It was all a lost cause, of course. Comics were typically printed on cheap paper that would burn itself to dust over the years from the action of acids in the paper pulp itself. There were always the legends of serious collectors who kept their collections bagged in Mylar in sealed boxes with the air replaced by dry nitrogen, but Jenny knew no one who had that much time and money. Her collection was still back at her parents' home in Amarillo—several long-boxes in the back of her closet.

The Legion of Super-heroes! She pulled out an old issue, and the cover triggered a flash of memories. There was Saturn Girl, and Triplicate Girl, and Brainiac 5, and all the others. This was close to what she wanted.

The Legion, based far in the future, was something like a teenage club of super-powered heroes, funded by an extremely rich industrialist, and with police powers from the interplanetary government.

Of course, all that could change from year to year. Occasionally, one of the dozen or so members would be killed off, or be banished. Regularly, there were auditions where all of the truly weird and exotic superpowered teens tried to join the group.

And if that wasn't enough (and for a series about a group of teenagers that spanned decades, it wasn't), the whole storyline would occasionally reboot, and start over from the beginning with the same, but different, characters in the same, but different, adventures. Being based so far into the future made them susceptible to changes in the contemporary comic book universe.

For example, the original version had been formed in homage to the teenage superhero Superboy in the distant past. This was done for a Superboy storyline where he traveled in time.

But by the 1980's when the Superman story itself was re-written, with Clark Kent not even becoming super-powered until he became an adult, there was a period when there was no Superboy. The Legion was re-written to have been inspired by a different teenage superhero entirely.

Jenny liked the earlier version best, with the heroes more noble, and the adventures more important, and fewer pages spent on the politics and romances in the clubhouse.

And she liked the costumes better, too.

She turned the page, reading afresh, and tickling old memories of when she had read it the first time.

Brainy's flight rings! The heroes had activated one of the many inventions of the super-brain of the group. Braimiac 5, a workaholic, green-skinned descendent of one of Superman's major villains, was the brains-over-emotion member of the team. He rarely did anything outside of the lab, but often managed to save the day with an invention or an insight. At the first of the series, the non-flying heroes used rocket belts, but later these flight rings were invented. Put on one of these rings and you could fly.

Jenny had always been queasy about the idea. She knew of a very real case of a girl at her school who had tried to slam-dunk a basketball and had caught her ring on the net. It had effectively ripped that finger off, and after reconstructive surgery, she had to adapt to a four-fingered hand.

But in my case it might work. Jenny looked down at the class ring on her hand. *If I could find a way to power a large enough electromagnet....*

The theory was okay. The ring magnet would not be pulling her. It would just be activating the dark matter throughout her body. The dark matter would cause her to fly, not the pull on the ring.

She shook her head. No, it wouldn't work. Maybe the dark matter could pull energy out of the vacuum, but that didn't mean she could create megawatts of electricity that way. Her original idea was still the best.

She picked out a half-dozen old issues and bought them. She shelled out the money with a guilty conscience.

It's research. But she knew better. She just wanted to read the stories again.

9

That didn't go well. Jenny sighed and headed for the bus station.

Two weeks after she had gotten the notice in the mail, she had gone to meet with her newly assigned faculty advisor. It had taken her that long to shake loose of the instinctive aversion to the campus.

Every time saw the opened letter on her table, she would have the overpowering urge to do something else—work on her costume design, or go to work early, or stare at her lab books fruitlessly for inspiration. Whether it had to do with Jase, or her experience at the plasma lab, it was as if she were allergic to the university. She forced herself to make the appointment and meet with the man who was now in charge of her scholastic future.

I shouldn't have bothered. It was plain that her chances for completing her masters project in the current year were nonexistent. She could have chosen a better advisor by throwing a dart at a phonebook.

He was Professor Ben Azrahid, and it was plain that she was just one more line item on his overflowing schedule. The administration had been willing to grant her some variance from the rules due to the death of Professor Williams, but she hadn't kept on top of what was happening.

Everything would have been much better if she had taken the TA position. Hausman would have been her advisor and they could at least talk. Instead, Ben Azrahid read from his list. Jenny had the uncomfortable feeling that he never looked up at her.

The partial results from her project did not look at all interesting from an outsider's viewpoint. The whole purpose of her detection array had been to avoid false-positive results coming from outside of the vacuum chamber. In summary, she had built a radiation detector that had detected nothing. She knew that her job had been excellent, but only someone familiar with the design and progress of the project would understand that.

Jase, I miss you so much. Why did you have to go away?

Ben Azrahid was, by reputation, a mathematician, not an experimentalist. The world of physics had a number of sects—warring factions at times, with different interests, different methods, and a common hunger for the limited pot of money available to fund their projects.

Unless she converted to this new church, she would never be considered worth much of her advisor's time.

He doesn't think my old project is worth salvaging.

Do I still want the degree? Yes!

Jenny had been tinkering with the universe since the day she had pulled the string on her mail-order gyroscope and watched the thing balance on the tip of a pencil. The Edmund Scientific catalog had been her friend and secret vice ever since—weather balloons, water rockets, prisms, and magnets.

The true worth of her high school science class had not been the facts taught—she had largely been exposed to those already from her toys and her own reading. No, its true value had been in the idea that the search for truth could be a respected profession and not just a game of trivia.

She could still remember the day in fifth-grade science class when her teacher was fumbling, badly, an example of how the sun was shining at an angle on the earth at the pole and straight down at the equator. The lady had her flashlight and the globe of the earth, but to her, 'down' was towards her feet, and not the 'down' of the example and so she was holding her 'sun' over the North Pole of the globe. Jenny had weighed in and rescued the demonstration.

Since that day, Jenny had an eye for mistakes in science, whether it was in her comic book universes, or careless teachers, or unforgivably, in the text books themselves.

By the time she graduated from high school, she was just beginning to understand how ignorant she was of the world around her. She had been living the encyclopedia fantasy—all the answers were known, and written down, and everything could be understood if she could just locate the correct books.

I am like Marie Curie.

It was a frightening thought. One day in high school physics, there had been a class discussion that turned argumentative when one person said that Mme. Curie had been stupid for playing with the radioactive substances that had eventually caused her death. Jenny argued for the great heroine of science. The effects of radioactivity were unknown then. That is what she was in the process of discovering. She didn't make much of an impact on the class, because *everybody knew* that radioactivity was deadly.

A hundred years from now, will everybody know that dark matter contamination is deadly? Am I a walking corpse and I just don't know it yet?

Jenny growled at her shadow as she walked. *I will never know the truth from reading in a book, because the truth has not yet been discovered. Only a physicist studying the effect will discover it. And I am that physicist! I may never get the degree, but that doesn't change who I am.*

"Hello Momma. It's Jenny."
  "Jenny! It's good to hear from you. How are you doing? Did you get the job you were after?"

Jenny had to think back to the last conversation. She didn't remember what she had said then, but it was before the copy center job.

"No, but I do have a new job. It's not much, but it will keep me from begging on the street corner at least."

"You know you can always count on us."

Jenny said, "Yes, I know." She said it automatically, but she didn't really believe it. She hadn't been able to count on them when she decided to get her Masters.

She let her mother talk, feeding her casual questions to keep the flow of hometown gossip coming. Most of it was about her parent's friends and co-workers. They both worked at a glass products factory there in Amarillo. Her father was a lawyer; her mother worked in the quality assurance lab. That is where they had met, and with the exception of the two maternity leaves, that is where they both had spent their everyday life.

Jenny knew a most of the names from long familiarity, although she didn't know their faces. With rare exceptions, she had never met her parent's friends. If she had an extended family of any sort, it had been their church friends. Three grandparents were dead, and her Nanna, her maternal grandmother, was living in Maryland with Aunt Billie.

There are not many of us left. She kept that thought to herself as well. It was just one more reason why she should never give up. Losing Joe had almost killed her mother. She shouldn't have to lose her only remaining child either if the dark matter proved dangerous.

"Momma, I've another favor to ask."

"What is it?"

"Do you think you could ship the sewing machine to me?"

"Sewing machine? I could never get you interested in sewing before. I'm so glad. Do you need any patterns?"

"No, I don't think so. I've already bought a few patterns and, to be honest, I don't think the styles are quite the same."

"You'd be surprised. These things come in cycles."

They chatted over clothes for another few minutes. Jenny was surprised at how the old jargon of bias strips and buttonhole attachments and hem-stitching still brought vivid memories back. There had been a time when her mother had a sewing nook no larger than a walk-in closet. Little Jenny went there to play in the piles of cloth with her dolls while the sewing machine made its whir-whir noises. She even remembered Granny Quinn's black sewing machine with the treadle underfoot to make the machine turn. *Where did that antique go?* she wondered.

After the phone call, she sat in the quietness of her apartment, and ached for someone to be with. Would she ever have a little girl of her own? Would the time ever come when she would want to sew up little outfits for her children, and let them come and play around her feet while she worked?

I always thought it was the money. They had not been rich enough to buy a lot of clothes, and she had resolved to be richer, so that she could never have to sew her own. *But there is more to it.* Her mother had been genuinely happy when she had been sewing. There comes a time when nothing eases the soul more than working with your hands.

Jenny frowned. *Well, I'll be doing a lot of that.*

She dumped the sack containing her latest purchases on the table. She had managed to return the car battery, and in spite of the restocking fee, she had gotten enough cash back to buy supplies for the next stage of her project.

She picked up the pattern envelopes, and looked again at the pictures on the front. *Those shoulder pieces are too 'Jetson', but I can leave that out.* She brought over the comic books and compared them to the patterns.

Spiderman was the first superhero she remembered who made his own costume. She remembered the reprint of the issue where he was working late at night, sewing his red and black spider costume with needle and thread. That might be too close to her own situation for comfort.

One version of Superman had been blessed by the efforts of Martha Kent, doing a superhuman task herself of unraveling unbreakable threads from his off-world baby blankets and re-weaving them back into a man-sized costume.

She also remembered a minor character in the DC comic book universe, a tailor who sold costumes to superhero and supervillian alike. *I could really use his phone number about now!*

In the comic book universe, a costume was required. She had wondered, back in high school, if there was a union requirement or something that said you couldn't do the super hero or super villain thing without one.

Some of the costumes made sense. A costume that held your gimmicky weapons or that concealed your identity was a good idea. A costume in bright colors for a bad guy intent on sneaking into a bank or a secret lab strained her credulity.

For the artists, costumes made more sense. Joe liked drawing girl characters in costume, because for him it was just a case of sketching a fantasy
nude and then adding a couple of lines and filling in the colors. She admitted to herself that she didn't mind the looks of a Superman or even a Robin
when done by a good artist.

Now, Batman had the most sensible costumes. Every one of them was
tuned for functionality, and Bruce Wayne was rich enough to have dozens;
bulletproof costumes, fireproof costumes, costumes built for gliding like a
hang-glider. Jenny had a memory of making her own utility belt, with little
pouches in a web belt, just big enough to hold film canisters.

Whatever happened to that? She shrugged. That had been when she had
discovered Batgirl in her pre-Oracle days, back before the attack by Joker
and the wheelchair. Back when she rode a motorcycle.

*I love the back issues; I always have. If I live through this and get to be rich
and famous, I'll be one of those legendary collectors with the nitrogen-filled
vaults. I'll have a quiet little reading room where I can pull out a long box and
read for hours and hours.*

10

Jenny placed the crimping vise in the center of her table. Unless she wanted
to do this on the floor, she would have to put her weight on the crimper,
and it was important that the table be stable.

She cut the light blue ribbon cable, about three inches wide, and pushed
the clean-cut edge into the connector. She leaned on the lever and dozens
of metal teeth bit through the insulation and connected 50 identical wires
to the 50 teeth in the connector.

A magnifying glass and a bright lamp confirmed that it was a good
mate. *Of course, I'll have to check every connection with the meter to make
absolutely sure.*

Ribbon cable was widely used in the computer industry to connect
hard disks to the interface cards. There were various kinds and counts of
wires to match the most common interface standards, but the pale blue was
cheap. It was going to be difficult to sew all the loops of ribbon cable into

a costume, but it was still a good idea. Wrapping her body in a three-inch wide ribbon was going to be a lot easier than winding herself evenly with fifty times as much single-stranded wire.

The sewing machine had not yet arrived—with something that heavy, she wouldn't be able to afford an over-night delivery. But idle evenings after work had given her time to start on the project anyway.

She had cut and stitched the inner layers for her arms and legs. *I should go ahead and try that out.*

She pulled out her sewing basket and looked at the leggings with a skeptical eye. *I wish they made spandex with integral cabling. It would be so much easier, and look so much nicer.*

Jenny hated the idea that her costume would look like something salvaged from a grade school Halloween party. The whole point of a costume was to conceal the hardware and to look good at the same time.

She unbuttoned her dress and with a glance at the window to confirm that it was shuttered, she skinned down to nothing and picked up the first legging.

It was a stretch fabric of very nearly the same color as the ribbon cable, and she was pleased at how it fit her leg. The other legging and the arms went on as well, although the right arm started to separate at the seam when she flexed it.

How do I fix that? She had picked up a textbook at the Co-op bookstore on sewing, but she had obviously skipped a chapter.

She walked around the room to test the feel and looked at herself in the mirror. *I really need to buy that bathing suit.* As it was, she looked like something from a low-grade porno movie.

The ribbon cable would have to be assembled in sections, and thus the reason for all the connectors she had bought. *I hope I can get it all done before the repairman at work needs his crimping tool back.* She would never be able to afford one of those as well.

She picked up the end of the cable. *I should at least lay it out.*

Duct tape to the rescue again. She started at her foot and began wrapping up her leg, taping the ribbon flat, edge to edge. The knee was difficult. She had to allow a gap so that the cable wouldn't bunch up no matter which position her leg was in.

I wish they made stretchy wiring as well. But that was very unlikely. High-speed electrical signals didn't like it when the wires moved. Ribbon cable was made to bend to fit the twists and turns inside the computer chassis box, but it was never designed to flex continuously. She frowned. *I'm going to have to add another connector here.* It wouldn't work to wrap the whole leg as one continuous run. It would be the same for the arms.

But she kept winding. This was just to get some measurements.

With one leg done, she started wrapping around her hips.

I don't know whether this makes me feel more decent, or more decadent. It looked ugly, with the irregular patches of duct tape she needed to keep the ribbon from spinning free. But the plastic on her bare skin felt interesting.

Breathing started to get difficult once the wrap got up to her ribs. She had to undo several turns and add more slack.

She stalled out entirely when she tried to wrap her breasts.

This just doesn't work! I don't want to look like a boy.

She limped over for another look in the mirror. Holding the spool of cable in one hand, and with her body half wrapped, up to the under side of her breasts, with the rest bulging out the top, she could tell that her original design needed a lot of work.

I am going to have to build a corset, with stays, to keep the shape right. Where can I get a period costume book?

Just then, her doorbell rang.

R ae Bellamy smiled as Jenny opened the door, and then stepped back in alarm.

"Jenny! It's just me."

Jenny was holding a pair of scissors dagger-like in her left hand.

Her right hand held her robe tightly shut. She glanced at the scissors.

"Oh. Sorry. I was busy—cutting. I was cutting, things."

"Oh...kay. Whatever." Rae shrugged it off. "Me and the guys are heading off to Threadgills. I needed another girl. Are you game?"

Jenny looked at the car still running at the curb. She could make out a couple of male faces. *No one I know. Thank God for small favors.* She was very conscious of how she was dressed.

"I'm not going to stand here in my robe. Come on it."

Rae waved to the guys in the car, and followed her in.

The apartment was a mess and Rae just stood in the middle of the room and rolled her eyes.

"Honey, are you sure you don't have a guy living here?"

Jenny winced as some duct-tape on her leg popped free and the ribbon cable started coming loose. She didn't dare move.

"No! Why would you say that?"

Rae crossed her arms and looked around. "Because I have never seen a room this much of a disaster area that didn't belong to a guy."

Jenny turned to follow her gaze, and then had to freeze when more of the cable started moving down her leg.

"I have been working...on a project."

"Yes. Cutting things. I know." Rae pointed to a pile of cloth scraps and pattern sheets. "Isn't it a little late for a costume?"

Jenny answered too loudly, "A costume. What do you mean?"

Rae shrugged. "Well, Halloween and New Years are both a long way off. If you are into amateur theatricals, I expect a ticket.

"So, are you up for dancing?"

Jenny shook her head, "I'm staying home for a while. Cash is really tight."

Rae looked concerned. "Girl, you have been in the lab too long! The guys will pay. They like to do that. It makes them feel macho."

Jenny still said no. "I'm not dressed."

Just then, another patch of tape came loose and a foot or so of ribbon cable spilled into view below her robe. The hard plastic connector went *thunk*, as it hit the floor.

Rae's eyes went wide. "What is that thing?"

"What thing?" Jenny could only hold the front of her robe tightly shut with a grip of death.

But Rae Bellamy would not be bluffed. She pointed a long finger with an ornate piece of artwork on the very long nail down at the curl of cable. "I am talking about that!"

Jenny looked down, and the motion caused the piece of tape that held the last few turns around her ribs to pop loose and she cinched her arms tightly to her side to keep the whole assembly from dropping around her ankles like discarded underwear.

"Oh that," she said lightly, although her entire body was tensed. "That's just a piece of cable. I was cutting it, with the scissors. You know, before I opened the door?"

Rae shook her head at the whole thing. "Whatever! Well if you aren't coming, I've got to go. But I'm warning you. I'm going to take you in hand and get you out more. You can't let yourself go like this."

Jenny simply nodded mutely, and let her leave. When she heard the car drive off, she let her arms relax, and the rest of the cable spun loose like a broken spring and collapsed to the floor.

11

"Just take my word for it!" Jenny said.

Her manager frowned. "Are you sure it's not just stuck in the program? If we re-booted..."

"No. The hard disk is wedged." She put her hand lightly on the top of the box. She could feel the magnetic spikes coming from the drive, as it tried, and dumbly re-tried, to move its internals to seek the new track. She was getting more sensitive to magnetism each day it seemed. But of course, she couldn't tell the boss that.

"You should be able to reboot from the CD, but that hard disk is toast. You will have to send it to the shop."

He sighed, "Well. You are the computer expert. I'll get Harold to move it into the storeroom. We can't have customers getting upset because of bad equipment."

No sooner had he left than she was startled by a voice behind her.

"Hello, Jenny. I didn't know you worked here."

It was Ben, holding a large stack of papers.

"Ben! Yes. I've been here since the TA gig dried up." She indicated his papers. "Do you have a print job?"

Ben beamed, the first time she had ever seen that expression on his face. "It's my master's thesis. I came to get it bound."

She put her hand on his arm and gave it a squeeze. "Oh Ben, I'm so glad for you. It is working out with Professor Hausman?"

A mix of emotions methodically worked their way over his face. "Yes. He is a great guy. Of course he is a busy man, and I don't get to talk to him much like we did with Professor Williams, but the group is great. I got lots of good advice on how to present my findings.

"But I'm real sorry it hasn't worked out for you. I hear Azrahid is a real jerk, and threw out your radiation detector project." He looked genuinely angry about it.

Jenny managed a small smile. "No, it wasn't like that. We just have different ways of looking at things. I wouldn't call him a jerk. He just hasn't been very supportive."

Ben nodded. "A jerk. Believe me, it takes one to know one."

Her mouth twitched a little. "Now Ben, I have never called you a jerk."

He shrugged. "Others have. Do you want to go out some time?"

Jenny smiled, "Why, I think I would enjoy that. But ... not now. I've been extremely busy lately. I have to work long hours to make ends meet." She waved at the row of computers. More than half had people working at them. There were a lot of school projects with deadlines to beat.

He nodded. "I still feel bad that I took your TA slot."

She shook her head. "That is not how it is. It would not have worked out for me."

"Well, then promise me that you will keep at it. It would hurt even more if I thought that I'd knocked you out of school altogether. You are good. Maybe better than me. You need to get your degree."

"Thank you. You are becoming a nicer person every time we meet. Now let's take your thesis to the counter and get someone started on it. I'll make sure they take good care of it."

She arrived with a bounce in her step and spilled out the roll of Velcro on her table. The clock said four. With luck, she could finish in time to try it out.

The costume had firmed up in her mind as the design settled in. Over the past few weeks, she had worked long hours; cutting and sewing, pausing only long enough to go back to work to keep the paychecks coming.

Jenny opened the closet and pulled out the heavy garment.

It was blue, a pale blue, like the sky in the afternoon. She would never have been able to hide all the ribbon cable, so the next best thing had been to make it look as if the color was intended. The only accent on the main body of the costume was a pencil-thin strand of white piping that ran from collar to ankle along the right side.

She was pleased at the way this asymmetrical look had come out. The entire right side was one long zipper. It had nylon teeth—no metal here. Over it were the connectors; there were twenty-four in all throughout the costume. And tonight's completing touch was a Velcro closure to keep the exterior flap closed around the connectors.

This three layer seam was impossible to conceal, and thus the piping, to make it look as if the costume were like one of Emma Peel's mid-60's boots and zipper outfits from the old Avengers TV series.

Boots would be really nice. Maybe I need to check the stores again. They would be tough to make.

She sat down at the sewing machine and got to work.

As she folded the un-wired flap down and pinned the Velcro in place, she thought, *I wonder why zippers are sexy? Maybe it's the implied invitation. Maybe I should add one of those large rings to the zipper, up at the collar end. It would need to be white.*

Jenny was surprised, sometimes, at the change in her. Every time she put the costume on, she had the strangest feelings.

I wonder, does Superman feel bold and sexy when he is in his skin-tight costume? Clark Kent is the timid one. Just like me.

It was past seven when she turned off the sewing machine and inspected the Velcro under a bright light. It was good.

Okay, am I ready for this?

She checked the fading light outside—an early spring evening.

Tonight is the night.

But there was still a lot to be done. She had to load the batteries and find a pair of shoes.

She took off timidity with her clothes and felt excitement as she put her left leg into the costume. Left arm came next and she twisted the rest of the wire-laden fabric around her and began the tricky task of zipping up the right side.

Once zipped in, she spent several minutes before the mirror tugging and adjusting, trying to make sure that everything fit and the parts of her body that were supposed to be symmetrical still looked that way.

In spite of the fact that she was layered like a mummy in wide ribbons of wire, it didn't show. The inner and outer layers of the costume were sewn with lateral pockets to contain and restrain the cable. She had taken great care to keep the seams secured to the under layer of cloth, with the outer layer smooth.

With my body, the extra bulk doesn't look bad at all. She ran her fingers down her belly. She could feel the wires, but unless she pushed against it, they didn't show.

The next step was all those connectors. She sighed, and sat down on the floor. *This isn't easy.*

One by one, snap by snap, she worked her way up. She had spent extra for positive seating connectors with little latches. With her life in the balance, she had gritted her teeth and spent the money. It would not be fun to have her suit fail a thousand feet up.

With each click, she sealed the Velcro flap tight around it. By the time she pushed the collar flap in place, she was stiff. She got to her feet and twisted her torso back and forth. She stretched and bent and waved her arms.

Everything feels secure.

Now the belt.

She had spent more time on the belt than she had on any other component of the costume. Batman's utility belt was her model. It was basically a battery belt with a wide control box in front. She had crafted it white, like the accent piping, with canisters containing batteries all along its length.

A connector from the suit snapped into place on the control box, and she twisted a metal tab that held that critical component in place.

The controls had an inelegant feel to them, but she had a strict budget. The switches were solid, with nothing that would snap off. The adjustments were simple white knobs.

Her heart raced as she made sure that all the dials were off, and then she turned on the master power switch.

Inside, the control circuit woke up. Three relays, each about an inch square and a quarter-inch thick, clicked on.

She carefully turned each dial to the minimum power position and then flipped the test switch.

Across the top of the belt-buckle/control-box, a series of LED's lit amber and then green as each combination was checked. Each test was timed to take a second, and as each one tested the wiring of parts of her costume, she could feel that part of her body twitch in response. At minimum power, it was like being brushed by an invisible feather. All but one of the little lights went green. There was a vacant circuit for a helmet, once she managed to build it.

It's live! Her heart was thundering in her ears.

She looked again at the mirror, and she straightened up at the sight. *I look good!*

With a white mask, and maybe with her hair longer, she would be perfect. Her eyes noticed her bare feet and she frowned a little. *I definitely need some sexy boots.*

Her fingers caressed the lower edge of the knobs and added some power. She could feel the weight lift away. She drifted up on her tiptoes and then lost touch with the floor altogether.

For an instant, she hung weightless, motionless, a foot above the floor.

"Whoa!" With an unexpected shout, she tilted over. Arms flailing, she turned upside down, and drifted towards the kitchen with her hair brushing the floor and her whole body swinging back and forth like a very slow clock pendulum.

"Arrgh! I'm top-heavy." *Maybe I'll need that helmet after all.*

She struggled with a flash of vertigo, and reached for the controls. By feel, she reached for the knob that controlled her upper torso, and added power. She flipped again, and started rising. *Reduce power to the legs.*

With a little practice, she trimmed her lift, and settled back down, right side up, on the ground. *I need some shoes, but it will work.*

She hit the master switch, and weight returned with a thump. *This will really work!*

Jenny paused just a second to note down the time and a cryptic "Need auto-bal. Suit works!" into her lab book. The lettering was barely readable. She snapped it shut and pushed it back into the drawer. Her mind wasn't on the documentation.

The Nike shoes definitely clashed with her costume. *But no one is going to see me anyway.*

It had gotten a lot darker, she noted. She peered out the half-opened door. Suiting up in her own apartment was one thing, but stepping outside was more frightening than she had expected.

Now is not the time to be timid! She slipped out on the tiny porch, more like an extended step, and locked the door behind her.

For an instant she stared blankly at the key in her hand. *Oh no. No pockets. I need to fix that.* Not even her 'utility belt' had any spare space to put the key. On impulse, she wedged the key up under her left sleeve. *It's brass. It won't make that much difference to the magnetic field.*

Her porch light was off, but there was still plenty of glare from the streetlights to make everything visible, too visible. There was enough for someone to see her as well, if there had been anyone about.

Honestly, the costume is no more remarkable than some of the things Rae wears.

But still, she would rather not be seen—not yet.

She turned to the left and followed the edge of the building. The apartments were an extended two story multiplex. Up above her porch was a balcony for the upper apartment. It was just enough room for a chair or a barbecue grill, but not both. The entrance stairway was the other direction. She headed towards the blank wall on which all the individual electric meters and fuse boxes were mounted. In a city with an unforgiving summer, it was a rare apartment complex indeed which included the electricity bill for all those air-conditioners in with the rental.

The narrow corridor between buildings was poorly lit—not the kind of place Jenny would visit, even in the daytime. But tonight, it would keep prying eyes from seeing her.

She touched the controls carefully. The pressure on her feet went to nothing, and she was standing on her toes.

She consciously tilted her toes up and bent her knees. Light as a feather, she drifted lower.

Then she jumped.

She grabbed for the aluminum wiring conduit on the side of the building, and more for control than anything, she climbed quickly up to the roof.

Another adjustment, and she settled down, her feet sliding on the slanted roofing tiles. She found her footing, and added some weight.

That was fun.

From her viewpoint, she could see several blocks in all directions. The cooling air of the evening had produced a light haze, and the streetlights each made a yellow fog that together dotted the residential neighborhood.

Without thinking, she crouched again and jumped, turning her weight negative with a touch on the dials. The night air rushed past. She spread her arms and used her hands to carve through the air, like she did out the window of her car sometimes.

More. She turned the knobs one by one, and the wind picked up, plastering her hair into her eyes. *How fast am I climbing?*

But no sooner had she formed that thought, than a sharp burning pain bit into her right thigh. "Ouch!"

"No. No. No!" She slapped at the spot, but it only made it worse.

Short circuit!

12

Frantically, Jenny bent forward, trying to see her control box with her hair and the blasting wind in her eyes.

One of the lights was barely lit. *Power circuit 2.*

The pain was unbearable!

In spite of it, she slowly and carefully worked her finger along the switches from the end. She stabbed at the right one.

Jenny felt the click—nothing could be heard over the wind.

I've got to get back down. The other two circuits could handle the load. She had designed three completely independent systems for just this kind of problem. One circuit alone should be able to produce the necessary magnetic field.

Still, her leg burned! She wrenched her mind away from the pain. A primitive desire to rip open the suit clawed at her. The instant she tried that, the whole suit would go dead. She forced herself to think about that, splattering herself on some darkened street below. Her hand clenched. She forced it back open. *The pain will go away. The pain will go away.*

Her left arm had no magnetic field. One band around her torso was on the problem circuit. And of course, the right leg was powerless as well.

There! She had turned herself to a face down position. It was a little unstable, but with effort, she could watch for landmarks below.

The wind dropped very slowly to nothing, and then she felt air on her face. She was coming down, far slower than she had climbed.

The pain eased. *Okay!* It was a short circuit. That was fixable. All she had to do was get back home and check on the damage.

She stretched her arms out, sliding through the air. *So this is flying.* At this reduced speed, it was less frantic than skydiving.

Where is my place? In this darkness, the streets were an anonymous maze of yellow dots. *I must be a couple of thousand feet high. I need a GPS navigator to tell for sure.*

Oh great! A pocket for my key, something to hold a GPS. No telling what else I'll need.

How many superheroes carried a purse?

Is that why Batman has the belt? A utility purse would look too sissy. Hard to keep up the superstitious awe that way.

"Hmm." She could make a white pouch strapped to her left leg, something like the holder Daredevil used for his cane.

Quickly, the streetlights were getting larger. She adjusted the lift, and pulled to a stop, a couple of hundred feet up.

Where am I, exactly?

Not that it mattered. She couldn't risk hanging in the sky. No only was there the chance someone would see her, but there was also a risk of other circuit failures. She could walk home.

There was not much movement in the air, but she let herself drift long enough to be confident that there was no one walking this block. As she came even with the street, she cut power to her left leg and settled down the remaining distance feet first.

Her toes touched down on the sidewalk. She cut all the power. The lights on her controls went dark. Weight had returned.

"Whoo, whee!" Jenny felt giddy. She almost lost her balance and tripped when her foot hit the edge of the concrete.

She felt like shouting aloud. *I can fly!*

S omewhere in the flight, Jenny had lost her sense of direction. She walked three blocks before she realized that she was heading away from her street.

Okay, the breeze is coming from that direction. If I head into it, I will find my street. Next time, I'll find my landmarks while I'm still high enough to spot them.

She toyed with the idea of popping back up for a look-see, but her leg still throbbed from the burn spot. Better to wait.

The walking felt good. The exercise kept her warm.

When was the last time I went for a walk on purpose? The campus was large enough that she had never felt the need for the exercise. But with her current job, she hadn't been back there in weeks. There had been time for nothing but work, shopping, and working on the costume.

But it is worth it!

She was conscious that, in spite of her limp from the burn spot, she was walking straighter, taller, than she usually did. I nice outfit had always made an impact on how she felt about herself, but this one was different.

She was special. She was unique. She was ... well maybe not a superhero, but she had a gift shared by no one on the planet.

Sorry you are not here to share this Jase. You would have had fun.

"H ellooo, there, missy." The husky voice out of the darkness sent her pulse rocketing. She started walking faster.

"Hey, don't be like that." The man stepped onto the sidewalk behind her. He started walking after her.

Another voice came from the darkness. "What's up Lou?" There was a creak, like a door on bad hinges.

Jenny ran. There were heavy footsteps behind her, and they weren't getting any fainter. She was too terrified to look back.

This was one of her nightmares—men chasing her in the dark—men who would hurt her. She felt her chest tense up for a scream. Where was she? Would there be anyone to help her? Would a scream only attract others like that dark presence closing in on her?

The end of the block. There was a fence.

She didn't even think about it. She rounded the fence, slapped the controls, and jumped for the safety of the sky.

There was a flash of pain on her burn spot, and she juggled the controls, but it didn't stop her rapid climb to a hundred feet.

She looked back. Her pursuer was a man as big as Ben, only in a black jacket and with a black scraggly beard. He rounded the fence, and then ran out of steam as his prey was nowhere to be seen. He never once thought to look up.

The second man arrived a few seconds later. They talked, but she was already too far away to make out their words. They stopped, and then turned back the way they came. When they went out of sight, she allowed herself to breathe.

She glanced around, and settled swiftly back down to the front yard of a dimly lit house. Almost as soon as her foot hit the ground, she was jogging. A familiar road was just two blocks away. Home was not far.

She pressed her hand on the belt, where every third battery was still radiating heat. *Technical details. The suit works. And I'm never giving it up!*

Issue 3: Angel

13

She put down her pen, after she'd documented the poor insulation and the crossed wire. A teflon replacement and new batteries had fixed everything. She looked at the clock. If she were going to make it to work on time, she really had to get some sleep. She pushed back the chair and took a step towards the bedroom.

She stopped, and looked back at the suit.

She picked it up and draped it over her arm. She held it close as she headed off to bed.

"Hey, Tinkerbell! Where'd you put the disk caddy?"

Jenny felt her face go pale. "What did you call me?"

Had he seen me? I only lifted an inch or two. Her hand went to the control belt under her baggy outfit. She was sure it was off.

Mike, the computer repairman, was in for his once-a-week check of the equipment. He smiled. "'Tinkerbell'. I've seen you flitting around, always granting customers' wishes. The boss said he wished he had more employees like you."

Jenny let herself smile. She knew it was a fib. It had been hard to keep her mind on work at all. Her mind was always on the flight suit.

"Okay, so you can charm people at the drop of a hat. What is it you asked for?"

"The disk caddy. My diagnostic disks are in there."

Jenny pointed him to the cabinet where she had stored the software, and forced her heart back down her throat. It was silly to wear the costume to work. Not only did it mean she had to wear her ugliest clothes over it, but it also tempted her to lift when she had to reach something on the top shelf in spite of the risk.

Hmm. I wonder if I could make a torso-only suit. Keep the arms and legs bare.

There was a burst of static behind her, and the thought scattered. She looked. There was an older man, thin, with the look of a farmer. He was twisting one of the knobs on a belt radio. It silenced the noise.

"Are you a policeman?" she asked.

He shook his head. "No. Just a First Responder for Smithville." His voice was gravelly, and his manner was charming.

"'First Responder'—what's that?"

His well-lined face cracked a smile. "It's a volunteer thing. We're the first to respond when there is a call for help."

"Like the volunteer fire department?"

"Yes. It's like that. There is a lot of overlap. First Responders fill the need for medical aid, especially in small towns that can't afford full time EMT's—Emergency Medical Technicians. The First Responder certification takes less time to get, so there are more volunteers. My wife and I are both certified. We do the CPR, stop the bleeding, treat for shock—that sort of thing."

Jenny had a sinking feeling. "How much training does that take?"

He scratched his chin. "I think it was a 40 hour course. Lots of weekends, as I recall. Plus there is some on-going training every now and then."

"And you get to carry a radio."

"Mostly a pager."

Jenny asked, "Can I look at the radio? I had been thinking of getting one of those scanners."

"Sure." He handed it to her. "Get a programmable one, so you can enter in the right frequencies. Are you interested in emergency services?"

She nodded, as she looked over the settings. "Do all the police use the same bands?"

"Not hardly. There's been noise about setting up a common band so all the different police and fire and medical people could at least communicate, but it hasn't really caught on."

She handed back the radio. And he handed her one of the fliers he was having copied. There was a fund-raiser coming up in a few days.

Why would I need a radio? It's silly to think I could be like Batman and swoop down on the crooks. I'd more likely run away—from the crooks and the police.

And the idea that she might need to get official certification to even help people—how did that work?

Superheroes aren't usually all that popular with the police. Unless you are Superman Himself. Even Batman is only quasi-legal. Without the secret help of Commissioner Gordon, he would be constantly at odds with the police.

Maybe she should cultivate that Davis character. She shuddered. *He scares me too much. Too much guilty conscience.*

Just then, a matronly lady with a gleam in her eye and a photo album headed her way. Jenny nodded goodbye to the First Responder, and went to help her.

Jenny snapped awake. *Five AM! I didn't get any sleep.* It was time for her limits test.

When the GPS arrived, yesterday afternoon, she should have guessed she would be too keyed up. She picked it up from the side table.

It was a lovely little gadget. It was a low end Global Positioning System unit, but it had the features she needed. She felt a pang of guilt that she had used the credit card to get this one. There were ones the same size that had detailed maps and lots of trip log features, but she couldn't justify the price.

But the best price was on the web. I had to use the credit card.

Now with the costume fully repaired, her GPS, a day off from work—it was time to do the limits test.

She padded on bare feet to the window. There were stars out. It would be a clear day, and she needed the visibility.

Dawn wasn't far off, and she slipped into the costume with the ease of regular practice.

She tightened the Velcro, pulled on the white slippers she had made, and put a checkmark beside that item on her list.

The shoes were crude, and she was far from satisfied with them, but they were really more for looks than durability.

Next came the battery check. All new batteries—and she checked each with the meter before securing them in place. Two days before, she had run a set of batteries to exhaustion on the empty suit, measuring the voltage and current every minute. She had to have a good idea of how long her batteries would last. She fully intended to never let the capacity drop below a third.

Batteries. Check.

She affixed her foot-long leg pouch to its Velcro attachment and checked it for a secure hold.

That had been a fiasco. The first time she had sewn the Velcro patch on her leg, she had put the side with all the hooks on her leg and the patch with all the loops on her pouch. Wrong move! With the hooks on her leg, every time she wore a skirt or jeans or her sweat pants over the costume, the Velcro snagged the overlying cloth. It had been a hard job to remove the Velcro and reverse it, with the loop patch on her leg—especially hard because she had to do every cut and stitch by hand to make sure that she didn't nick any of the cable wires beneath it.

Pouch. Check.

Into the bottom of the pouch went a spare battery set, enough to run one of the power systems. She hoped never to have to replace the batteries while falling out of the sky, but it would be a lifesaver if she had them.

Spare Batteries. Check.

Cell phone. Scratch.

With her original cell lost somewhere in Blanco county during that skydive, and no money to buy another, she kept putting off getting the replacement.

Police Scanner. Scratch.

Ditto. She would need to make sure that whatever she got was long and narrow and would fit the pouch.

GPS. Check.

Notepad. Check.

Jenny clipped her pen into the loop on the side of the cheap little scratch-pad and fit it carefully inside the pouch beside the GPS.

I'm ready.

She eased out the front door into the cool morning air and locked her door behind her. The key went into a special snap lock pocket in the back of the pouch.

A glance around to make sure she was the only one awake at this time of the morning, and then she jumped easily to the roof of the apartment. She walked to the center, where she couldn't be seen from the ground.

The GPS came on with a push button and she waited several seconds for the little hand-held unit to acquire a few satellites orbiting twelve thousand miles overhead.

The clock on the GPS had the added advantage of being dead-on accurate, since the satellite system used atomic clocks to create accurate timing signals. She noted down the time onto her notepad, and then affixed the GPS to a spare position on the Velcro leg pad. She pushed at it, testing it, but the Velcro held fast.

Good. I want to be able to look at it all the time.

She snapped the pouch shut.

Time to go.

Jenny jumped into the sky.

14

She dialed full power into the coils. She closed her eyes and concentrated on the feeling in her body.

If there are uneven clumps of dark matter in my body, I should be able to feel it. She tried to quiet the distraction of the wind noise and the sting of chill on her face. She really needed to know if there were any feelings of pressure, or the tug of dark matter trying to tear at her insides. *The more I know, the less likely it will kill me.*

But there was nothing that she could feel, other than disorientation. Where was up, and where was down? She opened her eyes, and focused on the glowing light of the dawn. It was enough. She would have to use her eyes to keep her brain happy. It was as she had expected, from all the astronaut tales of how they coped with weightlessness.

It didn't seem to be a severe problem. *Does that mean that the fluid in my semi-circular canals in my ears is not as affected by the dark matter as the surrounding tissue?* Something to check on later.

She noted her altitude and the time and scribbled the figures down, in spite of the wind. *Only three thousand feet, and it feels like my speed has stabilized.* Unfortunately, her GPS didn't have a readout for rise or fall velocity. It was designed for hikers or motorists who didn't really have any need for those numbers. She would have to do the math on the raw numbers when she got back down. It was important to keep recording.

The climb into the sky might have stopped accelerating, but it was not stopping.

I'm freezing!

She stuffed the notepad back into the pouch and put her hands over her ears. *I should have thought of this.* Of course, the air up higher would be cooler. And with this climb, the wind-chill was getting very uncomfortable.

No help for it. She folded her arms tightly together across her chest and protected her hands as well as she could. *I should have worn a jacket. I'll need one. A white version of the Cadmus Superboy's leather jacket? That would look good.*

She took a deep breath and with stiffening fingers, took another altitude and time reading. 6,250 feet, and still climbing strongly.

The land below was beginning to show texture and dramatic highlights as the dawn colors spread out over the landscape. She sniffed with her suddenly runny nose, and twisted her body around so that she could see the sunrise.

8,400 feet. She held on to the notepad as the sun came quickly above the horizon.

Oh! With her rapid climb, it was if the sun jumped into the sky. The sudden touch of warmth on her face was welcome, even as her eyes blinked away tears from the wind and the sudden brightness.

9,220 feet. *Am I slowing?* She tried a quick mental calculation from the nearly illegible numbers on her pad. *Yes.*

The batteries were still in the flat part of their power curve. The slow-down wasn't due to any drop off in the magnetism.

It has to be the dark matter field. It was something she had half expected. She was a physicist, and finding a theory to make complex problems simple was her delight.

Gravity dropped off by the square of the distance. If the dark matter repulsion followed the same relation, then her dark matter would be pushing and her climb would just keep going to the edge of space and beyond. The repulsion, for as long as the magnetic field held out, would be greater than gravity's attraction no matter the distance.

But if the repulsion fell off as the cube of the distance, or even some more exotic multiple, then she would only climb as long as she was close to the mass of the ground. She would only be affected by matter close by.

It could also explain why the dark matter was trapped inside her body. If dark matter particles were tiny, the size of atoms or smaller, then for each speck of dark matter, the shell of atoms around it would form a repulsive trap to keep it in place. That very close shell would have a much stronger effect than the repulsion of the ground below, and the dark matter would have to lift the normal matter around it, rather than slip through the atoms and evaporate out of her.

At 12,000 feet. Jenny held her arms tightly around her. It was bone-chilling cold, even if the wind was dying down, and the sun was shining.

If there is snow on the mountains at this altitude, I shouldn't have been surprised. I hope I don't get sick from this.

Her mind raced over the idea of a complete ski outfit, with gloves, a fur hat, earmuffs, and of course, good boots.

Or maybe, if I can make a suit with a stronger magnetic field, I should just go for a space suit. Sealed helmet, oxygen supply. Heaters!

That was a vision that caught her attention. Could she make it all the way to space?

14,000 feet. *This is what I set for a limit, but I went to Pikes Peak, and it is taller than that. I didn't faint there. Besides, I am almost at my ceiling. I can tell it won't go much higher.*

It was almost still. And with the sunshine, it was starting to feel much warmer. No wind chill to complicate it.

15,000 feet. Jenny watched the GPS digital readout. The numbers were starting to become erratic. The manual had said that the altitude readings were not very accurate, and she had seen that for herself at the 600-foot altitude of the city, with the GPS reading from 250 feet to over 800.

15,350. That is what it looks like. She noted the reading on the notepad and waited. She was definitely hovering. The readings were flickering higher and lower with no other evidence that she was really changing altitude.

"Good." She spoke aloud, just to hear her voice and to make this strange moment a little bit more real.

The sunrise had touched the ground far below, although there weren't many details she could make out, other than a few low patches of ground fog that seemed to twist along the tributaries of the rivers and creeks.

Jenny frowned. "Where did the city go?"

15

There was a buzzing sensation somewhere in the back of her head. *Altitude. I'm not used to this.* It would be very bad to faint right now. She eased off on the controls, and was instantly greeted with a rush of air coming up from beneath her. She still had plenty of juice left. No sense in dropping too fast and freezing herself.

She checked the GPS and looked at the breadcrumb trail on the little screen. She had to expand the scale to find the waypoint mark she had left to mark her apartment.

How did I get this far away? She changed the display again and was shocked to read her speed. She was heading northward at twenty-six miles per hour.

Okay. I'm traveling with the wind, so I can't feel it. There hadn't been any breeze she'd noticed when she started, back at ground level, but the winds aloft, a phrase she had heard often used by TV weather reporters, were much faster.

Jenny used her arms and the wind of her fall to orient herself towards town. She cut the power all the way, and started skydiving in earnest, using the slant of her body in the air to cut across the sky. She clenched her jaw as the fierce chill hit, in spite of her neck-to-toe costume. Why hadn't she given any thought to insulation?

Nearly a minute later, she checked the GPS.

What! The breadcrumb trail showed no progress, and the speed showed her still heading away from town, but now by five miles per hour. She pulled herself to a stop.

Oh no! I can't make headway against the wind. I can't get back to town.

The sinking feeling, made worse by the shivers that were wracking her body, forced her to face facts.

I can't fly. I don't have the power of flight. I can only float. I am totally at the mercy of the winds.

Her early confidence was shattered. The ease with which she could jump in any direction and the illusion of great speed while skydiving; it was just wishful thinking. Easy first steps had hidden the real facts.

Maybe I can zigzag—use a skydiving glide while going down, and then another while rising.

But even that could be no faster than what she had just tried. Using her body as a wing was directly dependent on her rate of falling and rising, and she had already observed that she could only rise at a slower rate than she could fall.

It tasted bitter. *I've just been fooling myself, playing out this superhero fantasy. I need to get down, and get home, before I kill myself.*

Jenny had planned to pop up to her maximum altitude, and then circle back down, using her skydiving glide, until she could land, hopefully unseen, in the city park that stretched along Shoal Creek. From there, she expected to walk the few blocks home, more confident that her costume was 'normal' enough to pass without comment.

But now, there was no telling where she would come down. From the looks of the land below, she would land in the middle of some farmer's field, many miles from even a bus stop.

She deeply missed her cell phone.

No good! No money for a taxi, and what address would I give? Taxis don't come to latitude and longitude. They need a street address.

More shivers shook even those thoughts away. She had to get down to the ground, quickly. *Worry about how to get home later.*

She reset the controls to put her into a slow downward glide. She had to minimize the chill.

There was a road. It was a long straight blacktop, running in roughly the direction she had come. The morning sun caught a glint from a distant car's windshield. She could hike to the nearest gas station and call Rae to come rescue her.

I'll need a really good story—maybe I should call Bob? She could imagine his frown too. She sighed.

No. For now at least, I have to keep my friends out of it. They are all too nosy. I can't turn this into a committee effort. This is my life!

A thousand feet up, she leveled out. *The ground is moving too fast.*

She glanced ahead. *No time to dawdle.* Her path crossed a highway in a couple of minutes and she had no idea how long it would be before she encountered another road.

Off on an adjoining field, there was a farmer hard at work on his tractor. His eyes were down on his field, oblivious to the strange bird in his sky.

Farmhouse. She dropped down to a hundred feet. She had to be ready to hit the ground running.

If there were anyone looking out the window, they'd see her. There was nothing Jenny could do about that.

Trees. There was a row of tall trees, planted as a windbreak, all along the front of the property. They were coming up fast.

Jenny hesitated; she wasn't yet oriented feet down. She grabbed for the controls, but her finger slipped.

There was a web of branches. She put up her hands to protect her face, and sailed into the stinging slap of the twigs. Her hair tangled instantly, and it felt as if it were coming out by the roots.

She grabbed a branch and held on. Then she grabbed another, and pulled herself up, to free her hair.

It was a blind fumble, with the tree trying incessantly to poke her in the eye with a twig. Finally, with a twist, she snapped the tangle free, and was able to turn her head toward the ground.

She twisted the knob to zero, then backed off a whisker. She came down hard, but still bounced when she hit.

Off! She hit the master cut-off, and collapsed in a heap on the ground.

"Ah! Chew!" With a sneeze that for a moment relieved the need to wipe her nose on her sleeve, Jenny trudged step by painful step down the edge of the highway. Her makeshift shoes were useless. She had not thought the design through. They looked okay, but the soles were murder on her feet. She had taken to reducing her weight slightly—just enough for traction, but not enough to rub any more blisters. She had to lean into the wind more than looked normal, but it was worth it.

What makes me think that I could be any kind of a superhero? Look at me. I have no strength at all. Superman has strength. He could do things.

All I could do is run away more effectively.

Batman was a 'normal' human, but he at least had a budget to build the tools he needed.

And who even needs superheroes, in the real world?

We have Star-Flight medical helicopters to get injured people to the hospital. We have a trained group of Emergency Medical Technicians. We have FEMA and the National Guard for big things like floods and disasters. What would Superman be able to do in the real world? After the first couple of rescues, he would be slapped down with a court injunction to stop until he at least got his First Responder Certification.

Batman would be hunted down by the FBI, and BATF forces would lay siege to the batcave. After all, he is a seriously insane vigilante.

No, superheroes are not needed nor wanted in this world. If I really wanted to help, I should get my own First Aid training and forget this costumed hero business.

I need to keep my feet on the ground.

16

The chills had gone. The morning was warming quickly, and she was starting to chafe. The costume had failed her again. The fabric wasn't smooth enough, and there were too many lumps due to the wiring. It wasn't designed for long distance walking. Too much more of this, and she would have to re-check all the wiring for wear and tear.

So much for crafting a superhero costume on the cheap.

The approaching rumble of a large truck changed to the hiss of air brakes. Jenny dodged over into the grass as the 18-wheeler slowed past her and pulled to the side of the road a hundred years ahead of her.

She kept her pace, wanting to catch a ride, but frightened of the idea. The face in the rear-view mirror watching her looked okay, but what could you tell about a face anyway? She looked the truck over. At least there were no naked girls on the mud flaps.

Below his window, in large letters, it said "Mandrake".

"Hello," he asked. "Do you need a ride?"

Jenny put her hand above her eyes to shade them from the sun. A bone-deep ache all over her body pushed the decision.

"Yes. Are you headed into town?"

"Next stop. Climb on in."

She moved around to the passenger side and climbed up the steps. Even opening the door seemed too much for her, but she managed.

"Manny Samuelson," he said. He offered a smile. Up close, he looked older, maybe near her father's age. He was a little overweight too, but not unpleasantly so.

Jenny hesitated. "Tinkerbell", she introduced herself. She had been called that more than once in her life and she had no intention of giving out her real name.

She sat quietly while Manny eased the truck back onto the highway. The cab looked well lived in. There wasn't an untouched foot of factory dash anywhere. In addition to numerous cup-holders, and what looked like a small refrigerator, there was a rack of radios, two big scanners, and a CB with a hand-held microphone dangling from a metal clip. Below that was custom aluminum box that looked suspiciously like a linear amplifier to boost the CB transmitter into the illegal power ranges. Up above it all was an ornate crystal goblet containing leaves and crystal chunks emitting a pleasant lemon smell.

Her nose twitched, and before she could stop it, she sneezed.

He pulled out a box of tissues and handed it to her.

Gratefully, she proceeded to clean out her congestion with several tissues and even more heartfelt honks.

"Thank you." She said, suddenly aware of how hoarse her voice sounded.

There were another few minutes of silence. Manny would look her way and smile, but he was leaving it up to her whether to talk or not.

Her attention was caught by the erratic blinking of the radio scanner. There were ten channels, and it blinked a red light for a fraction of a second as it checked each.

Finally, she asked. "Do you monitor the police bands?"

"Sometimes, when I'm bored, or when the CB starts talking about an accident or something. I make my living by keeping a schedule, and I can't afford to be held up for hours because of a ten-car pile-up. I've got the sound turned down. Play with it if you want."

She shook her head. The idea of a police scanner was really just part of the superhero fantasy. She wouldn't need one in real life. She had to get out of that rut.

"What do you haul?" she asked at last.

"It varies. I have contracts with distribution centers in San Antonio, Austin and Waco. I own my own rig—the front part of the truck with the engine. I hook up whichever trailer they have waiting for me and take it to the next city."

"Make much money at it?"

He laughed. "Depends on the price of diesel."

Jenny smiled. That made sense. It was a big variable, with most other things likely to be fixed costs.

Just then, they approached a highway intersection and he turned left.

She frowned, "All three cities are on I-35. What are you doing out here?"

"Now little lady, I may have my schedules, but I also make this run with painful regularity, and I have noticed that the restaurant owners have neglected to put their best places on the Interstate. Unless I want to eat yuppie at places that don't have parking spaces for my rig, or unless I just love greasy spoon cuisine, I have to do a little exploring." He nodded back towards the way he had come. "A few miles past is the best place for breakfast taco's I know."

He looked at her, "You look like you could use some food. Did you have breakfast?"

She shook her head. "No, but I really need to get home."

"Got a chill. I can tell. But there are some emergency rations in the box. See if there is anything you can eat."

Jenny hesitated, and then looked. She was trying to decide between an orange that was almost frozen solid, and a can of chocolate malt diet drink, when the radio crackled on.

"Hey Mandrake, what's your twenty? Come back."

Manny reached for the microphone and chatted with the other trucker for a moment. He apologized for missing the rendezvous and promised to catch him on the next leg.

"Am I making you miss your schedule," Jenny asked, after he had put back his microphone.

"No. I've got lots of slack this run. Rescuing a fair maiden is the high point of my day."

Manny wove his truck into the city traffic as Jenny sipped the odd-tasting chocolate drink.

"Where do I drop you?" he asked.

She considered the question.

"Come on," he said. "I know young girls are not supposed to trust strange men, but you are sick, and fading fast. I'll drop you anywhere you wish, but make sure you can get home quickly."

Jenny nodded, and directed him to a street just a couple of blocks from her apartment.

"Thank you," she said, as she stepped down to the ground. "I really appreciate it."

"And I really enjoyed helping. Tinkerbell, I want you to call me for rescuing any time you need to. Now go home, and take care of yourself." With a rumble of the diesel engine, he turned his eyes back to the road and started to move.

She waited until he was out of sight, and then hobbled the remaining distance to her door. She peeled the suit and left it piled on the floor. She went to bed, and slept the clock around, in spite of nightmares.

She had to take off work for four days, fighting the flu.

17

The phone rang several times before Jenny shook off her lethargy and pulled herself out of the chair.

"Hello."

"Hi. It's Rae. Get dressed. We are doing Berry's tonight."

Her shoulders sagged. "Oh, I don't know. I've been pretty droopy lately. I've had to work a lot of extra hours lately to make up for the days I missed sick."

"No excuse, girl. You wimped out last time, and I let you get away with it. Not this time. We will be there to pick you up in an hour. And show some skin! No more overalls."

Jenny held the receiver for a moment after the call ended, and then put it down with a sigh. Rae wouldn't be put off. She would be here, with friends, expecting her to be ready. At least she had something to wear. She hadn't changed sizes in years, and her clubbing outfit saw very little use.

Her apartment was still a disaster. Perhaps it was even worse, after being sick for a nearly a week. Her eye caught the blue pile next to the door. She hadn't even put up the flight suit since that disastrous test.

She picked it up, and slapped at the wrinkles. With the plastic ribbon cabling, it would take a while to smooth it out. She should at least hang it up.

She put it on a wooden hangar and detached the control belt. The suit went to the far back of the closet and she opened the belt over the table. The batteries slid out with a clatter. All except one. *Oh no. A leaker.* She fished it out with her fingernails. The side of the case had a slimy feel. *I had better clean this immediately.*

She dumped all the batteries into the trash, and then used a tissue to wipe out the inside of the battery case. She gave special attention to the contacts on the leaky battery's position. It was a difficult task to get every last hint of the chemical off the metal in the enclosed space. *Am I even going to use this any more?*

The whole superhero idea was dead, and she was grumpy about it. It had been such an appealing fantasy, but she was too realistic to give it any credibility now.

It was an expensive fantasy too. How many more months until Halloween, when I can wear this again?

She stuffed the battery container with wadded tissue and filed it in her dresser drawer next to the wool socks.

The nightclub was loud. Jenny had been surprised, at first, to see Bob Mitchell in the car, along with Rae Bellamy and Perry Thredwell. They had all been among the dozen or so people that had collected at the library study rooms Jenny's first year there. In various combinations, they had attended classes together, gone to movies together, and in some cases, paired up as permanent couples.

Perry was in his senior year, well on his way to collect his BS in Geological Sciences. He was more interested in job interviews than going for a Masters.

Jenny had been severely shocked when she found out that Rae Bellamy was a Ph.D. candidate in mathematics. She was specializing in some topological something that made no sense to normal mortals. Up until that revelation, Jenny had always suspected that she was a Business major or something like that, slumming with the techno-geeks.

Rae had always been the event coordinator for that group. If it had been up to Jenny, she would never have done anything more than conspire to spend time in Jase's presence.

None of her peer group males had impressed her much. Their major interests, football and time alone with her in darkened rooms, did little to inspire much respect for their brains. She managed to avoid both by tuning out most of the chatter and keeping to well-attended groups.

She frowned. The noise tonight was likely to put her to sleep.

Bob yelled at her, "Headache?"

She shook her head. The music was interesting enough, but amplified as it was, it made conversation impossible.

He held up one finger and then walked away. She smiled absently. Rae and Perry had already migrated out into the mass of people dancing. Rae looked at her, and for an instant, her eyes were poisonous.

The guitar section ended and some heavy bass wove its way into the song.

Deep inside her, she felt a resonance with the music. It was loud enough to shake up anyone's insides, but tonight it felt different.

Bob waved at her. He had staked out a sliver of table space and had acquired her standard drink, a Coke still in the can. She joined him, and they listened to the music awhile.

Space was limited and she was grateful that she had the outside seat. Wedged up next to Bob was okay, but squeezed between two people would be claustrophobic.

"Do you want to dance?" Bob shouted in her ear. She nodded, and they moved into the bouncing population on the floor.

Bob must have been practicing, because he took her hand and moved her through the motions with very little effort on her part. It was almost too fast for her. She skipped along the floor and a couple of times, almost tripped. His strong arm was always there to catch her, so there was no problem.

The huge black floor-standing speakers were doing her in. As Bob moved her across the floor, they came too close. The magnetic spikes caused her foot to miss the floor altogether and she collapsed on her side.

Bob had her up in a flash, but she shook her head and pointed toward the side room that was out of the main squeeze.

Behind a wall, they could even hear each other talk.

"Are you okay?" he asked.

"Yes. I just slipped. I haven't been dancing in a long while."

"I enjoyed it," he declared. "Rae said you had gained some weight, but I don't think so. You didn't weight anything out there on the floor."

Jenny felt her heart catch. *Could it be?* She didn't remember being affected so much by speakers before.

Bob asked, "Are you ready to go again?"

She shook her head. "I need to just sit here for a little bit. But why don't you cut in on Perry and give Rae a spin."

He looked doubtful. "Are you sure?"

She patted his arm. "Yes. I just need to sit still for a little while. I won't be doing much dancing tonight."

He shrugged and headed back onto the main area.

Jenny stared at the wallpaper pattern, blindly.

Could the dark matter be growing in me? The chamber continued to lose weight, even when we pulled the plug.

She looked around the room, filled with happy active people who wouldn't understand her panic even if she explained it to them. *Data. I need data.*

There had been a scale in the entrance to the club, she remembered. One of those antique coin-operated monstrosities that gave you a fortune and your weight for a nickel. Did it still work, or was it just decoration?

She was up and weaving her way through the crowd. *All these tall people—I need to get through!*

She made it to the scale and stood on it. A metal flag moved over the window that showed the numbers. In embossed brass lettering it said. "One Nickel Please!"

She patted her micro-purse. The little wallet on a long strap held her credit card, and a twenty-dollar bill, and very little else. She hadn't brought any change. She looked around, and made eye contact with a man waiting to enter the club.

"Hello," he said.

"Hi. Can I have a nickel?"

He smiled and nodded. "For you, anything." He pulled the coin out of a pocket and put it in the slot for her. The brass lettering moved aside, and she read the scale. It was just two tick marks shy of the 50.

She was very conscious of the warmth radiating from the man standing very close behind her.

"It must be broken," she said in clipped tones.

"Sorry." He held out a hand to help her down. She wasn't that helpless, but he had sacrificed a nickel for her.

"Thank you."

Just then, Bob came through the door. He looked puzzled and hurt.

"Bob," Jenny said, "I'm feeling sick. I'm going to go home now. There's a bus run just down the street and I insist that you stay with Rae and Perry. I don't want to ruin your evening."

He frowned. "Okay, but I'll take you home."

"No. I won't have it. I know exactly what I am doing. Tell the others." She turned and walked out into the night air. It had begun to rain. Inside, she could see a reflection of Bob's glare at the other man, but she almost ran down the street to get clear in case Bob tried to insist.

48 pounds! How can that be? Surely, I would have noticed losing half my weight!

Her foot slipped a little as she ran, and that part of the sidewalk wasn't even wet yet. How many times had that happened lately? A trip here, a slip there. A little self-depreciating joke to the people around her about how clumsy she was getting. Had this been going on since the dark matter explosion?

There was a brightly-lit storefront—a drugstore. She pushed her way in and walked the aisles until she found the bathroom floor scales.

She had never bought one before. Her weight had been rock stable since high school, 96 to 97 pounds. No matter what she ate, it never varied.

The scales were packaged in a cardboard wrapper, and she tore it loose from one of them and placed it on the floor. She stepped on it. The spring-loaded scale spun easily to 47.

"Can I help you?" A uniformed store clerk came up, a frown on his face at the demolished cardboard.

She stepped off the scale. "I'm buying this." She picked it up and handed it to him. She dug into her purse and pulled out the credit card. "Charge it, and hurry. I've got a bus to catch."

She followed the clerk, and it seemed that she was dancing on her tiptoes. *How soon? How soon until I lose it all?*

18

L OG ENTRY:
As is indicated on the previous chart, I should go to negative weight in eight days with an error bar of two days. This assumes that the rate of dark matter development in my body follows the same non-linearity as was shown in the original chamber. This cannot be certain, because of the change that occurred when we killed the power.

I am also beginning a periodic entry of my subjective body sensations. To date, I have felt no pressure that would be evidence of a hot-spot concentration of the dark matter. ~~This is a big concern, because of the possibility that the process could become painful before~~

This is an important issue. If there are irregularities in the dark matter inside my body, damage could occur when the forces of repulsion become sufficiently large.

JQ

She glanced at the clock. It was nearly dawn. The thunderstorm front had passed through finally. She had filled two pages with her weight, every few minutes, with special notes when she had gone to the bathroom and when she had drunk a glass of water. The scale wasn't very precise, but at least it had given repeatable measurements.

It is so much like that other night.

In her case, the weight loss wasn't as rapid as the chamber's, but she couldn't deny that the trend line was there.

Maybe I should just give it up—call in the university and the government. Let them study me, and try to save me.

She wished she had been taking measurements from the first day. One night's data, even if it had been a very long and soul-draining night, was not enough to make a very predictive curve.

"Oh Jase. What am I going to do now?" She rested her head on her crossed arms. She was too tired to think.

The alarm clock startled her awake an hour later. She didn't feel at all rested.

Picking up the phone, she called work. At the beep, she said, "This is Jenny. I am sick again. I'm sorry." Click.

She couldn't make herself care about her job. Not now.

The bed was unmade and the blanket was lumpy, but she fell asleep the moment she put her head on the pillow.

Jenny fastened the skirt around the flight suit, and then pawed through her closet for a jacket. It wasn't the best mix, but she wasn't going to the cemetery just dressed in her costume. She fished the tissue out of the control box. *Batteries? The spares!* She emptied the pouch and loaded up the belt. She glanced over the GPS and the other contents of the pouch, but she wasn't going to actually fly today, and the pouch wouldn't fit right under the skirt.

It's just for comfort, anyway.

The clock said it was two in the afternoon. The sleep had cleared her head, but it hadn't improved her spirits. She had a death sentence coming in about a week. There was very little that could cheer her up now.

I could go visit one of the caves, and on flip day, I could start walking on the ceiling with all the hanging bats.

But that wouldn't help much. If her chart were any indication, she would have her full weight, only reversed, within just a few hours. After that she would be crushed to death, flattened to a pulp against the roof of the cave an hour or so later.

If she had to die, wouldn't it be better to fly out, towards space, and a painless unconsciousness before the end?

Before then, however, she had some things to do. Today, she was going to visit Jase's grave. She should have gone there before now.

She managed to start the car, although it let her know how much it disliked her neglect.

Enough gas for this. She would just use the card to fill it up. That was one bill she probably would never have to pay.

The drive out to the cemetery was punctuated by a couple of moments of panic when she strayed into the wrong lane and other motorists let her know it. She was a little flustered by the time she drove through the stone gateway and followed the long sweeping curve towards the location where Jase had been buried.

An uneven array of stone markers, hundreds of little vases with flowers—the sight was familiar. Cemeteries were not her favorite places. She had despised the trips to visit Joe's grave that her mother demanded. It gave her a bitter pleasure that she would never have a grave like this.

A s she walked closer to the gravesite, she frowned at the sight of a dark-haired man working with a shovel.

Is that Jase's grave he is working on?

"Hello?" she called.

He paused in his work.

"What are you doing there?"

"Perdóneme señorita."

Jenny caught a bit of what he said. Her schoolbook Spanish wasn't the greatest, but she repeated, "¿Qué hace aquí?"

He tipped his hat. His hands were encased in heavy work gloves. "Me pidieron arreglar esta pozo. La tierra no está plana."

Jenny understood every other word, but it was enough to get the meaning. *Of course! Jase's body is contaminated just like mine. As it gets lighter, it just might cause the ground to settle differently. It will get a lot worse, when he goes negative.*

Oh Jase! You don't get to rest in peace either.

The workman stepped back from the grave, seeing the grief come over her face.

"Volveré luego."

As he stepped back, Jenny moved closer. She could almost feel the presence of Jase's body. She took another step, and the ground heaved.

"¡El diablo sale de la tierra!" shouted the workman.

She was thrown back by an eruption of dirt, as a large metal box broke free. For just an instant, it was stuck, with one end tilted toward the sky, and then with a shake, it slid free of the earth.

Jenny got back to her feet. The shiny coffin, shedding dirt clods, was climbing rapidly. She motioned to the workman to stay put, "Quédese aquí. Volveré."

With that she reached for her control belt and jumped into the sky. She pointed her arms towards the dark shape and began the chase.

The workman dropped his shovel. "Sí, mi angelita. Esperaré," he said, and sat down on the grass.

There were tears in her eyes, and she blinked them away as she climbed rapidly into the bright sunny sky.

"Wait!" she called. The coffin, in a slow corkscrew climb, flashed once per turn, catching the sunlight off the metal.

"Don't leave me!" She reached down to her belt, making sure that she had all of the controls turned to maximum.

Her chest was tight, with a hurt that made it hard to even breathe. *Jase, don't go. I have to talk. I have so much to say!*

A cry started. A wail. It crept out of her throat like a timid creature, startled at its own sound.

Then it grew. A great scream of pain, pain of the heart, emptied her lungs, and after a gasp, began again. He was leaving her, just like all the others had left her.

Joe had gone. Gone in the night never to return. Gone before she could ever tell him that she liked him, that he was a cool little brother, that his drawings made her proud, that she always kept one of his comics in her notebook to show off to her friends. Gone before she could tell him that she loved him, in spite of all the trivial little sibling fights and bumped elbows that came from being close family in the same house. Gone before she could tell him that he had been a part of her soul, part that could never heal, now that it was cut out.

And Dad had gone. She angrily blinked away more tears. Joe had taken him away, somehow. A light had gone out of his eyes. He listened and said a word or two of reply, but he was never there, not anymore. Joe's death had burned something out. And there was nothing left for her.

And then Gary. He had slipped away, silently, off to some new life, with never a word.

"And now you too! Don't do this to me!"

The coffin was getting closer, and she moved her arms slightly, and straightened her back to change her course.

Every man who ever meant anything to me. She gasped for air. The crying, and the altitude were taking it out of her.

She could make out details now. There was some stain on the box, either corrosion or just dirt that hadn't fallen loose. One end was higher than the other. The dark matter must have collected there.

There were handles on the coffin. *If I can grab one of those, and then kill my magnetism, maybe I can weigh it down.*

But first, she had to get close enough to grab it.

They were both climbing rapidly. Her increased dark matter had given her a higher climb rate. The skydiving skills were now becoming second nature, and she could slide through the air just as if the sky were some large swimming pool.

Soon it was within a hundred feet, then fifty.

She timed the coffin's spin, and accelerated towards it, ready to catch the handle just as it swung by.

But it didn't work.

When she was within a body length of the box, it suddenly pulled away from her. She lost ground, as her trim in the air was spoiled. She turned and headed back towards it.

Jase, wait for me.

It happened again. Just as her hand slapped towards the handle, the box jumped up.

Oh! My magnetic field. I'm driving it. Without her, only the residual magnetism of the metal box and the giant, but low intensity, magnetic field of the Earth were activating the dark matter in the coffin. The field lines that spilled out of her costume were more than enough to push its rate of climb even higher.

But I need the magnetism for my own lift.

She had a thought. Pulling away from the coffin, she concentrated on getting higher. It was a slow pull. Her own rate of climb was falling off more rapidly than the coffin's. She was only barely faster.

She moved above it. And waited for it to rise to her.

It came on like a battering ram. It hit, and she had to grab frantically for the handle.

I've got it!

But she was like Ahab on the whale. All that she could do was to hang on as the metal box leapt upward even faster.

Deep within her, she could feel his presence.

The sun flashed across her view, and reflected from the metal. It seemed as if there were a shimmering next to the box.

Jase?

First, like a heat haze, then forming into a body, she saw him.

"Jase! You've come back!"

He was smiling—that infectious grin she so loved. He was riding the coffin like an amusement park ride, enjoying the climb.

"Jase, I love you!"

He looked back at her. *Go back, Jenny. You need to let go.*

"No, Jase. It's going to kill me too. I'd rather stay with you."

Oh, Jenny! You are too much a physicist for this. It is just a puzzle. Solve the puzzle, Jenny.

She blinked away more tears. "I have to go with you."

No. Think it through. Anoxia, remember. Go back down and solve the puzzle.

Jenny frowned, "Anoxia?" She blinked again, and the image of Jase was gone.

Anoxia! The buzz in her head was loud and overpowering. She couldn't think straight. *Of course,* she remembered. She was too high. There wasn't enough oxygen. She wasn't thinking straight.

She let go. Her hand came free from the handle, and the coffin raced free. The deep burn within her vanished.

She hit the master switch on her belt, and began to fall.

19

The cemetery, a large green patch next to the interstate highway, was clearly visible, once she started shaking free of the oxygen starvation. She adjusted her trim and headed in that direction. The winds aloft must have been light, because it was well within her glide path.

It was an hallucination. Oxygen starvation, plus too much wishful thinking. Jase is dead. He didn't talk to me.

When she didn't immediately convince herself, she stopped trying. *I need a few illusions right now.* If Jase wanted her to solve the puzzle, then that is what she would do. Even the fantasy of his last words comforted her.

When she reached for her controls, to slow her fall, she noticed the workman, still sitting beside the opened grave.

I have a witness. Someone has seen me fly.

She adjusted the controls some more, and when she was very close, she turned herself feet down and managed to drop to a light touchdown just to the side of the grave.

He jumped rapidly to his feet. "Me quedé como me lo pidió." He bowed one knee to the ground. "Le pido su bendición a su servidor humilde."

Oh, no! I don't need a worshiper.

Jenny stepped over to him and grabbed his arm. "Levántese Señor. Soy mortal como usted. No se incline!"

He got to his feet, but he did not look up to her eyes. "Como usted duce, mi angelita."

"¿Cómo se llama?"

"Soy Carlos. Carlos Sánchez, mi angelita."

She knew that it would be a waste of time to argue with him. It frustrated her that he kept calling her angel, but she didn't have the time.

"Carlos, hecha la tierra al pozo. Sequí sus pasos hacia la gloria, y no tendremos más problemas con esta tierra."

He nodded. "Sí, lo haré."

"No tiene que explicar nada a sujefe. No lo entendería." She hoped he would keep the secret.

"Sí, tampoco lo entiendo." There was even a hint of a smile, and he ventured to look at her. He did understand the uselessness of trying to explain this.

"Gracias, Carlos. Hace buentrabajo aquí."

He dipped his head. "No hay de que. Mi angelita."

LOG ENTRY:

... and when I noticed that after the flight, I really felt light, as if the suit was still active some-how, I disconnected the control belt from the suit wind-ings. It made no difference. A check on the scales, once I returned home, showed the logged reading—36 pounds. Somehow, the incident had accelerated the growth of dark matter in my body by a full two days.

My supposition is that accumulation of dark matter is a function of some field generated by the dark matter itself. I 'sensed' some activity, like a warmth, inside my body when I was close to the body of Professor Wil-liams. While this only occupied less than a minute, over two incidents, it has produced a drastic acceleration in my weight loss.

This would also explain the acceleration of weight loss documented for the original chamber. The more the dark matter, the faster dark matter is produced, the faster the weight is nullified.

My problem is unchanged, but I must find a solution faster. I must solve the puzzle fast.

Reader—forgive me this rambling in print, but there

is still a very real chance that I will fail, and this may be the only documentation of what has happened to me. I have decided not to waste any time recruiting help at this stage. I am closest to the problem. I have the best knowledge of the situation. I have the most to lose. I dare not change myself from an investigator into a lab rat.

But back to the issue: I need a method of reducing the dark matter in my body.

1. Dark matter repels normal matter.

2. A magnetic field catalyzes the process, but there is no evidence that energy is drawn out of the magnetic apparatus. The battery consumption is consistent with simple ohmic losses—resistance in the wires turning the current to heat.

3. Work is done during the levitation. Normal mass is lifted against the gravitation field of the earth. A great deal of energy is expended—where does it come from?

4. Dark matter has been created. This is an unknown type of matter, but IF $E=mc^2$ is still valid, then energy is needed to create it. Supposedly, zero-point energy is being tapped for this process, selectively channeled into the production of more dark matter. Does the energy of item 3 come from decay of the dark matter itself? Does flying use up any dark matter?????

It's worth a shot. I'll test it. There is still enough daylight for a good flight, and today the air is very still. Ideal conditions—not that I have any options right now.

JQ.

She put down the pen. *I need to get more batteries.* She checked her purse. Cash was pitiful, but there was still credit on the card!

The last flight had brought one point home. Park land made a nice target—a large green area easily identifiable in the maze of the city. She would drive out to Wild Basin Park, and get the batteries at the mall on the way.

I am getting positively bankrupt, she thought to herself as she pulled into the park. There were very few other people here at this time of day, and they would be easy to avoid. Wild Basin was a chunk of Hill Country land within the city that had been bought and deliberately left untouched as a contrast to all the housing development around it. It was heavily wooded and with luck she could leave without being spotted.

She killed the engine and started unwrapping her latest purchase. It was a pony bottle.

There had been a scuba-diving supply shop in the mall, and she had gone in on impulse. The quart-sized air-bottle and its attached breathing mask was supposed to be an emergency breathing supply for a diver who had run the main tanks dry. But it had seemed like a perfect hedge against anoxia for her.

She had asked how long she could breathe on a full charge, and the salesman, even younger than she, gave her a sales pitch about how she could make a controlled ascent from 100 feet—like that meant anything to her.

A breathing supply under water was used up at different rates depending on how deep you were. The deeper, the more pressure, and the faster the air was consumed.

She, on the other hand, would be using the air at lower than normal pressure. *I really would rather have an oxygen cylinder, but I don't have time to track one down.* The only ones she had seen had been from a medical supply store and they were all too big for her to handle.

The salesman had asked for her PADI certification when she was ready to buy. When she said she didn't have it with her, he waffled about whether it was really required for the pony bottle, and she assured him it was not. Whatever the real regulations, he wanted the sale, so she got it.

She replaced her batteries, and re-packed her pouch. She turned on the GPS and let it acquire the satellite signals.

Just like before. Only this time, I'm bringing the jacket.

She locked the car and walked off the trail and into the woods. She thought she spooked a deer hiding through the daylight hours, but it vanished before she got a good look.

With a few pen strokes, she noted down the time and conditions. *Data. Get lots of data.*

One more look around, and she jumped.

She held her breath, as she raced up from the woods. Traffic on Loop 360 could still see her, if anyone was looking in the right direction. There were no obvious cars veering out of their lanes, so she blessed her luck and kept on climbing.

5,000 feet, then 8,000. *I am climbing much faster than before.* She fought the wind of her passage as she noted down times and altitudes.

10,000 feet. 12,000 feet. *I need to get the pony bottle ready.*

When she passed 15,000 feet, she put the breathing mask on and bit down on the rubber. She breathed in, and the stale tasting air came pouring into her lungs.

It had gotten cold, the wind giving her face the sting of frostbite, but at least she was holding that familiar buzz of altitude sickness at bay.

By the time she passed 20,000 feet, she could feel the climb rate start to drop.

23,000 feet. 26,000 feet. It was difficult handling the pen, and taking notes with the bottle hanging from her mouth, but it was doable.

At 28,000 feet, she started getting a bloated feeling. Gas in her intestines was expanding, with the fall of the external atmospheric pressure. Flatulence and a huge burp later, it was a little better.

30,000 feet. 31,000 feet.

She was using her air faster than she liked, but it was critical for her charts to get a true flight ceiling. She would just have to stand the high altitude effects.

When will blood vessels in my skin start to break? She didn't want an all-over bruise.

32,820 feet. Flight ceiling.

She noted down the numbers in the silence of the peak.

Done. She dialed her belt to zero, and began to fall.

It was good to breathe fresh air. She shut off the pony bottle as she dropped through the 15,000-foot level and let it dangle from the strap. It had proved its use, but she really didn't like it. If that meant she had to stay below 15000 feet, then she could live with that. High altitude was cold, painful, and dangerous. If she had to do it a lot, then she would need an entirely re-designed suit.

The Russians auctioned off some old spacesuits some time ago, but they were too expensive.

Not that anyone would have an off-the-rack space suit for someone her size.

As she passed through the 5,000 mark, she concentrated on making sure that she was still over Wild Basin.

I can fly. But there are limits. My forward velocity will always be much less than my rise and fall speeds. I suppose I could travel any distance, as long as the batteries held out, by bouncing up and down, using my body for thrust.

She dropped down to 2,000 feet, and then pulled to a stop. She had her data. She really needed to get home and plug her numbers into the chart.

But there were people down there, and she didn't want to have to deal with the high-speed drop and the hiding, not just now.

There is another way to find out, and a quicker way at that.

She dialed the magnetic field up and climbed.

I wonder if I could get faster side velocity if I added wings to the costume. Of course, that would make it harder to put a coat over it and pretend that I wasn't crazy.

She visualized some kind of folding wings, but that was definitely out of her experience.

Or how about a separate vehicle—a miniature glider, made of very light weight fiberglass. Make it aerodynamic and very streamlined. I bet I could get a good speed out of something like that.

She noted down her altitude and the time. She nodded. *Just as I thought.*

This time, the climb was slower. She peaked out at 21,200 feet.

I have less dark matter now than when I started. The energy consumed by the climb comes from the dark matter itself. Every time I climb, I use some of it up!

"Yahoo!" she shouted to the sky. She could control it.

I won't die!

Issue 4: Balloon Dance

20

As she copied her nearly illegible numbers from the wrinkled and smeared notepad into her logbook, she fretted over the analysis.

Her computer was ancient and nearly unusable. The lab computer had been so much more powerful, and had been loaded with number crunching programs that left her ten-year-old spreadsheet in the dust.

Somewhere in the numbers was an equation. That equation would reveal something of the reality behind the dark matter. With that equation, she could have a handle on how to manage it—how to predict what it would do, and on what time scale.

But the numbers were not clear. Other equations had their influences. Her climb velocity, for example, was influenced by her normal weight, the quantity of dark matter, however fast the dark matter was used up over time, her wind velocity, the drag caused by her body position and such things as whether she was wearing her jacket. Other factors such as the air temperature and humidity and the time of day probably were also somewhere in the mix.

It would take forever to decode this puzzle on her ancient machine. It was a shame that the lab computer had been re-allocated to another project. She was left with trying to work this out with pencil and graph paper.

In the back of her mind, behind her survival concerns, Jenny dreamed of stepping up before a crowded auditorium, and in a clear understandable presentation before physicists, revealing the existence of dark matter, and the unassailable theoretical basis for its behavior. She would call it Williams matter, and the name would stick. Jase would be immortalized for all time, enshrined by his discovery.

The phone rang. Jenny sighed. She had been enjoying the break from her worries. She almost set the paperback novel down beside her on the ceiling, before she realized the mistake.

She leaned forward slowly, and caught the pillow before it fell. With the pillow in one hand, and the novel in the other, she was stuck, so she sighed and let them fall all the way to the floor.

She touched the control belt and eased away from her resting position, lying on the ceiling. It had not been a comfortable hour; with the little plaster texturing bumps making little casts of themselves all over her backside.

By the third ring, she touched down on the floor, and picked it up.

"Hello?"

"Hi. It's Rae." Jenny could immediately tell that something was wrong.

"Oh, hi. I'm sorry I dropped out on you ... last night." Only last night, she mused. It seemed like a couple of weeks at the least.

"Well you should be! We hunted for you all over the place. You didn't go home with that man Bob hit did you?"

"What? Bob hit someone?"

"Yes. He saw some man with you, and they exchanged a couple of punches."

"I didn't know. The man was a complete stranger. I borrowed a nickel from him. Was he hurt? I was gone before this happened."

"Who knows. Young bulls in heat. It happens. But in any case, you should not have left Bob stewing like that. You really hurt his feelings. He deserves better than that after the way you came on to him!" The anger in Rae's voice was clear.

"I did nothing of the sort! You invited me. Bob asked to dance. That was all!"

"Hmm." She sounded unconvinced. "Bob was supposed to be my date! I invited Perry to keep you company."

Jenny bit back, "Well you didn't tell Bob! He had asked me out before. You show up with two men in tow. How was I supposed to know?"

"It'll be a long time before I invite you to come out with me again."

"Well, I never asked to be invited!"

"If you are going to be that way..."

"Bye. Rae." Click.

Jenny took several deep breaths, her heart racing. *I didn't know Rae was interested in Bob. It's not my fault.*

She turned and went to the scale.

62 pounds. *Not any loss at all.*

It was disappointing, but not unexpected. She had hoped that spending some time with negative weight in the confines of her apartment might use up dark matter, but the test had been a bust. The theory was holding. Lifting her mass up through the gravitational field of the Earth used up energy, and thus drained the dark matter, but just sitting on the ceiling reading a book didn't.

I will have to fly every day.

It would be tough. She had been lucky thus far, with only one witness, and that one not likely to be widely believed. But she was living in a heavily populated area. She would be spotted.

Could she move out into the country?

Away from the university. Away from computers. Away from the research libraries.

She had no money for a move. It would take time and effort she couldn't spare.

The phone rang again.

If she wants to argue some more, I'll just hang up on her.

She stalked back to the phone.

"Hello."

"Jenny, what in the world are you doing?" It was Mary Freitag, her supervisor.

"Hello, Mary. What do you mean?"

"You were seen! You're never going to get away with it."

Mary was talking loud and fast, "The boss was driving down 360 and saw you drive into Wild Basin. This was just after I had told him that you had called in sick again. He was furious on the phone."

"I just talked to him again, and he wants you fired. He doesn't believe you were sick last week either, and he wants me to hire someone else."

Jenny felt her stomach turn. "I'm sorry Mary. Last week was definitely the flu. Today, it was something personal. I needed the time off."

The lady sighed, "I am sorry Jenny. You were a good worker, but the boss is right. If we can't rely on you, then we will be better off with a replacement. I'll arrange to have your final check mailed to you. You don't need to come in any more."

Tomorrow, Jenny rubbed her forehead. *Tomorrow, I will think about this.* She had never been fired before, and it was a losing battle to keep from getting angry with Mary. Her mind was a churning cauldron of partial thoughts and emotions scraped raw. *I need that job! How am I ever going to pay my bills?*

But she had lied to them. *Such a little lie. Should I go to work on time just to die because I can't find time to fly?*

And Rae should stick to her own problems. I don't need her running my personal life. I don't need a boy friend.

I've got to survive. I have to fly every day. I don't have time for a job. Good riddance!

She glanced at the phone. *No! I am not going to call home. Not if it kills me. I can't ask them to send me any more money. They would never understand this.*

21

The pale light of dawn found her on the roof. She had a headache from crying most of the night, but the air was still, with a light ground fog. Her batteries were fresh and she needed to fly.

She didn't bring the pony bottle this time. Today wasn't for the numbers. She just had to burn off dark matter.

I will bounce from three thousand feet to ten thousand for as long as the batteries last. If I can get my weight back up into the 80's, then I might be able to keep the flying down to a weekend thing.

If she could control it in a predictable manner, then she could hunt for another job. With a regular income, then she could afford to tackle the long-term problems.

And somewhere in all of this, I might have time for a real life.

Maybe she didn't need a boy friend, but she wasn't totally dead to the idea either.

Maybe it had been a mistake to read that romance novel. It was a shame that people couldn't be pure intellects. Why couldn't people interact on a totally platonic level? Why did everything have to collapse back into the mire of who got whom into bed?

Yes, it would be nice to have a man take care of her. It would be nice to have a home, where she could have children. It had an undeniable draw.

But could she? That was one of the little worries that ate away at her heart in the dark times between wakefulness and dreams.

Has the dark matter contaminated every cell in her body?

Would a child growing in her be fatally infected with this plague as well? Would a child of hers be doomed to this fly or die curse?

Or even worse, would the internal pressures of the dark matter cause horrible deformities in the developing embryo?

Was she doomed to be alone and childless all her life?

She breathed in the cool morning air.

Probably. That was the way to bet. Stay alive, but stay alone, so that I never have to make those kinds of choices.

She noted the time, out of habit, and jumped into the sky.

Austin Texas had long been a university town. It had become a high tech center and had more than its share of well paid workers. With a scenic beauty that came from being on the edge of the Texas Hill Country, high tech workers stayed and built their lives there—lives that included high tech hobbies.

The other side of the city, the flat farmlands of the Blackland Prairie hosted a colorful event on those special mornings with no wind and cool air. With as few as five and as many as twenty or more, hot air balloons would often greet the morning skies. Motorists heading to work or church would often crane their heads, trying to count the brightly striped, slow cruisers of the sky.

Jenny broke out of the low morning fog to see that she was not alone.

Her first impulse was to turn up the controls and get up and away before she was spotted, but she probably needn't have worried. They were off to the south and east, and although they were clearly visible to her, she was tiny compared to their great bulk. With her sky blue costume, she would be hard to see.

As she climbed, she angled towards them. If she stayed above, there should be no problem, and it would be fun to watch them in their slow dance.

They too, rose and fell in the sky, but she was a speed demon compared to them.

Off in the distance, she heard the roar of the burners, as one of the six balloons turned on the gas to gain some altitude. She looked carefully and saw one, a yellow balloon, shine faintly with the light of its controlled fire. After a moment, the light went out. Several seconds later, the noise stopped too.

Sound travels a thousand feet per second. She did the easy calculation without thinking. *Two miles away. I wonder how hard it would be to go that far.*

She set the controls and stretched her body for a glide.

Wonder Woman, she thought to herself as she glided on the air, *it was Wonder Woman who rode the air currents. She couldn't really fly, but it made no difference in the story. Her powers were magic-based anyway. You don't have to explain magic-based powers.*

She started remembering bits and pieces of the Amazon's history. Just like all the other comic book characters, her history had been restarted and mutated over time. Her flying had been true of some versions, but not of others. In some variations, she flew an invisible jet plane. That was from part of her history that Jenny hadn't read much about.

Wonder Woman hadn't been much of a role model for her. Diana Prince had been big and strong and assertive. It was too much of a stretch to identify with her. Jenny preferred her female superheroes to be petite and clever.

WW was like She-Hulk. Another Amazon class, six-footer female with a perfect physique, She-Hulk was a green-skinned athletically beautiful lawyer. While Wonder Woman had been a noble-soul superhero, in some ways a match for Superman, She-Hulk had been an actor on a smaller stage, rarely saving the world. She had been as clever and intelligent as she had been beautiful, with an endearing quality that she was aware that she was a comic-book character and would frequently 'break the fourth wall' and talk directly to the reader.

She-Hulk was a cousin to Bruce Banner, the Hulk. She had gotten her green skin and super strength via a blood transfusion from Bruce. The radiation contamination had passed to her through his blood.

Oh. One more thing I have to think about. Don't be a blood donor. Not that she had been able to be one even before the dark matter explosion. The couple of times she had tried, the blood bank had rejected her because of the blood-iron test. A lot of women failed that. *Perils of being female.*

The roar of the burner lit up the balloon below her, and from this distance, it was much louder. Floating in the still air was a particularly quiet time. Every noise source was far away. Her own heartbeat had a chance to become the loudest sound around.

She checked her time. Only twenty minutes, she had traveled much faster than she could have walked.

Okay, I officially declare that I can fly. It isn't just floating. If I can control direction and get there faster than I can walk, then it is flying—so there! She had restrictions and limitations, but so did every other kind of flying.

If I have to be up here for my health, I might as well have some fun. She set her sights on the next balloon over, a red and blue striped one. Her fingers moved the controls to climb and headed off.

She knew she passed over her third balloon when she felt an upwelling of warm air.

That feels lovely. The morning chill wasn't too bad, but she had been out in it for some time. The hot air balloon below was spilling off heat into the surrounding air. She guessed there was more of a premium on a lightweight fabric for the bag than for any insulation effects. Heat loss was just part of the equation.

She looked down, and from her viewpoint, the top of the bag looked like a giant target, with big concentric circles in all the primary colors.

I can do that. She reached for her belt and started dropping feet first towards the bulls-eye.

There was turbulence from the updraft, but it felt very good, especially to her chilled fingers and nose and ears. She kept one hand on the controls.

This has to be a perfect landing. The surface was flexible fabric, but more than that, she could put the balloon, and its passengers in danger with a wrong move. She could vividly remember the news footage shot at one of those Albuquerque balloon festivals where a pilot had his burner running at full blast trying to re-inflate the collapsed bag. It had roared all the way to the ground. He hadn't survived.

She eased back on the controls as the fabric grew quickly to obscure the whole earth from her view. For a moment, she was fighting the heated air, and then as light as a feather, her slippers touched down.

There was some kind of a vent, with control cords at the exact top of the bag. She carefully let herself slide sideways across the cloth 'ground' until she was a safe distance from it, and then she added a few more ounces to her weight. It was just enough so that she could walk, if she didn't move her legs too fast.

It was an alien planet, she felt. A strange, tiny, colorful planet—warm under her feet. *Is this what it would be like to walk on an asteroid?* She had micro-gravity, and the curvature of the horizon was very very close.

She walked down to the red ring, taking several long seconds for each step. The balloon surface was inclined ten or fifteen degrees at that point, and she had the irrational fear of falling off.

I should be over that by now. But instinctive reactions could not be banished by simple experience. Instinct was learned deeper into the cells than logic could reach.

Her balloon world was like those 'Moon walk' amusement park attractions, where kids could bounce on an inflated bag. She had the urge to hop on the bag.

Suddenly, the roar of the gas burner below stopped.

"Hang on!" came a shout. "I'll get down to the ground as quickly as I can! Just hang on!"

22

Jenny froze in a panic. She had been spotted.

Stupid, stupid. Why did I ever come down here? Of course the pilot would notice something as she tromped around on the balloon above. They were all tied together. Every step would shake the whole contraption.

"No, I am okay!" she called down. "I will come down to the basket."

She wanted to turn the controls up and fly away as fast as she could, but it was too late for that.

"Don't try to bring your balloon down. You don't need to do that."

She walked toward the steeper grade, and then reached down to grab a control line. *Hold it gently.*

With the line for guidance, she slid slowly, foot by foot down the side of the bag and then towards the bag where a wide-eyed man held one hand on the controls lines, and stretched out towards her.

She slid gently down the rope. Strong arms were around her in an instant, pulling her roughly in.

Not by any means a giant, he was comfortably larger than she. His grip, and his warmth were nice. But he was shaking from his fear for her.

Jenny looked into his wide brown eyes and said, "You can let go. I am okay now."

Hesitantly, he released her, as she lightly touched her belt control. He felt the balloon start to drop, and almost unconsciously, he turned on the gas.

In awed tones he said, "That was the most amazing bit of climbing I have ever seen in my life! How did you get here?"

Jenny closed her eyes for a moment. *What can I possibly say?*

When she opened them, that earnest face, framed in light brown hair, was still focused on her, still waiting for an explanation.

"I was there all along."

He frowned, intent and shaking his head.

"No. There is no way in the world you could have been riding in the rigging all this time. No matter how small and light weight you are, the balloon would never have gotten upright when we initially inflated it."

He would focus on my size. She waved her hands to explain. "Well, it wasn't from the ground. Once you started, I jumped on from a nearby power pole...."

"I'm not that stupid! There were no power poles where we launched."

Jenny's mind was racing. She sighed, "Okay, I didn't want to say so, but I was skydiving and..."

"Oh, be sensible! If you were skydiving, and hit my balloon, you would have destroyed it. Even with a parachute open, you would hit so hard that you would have collapsed the bag. There's just no way!" He hit down on the railing with the side of his fist.

A thinker. I'll have to come up with something better.

"Calm down," she advised. "There is a perfectly logical explanation, but it isn't going to help you if you blow a blood vessel."

He blinked. Then, he eased back against the wicker and took a deep breath. When he spoke, his voice had mellowed. He held out his hand, "Hello, my name is Shawn Breaker. I am sorry. I just can't understand what's happened, and it bothers me."

She shook his hand and smiled. "I understand. Puzzles and me go way back. Just give me a minute." *A minute to think of something.*

"Okay, but before we land, I will have the real story or I won't let you go. You cost me this race, and I have to have something to tell the others."

Jenny looked over at the other balloons. "A race? How do you race balloons? I'm sorry, I didn't know."

There was an edge of a smile. As he thawed, Jenny realized he wasn't that much older than she was. Angry, he looked years older.

"Air currents," he explained. "You find air currents that are going the right direction and then raise or lower your balloon to sit in that air layer." He pointed to a roll of streamer tape. "I can toss a piece of that over the side and see which way it drifts. Lately, I have been using a GPS to find the currents. Climb fast and watch which way you drift, then drop back down when you find the best layer."

Jenny's hand drifted down to the white pouch on her leg, then stopped. Her first reaction was to compare GPS units with a like-minded techie, but that wouldn't be a good idea.

One look at the breadcrumb display, and he could see that I have been all over the sky this morning.

She still had to find a story he could believe. Or, maybe just distract him.

"Well," she asked, "were you winning?"

One corner of his mouth twisted into a grimace as he shook his head. "Nah. I'm not that good a pilot. This is only my third solo." He rubbed his face. "Sorry. You didn't cost me the race. I was just blowing off steam. This isn't my balloon either, but I would have some serious payback to do if I'd damaged it."

"Oh, do you rent it?"

"No." He looked off across the sky. "I would love to own one of these, but that's not the way it's done. Ballooning is not a one-man operation. You need a ground crew to launch, and a chase car to follow you from the ground and help you land. It's like a club. If you do your part on the ground, then maybe you can get some time in the air too. There's a crew down below right now, following me."

He picked up a hand-held radio. "And I need to call in and let them know what's going on."

Jenny grabbed for his wrist. "No, don't!"

His face went severe again. "Why?"

She shrank back. "It..." Her mind was like a mouse in a maze. "I can't reveal my presence."

"Why?"

"I was teleported here from the mother ship, and..."

"No." He grabbed the collar of her jacket and pulled it back enough to read the label. He was tall enough to do so with no effort at all. "Sears. Do not use non colorfast bleach," he quoted.

She pulled free of his grasp. She didn't like him tugging at her clothes, no matter what the reason. They glared at each other.

"Why shouldn't I use this?" He gestured with the radio.

"There is a coven of witches in the Speedway area next to the university..."

He threw back his head and laughed long and hard. Jenny tried to keep her own face fierce, although the laugh was infectious and she was on the verge of joining him.

He wiped some moisture from the corner of his eye. "Okay. Give me a better reason, or we'll just stay up here! I started ballooning for the peace and quiet, but meditation isn't as entertaining as you are. Another one?"

She felt a little irritation at his patronizing tone. "Just take my word for it. Don't tell anyone I'm here, or you'll regret it."

"Nope." He grinned. He pushed a button on the radio, and there was a burst of static.

"Okay! Put it down!"

He inclined his head to listen. "Well?"

She took a breath. "I have invented antigravity and I was out flying..."

He shook his head. "Nope. Try again."

Jenny felt her face turning red. There was just no pleasing this guy. *I'll show him!*

She reached for her belt, and dialed away her weight. Almost at once, the balloon reacted with a rapid climb, as the ballast of her weight was gone.

He grabbed for the rigging. "What!"

A grin forced its way all over her face. She reached for the rigging herself and before he could react, she pulled herself over the side of the basket.

He grabbed for her, but she pushed away. The balloon lifted away. His face, a mask of horror, peered over the edge of the basket.

Her triumph at the escape lasted only a second. She couldn't leave him like that. She touched the controls and moved up to match his flight.

He watched, with an open mouth, as she came up beside. Trying to match the balloon's position was tricky, but she was able to stay within ten feet.

"Don't tell anyone. Please don't tell anyone! I have to keep this a secret. My life may depend on it." She called over the roar of the burner.

His mouth was still hanging open, but he nodded. "I won't."

"Thank you. Bye now." She cut the power and dropped away.

23

The key missed the lock on her apartment door. She had to calm the jittering of her hand.

One little miscalculation and I would be dead now.

She had dropped away from the balloon, and below was the twisted, tree lined, limestone path of Waller creek. Now, she had a second witness and she didn't want to spend any more time than necessary where people could see her.

Jenny collapsed onto her bed, just taking a moment to disconnect the lumpy and uncomfortable battery belt and drop it on the floor.

As the strip of green had grown in her view, she had let desire for escape rule, and she had dropped too fast, too far.

I should never have tried that. I'm getting too comfortable in the air. With the dark matter changing all the time, why did I even think I could pull off a max-efficiency landing?

Lunar Lander. That's the culprit.

The game was probably on every brand of digital computer ever made. She had even seen it built without a CPU, using op-amps, resistors, capacitors and voltmeters as a simple analog computer. The game idea was simple and made even more popular because it was just like the Apollo moon lander.

To land on the airless moon, the lander had to kill its speed by firing a rocket. The complications came with limited fuel, and the laws of physics. If the pilot fired the engines a lot, to ease the lander down to the surface gently, then the fuel ran out. Worst case was to hover the lander. You made no progress and burned all the fuel.

The most efficient landing was the most dangerous looking—let the lander fall freely until the very last second and then apply full power. If your calculations were exactly correct, you would touch down perfectly with minimum fuel usage.

Of course, if you were a second too late, then you crashed, but in computer games, there were an infinite number of 'lives' to burn so that you could learn the correct play with no real penalty. With a physics gene even in her teens, Jenny had done just that on the school computer until she knew the strategy by instinct. She played it on other computers over the years, but never for long. It was like tic-tac-toe, once you knew the rule for winning, there was no real excitement in the play.

But old habits had come back in her dive for the secrecy of the creek's woods. Jenny had held off killing her speed until the ground suddenly looked close, too close.

She had turned the magnetic field on to highest power—it was too late for niceties like lower power for her legs so that she could land upright. Her glide tumbled instantly. The last hundred feet was just a streaky blur as the landscape bloomed toward her.

A tree must have been her first impact, because she distinctly remembered the sound of a loud crack, but none of her bones appeared broken.

She remembered waking up, flat on her back with a sore right hip. How long she had been out, she didn't know. Agony greeted her when she got to her feet, and she was none too steady as she forced arms and legs to move her towards the street and the nearest bus stop.

Never again. Calibrate it. Use a stopwatch. Never just wing it. Not until I have more experience. This was not a game. She wouldn't get another life.

It was rare that she regretted not having a TV, but as she hobbled to the bathroom after having slept for several hours, she wished she could just sit a comfortable chair and dull her brain with mindless entertainment.

71 pounds. It was progress, but she would need to fly again within the next couple of days.

The problem was that she had two witnesses, all because she was being risky and flying in a metropolitan area. *How many witnesses is enough? When will the idea that someone is flying through the sky become believable?*

But could she drive out into the country and fly there? If the wind blew her too far, how would she get back? At least in town, there were busses.

I need something like a balloonist's chase car. She frowned. That would require an assistant, one more person in on the secret. There was no one she trusted that much. The idea of recruiting Shawn came and went in an instant. He looked nice, but she couldn't trust a chance-met stranger.

The suit was dirty, and she sighed over it. She held it up and looked over the area that had absorbed the impact. She would need to give it a complete electrical check before dared fly again.

She used a hand mirror to stare at the large discoloration on her rump. There was another on her shoulder, and her back ached. Time alone would fix that, but some pain pills would be necessary for a few days. Luckily the bruises would all be hidden unless she went swimming. That was easy enough to avoid.

Her eyes went to the clock. She was hungry, but she had to work on the suit now. It was penance for being stupid.

I wish I had come here with Rae or Beth. Jenny looked over the assortment of tables arrayed in front of the large screen TV; before choosing one at the far left and laying claim with her two plates and her drink. There was a baseball game, and most of the tables were occupied. A dozen male eyes turned from the screen to watch her.

She did her best to ignore them and picked up her plate to make a first pass at the all-you-can-eat salad bar. Men were nice enough as individuals, but as a group they were intimidating. At least with her friends she could be social with her in-group, and put up a screen to inhibit strangers. Alone, she had to stare at her food and fiercely cultivate an aura of maniacal introversion to achieve the same effect. It wasn't comfortable.

I wish this place had trays. Making multiple trips to and from the table to pick up her salad and pizza slices just made it that much harder to be invisible. *No wonder I stay at home and eat TV dinners.*

Jenny wanted to be sociable, but being small, alone, female, and even, she admitted to herself, pretty, made her particularly vulnerable.

This was a mistake. TV's are cheap. Either that or get a boyfriend.

Brown eyes intruded into her thoughts. She shook her head. *No. Not now.*

The screen was alive with mutating scenery. At first glance, she thought it was a fantasy movie, but soon enough it was clear that it was an automobile commercial. That was one thing she noticed living without a TV. Advertisements were getting more fantastic and creative, at the same time that the shows were getting increasingly crude and boring.

Oh well, I asked for this. Mindless and boring is why I came here.

She munched on her meal, relishing the cheese and the sugar cinnamon sticks. If she ate slowly, perhaps she could get through the show and glean some entertainment from it.

P redictably, the episode ended with the family jerk embarrassing himself in front of the beautiful neighbor he was trying to impress, at the same time that the younger daughter learned her mother was right all along about which of the two boys could be trusted.

Jenny squirmed on her sore rump, lasting out the show as a matter of duty. As far as the story line, she could not spare enough emotion to judge it.

There was one untouched sausage pizza slice and part of a ham and pineapple that she debated finishing. The meal hadn't been as bad as she had feared. She had managed to achieve her invisibility and be mindless in front of the TV, which had been her goal.

Time to go.

There was still quite a bit of work to do on the flight suit. A close inspection showed that one section of ribbon cable had part of its insulation scraped off. She must have landed on a sharp section of rock, and the wired fabric had provided protection for her skin.

An electrical check had missed the damage. As much work as it took, the detailed inspection was worth the effort.

"Tonight on City Beat, a deepening mystery over the falling death of a hot air balloonist!"

Jenny's eyes locked on the large talking head. The image switched to a picture of a sky full of balloons.

"This spectacular footage of the tragedy was acquired by Channel 8 news."

It was Shawn's balloon, and in spite of the hand-held unsteadiness of the image, she could clearly see two people in the basket. The larger was waving his hands, and in her mind's eye, she remembered him doing just that.

The smaller individual could not be identified from that distance. The video was obviously shot from one of the other balloons. There was a pan away, as the cameraman took pictures of the other two people in his basket. Suddenly one of them shrieked and pointed.

The camera zoomed back to Shawn's balloon, and the body that was rapidly falling away from it. The camera unsteadily tried to follow it all the way to the ground, but lost track. Then the shot went back to Shawn's balloon, with only the one person. Shawn was leaning over the side, looking down.

"Police report no statement from the other passenger of the balloon, and an extensive ground search has turned up no sign of the body.

"In other news, the City Council has approved..."

Jenny tuned out the rest.

I have been seen, and filmed, and everyone thinks Shawn Breaker killed me.

She had a moment's relief, as she realized no one could be identified by the tiny image, but it lasted only a second or two. *If there was one camera, there might have been two. And in any case Shawn is in trouble. What will he say?*

She sat stone-faced though the rest of the news. After suffering agonies waiting though the useless drivel that was maybe important news for someone else, they came to the main story.

They re-ran the home video, and then cut to an interview.

The face of Officer Davis blandly repeated the police no-comment line: They had a suspect in custody, there was no official statement, investigation was still in progress, and the victim had not been identified.

So, you are a Homicide detective. That makes sense. He was creepy enough. *Now you have two reasons to hunt me down.* She didn't like that thought at all.

But Shawn was in deep trouble because of her. She needed to do something. Ruining his life was not something she wanted on her conscience.

Even if he tells the full and unvarnished truth, no one will believe him. Should I go public?

She shivered. She just wasn't brave enough to do that. How could she close her eyes and turn over her future to people who didn't know her and who wouldn't care about her? She was one little girl with a zero bank account, and she would be pitted against big government, and big business, and maybe the university as well.

It was clear whose priorities would be lost in the shuffle.

She looked at the people in the restaurant with her. She didn't know a one of them, and they didn't know her. It was better that way. She liked people, but mobs, even official mobs, were a force to be avoided. Stay invisible.

She got up and walked out.

The parking lot was getting darker by the minute, as a bank of clouds was accelerating the evening.

No. I can't just abandon him.

She thought again of Officer Davis. He scared her, but maybe, just maybe, there was a way.

Of course, it would cost more money.

Surprise, surprise. Everything costs me more money.

I n the pre-dawn darkness, she heard him before she saw the headlights of his car. The police scanner coming out of squelch into her earphone caused her to jump.

"C-12 approaching the Zilker end of the footbridge."

"Roger."

Jenny turned the volume down, and noted with satisfaction that she had guessed the correct frequency. The list of local police channels at the store where she had bought the pocked-sized device was vague about which type of police had which bands.

She peered into the darkness and knowing where he was, she could see the darkened car pulling into the little parking lot.

Davis was early, but so was she, waiting on the footbridge that crossed Town Lake beneath the Mopac expressway.

She cautiously lowered the visor on her freshly purchased motorcycle helmet. *Blind as a bat.* But if she couldn't see out, neither could Davis see her face. She lifted it back up.

The helmet was bulky and uncomfortable and didn't fit well.

My own fault. She had to make a choice between the white one, which matched her outfit, or the one with yellow and black swirls, which actually fit. Maybe if she padded the inside with tissue, she could make it fit better.

There was a rumble as a car passed overhead. Traffic was very light this time of morning, which was why she chose it for her meeting. As it passed, she heard the distinctive *chunk* of a car door closing. After a bit, she could hear him approach.

She got to her feet, and made sure the radio was turned off, and stashed into the pouch.

Davis switched on a flashlight, and caught her in the face. She lowered the visor instantly. He couldn't have seen enough to recognize her that way, but it was a clever trick. She put her hand down on her controls. She set her effective weight to ten pounds, and then rested her hand on the railing.

When he was a dozen feet away, she called out, "That's close enough. We can talk like this."

Her voice worried her. The helmet muffled it—she had made sure of that—but that might not be enough. Davis had spoken to her before.

"I hope you have something to say. I can't say I like having my beauty sleep upset like this."

"You do want the truth about the balloon incident don't you?"

"We already have the person who can tell us that."

"What did Shawn Breaker tell you?" It was a probe on her part. It had been interesting that the news outlets were not giving out his name.

Davis showed no reaction. "Oh, he's talked. What do you know that he hasn't already said?"

"I'll tell you enough. But first, tell me what Shawn said."

"I thought you were in possession of the truth. Why do you care what he said?"

Jenny's heart was beating away like a jackhammer. This verbal sparring wasn't her thing. It would be all too easy to make a fatal blunder.

She raised her voice. "Do you want the answer or not? Just tell me what he said, and then I'll tell you the truth!"

He waited a few seconds. It lacerated her nerves.

"Don't get so agitated little girl. For your information, Breaker was a very dull character. He just said the same three sentences over and over and over. It was a big waste of time for all concerned."

"And what were these three sentences?"

"You haven't told me a thing thus far. I'm a busy boy. I need my sleep. I'll make you a deal. I'll tell you each sentence, and then you tell me something I don't know. Deal?"

Jenny gripped harder on the railing. She was out of her depth. She should never have called him here. She should have stayed invisible no matter what.

"Deal."

Davis raised one finger. "He said 'I took off from the landing site alone.'"

"That is true. The girl in the video joined him in the air."

"How?"

Jenny opened her mouth, then paused. *Play the game.*

"Next statement."

He grumbled under his breath. He held up a second finger, "Okay. He said, 'I landed alone.'"

She laughed. "That's no surprise." She pondered what info to trade. *Something innocuous.* "Shawn had never seen the girl before they met in the air. What was the third statement?"

Davis held up a third finger. "He said, 'Nobody fell to her death from my balloon.'"

Jenny smiled. Shawn had kept his promise, and had kept to the strict truth at the same time. Good move. She was absurdly grateful that he had kept to his word. He hadn't owed her a thing.

"Okay, here's my little tidbit. The girl didn't fall to her death."

"Oh, give me a break! We aren't playing games here! This is a murder investigation and if you won't cooperate, I'll just have to take you to the station and make you talk."

She held up her free hand. "Okay. I'll be fair. I have to tell you something new, don't I? How about this?

"I know she didn't die, because the girl is me. I was the girl in the balloon. You never found the body because I walked away to the bus stop and went home."

Davis shook his head. "You'll have to do better than that."

He took a step towards her.

"Stop!" She shouted, and pulled her self up and over to the outside of the railing in one smooth motion. "Don't come any closer, or I will jump."

"Now, calm down." He stopped. The drop down to the lake water below was not that far, but it was still enough of a drop to be hazardous. "There's no need for this kind of theatrics. If you fall, it won't help your boyfriend."

"Who said he's my boyfriend? Didn't I just tell you that we'd never met before? It's clear you don't believe me. Maybe you need some convincing."

With an elaborate swing of her arms, she released the railing and started to fall.

Davis gave a shout and raced to the side.

Jenny had already reversed her weight, and came back up to eyeball height by the time he got there. She slowed to a hover just out of his reach.

"I told you the girl didn't fall to her death. You have trust issues, don't you? Sometimes people tell you the truth.

"One last point before I go. Just because someone goes over the railing doesn't mean they have to go splat when they reach the bottom. New things get invented all the time, and sometimes they have to stay secret for a while.

"Shawn Breaker did nothing wrong, and told the truth. If you don't release him, when the time comes for my press conference, I will make sure people know that you were told the real facts today."

She didn't wait for his response, increasing the magnetism and heading up.

"Hey! Hold on!"

Jenny didn't look back. She had to shove against the concrete of the highway bridge above, but she cleared it smoothly, and accelerated as fast as she could.

There was another car below—a police car—idling its engine while waiting on the shoulder. She looked up, and was relieved to see the low hanging cloud layer within a short climb.

As the visibility dropped to nothing, and the air dropped in temperature a couple of degrees, she reduced her climb. She reached for her scanner and turned the volume back up.

"... told me to watch the south shore and that was what I was doing. I didn't see anyone on the bridge."

Davis responded with a word that used to be banned from radio. "Stay where you are and search every inch of the east railing."

"What am I looking for?"

"The girl, or anything that looks like a cable. She used a high-tech winch or something. I couldn't tell in the light."

"Roger."

There was silence for a while, and the scanner started roaming through the other channels, she fumbled over the buttons and forced it back to the right one.

"Davis. There isn't anything here." In the background, a truck rumbled past. The morning sky was getting brighter and traffic was picking up below.

The response, when it finally came, had static in it. She used the belt control to zero out the wind around her. She didn't need to climb anymore.

The other voice asked, "Did you get anything to satisfy Blane?"

Davis sounded irritated, "Maybe. Tell him I'm willing to release Breaker. I won't be in 'til later. I want to check on some other things."

"He'll want an explanation."

"Just say I have reason to believe that there might not have been a fatality. It may have just been one of those student pranks. You know, throw a dummy off a building and watch people panic."

"So you think Breaker is innocent."

"Bill, you are new. Let me tell you the facts of life. No one is innocent. Everyone breaks the law. But we only get to keep the ones who leave us enough evidence."

The other voice began to reply, but there was so much static that the scanner thought it was a bad signal and moved off channel.

Jenny was suddenly aware that there was the sound of wind again, and it was coming up from below her! With nothing but white fog in every direction, she was disoriented. She grabbed for the controls. She must have over-corrected last time. She had to stop her fall!

Jenny pulled the visor open, but it made no difference. She was deep in a cloud layer and there was nothing at all to see. There was a moment of vertigo, and she wasn't sure which was up and which was down.

The controls. Zero the wind, that would be safe. She increased the power and the wind dropped. *I was falling.*

But why? Were her batteries giving out?

Surely not. She had put in fresh ones before starting out, but she regretted that her crude control box didn't really have any battery level meter other than the simple LED lights.

The helmet annoyed her. She unsnapped the latch, and pulled it off her head. With difficulty, she looped the strap around her belt.

The air was wet and cool. And there was still a faint updraft. She increased the climb another notch. She did not want to crash into the ground blind.

How do I get down?

She had been so focused on the interview with Davis, and escaping from him afterward, that she hadn't planned this part out.

At least it worked. Shawn will go free. She just hoped the news media would be as fair about it as Davis.

What a hard-nose he is! Nobody is innocent, everybody is a crook! I have to stay clear of him.

A strand of her hair tickled her forehead.

Again? She added more power, and reached for the GPS.

It took its usual laborious few seconds to acquire the satellites and download the orbital and clock data from them. The screen finally changed, and she turned to the numbers. The altitude just kept increasing.

She was climbing at over 100 feet per second!

Jenny tugged her glove free from her hand and reached out to feel the air. It was truly motionless. She was at zero velocity with respect to the air

She had more respect for the technology than her senses.

The GPS says I'm climbing, so I am climbing, so the air around me is climbing.

She shook her head to clear it. With no sleep, maybe she was dopey.

She was used to normal wind, moving from any sideways direction. She was not used to a vertical wind.

If I feel wind from above or below, it means I am rising or falling, doesn't it?

Not really. Her instincts were built from living on the ground. Air masses did rise and fall. A childhood memory, watching the weather report in Amarillo, back where the land was flat and weather was a much more entertaining spectator sport than in the relatively tame Hill Country.

She could remember the popular weatherman, as he diagramed an incoming cold front as a wedge of heavy air forcing the moist warm air higher, triggering rain and a storm.

Her hair was tickling her forehead again. She brushed at it, but she was suddenly aware that it was not behaving normally. Her hair was sticking out in all directions.

Static electricity. She was charged up. There were eddies in the air. She could feel them now. Friction in the air was building a charge on every droplet of water, and on anything else in the cloud.

The cloud was building towards a lightning strike, and she was right in the middle of it.

I've got to get out of here. She turned the power down and began to fall. She glanced at her GPS. She was at 8000 feet.

It happened too quickly. There was no warning.

The world flashed. Her body convulsed. She had no time for any last thoughts.

Issue 5: Mandrake's Magic

26

Whiteness, and tears—the wind roared in her ears.

I'm falling. She formed that thought with difficulty. The past seemed disconnected. There was the hint of memory. Davis, the wind, the radio, the lightning!

There was pain in her arms and legs, an ache. *What happened to me?*

Her mind worked slowly, but she struggled to shake it off. *Falling.* She reached for her belt and turned the controls full on.

Nothing happened. She could feel it in her gut. Frantically, she turned the controls back and forth, and toggled the switches. Nothing.

She ripped the GPS from its velcro. The screen was blank. She pressed the on switch. There was a flicker of something on the screen, like static, and then it blinked back off. The GPS was fried.

The lightning had taken it out. It must have fried her control belt.

How long have I been out? Was she a minute from crashing into the ground, or just a second?

I need magnetism! She let go of the GPS. It tumbled away into the sky.

If the wiring in her suit was fried, she was dead. But if it was just the control circuits in her belt....

She unbuckled the belt, careful to leave it plugged into the suit. The helmet was in the way. She let it fall away. No time for anything but the belt.

The belt was several boxes, linked with the webbing and connecting wires. She tugged off her gloves with her teeth. She needed the dexterity.

The controls were in the large box in the front. The lid popped open, a simple plastic latch and hinge. She blinked her eyes to clear the wind-caused tears.

The insides were charred. Everything was fried. She jammed a finger against one of the control pots, and a chunk of its material broke free and vanished in the air turbulence.

Forget it. The controls were gone, unsalvageable.

Which wire? She had not used a color code to keep the battery wires separate from the control wires—she hadn't been able to afford it. Everything had come off one spool.

Try that. She crooked a fingertip around a wire soldered tightly to one of the switches. She twisted back and forth, until the wire fatigued and broke off.

She tugged at the wire, taking out all the slack. The costume windings were fed from the left side, she remembered. She scraped the tip of the wire across all the connectors, one at a time.

Nothing. Not a twinge of her dark matter, not a spark. Nothing.

She wasted no time, breaking the second battery wire free.

This time, she felt a tug on her leg the instant she touched the connector. There was a slight spark too. She tumbled to a head down orientation.

She held it for a couple of seconds. Was she slowing? Was just one leg enough?

She moved it again. A quick set of trials confirmed that the windings were good to both her left arm and leg and to the torso. Her right arm and leg didn't respond.

The torso was a no-brainer decision. More body mass—more dark matter. She stripped the wire free of insulation for an inch, and wound it as tightly as she could manage around the connector.

The ugly knot of wire was warm to the touch, a bad connection. She tried to crimp it even tighter with her fingernails, but she didn't know if it helped.

The wind is dropping. She could feel it working.

Her fingers were cold and painful. She paused to let her heart recover, and to see if she would hit the ground before she stopped her fall.

She panted, looking out into the featureless white. Her own sniffles and heartbeat were becoming louder and louder as the wind sound dropped off.

Everything went still. And then the wind started up again, from above. She was climbing again.

Now what?

Jenny let her mind go blank. She wasn't in any danger of crashing in the next few seconds. She had to collect her wits, and now was the time to do it.

A cold front had come through, and she had been so caught up in her plans that it took her unaware. Now she was lost.

Cold fronts came from the north, so she had to be traveling south. With her GPS gone, she would have to get low enough to spot landmarks before coming in, and without a good altimeter, she would have to drop carefully, especially now that her controls were shot.

And I have to work swiftly. I am running on one-third of my batteries, and only using part of my windings. I must have lost a lot of altitude, and I won't have the time to mess with the wiring if something else gives out.

Jenny formed a plan, and started a *tick, tick, tick,* a mental clock so she could time what was happening.

She flipped open the battery case, breaking the circuit. Carefully, by opening and closing the battery case, she brought herself to an erratic stop in the air.

Timing everything, she dropped freely for three seconds, and then waited the long 14 seconds for her lift to kill the fall.

Okay. Drop for three, then kill that velocity. That should bring me down, without ever falling fast enough to be fatal. When it starts taking longer than 15 seconds to bring me back to rest, then I'll know the batteries are giving out.

She didn't try to think past that point. She wouldn't have time to re-wire, but she might be able to swap the actual batteries from one container to the next, if she were prepared. When the first set started to go, then she would act. Until then, this set ought to be enough to get her to the ground.

She did the math in her head, and predicted she should definitely see the ground before she had to go through another eight cycles.

27

Ten cycles later, she was still wrapped in the misty grey-white.

How high was I? She had been at 8000 feet before the lightning strike. It had taken her several seconds to get power back to the coils. That alone should have dropped her significantly. She was unconscious, but that could have been one second or much longer.

Unless the lightning threw me even higher. She had assumed the coils had protected her. Rapid electrical spikes had trouble going through coils of wire. That is why they were universally used to dampen out electrical noise on wires.

Maybe I hadn't been electrocuted because the windings turned it into a magnetic spike. If so, who knew how high she had been thrown, or how long she had been unconscious?

There was nothing to do but keep up her routine. She was tempted to drop longer—to get down faster, but that was suicide. The clouds could go right down to the grass. She had to be patient.

The first thing she saw was a dark band of trees moving swiftly by. It was in the last few seconds of the braking part of the cycle, so she let it nearly time out before beginning a more manual, eyeball controlled drop.

But as she reached clear air, and forced her eyes to focus on the patches of darkness below, she realized that she was still higher than she had thought.

I am really traveling! Just how fast is this wind?

She kept a hand on the battery case, cycling the power to the windings as she maintained a nearly steady drop.

At a hundred feet up, she stopped trying to get lower.

This is too fast. I'll break my neck if I touch down at this speed. It had to be thirty miles per hour, at least. She remembered the story of when steam locomotives gradually started traveling this fast and all the fatalities the greater speed caused. When the train had only gone ten miles per hour, it had been good sport to jump from the train, but only incremental speed increases had changed sport into suicide. It was the square law again. You hit four times harder when you doubled your speed. Nine times harder when you tripled it.

I can't get down. She could only watch in horror as the bands of trees whipped by, ready to swat her out of the sky. She had to climb.

The terrain was generally flat below. Jenny occasionally had to climb to avoid a rise, but it wasn't like the Hill Country. She had to be traveling southeast. With the exception of an occasional two-lane blacktop road, and the dark green of the water-loving trees that followed the streams and creeks, most of the land was covered with the springtime fresh green of a broad mesquite thicket. Twice, she lowered herself to the crest of a wooded stretch, nerving herself to catch a branch and slow herself down that way, but her previous run-in with a tree was still too fresh in her memory. And mesquite would be a hundred times worse, with inch-long thorns that covered every branch. Her costume would be no protection. Even automobile tires were regularly defeated by the wooden needles.

Hill. She climbed.

But no, it wasn't a hill. It was a dam.

As she popped up above it, there was a several acre expanse of water, frothed white from the winds.

I can do this, she thought, but before she could drop down to get her feet wet, the curve of the shore put her over the ground again. An opportunity lost.

Water paralleled her for several more seconds, before it shallowed out. Right now, she was at the mercy of the wind. She couldn't risk the big rise and fall that would be needed to steer her course.

Still, she was following the watercourse. In this part of the country, ponds were common. Every farmer with more than a few head of cattle or a stand of pecan trees needed the long-term water supply. She had to be ready.

Water. This time, she had the altitude and could see it coming. This pond was larger, but she was heading crosswise to the irregular triangle. She dropped, and was in place when the shore gave way to the froth.

In her mind's eye, she had expected to skid in feet first, like a barefoot water-skier. With her torso lift, she had been holding a feet-down posture.

But that first, cold, impact sent her tumbling. Cold water slammed into her. She gasped from the chill, and inhaled a mouthful of water. Her face stung from the wet slap at high speed.

If she had been normal, she might have drowned. Today, however, her average body weight was much less than the specific gravity of water, and she wouldn't have been able to sink if she had tried.

With the wind pushing her, she quickly scraped ashore, wet and cold and shaking.

Jenny was bone tired when she followed the road around yet another curve. She was greeted by the sound of a lone automobile in the distance, and the gas station marking the junction of the two roads.

"Ginger's Grocery", read the sign, and under it, "Electrical, Plumbing, Feed, and Fuel". In any case, it was civilization. She leaned into the stronger wind and pushed closer. She appreciated the protection the woods had provided, both from the wind-chill on her still-damp clothes, and from her low traction.

Something had definitely happened in that lightning strike. The dark matter had grown again. She walked like she weighed nearly nothing.

All the trouble I've had—all caused by too many public flights, and now I've got to find a way to do it all over again.

She entered the store. A middle-aged lady in graying hair looked over her with a flat expression as she sat on her stool behind the cash register. Jenny nodded, and the lady may have nodded back, but if so, it was hardly visible.

If her greeting was lacking, the long line of shelves was a warm welcome. Much larger looking inside than out, the place looked part grocery store, part eatery with tables and benches, and down at the far end, part hardware store. Ginger's was a general store.

Jenny opened the flap on her leg pouch and was reminded again that there was nothing in there but a freshly purchased radio scanner, soaking in water and probably fried beforehand in the lightning. She checked the two pockets in her jacket, and was relieved to find a soggy, but spendable twenty-dollar bill.

Leaving her wallet, with all her identification, her driver's license and her credit card, had seemed the prudent thing to do before confronting Officer Davis, but now it seemed foolish.

But past mistakes aside, what she needed right now was something warm. She moved to the food counter and microwaved a sweetroll and following the terse instructions penciled on a sheet of paper, heated water to mix with a packet of hot-chocolate mix.

"Are you Ginger?" she asked timidly as she brought her purchases to the counter.

"Yes." The lady took the proffered twenty, and with a frown spread it out to dry next to her register. She made the change with no other comment.

Welcome or not, Jenny had paid her entrance fee and moved to one of the tables and began slowly munching on the warm food, forcing herself not to down it all in one gulp.

After a few minutes, Ginger left the register and began stocking a shelf on the other side of the store.

Jenny put off thinking about what to do next. Right now she had to warm up and shake off the chill. As long as she wasn't evicted, this store was a good place to recuperate.

She made a slow survey of the place. In addition to the expected beer company banners and promotional neons that you saw in every road-side eatery, this place had farm implement calendars, advertisements for something she could only guess was a seed variety, amateur posters for a dance at the 'Sons of Herman' and her favorite, a photo poster of two tots standing in a field, dressed in overalls. One was asking the other, "Been farming long?"

Jenny surreptitiously fished a half-dozen napkins from the dispenser and tried to wipe the scanner dry. She had removed the batteries earlier and put them in her jacket pocket, but even with everything superficially dry, there wasn't a glimmer of activity on its LCD display. Just like the discarded GPS, the scanner was totally useless. If the lightning hadn't gotten it, the lake water had.

She feared her costume would be just as fried.

Of course, the control box would have to be rebuilt, but how severe was the wiring damage? If she had anything to change into, she would have tried to examine it, but this was not the time or place.

Where is this place anyway?

She looked along the wall, and yes, there it was. She walked over to the map. Layers of dirty hands had marked the location of Ginger's better than the penciled star. *There's Lockhart. How did I get this far out?* She shook her head. One more piece of evidence that she had been flung higher and farther by the lightning strike than she had first thought.

There was a *ding-dong*, as a vehicle drove up. Ginger headed back to her register. The door opened.

"Well, hello there Bud!"

"Howdy, Ginger."

Jenny was amazed at the change in the lady's appearance. With a cheerful smile, and a gracious manner, she and Bud began doing business and exchanging gossip.

Is it just me? thought Jenny, *or is it because I'm not a local?*

She moved back to her bench and finished off the sweet roll. *Somehow, I've got to get back home.*

She could stay here until her money ran out, or try to make a call back to town. *But who? Rae is out of the question. The people at the copy shop don't want me around.* Indeed, there were a limited number of people whose numbers she had memorized. A taxi would want a fortune, up front, before coming out this far, and she didn't have the cash. Her parents were five hundred miles away, even if she dared ask for help from them.

Who was left?

She moved towards the front of the store, and looked out into the parking spots. Bud's pickup truck was the only occupant, and it didn't have what she wanted.

I'll just wait it out, and when I use up all my change, I'll cry and plead for some macho local farm boy to help.

The plan left a bad taste in her mouth, but she didn't have many options.

28

The hiss of air brakes, and the *ding-dong* shook her awake.

She was immediately aware that she needed to go to the bathroom, and that her costume was chafing horribly.

I have to check first.

Casually, she got up and walked over to the window. This time, she was in luck. It was a big truck, and CB radio antennae were mounted on either side of the cab. She watched in anticipation as the driver got out and went though the process of pumping diesel into the big square tank on the side. When she turned back toward her seat, she noticed Ginger looking at her with a decided frown.

I can't worry about her now.

Jenny waited until the driver came in to pay his bill. She waited while Ginger chatted with him, then he browsed the cigarette display and made his selection. She almost waited until he left.

It went against her nature, but she had to.

"Excuse me."

The trucker turned, looked her over, smiled broadly, and asked, "No excuses necessary. What can I do for a fine little lady like yourself?"

"Can I look at your truck?"

He opened the door and said, "Be my guest."

Jenny could feel the glare of the storeowner on her back, but she walked out with the man. She moved a little faster than he did, sensing that he would have an arm around her as soon as he could manage.

She hopped up to the door easily. She felt like she could have hopped right over the truck at her present weight. She made a mental note of the fact, just in case.

"Can I use your radio?"

He looked dubious, but he was willing to go along if it meant she would get into his cab.

She had him turn it on and set the channel. She took the microphone. "Hello. Is Mandrake in range? Can you hear me?"

She released the switch, and listened to the static, and chatter of distant voices. There was no response.

"Mandrake. Can you hear me?"

She looked over at the trucker. He smiled innocently. The next obvious step was for her to ask him for help. He knew it and she knew it.

The radio made a burst of static, and then a distant voice asked, "Mandrake, got yer ears on? Someone's callin' for you."

There was another burst of static, and then the voice said, "This is BillyBeer, relaying for Mandrake. Who is calling?"

Jenny had her heart in her throat, but she pushed the button on the mike. "Hello BillyBeer. Tell Mandrake that Tinkerbell is calling for help."

Ginger stood in the doorway, arms crossed, with a glare on her face that could start a fire at ten paces. Jenny smiled, grateful to hear the release of the brakes and the sound of the disappointed trucker moving on.

"Ginger, Mandrake told me to tell you that my name is Tinkerbell and that he is coming to pick me up in about two hours."

The lady's glare softened immediately.

"Manny knows you? Why didn't you say so? Come on in out of the chill."

With the vouchsafe of one of her regular customers, Jenny was pulled in and treated to several minutes of gossip about her favorite trucker.

By the time Jenny excused herself to go to the bathroom, she had a firm welcome and assurance that she could stay as long as she liked.

The relayed message had been necessarily brief, but although he offered to come get her immediately, he needed to make his delivery first if possible. Jenny had told him that there was no hurry.

But now, she had an idea of how long she would need to wait and suddenly, the fifteen dollars and change she had left seemed more than enough.

Wandering the shelves, she picked up a discounted T-shirt advertising some brand of tractor she had never heard of, a toothbrush and a roll of paper towels. The tax pushed her a few cents over her limit, but Ginger fished the difference out of the 'take-a-penny-leave-a-penny' bowl and rang up the purchase with a smile.

With the XXXL sized shirt more than large enough to keep her decent, she retired to the restroom and peeled off the flight suit. Back at the table, she set up shop—removing each ribbon cable from its cloth sleeve and checking for melted or burned spots, and then using the paper towels to dry everything out. The connectors got a thorough scrubbing with the toothbrush. She was dead tired, but the work was repetitive and didn't need her brain.

It was a long wait, but only once did she hear anything from Ginger. That was a rebuke to a couple of teenage boys who had sat down at the next table and tried to start up a conversation with her.

"Jeff, leave her alone. I have your mother's phone number right here next to my register."

They left in a minute.

With the suit dried out, and the ribbon cables replaced, she took a little break and rested her head on folded arms. She was deeply asleep seconds later.

There were voices, talking about her, and then Daddy picked her up and carried her from the playground. "No, she doesn't weigh a thing. Could you get the door for me? I'll tell you the story when I know it." And then he tucked her in and was about to read her a story when it all drifted away...

Jenny woke, startled by the brakes and the bump of her head against the wall. The first thing she was aware of in the darkened compartment was the baby-blanket softness of her covers and the fact that she was nearly naked except for a T-shirt.

The truck was building back speed as she remembered where she had been, and figuring out where she was now.

She was in Mandrake's truck, in that little cabin thing behind the cab. There was a nightlight, and from its illumination she was able to locate the reading lamp.

It was a comfortable little world, spacious for someone her size. There was a little bookshelf, with an elastic strap across the front to keep the books from sliding out. There was a sound system, and a TV with VCR. The walls were decorated, with pictures of far away cities, and portraits of several people. A large digital clock graced the far wall. There were latched compartments on one side, and she suspected his clothes and other possessions were hidden there.

There was also an intercom speaker with a red push to talk button.

Jenny hesitated. If there were anything she wanted to know about Mandrake, it was all here.

She read the spines of the books; John D. McDonald mystery novels, a Bible, a TV guide from three weeks back, *Field Guide to the Birds of North*

America, and *The Nine Nations of North America*. Not exactly her taste in books, but decent enough.

The videos had less variety. Gene Kelley and Audrey Hepburn accounted for seven of the ten, two were labeled 'One' and 'Two', and the third was hand labeled 'June and Jake'. She hesitated to actually run any of the ambiguous videos. Anything more than looking at what was in plain sight felt like invasion of his privacy, and the contents of a man's private video collection might just be more than she cared to know.

There was a large paper sack, and a quick look revealed it to be her possessions, including the roll of paper towels and the toothbrush. She grabbed at it gratefully, and got dressed. A T-shirt was okay for emergency wear, but she felt naked even if she was officially covered.

Only then did she push the red button.

"Hello?"

"Hi there Tinkerbell. Did I wake you?"

"No. I'm okay. How long have I been out?"

"I picked you up about four hours ago. Want to come up front?"

"Yes."

"Wait a moment. I'll stop."

She could feel the rig slow, and then move to the right. The door opened. The afternoon sun was bright, and Mandrake's smile was brighter.

"Once I drop off the Waco load ... Tinkerbell, are you awake?" Jenny looked up at the big man and smiled. "Sorry, I was off in a daze. What did you say?"

"Just that I'll be able to head back to Austin after we drop this trailer in Waco. It might be close to midnight before I can get you home. Is that okay with you?"

"Fine. That's fine."

But it wasn't. Jenny had felt her world collapse when she jumped down to the ground beside the truck. *I must weigh less than ten pounds.* She had practically floated. Mandrake had a ready hand to steady her when she wobbled on landing, but she covered up the incident with a smile and the assurance that she was okay.

By midnight, I will be too light to even walk. I will be negative by morning. I will be dead before noon.

She started the mental calculations. What would it take to get back into the safe region? How much longer would the current batteries last? Would her emergency wiring last?

Did she have a chance to pull it all together?

She closed her eyes again. The comfortable ride in the big truck, the pleasant company of Mandrake, the illusion that everything was okay— why should she try?

She moved in her seat, until she rested up against his side. He was driving with his left hand, and he put his right arm around her.

"You feeling okay? I can call the dispatcher and they can send out a replacement tractor if I need to get you to the hospital." He pressed his fingers against her forehead, feeling for a fever. "You are a little warm."

Probably the dark matter. She remembered the warmth that she had felt when she had moved into the influence of Jase's body. There was some heat generated as the dark matter bred itself. Normally, it was too small an effect to be felt.

"I will be okay soon enough. Just keep driving. There's no need for you to miss your deadline."

"Appreciate it. The company can handle these things, but it cuts into my completion bonus if I call for help."

"I guess I should stop pestering you to bail me out when I get stranded. It's not fair of me."

He gave her a little squeeze, "You've only asked once. I volunteered the first time, remember? And if I recall, I asked you to call for help back them. You don't owe me a thing." He glanced at the mirrors and pulled his arm free to work the gearshift.

"Of course," he added, "I can't help but wonder how you manage to get yourself stranded so far from home, with not a hint of how you got there, twice, and dressed in the same clothes. Not that I need an answer, mind you. I'm just curious."

Jenny was silent for more than a minute, wondering to herself how she had gotten herself off on such a dead end tangent. *A tangent. That's exactly it. Come tomorrow, the world will still be turning, but I am off on my own course. And it will be a relief.*

She blinked away an upwelling of tears. *Don't cry on him, he doesn't deserve that.* Vividly, the memory came back of Shawn, and her extravaganza of lies. *Fiasco. Just tell him the truth.*

She looked at the side of his face, and he took his eyes off the road long enough to give her another of his big comforting smiles.

29

"You've heard of anti-gravity?"

"Sure. I read science fiction. Standard stuff."

"We ... my university professor and I, we discovered it. This," she fingered the pale blue sleeve, now discolored by muddy water, "This is a suit that lets me use it. Twice now I've been caught by high winds and blown off into the countryside. That's how I've gotten stranded."

There was a big long silence in the cab. He gave her a quick glance, but the smile was tempered with a somber puzzlement. He didn't say anything.

Jenny felt her chin quiver. "You don't believe me?"

"Well ... It's not a story I've heard before, although to give you credit, it does cover the questions nicely."

"But you don't believe it."

He gestured with his hand, a small gesture, never getting too far from the steering wheel. "I'll consider all kinds of things. I've had people tell me stories about everything from the Kennedy assassination, to cloned dinosaurs hidden away in Hill Country exotic animal ranches. I don't dis-believe in any of it. It doesn't cost me anything to not dis-believe.

"But the things I truly believe are few and far between. To believe something makes demands on what you do in life. I don't willingly give up control over my life to anyone, no matter how well their story hangs together." He gave her an apologetic shrug.

Jenny felt a surge of resentment. "Stop the truck."

"Now Tinkerbell, don't get upset over..."

"I'm not mad at you. Just stop the truck. I have to show you something."

He sighed, and said, "There isn't much of a shoulder here. Be patient." It took another minute, but he found a stretch of the road with a wide gravel shoulder and stopped.

Jenny had spent the time unwrapping the batteries she had put into paper towels to dry, and then reinstalling them into the belt.

She opened the door and jumped down to the grass. Mandrake came around from his side.

Jenny looked down the road in either direction and waited for a clump of a half-dozen cars to pass by.

"I am tired of sweating blood to keep this secret, and then, when I tell someone the truth, they don't believe me!"

She snapped the battery compartment lid shut, and launched herself a hundred feet into the air.

The air was cool, and it brushed aside some of the comfortable warmness that had invaded her spirit, but the speed at which she climbed was chilling in itself. She killed the magnetic field, and concentrated on getting back down to the ground.

Luckily, although there was still a wind from the north, it had eased quite a bit, and she had no fear of another high speed dunking.

She looked down, and smiled to see Mandrake, running faster than she imagined he could. All she had to do was give the battery box the slightest of taps to kill her fall, and suddenly he had her.

"Gotcha!" he cried.

It was very nice to be wrapped up in his arms, and she didn't object as he carried her back to the truck.

When Mandrake climbed up into the cab beside her, he sat facing the nose of the truck for a moment.

"Do you believe me now?"

He looked at her. "I'm closer. But now I want the whole story. Start from the beginning." He put the transmission into gear, and for the first and only time, Jenny heard the metallic grind of a missed shift.

Mandrake was an active listener, asking lots of questions. Some of them, Jenny wouldn't have answered for anyone else.

Before she was half through, she had to take a break and get something to drink. Her throat was getting dry.

As she sipped on the square box of mystery fruit juice, Mandrake frowned at the road, and then asked, "You think this cop still suspects you of your professor's murder?"

"No, I don't think it's murder he has in mind. There were too many witnesses. He just expects people to be crooked, and he could smell that I wasn't telling him everything."

He nodded. "I know a cop like that. Even if you stay right on the money, he doesn't trust his ray-gun. If you go-slow, he thinks you are running something illegal in the trailer. I just avoid his town these days.

"But back to your problem. I understand about logbooks. I have to keep lots of records myself, but I take it you didn't break any laws by copying the book?"

Jenny shook her head sadly, "No, but what I did was much worse. Falsifying data is the one true sin of science. Once people know you've done that, no one will ever believe you again. I killed my chances to be a respectable professional physicist. I think I've known that all along, I just didn't want to admit it to myself."

They went on, with Jenny telling about discovering the truth about the dark matter contamination, her super-hero fantasies, her costume.

Mandrake told the story of his mother, and his true given name and the Sunday paper comic strip that gave him his nickname.

Then Jenny told him the dark side of the gift.

He held up his hand, "Let me get this straight. You, Tinkerbell, have this pixie dust stuff, which lets you fly, but it grows inside you, and unless you do a lot of heavy lifting, it will take you off to Never-never land, for good?"

She sighed, "That's about it."

He continued, "So you have to make these flights, even if people see you, or you get blown off course, or you get struck by lightning."

She closed her eyes, and nodded.

"Bummer."

They rode in silence for a few of the *thrum-thrum*'s of the highway dividers.

Mandrake asked, "So, how soon do you have to make another flight."

She didn't answer. The words wouldn't come to her lips, just a deep, deep sadness filling her chest.

"Tinkerbell?" He looked at the tears trickling down her face.

"Oh, no. I thought you were extremely light, when I carried you. You are close aren't you?" He grabbed her arm and shook it, until her eyes came open. "Aren't you?"

"Yes! Yes. Yes. I lose it all in a few hours. Are you happy now?" She could barely keep the words coming. It was okay when she could just ignore it all and pretend.

"They why aren't you flying? Why did you say we had time for this run?" He shifted gears and the truck started moving faster.

"Because I'm tired! Everything I try just causes more troubles. I try to get it under control, and then something like the lightning hits out of the blue and I'm worse off than before. I give up!"

"No!" he was angry. "You are not giving up! You listen to me. I'm in charge now. You are not allowed to give up. I'm going to make sure you get through this, and you're going to let me. Understand?"

She sniffed, upset by his sharp words, hurt by his anger.

"I said, do you understand me?" The words were strong and firm.

Jenny nodded. "I understand."

"Okay, first off, give me a better schedule. Tell me exactly what is going to happen."

He was a force of nature, unbendable. Jenny closed her eyes and recited her best guesses about the dark matter and its progression. In a way, it was a relief. She didn't have to think anymore.

30

They dropped the trailer in Waco, and then made a couple of stops, one at a sporting goods shop and another at Radio Shack.

Jenny was starting to feel a little better, now that she had gotten a thirty-minute catnap. Maybe it had taken a kick in the rear to get her moving again towards survival, but now that the decision was made, action made her feel better.

She took the new switches and spool of wire and began building a crude control. It was simply on/off from each of the three battery banks to all of the good magnetic sections of the costume. There was hardly any redundancy, but Mandrake told her to stop worrying. Duplications and good design in her original wiring had let her survive to this point. But she was still in the action stage, and re-design would come when she had time for it.

Soldering in a moving vehicle had its trials, but she was willing to put up with the occasional burned finger. At least decisions about where to go and how to hide her next flight were not her problem. Mandrake knew the territory better than she ever would. If he said he knew where to go, she would trust him.

They arrived sooner than she suspected. She ran her continuity checks again, even as he pulled into a roadside picnic ground and called for her to get dressed.

She felt more like a first-grader being sent off to school, than like a superhero.

She took a step, and the heavy bag of lead shot strapped to her leg shifted. "I guess this'll work."

He shrugged, "Your equation. The more weight you lift, the more pixie dust you burn."

"Just so long as I can reach the controls." Her arms were weighted down the same as her legs. And on top of that, she was wearing his heavy overcoat, nine sizes too big for her.

"You'll do fine. I bet you don't weigh any more than your original weight, now do you." He pulled a wool cap down over her ears, and had her step up on the bathroom scale he had brought down from his truck bedroom. Even with all the additional weight, it registered a dismal 65 pounds.

"Now," he coached. "Go up and down until you see the moon rise. Call me on the walkie-talkie at least every five minutes. On your final approach, turn on the flashlight and try to keep it pointed towards the ground. Can you do all that?" She nodded. "Good girl. Now go."

She reached in through the coat and flipped the switches all on. The strap-on weights pulled hard as she climbed rapidly.

I'm going to be heads-up the whole flight. At least that was better than his first suggestion—strap on his backpack and fill it full of bricks. She had disabused him of that tactic. Since the lift came throughout her body, she couldn't balance a load like that, and it would have left her head down.

The coat started whipping in the wind, but she was warm. He was worried she was going to come down with an infection. So was she. An extended illness was deadly until she had her weight stabilized.

Handling the walkie-talkie was difficult, with the arm weight to unbalance everything.

"Tinkerbell here. Can you read me?"

Down below, she could see a flash of headlights. He would talk if she needed help, or if he lost sight of her, but the intent was to keep radio traffic to a minimum, especially for him. Mandrake was well known, on practically all of the CB channels.

Falling was not so easy, with the coat trying to slap her in the face, but she had more motion control than she had thought. At least she was able to see enough of the ground to tell, within a few thousand feet, how high she was. She missed her GPS, with its satellite-based altimeter.

"This is Tinkerbell. I'm coming in."

Off in the distance, she saw the headlights blink. She wondered if he had lost her. His had been a slow road trip, moving down the road a half or a quarter of a mile at a time, following her drift with the wind. For her part, she had lost track of the number of times she had done the bounce. With no idea of her true altitude, she hesitated to climb too high, and with nighttime visibility, she feared to drop too low.

But this time, the moon had come up, and the light had given a texture to the trees and fields.

Mandrake had chosen the right road as well. With its twists and turns, her drift in the wind kept her always within striking distance of the road. Bundled up as she was, she had little chance to do any cross-drop glides, but at least she could control her drop rate, and attempt to land close to a road.

As it was, she hit the furrowed field a hundred feet from the asphalt and stumbled to her knees. The hiss of air brakes was a welcome sound and he was there in a couple of minutes to carry her back.

"Step here."

78 pounds. It was progress,

He lifted her to the bedroom. His breath was visible in the cool night air. "Get some sleep. You get to do it all over again in about two hours."

She groaned. But the promise of his soft blankets made her nod and climb in.

31

Daybreak found them at an omelet shop well off the Interstate. Mandrake liked his cooked with a half-dozen ingredients, but Jenny, in spite of the aroma, ordered cheese only. She was so starved that she didn't want any unusual tastes getting between the food and her stomach.

"I think," she said, "that I'm stable now. I won't need another flight for at least two or three days, and I could stretch it longer if I had to."

He nodded. "That's good. But I want you to keep the radio, and give me the code whenever you are up. The range on these things is pretty well line of sight, and I think maybe you could talk all the way to Dallas if you were two miles up. You have been thinking you are the Lone Ranger for too long. It's great to be independent, but people need people. You need a partner. You yourself said that we did more concentrated flying last night than you did by yourself in several sessions. You didn't get lost once, and you had rest and food," he gestured at the scraps of egg that were vanishing from her plate, "when you needed it."

Jenny had been thinking the same thing. Mandrake was a big, comfortable man, with a little gray hair maybe, but that didn't bother her at all. She liked him, and she was sure that he liked her as well.

He scratched his chin. She could hear the rasp of his fingernail over the stubble. He had been up all night, never sleeping, driving her from one rural road to another as the wind changed direction, giving her untouched skies to fly so that no one would see her twice, and someplace where he could pace her on the ground with no difficulty.

How much has he spent on me? The radio, the weights and all the other gear, and then there is the fuel. How will I ever pay for it all?

"You know," he said, coming out of his musing, "you should get a boyfriend—someone you could confide in, someone you could trust. How about that balloonist fellow? He didn't break his promise. You could use help from someone like him."

Jenny twisted her lip. *Men!*

"Or how about," she said, "a truck driver? Flexible hours, knowledge of the roads, demonstrable trustworthiness, and with a lovely comfortable bed big enough for two behind the cab!"

He visibly shifted back in his seat.

I shocked him. Jenny hadn't expected that. She was suddenly fearful that he would get up and leave.

The silence lasted long enough for him to take a deep breath or two, and for his smile to edge back onto his face.

"Now," he began, "I'm going to interpret what you just said as an invitation to a life of hot lust on the road. I can make that interpretation, because I'm going to turn it down."

He put up a finger as she started to protest.

"No wait. I can understand it, because I have an appreciation of my great personal virility and deep animal magnetism, and I must admit that you have crept into my dreams more than once since we first met.

"However, it wouldn't work out, and while I deeply appreciate the sentiment, more than you can imagine, it's a no-go."

Jenny was on the edge of angry. She had never offered to bed anyone before. Her usual problem was letting the guy down easily. But this time, it had just slipped out. She had never been so overt before, not even with Jase.

And he had turned her down. Forget fairness, forget justice, forget that she had presumed too much, too fast—she had offered, and been rebuffed!

Her lips tightened, and several angry jibes bubbled through her head, but he was watching her with a gentle smile. It was if he could read her thoughts, and she knew, suddenly, that there was nothing she could say that he wouldn't understand for what it was. She couldn't hurt him with words that weren't true. He had set himself up for that, on purpose.

She let out an angry, hard sigh. She could feel her face burn with the heat of her flush. He started to shimmer.

"Now don't cry on me, Tinkerbell." He plucked a napkin from the table dispenser and dabbed at her eyes with it. Gently, he said, "You are young and pretty, and if I were twenty years younger, I'd turn my life upside down to make it happen.

"But the fact of the matter is that twenty years ago, I did build my life around a young and pretty girl. For a dozen years, and two kids, and three different jobs, I built a life and a family.

"It wasn't perfect, and in spite of all my efforts, Gail wanted more stability than I knew how to provide her. Truck driving was my escape from her, and divorce was her escape from me."

He eased back against the wooden bench of the booth. She was surprised to see a tiny trace of moisture around his eyes as well. He was looking into the past.

"I've been able to provide for June and Jake, and I have a good relationship with the kids that Gail doesn't try to poison. They are proud of their Dad, and I will never, ever do anything that will change that."

He looked Jenny in the eye. "I wouldn't know how to introduce a new lover or a new wife to my daughter, one that looked barely older than she is." He shook his head, and for the first time ever, Jenny saw fear in his eyes. "I couldn't risk it."

He shook away some imagined ugliness, and then his smile came back. "So, little Tinkerbell. Let's get this straight. I'm your Uncle Mandrake. You can call me Manny."

Jenny smiled timidly. "I think Gail was not very smart."

A flicker of darkness startled her as it passed over his face in a fraction of a second. *So. He is still in love with her. Never criticize her again.*

They sat and talked in the cab for more than an hour, parked in front of her apartment. Jenny was glad it was in the middle of a school day, and the traffic on the narrow street was minimal. With difficulty, he had parked between an old tan Dodge and a mid-seventies Ford pickup. They scraped under the tree branches, but he didn't seem to mind. She now understood why truckers who had their own rigs tended to live in the country. It was murder to find a parking place for one.

"You're a messed up kid, did you know that?"

She sighed, "Yes, but is it that obvious?"

He nodded. "You are a young, sexy, bright, capable girl, and yet you go out of your way to annoy your friends."

"I do not!"

He nodded. "Yes, you do. But let me finish. You are young and in the prime age to be sizing up potential mates, but instead, you fall for older men. Unsuitable older men. If you were a tad less smart, you would already be stuck in a dead end relationship with some mid-life crisis refugee with a menopausal wife and a yen to make more babies."

She winced, hurt and at the same time, sickly convinced he was right. She did like older men. A series of faces flickered through her memory. Except for Jase, and Uncle Manny, she hadn't consciously thought of them as mates, but there were many others she had talked to in school and at the copy center. She would have conversations, long conversations with an older man. They always seemed to be more interesting people than the boys her age. They had been places, done things. Her peers didn't even know where they were going, most of them.

"It sounds like," he continued, "that you have at least three young men who could be molded into shape, if you took the time to do so. They are interested in you."

Yes, but I'm not interested in them.

"Uncle Manny, I don't think this is the time in my life to go boy crazy. In spite of your help, I'm still walking a ledge. If I fall one way, I'm dead. If I fall the other, then I'm some else's lab rat. I'm not sure I can keep my balance and have a social life as well."

He nodded, then smiled. "'It's none of your business, so stay out of my life'?"

Once again, she blushed. "I said it more tactfully than that!"

"I know, I just wanted to make sure I heard it right."

She picked up her sack. "I have to go now."

He nodded. "One last thing. You are too young to understand this, but relationships are permanent. Friends, co-workers, chance-met-acquaintances, mother, father, brother—favorite uncle. You can never destroy them. At worst, you can muddy the waters. Listen to the wisdom of an old hermit. The friend you ignore drains you. The friend you care about builds you up."

Issue 6: The Warning

32

The next morning, she perused the papers, but the story about the balloonist seemed to have vanished. He must have been released, and maybe the hoax theory of Officer Davis had been believed. If she were the police, she would have apologized to Shawn Breaker, but she doubted that Davis knew how to do that. Someday, she would have to apologize herself, but not until things were resolved.

Morning also brought the mail. One was the bank card bill. She tore it open with a sinking heart. It turned to lead when she saw the total. The monthly minimum was bad enough.

She went to her desk and pulled out her checkbook.

I thought I would never have to do this again. It was hard to be alive, with a future.

She made a guess at her last check from the copy place and ran the numbers.

Do I give up food, or batteries?

After an hour, juggling figures every way she could imagine, she put it all aside for later. She could keep a roof over her head, or fix her flight suit, but not both.

The other mail was advertising flyers, which she immediately trashed, a postcard offering her a trip to visit a timeshare and a letter from her mother.

The remembered dark comfort of Mandrake's bed felt infinitely inviting, but that was an illusion.

But was he right? Should I cozy up to Ben or Perry and let one of them take care of me? She wrinkled up her nose. *Why don't I just go down town and find out what I could make in a tight dress hanging around the convention hotels?*

Romance either happened or it didn't. Mandrake had to be wrong about that.

She looked at the postcard promising a thousand dollars or a TV or a new car. *Which is the ringer?* At first, the TV seemed the lowest cost item, but she had heard of one of those places that gave out certificates that could be traded for a bond that matured to $1000 in twenty years. The net present value of that was probably next to nothing. The timeshare condo they were peddling was on a lake she had never heard of. With no real regret, she tossed it into the trash.

Which left her mother's letter.

She picked it up, then turned her eyes back to her bill calculations. There was no new inspiration there.

Uncle Manny's words came back to haunt her; a relationship ignored drained you. That was exactly what she felt about her parents. There was so much emotion there. It tied her up in a knot and she tried not to think about her life back in Amarillo. But even the instinctive avoidance reflex drained her energy.

But was the inverse true? Resolutely, she opened the flap, and tried to read it with a clear mind.

There was news about Aunt Billie, and her gallstone operation. It was an update, but Jenny didn't even know that she had gone into the hospital. Had she ignored some other letter so long it had been lost? What an unnatural daughter she was.

I will call her. The thought of the phone bill came immediately to mind. *Soon. I'll call her soon.*

Jenny put down the soldering iron and reached for the phone.

"Hello?"

"Is this Jan Quinn?" The man's voice gave her just a hint. He wasn't a telemarketer.

It wasn't her real name, but "Yes, this is she."

"This is Sergeant Russel with the University Police. We have been searching for the missing equipment from the Williams project, and we have a report that may be it. We would like you to come identify it."

The chamber! They couldn't have found it, could they?

"Yes. I'd be glad to help."

She was given the directions. A farmer had found it in his field and had brought it in to the university to see if anyone knew what it was.

She looked over the kitchen table, where her re-designed control belt was nearly assembled. She didn't have time to finish the job—and now was not the time to show up in her flight suit.

Still, she was nervous about walking into the police station. With a guilty conscience, it was too easy to imagine being detained for a day or two—long enough to have her walking on the ceiling.

I would love to have an invisible flight suit, one that I could wear anywhere, under my regular clothing.

As she drove to the station, her brain started putting together a design. *Something simple, something that could be mistaken for something ordinary. It wouldn't have to give me the full capabilities of the flight suit. Lightning-zapped, and half burned out, my suit is still good enough to do most things.*

By the time she parked down the block, she was in good spirits. Things were happening again. Her brain was working clearer.

She identified herself and a rotund black woman, not much taller than she was, dressed in the campus cop uniform, led her to the back entrance.

"The chamber!" Jenny spotted the two large orange slice chunks of steel at once, among the collection of recovered bicycles. She stepped quickly to the nearest, and noticed that they were still connected by a pair of bolts, bent back by the force of the escaping dark matter.

"So this is your equipment?"

Jenny glanced at her nametag, a terse "Johnson".

"Parts of it. There were six segments in total. This stuff lining the insides was my radiation detector."

"It's radioactive?" the lady cop took a step back.

Jenny shook her head. "Not very likely. Right up to the very last, we didn't detect anything." She reached down and tugged on the edge of the metal. It was still massively heavy.

But just how much does it weigh? She had the original figures in her notes. If there were any of the dark matter embedded into the steel, then it would have been growing lighter too.

Maybe the steel is too dense. Maybe only low-density matter like human flesh was penetrated.

Her eyes went to the remnants of her radiation detector. There was a wide range of materials there, from plastic foam, to Teflon rods, to glass, to copper. *I could tell so much from this.*

"It looks ripped apart, like an explosion," said Johnson, "but I don't see any burn marks. Was there anything flammable inside?"

Jenny shook her head, "No. No chemicals. No pressurized gasses. Nothing. That was the point. We were examining the vacuum."

"Vacuum?" She barely had time to react to the news.

The door behind them opened so fast it banged against the stop.

Ben Mitchell strode in. His eyes went immediately to the heavily damaged chamber segments.

"What did he do the thing!" He ignored the both of them and went immediately to the bent pipe that had been its vacuum connection.

Jenny gestured, "Officer Johnson, meet Ben Mitchell. He was the vacuum expert on the project." Ben didn't seem to notice they were there as he put his weight behind it and rocked the shell up enough to look at some other fixture.

The policewoman put out her hand; "You need to leave this alone for now, Mr. Mitchell."

He looked up. "Why?"

"Because this is evidence in an on-going investigation, and the property of the Texas Energy Consortium."

Ben frowned, then stood up. "Okay, I guess. I don't really need any of it. My thesis is all done. It's only good for scrap metal now."

"But the both of you agree that this is the missing—parts of the missing equipment?"

Jenny nodded. Ben said, "Sure. But it's junk now."

Jenny asked, "What happens next?"

Johnson waved her hand, "Austin PD wants to look at it. No idea how long that will take. Then it's up to the TEC what they want to do with it. I hope it doesn't take too long. We need this space."

Ben left shortly thereafter, just walking away with no goodbye. Jenny wasn't sure that he ever said anything directly to her. Maybe Rae was right and he was still upset. With Ben, it was hard to tell.

But I've got to find a way to get that equipment. If there is some dark matter trapped in it, then I can experiment with the pure stuff and get some hard data. All I've got thus far is rules of thumb for flying.

It would also take some time in a real lab. How much could she accomplish on her kitchen table?

I should never have dropped out of the university.

"Officer Johnson?"

"Yes, Ma'am."

"If I had access to this equipment, even damaged as it is, I might be able to salvage my Master's thesis. This event has really disrupted my education."

The cop nodded, "But what I told him," nodding in the direction of the departed Ben, "it'll be tied up as evidence, and then turned over to the owners of record. Nothing can be done until then."

Jenny didn't argue. They went back inside. As they walked, she felt a magnetic flicker as her hand moved close to the lady. *She must have a radio.* Jenny had gotten so she could recognize such common objects as the speakers in music players, and the tension in the air next to her pocket was something like that.

But there was something else. If she hadn't been so paranoid, she wouldn't have given it a second thought, but on a hunch, she moved a little closer to the lady cop and felt the flesh of her arm crawl.

She has a tape recorder. That's an electric motor running. Why would she be taping? She had scribbled Ben's and her comments on her notepad.

Unless it is for someone else.

Jenny forced a smile and said goodbye. She walked back to her car, and then moved it down a block.

Keeping next to the buildings, rather than on the sidewalks, she walked back to a two-story building close to the police station. With a quick look to make sure no one was looking, she grabbed the drainpipe and climbed. With her current weight, even without the suit it was nothing to pull herself up hand over hand. The roof was flat, with a graveled tar surface and a one-foot-tall edging all the way around. It wasn't comfortable, but she found a place to wait where she could watch, out of sight.

It wasn't long. Thirty minutes later, an old tan Dodge drove up and Officer Davis got out. A few minutes later, he left, carrying something in his hand. She had no doubt it was the recorder.

33

If I were Spiderman, I would toss one of those spider-trackers down on top of his car, so I could keep tabs on him.

Davis was too close, and she had no doubt he could find some law or another that she had broken.

I need my flight-suit fixed today. It was urgent she burn as much dark matter as she could, as fast as she could. Who knew when the police might decide to detain her?

And it would help if I could be someplace else.

She thought of her parents, five hundred miles away, but quickly dismissed the idea.

All the resources are here. She needed the chamber in a lab, with good equipment, and the university was her only chance to have that. If she did hide out, it needed to be someplace close.

No, hiding in plain sight was likely her best bet. Look honest, follow all the rules, and don't give Davis any hooks to snag her with.

Get another job, and this time don't mess it up. She could let the bills slide a while before collection agencies started coming for her, but if she were going to stay here, she needed income.

I have to get the chamber too, and even if I did try to steal it from the police, I would never be able to lift it. I have to follow the rules on that as well.

That was a stumper. What were the rules?

It would have to be through the university, probably. Either that or a direct appeal to the TEC, an organization she only saw in print once or twice when she was doing paper work for Jase. As a grad student, sources of money were very important when you start, and then invisible until the end. She knew Jase had his finger on that pulse, but it was something she had been very willing to leave to him.

Professor Hausman should know. Big-iron physics like his plasma confinement project required serious money, far beyond Jase's project. He had to be good at it, or he would never be in the position he was. That was one of the perils of the profession. Get too famous, and you have to spend all your time with the paperwork and handshakes, and have no time left for the lab.

She walked back towards her car, then stopped. *Hausman's office is near here. Why wait? Get the ball in motion.*

His secretary checked her calendar, and offered to schedule her an appointment.

"This is time-critical," Jenny complained. "It has to do with Professor Williams' project."

Those must have been the magic words.

"There is a young lady to see you, a Jenny Quinn, about the Williams project. She has no appointment..."

She set the phone down. "He said that if you can wait another fifteen minutes, he can see you then."

Jenny was grateful, and tried to wait quietly in the outer office. She looked at all the pictures on the walls. Most were of Hausman's projects and teams of co-workers. He had been in the plasma physics job for decades.

She was grateful someone was doing it. Someone had to be hunting down the final formula for controlled nuclear fusion. It was the El Dorado of plasma physics. Almost from the beginning of the nuclear age, the idea that the world's energy problems could be solved by safe, clean fusion, converting a fraction of the planet's seawater into unlimited power, had been there. For the past fifty years, it had been only twenty years away. She hoped it wouldn't still be twenty years away in another fifty years.

The other sciences, and indeed other branches of physics, had long been jealous of the big chunks of money needed to fund fusion research. That didn't bother her. Jase had always managed to find money for his projects, and to pay the salaries of his grad students. There were advantages in working on projects that promised less, but had a smaller price tag. Hausman probably spent Jase's annual budget every few weeks.

But now, she had a project all her own, with no one to write the checks for her.

"Professor Hausman will see you now."

Her first impression was that his smile looked a little forced. She resolved to get to the point quickly and let him get back to his regular schedule.

"I am sorry to drop in like this. I know I should have made an appointment."

"Not at all. The rest of the day is paperwork, and you are a welcome excuse to keep it at bay. Esther mentioned something about the Williams project?"

Jenny leaned forward in her seat. "Yes, do you know that part of the vacuum chamber has been recovered?"

He nodded. "I was notified, since I'm handling the final shutdown of his project." He gestured at the pile of papers on his desk. "Of course it is all just paperwork now—making sure that all the bits and pieces are put back on the proper shelves. The report I got was that it was quite a wreck."

She nodded. "The police called me in to identify it. It is only two of the six segments, but there is no doubt it was Jase's chamber." She paused, then pushed on. "I would like to analyze the pieces and prepare a final report on the project, but I don't know where to begin. The police won't let me do anything with it."

He glanced over at the papers, with a frown. "I understand your desire. My final report to the funding organization is sketchy at best." He looked back at her with a smile. "I always like to put a good spin on the results of a project, even if the evidence is all negative. It helps to keep them happy with you.

"But, with Jase's project, expecting negative results, but with not even a good time-base on the run ... you know what I mean. I am quoting the interim results from your logbook in my report, and you hadn't managed to beat the previously published lower limits. As it is, I couldn't even justify publishing the results."

Jenny nodded, well aware of what it said. She had done the calculations herself. "I know where we were, but if I had the opportunity to analyze the chamber, there might just be some evidence that we have overlooked. There is still a mystery here. Why did Jase abruptly decide to move it? Why was the chamber found ripped open?

"With time in a lab, I feel I could find some of the answers. Jase deserves something better for his last project—something better than having the parts hauled away with the trash and having the report filed where no one will ever read it."

He nodded. "I feel the same way. It is a crime, really a great abomination, to have a man's life work swept aside like that." She noticed his hand was clenched in a fist, white knuckled. He continued, "I had even considered proposing something like you are suggesting—an in-depth post-mortem on the project.

"Unfortunately," he shrugged sadly, "the agenda of science is set by its patrons, not by its practitioners. I know I could never get funding for this."

She sighed. It he couldn't do it, who could? But she had to get that chamber!

"But what if I did it, on a shoe-string? It would take longer, but I'm the only one left who really knows what the project was all about."

He tapped his fingers on the desk top. "Tell me about you. I had heard that you had dropped out of the program."

She nodded, "Not officially. I just stopped coming here. With my project gone, and my job non-existent, I had to concentrate on paying the rent."

"I wish you had accepted the TA position. Everyone has spoken highly of you. I take it your new advisor wasn't able to help?"

She looked down at her hands. "That didn't work out. Not his fault, but I have always been an experimentalist."

He sighed, "That one is my fault. I should've pushed harder to get you into a program that would let you grow. Of course, it's too late to do anything about this session, but if you want to re-apply in the fall semester, I would be pleased if you would let me try to get you into my organization."

"Thank you. Fall seems so far away, but I will certainly give it some thought. There was a time, not too long ago, when I thought I'd given up physics forever, but I now realize it's in my blood.

"That's one of the reasons I want to do this last research on the chamber. There are too many puzzles left. I know if Jase were still alive, he would want me to solve them."

He nodded, "Good girl. That is the spirit I like to see in the new generation. I know I can't promise you a thing. I don't even know if the TEC would turn the equipment over to be analyzed. To them, this is just one more tax write-off.

"But if you do come up with a final report, using your own notes or your own insights, I would really like to see it. Come up with results, and we might even get it published. I do have some influence around here, and as I have said before, I can get a little pushy. Is it a deal?"

She nodded. Publication was just what she wanted. "You will ask about the chamber?"

"Just as soon as the police let go of it."

34

The bus hissed, and she wrapped her coat around her as she stepped down. It wasn't all that cold, even at four AM, but she had a hint of the sniffles from her all-night flight, and her last bout with the flu was just a few days ago.

Still, getting out in the night air had cleared her head and lifted her spirits. It had been the perfect refuge from the disappointing task of finding a new job.

The ground felt firm beneath her feet, and she walked briskly, confidently, towards her place. She must have gained several pounds if she could feel the difference.

When the weather co-operated, and she could get a night like this, with clear still air, and the mosaic of lights beneath her to keep her oriented, she could believe that things were going to work out.

She fished her hand beneath the coat and pulled out her new GPS unit. She paged through the displays, looking closely at her path through the sky and the statistics the unit had collected over the night. This was a more sophisticated gadget than her first one, with a detailed street map and much more memory for storing custom waypoints and routes. She was even deeper in debt, but she needed it.

Flying is so much easier with a map. I wish life had a map.

She changed the map scale so it didn't look like she was already at her apartment. It had been tempting, on a night like this, to attempt a landing on her own roof, but she had started the night with a goal of landing in Pease Park, and that is what she'd done.

The sight of the yellow paper advertising flier wedged in her door immediately soured some of her good spirits. She looked around. All the other doors were likewise blessed.

Jenny steamed. She hated fliers, whether stuck in her door, or under her windshield wiper. It was just like email spam or telephone solicitations—theft of her time so someone could try to get her money. Fliers were particularly evil, since it was organized littering. She would have to take the extra time to pick it up and trash it. She would not read the advertisement, on principle.

By the time she had ripped the paper from her door and stomped into her apartment, she found her hand shaking from the reaction. She dropped the paper.

What is wrong with me? Standing still in the silent room, she could feel her heartbeat pounding away. There was a flicker of fear. Had she finally started to feel the medical effects of the dark matter?

Or was it just stress? There was really no reason for her sudden anger. *I am tired of being afraid. I am afraid of being powerless.*

She took a deep breath, and tried to bring back the calm of the night sky.

The flier was a rude reminder of her job hunt.

There were jobs available, more than she had expected, but so many of them were not for her. With all the good will in the world, she couldn't handle most of them. She was too small and weak for many jobs. She had been discouraged when the first two job postings had mentioned, in the fine print, that the applicant had to be able to lift a certain amount of weight. She could handle a mop, but hauling the bucket of water around might be more than she needed to attempt.

Clerical jobs were fewer in number, and her first interview had been difficult. When she was asked to answer the phone in a test, she had failed it. She had thought it was a receptionist position, but it turned out that the company was a telemarketing firm. She had walked out. It was a bad match all the way around.

But I am still mad that they didn't want me either.

She shook her head. It would be so nice if she could count on her emotions behaving like they should. They had been all over the map this past month, from elation to suicidal depression.

Not that she didn't have reasons for feeling like she did, but so often the reasons seemed like rationalizations after the fact.

Chemicals in the blood. That's what emotions are. Maybe I need to see a doctor.

But no, that wouldn't do. The first thing they would do would take her temperature and blood pressure, then have her step on the scales to check her weight.

Just keep my calm. If I can. I still have to make a good impression on my interviews today.

Something is wrong.

Jenny looked at her porch, as her car's engine started to make little popping sounds in the sudden silence. It had been a long second day on the job hunt and it was already dark. Too dark.

The porch light is out. She sighed. One more job to do. She tried to remember if she had another bulb left over from the last time.

She locked the car and trudged up the walkway.

The crunch of broken glass under foot brought her sharply alert. She looked up. The socket was jagged fragments of glass, and charred wire filaments.

And it wasn't just the lightbulb that had been broken.

She backed up a step. Even in the dark, the door showed chipped paint and frayed wood where it had been attacked.

Jenny stood silent as a mouse, but her hand reached down through the folds of cloth to finger the switch on her belt.

I should call the police and the apartment manager.

Not too many weeks ago, she would have already been running for help.

But I can't have people digging through my stuff, not until I get the lab books secured.

For an instant, she considered calling big strong Bob, to back her up when she walked in, but she didn't know if they were on speaking terms.

Mandrake was a couple of hundred miles away, and she had soured that parting as well.

It's just me. I have to do this.

She put her hand on the knob. It wobbled, like it had been wrenched in its fixture, but she still needed her key to open it up.

The inside light didn't come on when she hit the switch. By feel and the faint light coming through the open door, she located a lamp, its shade missing, but its bulb still intact.

She turned the knob, and its timid light showed the full extent of the shambles.

35

Jenny held the shredded paperback novels in her hands. Her meager library had been torn apart. Not a single book, not her first year Spanish text, nor her novels, nor the white bound Bible she had received when she was ten—not a single one had survived. Each had at least some of its pages ripped out of the bindings.

Her clothes closet was empty of hangars. Everything had been pulled out, and each had been ripped with a knife. Her dresser drawer with her underwear and foldables had been dumped on the floor and something with an acrid smell, perhaps her drain cleaner, poured over the pile.

The draperies all had long rips in them. The walls were dented, probably by the dishes that had been thrown at them.

Somehow, she surveyed the damage with a cool eye. The emotions she expected—rage and fear—seemed to be waiting for another time. She walked through every part of the small apartment, finding new atrocities with each step. In her bedroom, the pillows were ripped open, and the mattress was soaked with various soaps and lotions. In the bathroom, the drains were stopped, and the water left running. There was a flood, but not as bad as she imagined it would have gotten. The vandal must have left just before she arrived.

How long did this take? The destruction was so complete. It was more than just random vandalism.

Someone hates me. Someone really hates me.

She felt a shiver. Some of those blocked emotions were knocking, wanting out.

The lab books were buried among the other books. Pages were ripped out and scattered. Her private log, with all the details of the dark matter discovery and her contamination, those pages were ripped out too. She picked at the clutter, trying to salvage what she could. Jenny located an intact grocery bag among the pile of dented canned goods and smashed boxes of breakfast cereals. She started collecting the important pages, everything from the lab books. She found the broken data disks as well, and added them to the bag, even though she knew she would never be able to recover the files.

It was the useless things that caused her the most trouble. Her Bible, so neglected since she had left home, brought back all the memories of home, and the long years she had toted it to Bible class every Sunday morning.

Every torn novel brought back vivid flashes of the romantic lives and far away places that they had shared with her. Old clothes, gifts and special purchases—they all gave up old memories at this final disturbance.

She picked at everything, hunting for some reason for it all.

Why?

It was nearly midnight when she righted a chair, and sank, exhausted into it. From this tiny island of comfort, she looked around her destroyed little home.

It would never be the same. Everything would have to be trashed. It would have been kinder if the place had burned to the ground.

She spotted torn scraps of yellow paper. Even the advertising flier had not survived. On impulse she picked up the fragment. In big block letters, there were just enough hints to suggest it had been a band advertising a gig at some local club.

She turned it over.

In blue ink, someone had lettered, "Ginny, they..." and below that, "mentioned your" and below that "careful!"

She stared at the five words as if they were the secrets of the universe. She was instantly down on the floor, pawing through the rubble, hunting for more yellow scraps.

Who left this? Why "Ginny"? All of her friends were used to seeing her nickname spelled "Jenny".

An intense search revealed only two more yellow scraps. One had nothing on it. The other had some chemical spilled on it—she could make out a blurred "are" and "work" among the dozen words that had been there originally.

Jenny arranged the scraps, like a jigsaw puzzle with most of the pieces missing. Was this a warning? Who was the writer? Who were 'they'?

And who hated her?

She tried to make a tally in her head.

Maybe Rae, because she thought she was stealing Bob.

Maybe Bob, because she had rejected him.

Maybe Shawn Breaker, for all the trouble she had caused him.

Maybe Officer Davis, because he thought she was crooked.

Jenny shook her head. None of them made sense. No one really hated her. They were all basically normal people. Perhaps it had been a random crime, kids vandalizing for the fun of it?

Her eye caught the broken case of her telephone on the floor. The cord had been ripped from the wall.

She picked it up. It was bent, but nothing looked broken other than the plastic case. The cord was frayed, but wires held no terrors for her. A couple of minutes exchanging the yellow and black pair for the more damaged red and green pair, and she had a dial tone.

Holding the keypad carefully, she punched in Rae's phone number.

"Hello?"

"Rae, this is Jenny."

There was a loud slam and then the line went dead.

She let the phone drop.

There was an echo of Mandrake's voice. "You are a messed up kid ... you go out of your way to annoy your friends."

People did hate her. They hated her a lot. And it was all her fault.

She started shaking. The blocked tears came, spilling out for a long time. She finally collapsed into sleep in her chair.

It was about three AM when she came suddenly awake.

Something is wrong. And it was something more than her traumatized surroundings.

She sat silently in her chair, aware of the distant traffic noise, and the rustle of tree branches. Everything inside was motionless, with sharp-edged shadows from the single lamp bulb.

Her eyes were drawn to the unknowable blackness between the shreds of her drapes, where anyone could be watching from the darkness of the night. *Someone is out there.*

She leaned forward, and then she smelled it. Gas.

On tiptoe, she moved quickly to the kitchen. *There.* She could hear it, and the smell was much stronger. All of the knobs on the gas range were on full. She had missed it in her first survey, so overwhelmed by the other destruction.

Quickly, she turned them all off, but she could still hear the hiss. The pipe itself had to be broken. *But I would have smelled this earlier.*

She couldn't believe that her vandal had re-entered the room while she slept. That left only one alternative.

The place was booby-trapped. The gas was turned off outside, and then turned back on when I went to sleep.

Someone planned this. Someone is trying to kill me.

There was a crash, glass shattering. The kitchen's one lone little window belched forth a rock. For just an instant, in one glimpse, she saw it wrapped in smoldering cord, the burning ends glowing red.

Without thinking, she jumped towards the door to the living room. The explosive wall of flame caught her in mid air.

36

The blast wave shoved her well into the living room. Her ears rang, and the world turned nightmarish orange. The ignited gas had exhausted itself in the one blast, but the gas pipe still roared in the kitchen, flaring with burning gas. All around her, the scattered and torn pieces of her life were catching fire.

The drapes and the papers on the floor were already sprouting their own flames. A bite of pain on her head snapped her out of her daze.

My hair! She slapped at the burning side of her head, frantic to put it out. She coughed, as the air had become unbreathable.

I've got to get out of here! Above the growing roar of the blaze, she heard the raucous noise of smoke detectors.

Her eye caught the sack, with her salvage, and she slapped at the edge of the sack to put out the two inches of flame that were trying to complete its destruction. She held the sack to her chest, ignoring the embers.

The door beckoned. *Outside!*

But before she had taken two steps, carrying her prize, she had second thoughts.

It's just what they will expect me to do. She could feel her spine itch. If they were ready to burn down the place, they wouldn't hesitate to shoot her as she ran.

But there wasn't any choice. Her lungs were aching from the impossible air. Holding her breath was only making her panic rise that much faster. She had to get out.

She glanced at the blackness outside. They could be watching her every move. She reached for the lamp, still doing its job in spite of everything. A quick jerk yanked the cord from the wall.

With a yell from the panic bubbling inside her, she threw the lamp hard against the window. The crash of broken glass was all the confirmation she needed. Holding the sack tight, she ran for the window, ducking her head down and jumping for the jagged hole at the last instant.

Something, for an instant, snagged her left arm, but it came free. She was out. Instinct flipped the switch on her belt, and she rose quickly, silently into the darkness.

She drifted, for more than a dozen blocks, looking back to see the flames and smoke grow larger by the minute. Fire trucks, lights flashing, were already starting to converge on the site.

I hope the others got out. Whoever was trying to kill her didn't care about innocent bystanders. She was dealing with someone ruthless, someone who would stop at nothing to get rid of her.

What do I do now? Everything she owned, except her flightsuit and the smoked and charred sweater she was wearing over it, was gone. She held the sack tighter. It was all trash, but maybe somewhere in the scraps of paper was a clue to her survival.

My car is still back there, she realized. But her attacker had to know that too. Going back for it was senseless.

There was a deserted lot below her, and she dropped quickly down to the ground. *What do I have left?*

A quick inventory showed her flightsuit with GPS and reasonably fresh batteries. No clothes at all except for her sweater. And her sack of torn papers.

This isn't enough. I'll have to go to the police, let them treat it as a murder attempt, and hope that some victim services group will point me at food, clothes, and a bed.

That was sensible, but she couldn't bring herself to take the first step.

Davis will investigate. He already had her on one suspect list. He might have her on two, if he had recognized her at the bridge. Three would be too many.

I do not trust him. She had heard his speech. Everyone was a crook. He believed that. She could not get justice from him.

In desperation, she checked again, looking through the sack, and reaching into her pouch. The tip of her probing finger felt hard plastic—her credit card and her bank access card.

So. I'm not totally destitute. She could at least get out of town. She could at least hide from the murderer.

Unless it's some fancy secret agency. That was a possibility. Jase could have contacted a number of people in those few hours before he died. Maybe the CIA or some other acronym already had the dark matter working in their secret labs, and just wanted to tidy up the loose ends. Someone was certainly ruthless enough to burn down the place to get at her.

The instant I use the cards, they can track me down.

So, she had to move now. There was less than $200 in her bank account; she could pull all of that out in one ATM withdrawal. She could also make one single credit card purchase. And she had to do both at the same time, and then be gone within the minute.

Dawn was still some time away, but she felt the need to move before then. If this was some government agency, then the longer she waited, the more likely they would have people in place monitoring her accounts.

A 24-hour Wal-Mart was less than a mile away. She started running.

Issue 7: Cotton Candy

37

Carnival sounds and noisy people cheered her spirit, but one whiff from the hot dog stand drew her like a magnet. Her cash, after this long first week on the run, was down into the double-digits, and her easy resolve to eat only one meal a day was proving harder than she had thought.

I shouldn't have come here. She said the words in her head, but a smile she couldn't shake told her it was a lie.

I remember that. The paintings of a two-headed snake—it was just like the show that came though town when she was a child. There were bright lights and rides, with more games of skill and chance lining the way than she could count.

And people. I miss people. Just over a week on the run, hiding from everyone—she was less of a hermit at heart than she had thought. Walking through a crowd felt good.

Food stands dotted the area and it took all her resolve to keep from digging into her pouch for one of her remaining dollars.

I probably owe them something. She felt guilty for hopping the fence to get in, rather than pay for a ticket. That was another thing that was coming hard—a life of crime.

Her accommodations were likewise fenced off from everyone who couldn't fly. It was hard, living off a dwindling bit of cash, with no job, and no hope for one. Buying food was tough enough; spending money on a place to sleep was impossible.

She had camped out, under the stars, and that worked for a few days, but there was more to a home than a bed.

"Let me guess your weight!" a man called, standing beside a large scale. "Win a prize if I can't guess your weight within three pounds!"

She stopped to watch his pitch, smiling. *You could never guess my weight.* Of course, she didn't know either. Not only were scales unavailable, she had flown so erratically lately that she didn't know what to expect.

The trip across country to this West Texas town had kept her in the air for many hours on end, but it had been just drifting at a constant altitude, head up, wrapped up in the sleeping bag she had bought. *It is the climb that burns the dark matter.* Her long test sitting on the ceiling had proven that. Another serious flight was needed soon, just to keep her weight up, but she had been reluctant to start. She could stay in this town as long as she didn't bring attention to herself. Every flight had the risk of discovery, and she needed to wait for a perfectly still night, if she didn't want to wear out her shoes getting back to her baggage.

"How about you, miss? Guess your weight? It's only a dollar, and see what prizes you can win!"

"What prizes?" she asked.

He showed her. There were useless trinkets, if he missed by three pounds, and progressively more expensive stuffed animals and shiny, but probably worthless jewelry, and knives, and watches, if his guess was off by more. She could see the gimmick. Even if he weren't terribly accurate, by paying off with cheap prizes, he could still come out ahead.

Still, there was no risk, and she did need the information.

"Okay, I'll do it." She fished for a dollar.

He looked her over, frowning at bit at her flight suit. "Ninety-seven pounds," he said, and then wrote down the number of a little black board next to the scale.

Jenny stepped up on the platform, and watched carefully as the large dial rose up to sixty-three, and then stopped.

"What the..." he said, and advanced up to the scale and gave it a shake. The needle wobbled, but stubbornly refused to move any higher.

"Off by thirty-four. I'd call that a miss," she said.

She moved aside, and he stood on the scale, watching as it rose sharply to his weight.

"Medical condition," she explained. "What did I win?"

The thirty-pound mark gave her a choice of any prize on the top shelf, some of which would have been tempting, back when she had a normal life. "I'll take the Disk player."

The man gave a deep sigh, and dug out the key that secured access to the prize shelf. It was not an easy task. Jenny quickly realized that the items were for show. They were never intended to be won. By the time he started dismantling the shelf, to get to the bolts that secured the items in place, she spoke.

"You know, it will cost you to replace it—not to mention the time you will have to spend to dismount this one, and to mount the new one. Why don't I just sell this one back to you, right now, before you go to all of that trouble."

He stopped his work, and gave her a hard look.

She help up a hand to ward it off, "Don't worry. I'm not a cop. You set the rules, I won, and you were going to pay up fair and square. It is just that I could use a little cash more than I could use the player. What will it cost to replace it?"

He shrugged, "Thirty bucks." She had thought it would be more, but she didn't really know.

"I'll sell that one back to you for twenty."

"I don't know."

"It's legal, and we both come out ahead."

He looked her over again, harder than he did before guessing her weight. "I feel like a sucker."

She smiled. "Don't feel bad. I've never done anything like this before. Your job is to play the averages, and I'm way beyond being average."

He gave her the twenty, with more grumbling. "Wait." He dashed over to the next booth and returned with an instant camera.

As the picture came out with a motorized whir, he said. "Advertising. What's your name?"

"Jenny ... Jenny Bell."

He took a marker, and wrote "Grand prize winner! Ginny Belle." With a little more force than necessary, he tacked it up next to the rules list.

38

With extra cash, and just a little twist of guilty pleasure, she got a fajita from one stand, and a large Coke from another, and then wandered the midway, enjoying the sights.

It had taken her a day and a half to get up the courage to come here. She had seen the truck caravan come into town, and then watched from a distance as the various structures were erected. The Ferris wheel was the biggest surprise. She hadn't realized anything so big could be assembled from truckable pieces.

She bought a ticket, and handed it to the elderly black man who ran it. Just for an instant, the old man, his worn-ragged chair, and the metal structure around him seemed to be all of one piece. Dennis, for so his nam-etag proclaimed him to be, slowed the wheel to a stop and held the swaying steel car for her to get in.

For the first time around, stopping frequently to let other riders on and off, she enjoyed the sights, looking over the town and the midway. It was different from when she had flown in, trying to keep out of sight. Now she could see and be seen and no one would think a thing about it.

Off in the distance, she caught a flicker of light reflected from the water of the community swimming pool, her current residence.

The pool was closed for the season. By reading the posters there, she knew it would open back up in a few days, probably the minute that the public schools let out for the summer. By then she would have to be gone.

But for now, the place was perfect. It had tall stone fences and pad-locked gates to keep the adventurous kids from trying to sneak in. For her, it was wide open. Even the dressing rooms were open, with no doors, just strategically placed walls and corridors to keep the area private. There were benches, which made a firm but totally satisfactory bed when she spread her sleeping bag over it. There were also bathroom facilities, and running water. Even the electricity was still on, although she had sense enough to keep from using it.

But for the first time since her apartment had been destroyed, she could bathe and wash her clothes. There were even a few random slivers of soap left by last season's swimmers, and one true treasure, a bottle of shampoo.

Even her flight suit had benefited, with a full two days spent on it, washing everything that could be washed, and checking every pin of every connector for corrosion.

Everything was clean, and she was glad to be rid of the last of the stench of smoke. Her hair was still a little uneven from the fire, but that would grow out quickly enough, and it wasn't very noticeable.

She looked carefully from her seat on the Ferris wheel, but her things were well hidden, up on the roof out of sight from this direction.

It is like flying, she thought, as her car rotated down to the bottom and started back up.

Say, what if I... Reaching for her belt, she turned on the magnetic field. Immediately she lifted harder against the restraining bar.

Would it work?

At the top, she switched off the current and rode back down normally. At the bottom, she turned it back on.

Through the remaining turns of her ride, she cycled her flight suit. If her understanding of the process was correct, she could burn dark matter, and no one would ever suspect she was doing anything unusual. It was the perfect solution.

When Dennis stopped her car at the bottom, she was out like a flash, running over to the ticket booth and buying ten dollars worth of tickets.

"Here!" She handed him the whole string of tickets. "Just keep me going until these run out."

"You like da Wheel?" he grinned.

"I think I do!"

It was dark by the time he apologetically stopped her car. "Times up Miss." She took his offered hand and stepped down to the ground. She was stiff, from sitting on the hard metal, but she could feel instantly that she was heavier.

"Thank you, Dennis."

"My pleasure. Da wheel likes you."

She puzzled over that statement as she walked back toward the 'Guess Your Weight' stand. Could he tell a difference in the way the wheel turned? If so, that could be a good sign.

"Hello."

The weight guesser turned towards her and his face dropped. "What do you want?"

"I want you to guess my weight." She handed him a dollar.

"I don't understand. It is sixty-three. I remember that number right enough."

"But I've eaten since then. Don't you want my money?"

He reached for the dollar like it was being held in a snake's mouth. Taking his chalk, he hesitantly wrote 62.

"You don't trust me?"

He shook his head.

She stepped up on the scale, and watched the big needle swing up, stopping at 69. Her heart pounded. It worked! She had a way to keep her weight under control, in public.

The man whispered a word that had gotten her brother Joe a two-week grounding.

Then he added, in a well-worn chant, "You are entitled to any prize on the bottom shelf."

She glanced down at the pennants and little stuffed animals. She picked up a white rabbit. "I'll sell it back to you?"

He shook his head. "No."

39

The noon sun was bright and warm. She felt an itch on her belly where the pool water had dried, and scratched at it. Sunbathing was pure luxury, although she couldn't stop herself from checking the sky every few minutes.

Nothing but blue. Her bench was positioned for privacy, and not even the Ferris wheel riders could see where she was.

The traveling carnival had caught her imagination. That ride was the perfect solution for keeping her problem secret, but it was too expensive. Plus, the show would be leaving in another day.

She felt a familiar tenseness on the skin of her leg—sunscreen was a luxury she couldn't afford, and she had to watch her exposure. Time to turn.

With her head propped on crossed arms, she tried to clear her mind of everything but the warmth on her back.

Is there even a way that I could follow the show? And I would have to give up this place.

Knocking at the back of her mind was the unpleasant idea she had been attempting to banish. She had no plan. At the rate she was going, her money would be gone this week. She could not exist without food.

And this poolside spa will be usurped by a thousand school kids any day now.

She sighed, and buried her face in the darkness of her arms. *I can't play it safe. I don't have the resources.*

"Excuse me, Mr. Dennis?"

"Is jus Dennis, Miss. Da boss wants us all 'first name friendly'."

She smiled, and held out her hand, instinctively reacting to something in his bearing. It was like greeting an elder at her old church. They shook hands.

"I really like to ride the Ferris wheel, but I was wondering if there was any way I could get a volume rate? I'm very short on cash."

"You're da girl who rode ten dollar worth, yesterday." He smiled. "You new in this town?"

Her mind raced for a response, "Uh. Yes, I'm just passing through, actually. I don't live here."

He nodded, "Thought so. Been to this town nine years running, and I'da 'membered you. You like da Wheel?"

"Oh, very much, but like I said, I'm between jobs, and I have very little cash."

"Well there. We can work som'n out. Gimme a five, and I'll let you ride til clos'n. But only for you, since da Wheel likes ya."

"Thank you." She fumbled in her pouch, and extracted a wrinkled five-dollar bill.

He stopped the wheel and opened the door to the metal car with a pleasant bow. Jenny hopped in and started fastening the safety bar, when a small white card fell out of the latch. She snatched it up.

On the back was a #12883 marked in ink. The front of the business card was the contact information for someone at an insurance company.

"Dennis," she called.

"Yes, Miss."

"Is this important?" She handed him the card.

He squinted hard at the text, and then fumbled at a pocket for a pair of very worn spectacles. He read the text and then sighed, and handed her back her five-dollar bill.

"Sorry Miss, but would you take dis over to da boss tent?"

She nodded, and he pointed at a trailer parked up against the fence. Dennis turned the 'OPEN' sign to the reverse side, with a 'Sorry, closed" message.

Jenny reassured herself that it couldn't have anything to do with her, as she walked quickly over to the office.

She knocked on the door.

"Yes, what is it!" came the gruff response.

She opened the door. 'Da boss' was a tired man in a well-worn business suit. His desk, with metal straps that secured it to the wall of the trailer, was piled high with papers. He glanced up at her as she walked in, but his main concern was some bound ledger he was working on.

"Dennis sent me over with this." She handed him the card.

He looked up, and his expression dropped a bit more.

"Dennis." He was not pleased. "Where did this come from?"

"I found it. It was in the safety bar of the Ferris wheel car I was starting to ride."

"Which car?"

"Uh." She thought, recalling the large red number painted on the metal. "Car number 6."

He nodded, and opened a drawer in his desk. From it, he pulled a frayed manila folder and began copying from the card to a multi-generation photocopy of some form.

The door opened behind her, and Dennis entered.

"Why didn't you find this?" the boss demanded.

Dennis shook his head, with an amused smile. "Can't take no time for busywork. Da Wheel's in good shape."

"Well, it will cost you now. Shut it down until Morgan can do a full safety inspection."

Dennis nodded. "I tole him. He's work'n on it."

The boss looked at Jenny. "Thank you for spotting the card."

"What was it?"

He grimaced. "Insurance inspector. They think it's cute to hide their business card in the works, and they'll shut down the whole show if we don't find every last one of them. Some girl in Austin was killed in a ride a few years back. The legislature made the insurance company liable. Now, they're worse than the local officials ever were."

She nodded, remembering bits of the story.

She turned, but Dennis shook his head, confidently blocking the door.

The boss sighed loudly. "Okay, Dennis, what is it?"

"Miss here, she needs a job. An seein' young Pat left, and seein' as how you owe her a favor...."

He sighed again. "She's not a carnie." Dennis said nothing. "Okay! You go help Morgan. I'll talk to her."

Dennis smiled broadly, and with a deferential nod, he left.

"My name is Forester. I'm the general manager of Western Extravaganza Shows." He extended his hand.

"Genevieve. Ginny Bell. People call me 'Tinkerbell'."

"Well, Miss Bell, do you think you can run a cotton-candy stand?"

The negotiations took fifteen minutes, and Forester was obviously ready to shoo her out of his office before then. It was all she could do to keep from clapping her hands with joy.

Forester was paying her practically nothing, but as she explained her circumstances, he didn't bat an eye at the idea of a homeless girl joining up with the show. He even had a place for her to stay, an old six-foot travel trailer that one of the other trucks towed from town to town. She would have to clean out the junk it was currently carrying, but it would keep her out of the rain.

She was expecting problems when he asked for her Social Security number, and she claimed not to remember it, but he just shrugged it off.

He finished by handing her a key. "Go tell Dennis I hired you, then get started."

She picked it up. "Thank you. I really needed the job."

"Thank Dennis. If he says you're in. You're in."

"Why?"

For the first time, he cracked a smile, for just an instant. "You ask a lot of questions."

"Sorry. I am new here."

"You'll learn quick enough."

The key, it turned out, wasn't for her room, but for the stand. Open on all sides, the little cart held a couple of tubs, which she suspected were the cotton-candy machines, and shelves. A quick search turned up a splattered card with step-by-step instructions on how to make the candy. More checks located the sugar and food colors.

She half expected someone to come by and give her instructions, and she raced to prove herself by being ahead of the game.

However, she was just warming up the equipment when someone came by.

"Hello, I would like two please."

The mother, with one little child tugging at each arm, waited patiently while she poured the sugar into the opening. She remembered paper cones as a child, but there were none here, just plastic bags to hold the confections. The first one was, frankly, ugly and lopsided, but Jenny was happy that it worked at all. She made the mistake of making the second one larger than the first, but the mother fixed it by taking a pinch of the second one for herself.

It was only after she collected the money and had a moment to breathe, that she looked again at the trio and realized that the mother was probably her age, or maybe even a year or so younger. If fate had turned a different corner, it could have been her, walking her own children though the midway.

40

Her new home was slightly larger than a closet, and it smelled heavily of mildew. A couple of decades earlier, it had been a cute little travel trailer, sized small enough to be towed by an ultra-compact car. It had seen considerable wear since then.

Practically all of the space inside was taken up by the bed. There was a sink, but she was told that she had to fill the water tank herself, and that she wouldn't be able to use the drain unless she had a catch-pan underneath. Most of the campgrounds the caravan used had regulations about gray-water run-off.

Still, it was a roof over her head, and she could wash her face without listening for the police.

When the show closed its gates well after midnight, she still had cleanup to attend to, and then she flew (literally) back to the swimming pool to collect her hidden baggage.

She barely had time to stash it in her new home, when Forester came by, angrily demanding to know why she hadn't reported in with the day's receipts.

"Here it is." She handed him the crisply lettered tally she had kept, along with the shoebox containing the money. "I will need some of this change tomorrow, but let me know where to turn this in, and I will have it there on time, every time."

She had her response rehearsed. She knew she needed to be a little aggressive. He had left her to sink or swim, and she needed him to know that she could handle herself.

He looked over her paper, and grumbled something unintelligible. "Thirty minutes after the close. Turn it in at the office. Did you lock up?"

"Of course. What about supplies? Two or three good days, and I'll be out of sugar."

"Tell Betty what you need."

"Who is Betty, and where can I find her?"

He looked puzzled. "She's the cook, of course." He glanced at his watch. "Yes. She'll still be serving." He took the box and walked away. "Come by at noon for your change."

Rude, but she shook it off. *When I'm no longer on the run, then I can afford to be offended.*

But the news that the show people had their own meals, and served after closing was welcome.

She looked in vain for a way to lock her door, and then gave it up as a lost cause. There was an inside latch, but she would just have to hope that all the thieves were outside the gate.

"Hello. You're the new one." Helen's nametag was pinned a little crooked on her simple dress. Jenny suppressed a little flash of jealousy at the tall blonde. Helen was the kind of woman who would look good in a potato sack.

"Yes. Dennis recommended me."

She put her hand to her mouth, "Oh, so that explains it."

Jenny kept moving toward the counter where a large woman, in her fifties, presided over the pots. Apparently Betty didn't need a nametag.

Helen followed her. Jenny asked, as she followed the cook's gestured instructions to pick up a plate and serve herself, "Are you Betty? Forester said to tell you that I need more..."

Betty shook her head and tapped her throat.

Helen said, "Betty doesn't talk, and she hates trying to remember things. You need to write everything down and give it to her." Betty nodded.

"Okay. Sorry, I'm new."

Betty nodded, and smiled, briefly.

Helen led her to a table. "This is *Lady* Veronica."

"I am a Reader." She nodded.

Helen continued, "I run the ducks. Over there is Bill."

Jenny grinned. "I've met Bill already. He may not like to see me here."

"Oh, so you are the one! He was stomping dust something fierce yesterday. How much did you stick him for?"

She ducked her head, "Twenty dollars. I have a medical condition. I'm a lot lighter than I look."

Lady Veronica laughed. "He'll get over it. Being a sucker again stings. He only joined the show last year."

"How long do you have to be here to get past being new?"

They both laughed. Helen said, "Never. Dennis considers Forester a sucker." She added, "We are carnies, outsiders are suckers. It's not as much an insult as you might think. It's just the names we use."

Jenny nodded. "Is that why Forester doesn't like me, because Dennis suggested it?"

"Something like that. Dennis does what he wants, and Forester hates it."

"Is he too senior to fire, or something?"

"Oh, no. Forester would fire him in a minute if he could afford to. No, Dennis owns the Ferris wheel, and it's hard to book a carnival like ours without a Ferris wheel."

They explained in more detail. Western wasn't a one-owner operation. It was more like a flea market. Each stand and ride was independently owned, sometimes by the people who ran them, like Dennis with his wheel, and sometimes by absentee owners, like the cotton-candy booth. Jenny's new job wasn't a salary deal. She would split the net with the real owner of the booth, someone named Old Sam, who had retired to stay with his family a couple of years earlier. Her supplies, the trucking fee, and even the supper fee had to come out of that as well. Jenny privately hoped there would be enough left over to buy batteries. With food and shelter taken care of, and with the help of the wheel, her most basic needs would be taken care of.

Lady Veronica left, but Helen seemed content to stay and watch her eat, and to point out the other people who drifted in and out.

"H is back, I see."

The man looked wrung out. He retired to the far seat of the last table and kept his head down over his plate. Helen whispered, "He's a trucker. He disappears into the local bar every new town, and then shows back up, hung over, before we move out."

"You said his name is H?"

"Yes. Just the one initial. Not even Forester knows any more than that. As long as he's sober on moving day, he doesn't care either."

Jenny filed that bit of info away. Maybe she could survive in the place without coming up with a Social Security number.

As she was finishing, Helen perked up. "Here is my Jim. Jim! Come over and meet the new kid."

Jim was tall and smiling. He sat down next to Helen and nodded. "Jim Morgan. Thanks for spotting the business card. There was another one in the Tilt-A-Whirl, too. It must have been a new inspector. I thought I recognized all of them by now."

He was the safety boss, and second in command to Forester in most other matters having to do with the show. Helen latched onto his arm as he talked.

"You will need to come by the office to get your name tag. What was it? 'Ginny'?"

"Oh, could you do it with 'Tinkerbell' instead? That's my nickname." She would also rather keep her real name as restricted as possible.

He nodded. "That's fine. Around here, a person's name is whatever they say it is."

Helen and he got up from the table when she did, and Jenny was almost sure he gave her a wink as Helen led him away.

Nothing makes an old, worn-out mattress feel good like having spent the last few nights on thinly padded concrete. It also helped that she hit the pillow at three in the morning.

Get used to this. The carnival is always going to be a noon 'til late job.

She double-checked the latch, and then flipped off the lights.

"I told you the cave would be perfect," said Jase, as they both fell up to the ceiling.

"But what if we can't get out?" she cried, as she stretched out on the rocks. Pressure was building on her chest. The cave itself was breathing, and each warm breath was rank with decay.

"The pressure! It is crushing me," she cried, but Jase had vanished.

She woke suddenly, in the darkness, panicked by the weight on her chest. She tried to get up, but couldn't.

"No!" she cried.

Hiss! A beast, right in her face, became a scrambling thing of feet and claws, and then abruptly vanished.

She slapped a couple of times at the wall, before she hit the switch. In the glare a 40-watt bulb can only produce on totally dark-adapted eyes, she looked frantically around the little room, but there was nothing.

If the lingering cat-smell hadn't confirmed the incident, she would have thought it was a nightmare. She got out of the bed and looked all around, in the cabinets, and checking the door and window. There was no place for a cat to hide, and no way for it to enter, or leave.

She even looked up at the ceiling. *Unlikely, but who am I to judge?* But even there, she couldn't see any opening.

Jenny sat back on the bed. Weariness, and reaction to her sudden encounter, came crashing back down. She pulled up the cover and turned off the light. The impossible was not important enough to keep her from sleep. Not tonight.

41

She woke to birdsong. She had slept late, by her standards, but she realized quickly that the camp was not yet up. She walked around, trying to match up the different attractions with the people she had met.

Even with the awnings down and windows shut, she could see the place with more personality now. Lady Veronica's fortune telling booth had a decided gypsy motif that had been absent in the lady herself. Maybe it was part of the act.

There were Helen's ducks, and there was nothing that could be done to make a bunch of floating plastic toys glamorous.

Nor a cotton candy stand either.

As she thought about it. The actual sideshow performers she had met had all had an aristocratic air about them. It wasn't heavy handed, but Helen had deferred when they had spoken.

So I have a second-class job. At least I have a place to sleep.

And a teleporting cat to visit during the night. Or is it a ghost-cat? She smiled, and took another look around, only this time at ground level, looking for her visitor.

"Up so early?" It was Jim, striding across the grounds in her direction.

"Haven't adjusted yet to the hours."

"Well, we might as well get your name tag taken care of. Come on."

They went to the office trailer, and he fired up the little engraving machine that cut the letters into a multi-layered plastic.

"Here, let me put this on you." He stepped closer.

"No!" she backed up.

"What's the matter?" He smiled. "Afraid I'll poke you?"

She nodded, suddenly aware that he was still too close, and reached out for the tag.

"I made these clothes. I have to be careful with them." Which was the truth, and the reason for her first, instinctive reaction. But, he was also very attractive, and he knew it well.

She carefully slipped the pin through the outer layer of the flight suit. TINKERBELL.

"A costumer. I wondered about that last night. If you let this crew know about it, you will be inundated with requests for help. Everybody has an act. Everybody wants to be a specialty.

"What is yours?"

She shook her head. "Nothing."

He grinned, and it was hard to resist that look. "Okay. If you want to keep it a secret, that's all right by me. But no one wears a costume every day, just for fun."

Jenny took the hint and wore her sweater over her flight suit that day. A late cold front with intermittent rain showers really damped the business for the day. Her intent to get several cotton candies prepared in advance and hanging from the rack left her worrying about wasting supplies. The previous vendor had left the cabinets bare of practically everything, including anything to wrap the candy in. Raw materials were plain sugar, and electricity to run the spinner, and those were available everywhere.

It was a long day, with few customers. Helen came by, to warn her about the move.

"I'm already shutting down those dizzy ducks. I have to drain the water and get ready. Forester has already posted a 9 PM gate closing. Your stand will have to be packed up and ready to move soon after that."

Jenny asked how the stand and her trailer would make the move.

"Cobb is the truck boss. He'll have that covered. Just get your stuff secured. If the trucks start to head out the gate, and no one has made a seat for you, just come over to number 8, that red one over there, and we will make room for you."

J enny followed the advice, and had the stand secured, and anything movable locked down well in advance of closing. When the locals gave it up, she locked the stand and raced over to her trailer to secure her stuff for the move.

When she opened the door, a large yellow cat jumped out of nowhere and raced off.

She put her hand on her chest, to quiet her heart beat.

"You are a teleporting cat, aren't you? How did you get in?"

J im knocked on the door a few minutes later.

"Yes?"

"I just wanted to invite you to ride with me. I have that pickup over there." It was a large one with dual tires on the rear axle, towing a gooseneck flatbed with several of the smaller stands already loaded on, and strapped down.

She smiled, "Thanks, but I already have an invitation."

"Maybe next time."

"Yes."

A bout one AM, after the big field lights went dark, after the crew had disassembled the huge Ferris wheel into compact stacks of truckable components, one of the big eighteen-wheelers gave three long blasts on its horns, and a chorus of diesel engines revving up echoed through the fair grounds.

Jenny dashed over to truck 8.

"Hi, Tinkerbell!" She was greeted by Kelly, who ran the darts and balloon stand. "Helen said you might be joining our hen-party."

She climbed up, and found that instead of a bedroom like Mandrake had on his truck, this one was fitted out with front and rear facing bench seats, with a tiny little table between.

"What's your game," Helen said, brandishing a deck of cards. "We play everything from poker to go-fish."

If packing up for the move was hectic, unpacking was even worse.

"People, listen up!" Forester shouted to the mob. "I told you when we booked this place, Colorado City doesn't want us to draw customers away from their downtown celebration, so we have to set up the rides and stands in the parking areas they have designated. All personal trailers and all the trucks have to stay at the campground over by the cemetery. Ed and Lee will be guarding the place. Morgan will be running ferry service."

Helen whispered to Kelly, "Awful flat for a place called Colorado City." She nodded.

Jenny thought it was nice enough, for a West Texas town. She was just glad that her stand was considered important enough to make the cut.

The rest of the day was tough, with many of the show having missed out on the night's sleep altogether, and most of the rest having slept sitting upright in truck cabs.

Dennis was the most active she had ever seen him, prowling around his wheel, and the crew re-assembling it, making sure everything was perfect. He spared her a nod, but he didn't take his eye off the workers.

By nightfall, the brightly lit wheel was turning, the most eye-catching thing in town. Her secret plan to get her stand set up next to the wheel was aborted when she found out that it wasn't a new idea, and the others were quicker at it than she was. As the newest of the new, she had no status, so she just smiled and set up as close to the main street as she could.

There was no entrance fee, this time, with no fence and no resources to surround the place with guards. That was fine with her, as it meant more walk-in traffic. She made up for the light day before, and more so.

By closing, she was barely able to turn the key and find a place in the back of the pickup with others heading for their pillows.

She paused, with her hand on the door. *No. He was probably a local cat, and I made sure the place was empty when I closed it up.* She pulled it open.

Purr?

He stood there, in the center of her bed, blinking his eyes, as if she had disturbed his sleep.

"Scoot. That pillow is mine." She had to push him to one side, but with no more argument, she was under the covers and asleep in seconds.

The Saturday business was less hectic than Friday's half day, and she was very glad when Jim came by, with a grocery sack.

"Betty said this was for you, Tinkerbell."

After a quick glance at the contents, mainly bags of sugar, she gave him a thumbs-up. The people waiting in line for their treats gave her a good excuse to ignore him, but even then, he stood to one side, watching her, until there was a break.

"How is the life suiting you, little one?"

"Different from my last job, that's for sure. Stickier."

"What was that?"

She just shook her head. He didn't pursue it.

More customers arrived, and he smiled and wandered off.

It was strange how the work could be so mind-numbingly boring, and yet satisfying at the same time. She loved the little kids, especially the ones barely able to walk. The burst of sunshine that came across a pudgy little face when that first taste of cotton candy crossed the taste buds was something she watched for. It gave her a thrill every time. She was growing a theory that all the older kids and the adults bought her fluffy confection in a vain attempt to recapture that first-time burst of sensation.

Business was good, so good in fact that she barely had time to break for lunch. She wasn't really sure what Colorado City's "Railhead Trading Days" were, but there were certainly a lot of local shops where trading was happening fast and furious. She would have liked to join in.

But, she had to make her nut. That was a new term for her. Kelly had explained that bit of circus history.

Local officials, then and now, were notorious for expecting a cut of the proceeds from the show, in exchange for allowing them in their town. One Sheriff removed the nuts from the wheels, keeping the circus from leaving before he had received his fee. So 'earning your nut' meant making enough money to cover your fixed expenses.

Jenny was new. But it was plain she had to make money when there were people ready to buy, because there would be days when they were traveling, or rained out, and those fixed expenses wouldn't stop.

42

"Let me drop you off at your trailer," Jim suggested. He had a deep mellow voice, when he spoke quietly.

Jenny shook her head, getting out his truck. "You have another run back to the show grounds. I couldn't keep you."

He glanced at his watch, and frowned. "I'll be back later then." Without waiting for her response, he drove off.

There was a tension in her chest. It threatened to eat away at the glow that came from shutting down after a long and profitable day.

He is going to keep after me. This is just like Ben and Rae. Am I going to be doomed to have people hate me?

She looked down at the row of trailers. All along the left side, they were brightly lit. Tourists were all on the other side, and dark for the night.

The carnies were, for the most part, friendly to her, a sucker in their group. Oh, there were two or three of the male contingent that had been quick to start flirting, but Jim was certainly the most insistent, and also the most influential of them. There were so many ways in which he could sabotage her little free-enterprise operation, if she overtly offended him. Everything from the order of trucking to where her stand was allowed to set up was under his control.

Not that he had said one thing about it. But was that because he was too much a gentleman to threaten her, or was it that he honestly didn't expect any rejection?

But it was Helen that occupied her mind. Maybe she had just been naturally friendly that first day, but perhaps she was perceptive enough to know that 'her' Jim was likely to zero in on the new girl, and she had positioned herself to be there to clearly stake her claim.

She was walking the edge here. Should Helen react like Rae had done, her time at Western was likely short-lived. She already had enemies here. It wouldn't take much to convince the female population that she was a seducer and too disruptive to be permitted to stay. Especially, if someone as popular as Helen was doing the convincing.

Her fingers crept to the controls on her belt.

No! I am tired of being alone.

I've been running too much. It only gets worse each time. This is a good place. I will have to find a way to stay.

43

Jim's truck rumbled up next to her trailer, and stopped with a pinging noise of metal cooling down.

He knocked. "I'm here little one. It took me longer than I thought."

Jenny said, "Come on in, the door isn't locked."

Jim opened the door with his face beaming. Then, like a rock it fell.

Helen cooed, "Oh, Jim dear. You found me. How nice."

Jenny thought she could detect the edge of gritted teeth in Helen's words, but it was slight.

Helen continued, as Jim just stood there, his mouth open. "Tinkerbell and I were treating this stray cat. It has a cut on its leg. Be a good boy and go get my first aid kit, will you."

He nodded and walked away.

The two girls looked at each other and held their giggles until he was out of earshot.

"I could have sworn his chin was scraping the ground."

Helen was laughing so hard, there were tears. At least Jenny thought that was the reason.

"Are you even sure he is worth it?" she asked.

Helen sighed, "Oh, he's a good man, as long I'm around to remind him of it. His problem is that he's been on the prowl so long it's just second nature to him."

The cat scratched at her arm.

"No, I wasn't talking about you."

Helen thought she recognized the cat, but she hadn't thought anything about it. Strays were common in the campgrounds, and it didn't occur to her that it was the same cat she had been seeing in various towns.

"Do you see any way he could get in or out of here?"

Helen shook her head. "Are you sure you latched the door?"

"Well, it won't lock, but it was certainly firmly closed. I'm beginning to think he teleports. I have started calling him 'N-space'."

There was a blank look on Helen's face. Jenny waved it off. "Just a science joke. Like in science fiction. Teleporting though n-space."

"Oh, you mean like Star Trek."

"No, that is a different kind of teleporting ... have you ever read 'Flatlander'?"

Helen paused, "Is that a novel, or a magazine?"

Jenny shook her head, "Forget it. I used to be a techno-geek and it still shows. It's not important anyway."

"So you do computers? I had a boyfriend once who carried a computer around with him *everywhere*."

They talked for another ten minutes before Jim returned with the first aid kit. He offered to help with the cat, but there was barely room for the two of them and he was sent on his way.

They talked almost until dawn. Helen was the daughter of a card dealer at a Las Vegas casino. Growing up exposed to the glitter of the show world, she had always wanted to be a part of it. Her father, however, would have nothing to do with it. She didn't detail how it happened, but her joining Western was a refuge from the family dispute that happened when her father pulled strings to keep her out of a casino job.

Jenny couldn't bring herself to open up with all her problems, but she did relate Rae's anger over Bob.

"...which is why I risked bringing you here tonight. I would much rather risk being despised for something I did, than for something I didn't do."

"Your problem," declared Helen, "is that you are terminally cute. Until you get a man of your own—preferably one with big muscles—every male in sight will hit on you."

Jenny sighed, "And I can't encourage anyone. I have this medical thing..."

"I know. It's already all over the camp that you have cancer, or..."

"Oh, it's not that! No cancer, no viruses, nothing contagious. It's not even a disease, really."

"Then what?"

Her face twisted as she struggled to put into words something true, because Helen deserved that, but something that also kept her basic secret.

"It was an accident," she said at last. "A lab accident. There was an explosion, and ... and I..."

"You can't have children?" Helen guessed, her face a study of horror and concern.

Jenny could only nod.

Helen gave her a hug, and Jenny started crying. The simple warmth of a friend and the stress of trying to put into words what had been running around in the back of her mind broke through her defenses.

"You ought to sue!" Helen said as Jenny tried to rebuild her composure with a handkerchief.

"No," she said quickly. "It was my fault, as much as anyone. Besides, there's no one to sue. The only other person involved, Jase, is dead."

"From the accident?"

She nodded, and broke into tears again. The memory of his smile and the simple good times they had shared washed over her. What would he think of her now, a basket case, on the run?

Helen probed, with the long experience of a campground gossip, "This Jase, was he a good friend?"

She nodded. "My professor."

"More than that?"

Jenny shrugged, "In my dreams."

"So you are some kind of scientist."

"I used to be."

Helen ran her fingers over the sleeve of her flight suit, feeling the wiring in the layers. "And this ... costume, you are always wearing?"

"I need it. I need it to survive."

Helen shivered. "Scary, scary story."

Jenny dipped her head, and said nothing. N-space chose that moment to wake up, and slipped silently off the bed.

"How much of this can I tell?"

Jenny didn't look up. She hated the past. It was all a long series of trauma and pain. Even the bright moments brought a sharp pain of loss.

"I don't want to be a freak. I like Western. I want to be a part of it. I need a family. Doing this job, and doing it well, and fitting in with all of you. That's what I want. It's what I need."

Helen nodded. "The science stuff aside, your story isn't that different from mine or a half-dozen others here. You'll fit right in.

"An accident. Hmm. Do you have scars?"

"No, not that show."

Helen looked her over thoughtfully. "I can come up with something that leaves out the lab stuff, but do you mind if I tell Jim that you are broken up over a doomed love affair and that he shouldn't take it personally if you don't fall for him?"

"No, that's fine. But can you say that to him?"

Helen grinned, "If I pick the time and place, I can tell him anything."

44

The stay in Colorado City was only three days, and there were some grumbles from one side of the camp. Jenny kept quiet. It didn't matter to her how much they relocated, but was plain Dennis was angry about the situation. A major part of his expenses were the disassembly, trucking, and re-assembly of his wheel. Short stays were hard on his pocket.

The camp had various factions trying to second-guess Forester's bookings. Western was a small operation, and thus excluded from the bigger cities. County fairs and small cities like San Angelo, Big Spring, Victoria and Del Rio were the bread and butter of the operation. Lubbock, Amarillo, or Abilene were places to be dreamed about. Dallas and Houston were unthinkably out of their class.

Forester, in a good year, could find them enough one-week bookings to keep everyone afloat. This wasn't a good year.

She asked, "So what do we do now?"

"Sohelsky's ranch."

The next booking was still several days away, and the Texas Department of Public Safety had made it abundantly clear that an entire carnival could not camp out at the picnic areas and rest areas that dotted the numerous highways. Years back, Western had made a deal with a rancher with more flat land than he could keep sheep on. The fee was more then they liked, but there wasn't much of an option.

It was a quiet time, the first couple of days, as everyone took the opportunity to catch up on some sleep. This was also a good time to do a little repair work and repainting. Jim's truck was scheduled to make daily 90-mile runs into Big Spring for supplies and occasional novelties for the carnies like trips to see a movie.

Not that Jenny could afford to participate. Her cash was still much too lonely to be let out of her pocket. The sleep was nice, but when she woke, wide-awake at two AM, she had already swept her trailer and stall spotlessly clean. She didn't even have a book to read. Restlessly, she walked out into the moonless night and stared up at the brilliant swath of the Milky Way stretched across the night sky.

She breathed in the air, and was pleased that the scent of the roadside flowers and mesquite were stronger than the residual diesel and warm grease.

It had been a week since she had used the flight suit. In spite of her plans, the push to make good as a cotton-candy vendor had left her with little time to ride the Ferris wheel.

I wonder how much I weigh today. She really needed to repair relations with Bill the weight-guesser if she were to keep a proper handle on her problem.

But tonight, the air was still. Should she?

Her fingers found the control switches at her belt, and she held them there for two or three minutes, straining to hear the slightest crunch of gravel under a boot.

The moment came, and her finger flipped switches.

She rocketed up, thrilling at the rush of cool air, and the feeling of limitless freedom.

Ahh! This is my element. She arced her back and reduced her lift, throwing herself into a smooth sweeping curve, caressing the air, made tangible by her speed. It was a perfect sky, and she didn't feel like trying for an altitude record. *Just play here in the sky—swim between the camp lights and the stars.*

She threw herself into an overhead tumble, drifting lower towards the north. There was a small hill a half-mile from camp, which she could see by its silhouette against the dusting of stars. She reached out with fingertips and toes, stalling the tumble and with a little bend of her knees, she stopped almost dead in the air, drifting with the speed of a dandelion seed.

"Wait." It was a whisper, shockingly close, down on the ground below. It was Helen's voice. Jenny's heartbeat tripled in fright. Not even daring to breathe, she drifted on, a dozen feet above the vegetation.

Click. There was a flare of light to her left.

Jim rolled to the side, and Helen tugged at the edge of their blanket. He trailed his fingertips lightly across the sheen of sweat on her belly. Neither of them paid the stars the slightest attention. Adjustment done, Helen clicked off the flashlight, and Jenny closed her eyes. She drifted on, the roar of her blood in her ears not quite canceling out the night sounds of her friends below.

When she felt safe, she launched higher and arced back towards the far side of the camp. Landing with barely a crunch on the crude roadbase, she walked back to her trailer.

It's just the fear. She told herself, to excuse the jitter of her muscles. The vivid image of Jim's body, outlined by the flashlight beam burned in her mind.

She shook her head. *These are my family now. I am not jealous of Helen. I can't let what I can't have mess me up.*

As she reached the door of her trailer, she saw a flash of motion on the ground, and by the time she opened the door and stepped up, N-space was already on her bed.

"All right!" she said firmly to the cat. "I saw you. How did you get in here?"

It took her the better part of an hour of hard work, searching and testing every inch of the trailer, but at last, she found it.

The original floor of the trailer had rotted out ages ago, and a second floor of plywood had been laid down on the original, held in place by only a couple of nails and by its own weight. The fit wasn't perfect, however, and there was a gap of two or three inches back up under the bed, where claw marks showed a path under the new plywood where the old floor was warped.

"So, you are only a cat," she said, hugging the unappreciative beast to her, "and I am only a girl."

She let him escape out of her grasp. A sudden wave of weariness washed over her. Maybe she would be able to sleep the rest of the night, after all.

"Only human, and that's good enough for me."

Issue 8: Queen of Hearts

45

Navasota, in eastern Texas was a long journey from their layover, but the deeper green was a welcome change. Jenny kept quietly in the back of the truck when the caravan stopped for fuel and food near Waco. Austin was only about a hundred miles to the south on the major regional highway. Skipping a meal was an easy exchange for staying out of sight.

Everyone was looking forward to this week. Not only was Navasota a refreshing change from their usual West Texas and New Mexico bookings, but it was also an easy drive from College Station and everyone expected to see a lot of business from the Texas A&M students.

It was a nerve-wracking week for her. There was a very real chance that someone she knew would spot her. Every moment that she was on duty, she tried to be inconspicuous. Even more than usual, she pestered Dennis for time on the Ferris wheel. Unfortunately, the gate was much larger than usual, and the old man reluctantly had to turn her down for much of the weekend. There were too many paying customers.

However, when the lead truck gave its three blasts on the horn to move out for the next booking—back to the dry side of the state—she had not seen anyone familiar. She was too tired to join in another of Helen's card games and spent the trip drifting in and out of nightmares.

Far too quickly, after only three more bookings, they were back at Sohelsky's ranch.

"Can I join you?" asked Bill. Helen and Jim both said "Sure" in unison. They made room at the table.

"How are you today, Tinkerbell?" he asked.

"No sale," she sighed.

"Tell me about it."

She had gotten back in the good graces of the weight guesser a couple of weeks earlier by offering him a twenty dollar bill to use his scales whenever she needed to. Helen's careful management of the rumor mill must have been doing its job, because after a first flip-flop from sullen to sunny, he backed off from cheerful flirtation to a comfortable friendliness, just as Jim had done.

Someday, she thought, her untouchable status might get in the way, but she was grateful for it now.

"Any news?" she asked. She didn't need to elaborate. There was really only one question.

Jim looked up from his burger, still hot and juicy from Betty's grill, and shook his head. "Forester was making calls to Eden, but there is no news yet." From the other tables, a few other heads looked up.

Helen asked, "How big a place is Eden?"

"Not very. Other than the state jail and Venison World, I don't really remember much from the last time we drove through there. Even if they pulled in everyone from the neighboring communities, I doubt there would be much of a gate."

Jenny asked, "So do we wish for a booking there or not?"

Helen said, "My ducks are gathering dust. I would rather have a little business than none."

Jim shook his head, "Dennis is making retirement noises again. If he could find a permanent site, say a kid's park near a major city, he just might pull out. Last time he and Forester went at it, he even threatened to put the wheel up for sale. I would hate to have a bad booking that would drive him away."

"Is it always this bad?"

Jim said, "It is getting worse. We had more rides and acts last year. Forester has less to advertise. It just isn't as profitable for some people to stick with a small show like Western."

Helen sighed, "I wish I had an act."

Bill nodded, "Doesn't everyone."

Jenny was quiet while the others chatted. Something about the way Helen had talked about an act triggered an old memory. She looked again at Helen. She was really very pretty, in a tall blonde sort of way. Dressed in her workday clothes and with not much in the way of makeup, she looked rather drab, and Jenny had started to think of her that way.

When Jim and Bill left, Jenny asked, "Did I ever tell you about my brother?"

"You said he was dead."

"Yes, in a car accident. It was tough on all of us. He was still in high school. But he was an artist. He drew cartoons, good ones. Back at home in a trunk are a huge stack of his work."

Helen listened, a slight smile on her face. Jenny continued, "One thing he did well was to draw superhero comic books. He had a million characters—all the heroes and villains."

"You remind me of one of them."

"Me?" Helen laughed.

"Yes. Do you have a deck of cards?"

It wasn't surprising that she did. Jenny took the deck and located a face card. She then took a napkin and laid it down over the bottom of the card. As she sketched, she talked.

"This one was a villainess. She had some magic trick with cards, and was dressed up like one. I forget the story line." She struggled with the pen. She didn't have Joe's artistic talent at all, but she had developed a decent drafting skill. If she could visualize it, she could make a fair sketch of it. And in this case, Joe had done the creation, and she could copy it.

"'The Queen of Hearts', I think it was." She moved back from the drawing. "Done up seductive, as you can see."

Helen looked over the collage of card and sketch. "This is your brother's design?"

"Oh, yes. I have no design sense, just a good memory."

"He was good then. I'd love to have a costume like that."

"Then why don't you?"

Helen looked at her, "What do you mean?"

"You have said you want an act. Why don't you go for it? I've seen what you can do with cards. I sit through all those card games and you handle them like they were part of you. You even do magic tricks. Let's make up the costume, call you the Queen of Hearts, and you can do a magic act. Forester needs more glitter to book Western in more towns. Don't you think a picture of you in this costume and the name 'Queen of Hearts' wouldn't do a lot to help him out?"

Helen stared intently at the table, and there was a glimmer in her eyes. She looked up. "Do you really think I could do it?"

"No, the question is 'Do you want to do it?' I think you have the talent and the looks for it."

"The costume would be expensive, and I don't really have a magic act. I can just do a few things my father taught me."

"We can make the costume. I learned a lot making this," she said, fingering the collar of her flight suit. "You already know enough tricks to entertain your friends. How much more do you really need to learn to put together an act for random strangers? Dress up professionally, and smile confidently, and they'll buy the act."

Helen looked worried. "I don't know."

From the next table, Lady Victoria spoke up. "Helen, Tinkerbell is right. Go for it. You can do it. I only ask that you stick to playing cards and leave the Tarot for me."

Over at the counter there was a tap-tap-tap from Betty. The three of them looked over at the cook. She pointed her knife at Helen and nodded, and smiled.

Helen laughed, "Well, that settles it then. I'll put together an act."

46

They worked into the night on the design of the costume. Jenny even changed into normal clothes so that she could point to different features on the flight suit when they got deep into the details.

"It's still going to take money, especially if we go with the satin contrast," Helen fretted. "I don't have any money. The ducks haven't exactly been a gold mine."

Jenny frowned, "I have about thirty dollars, and I absolutely have to have about ten of that. Does Jim have any money?"

"I don't know." Helen shook her head. "I don't want to ask him. This is something I need to accomplish without his help."

"Could you get advance money from Forester?"

"It doesn't work that way. Even with a finished costume and a polished act, the most he would do would be to guarantee a place in one of the side tents. Not that I blame him. I've seen a half dozen acts that sounded great, but didn't bring in any customers."

Into the silence, Jenny said, "We need to start with the material we can afford. It's going to take some time to get it done anyway. We'll find a way to scare up the rest of it."

Helen cocked her head to the side. "Tink, would you come into town with me tomorrow?"

"Sure. What do you need?"

"Just moral support."

Sohelsky's ranch had a single telephone connection, and it was explicitly not available for personal calls. Helen, like many of the others, used long distance phone cards purchased at the convenience stores. The best rates had inconvenient restrictions on when and where calls could be made, but when every nickel counted, they were appealing.

Jenny waited outside the booth, trying not to overhear as Helen called her father, but that was hard to do.

It took a couple of minutes to get her father to the phone, and only a couple of sentences before they were shouting at each other. After that, the conversation got too quiet for her to understand.

Jenny could imagine her own father on the other end of the line, and it caused a pang in her chest. What must her parents think, after all this time? Did they think she was dead? What had the police told them?

It had been far too dangerous to make contact. That attempt on her life had been very real. It was a nightmare of crystal clarity, and no amount of wishful thinking would make it go away. Being a fugitive was hard on her, and it was hard on her parents, but there was no help for it.

She stepped away from the phone booth, and walked into the store. There was a rack of picture postcards, with Jackalopes and sexy Indian maidens, and the map of Texas 'The sun has riz, the sun has set, and here we iz in Texas yet.'

No. It would be traced.

Still, the temptation was strong. They didn't deserve the uncertainty.

There was a motion in the phone booth and she hurried back. Helen looked like she had been crying all day.

"Are you okay."

"Yes," whispered Helen. "It was a good call. He won't send me money, not to help me in an act, but I didn't expect that, not really." She smiled, and sniffed. "But he is sending me my books."

"Books?"

"My magic books. He gave me most of them, when I was growing up. If I'm going to do an act, I might as well do it right!"

A little while later, Jim arrived in his truck. His smile dropped when he saw her face. "What's wrong?"

"On nothing. I just called my father."

His face got a little pale. "About what?"

Helen laughed. "Not about you. And no, I'm not pregnant."

He blinked, and when Jenny joined in the laughter, he growled, "You two are getting on my nerves."

Helen took his arm. "Oh foo! I still love you, you big lug."

Jenny took the other one. "Me too." Then added severely, "But like a big brother."

He shook his head and sighed. "I just wish I knew what the big secret was."

Helen smiled, "You'll learn soon enough."

They were twenty miles out from the ranch when the truck's CB radio came out of squelch.

"Morgan, are you there?"

Jim reached for the microphone. "Yes boss, what is it?"

"I just got a call from the county sheriff. H has been arrested."

Jim sighed, "What for?"

"There was a fight at a bar. He wants us to come bail him out." The truck started slowing.

"I'll go check on him."

"Any bail comes out of his salary."

"I'll tell him."

They reached the courthouse by sunset, and Jim, from long experience, identified the sheriff's office by the cars parked around it. He went on in, but came out alone after about twenty minutes.

"What's the problem?" asked Helen.

"They want damages paid before they release him. Supposedly, there was a lot of breakage, and they want $2000. I'll have to find a phone to call Forester. We are out of radio range here."

"That's a lot of money! "

Jim looked grim. "Yes. They got his picture on a surveillance camera, so they are going to stick him with the whole bill."

Helen shook her head. "It's not fair. H is one of ours. We will have to do something."

"I agree, but who has that kind of money."

Jenny found herself incensed as well. H was a quiet man, and rumor had it that even when he was drunk, he was a quiet drunk. She remembered Officer Davis's view of the world, and wondered if H really was the cause of it all, or if he was just the one they had evidence on.

She looked at the jailhouse, a two story building off to the side of the main square. Now that she was looking, it was plain that there were bars on one of the windows.

"Maybe you should go with Jim," she suggested to Helen. "Forester might need some convincing, and you might help."

"You're probably right. Are you coming?"

"No. I'll stick around here."

J enny had her heart pounding in her throat. There was even a little head-ache from the tension.

What am I doing?

She walked over to the jailhouse and waited in the shadows, until she was sure there was no one out.

I couldn't break him out, no matter what. Still, she had to do something. H was part of Western, and right now, that demanded her loyalty.

She reached for her belt, and dialed her weight to nothing. The building was made of rough stone blocks, and her fingers were strong enough to find handholds, and guide her up to the window without the bars.

It was an office area, and in the back were several cells. Only one had an occupant.

The window was unlatched and partially open. *If this isn't an invitation...*

She pushed it open wider, and eased herself in. Only when she dialed her weight back to normal, did she realize H was watching her.

"Hi," she tiptoed over to his cell.

"Umm."

"Do you know me?"

He nodded. "Candy girl."

"Is there anything I can do for you?" She didn't offer to break him out. She didn't have that much nerve, when it came down to it.

He shrugged. "They got me on tape." He gestured over to the television cart in the office area.

"Did you really cause $2000 in damages?"

"Me'n some other guys. It's an accident."

She noticed the bandage across the left side of his face. If he was stuck with the charges and the others went free. It wasn't fair.

"Is there anything I can do for you?" she asked again.

He shook his head. "No. By the way, how'd you climb up here?"

She shook her head, and looked over at the television and VCR. Then she glanced at the open window. She wanted to be able to escape in an instant if she heard someone coming.

She walked over to the set, and made sure the volume was turned down to zero. There was a tape in the machine, and she turned it on.

Someone must have been reviewing the evidence, because it was already cued up to the fight scene. She ran it back and reviewed the evidence herself.

The camera had been positioned directly over the cash register, probably to watch for pilferage, so she didn't see the beginning of the fight.

But, it must have been exciting there for a while, because several items went flying past, and then one of them hit the camera itself, and re-aimed it. There was H, trading slugs with someone else. They moved out of the frame, and then there was another blur of motion, with H crashing up against the counter and knocking over a row of bottles.

She looked back at him, surprised that he wasn't cut up more than he was. After that, the fight wound down, and a man in uniform showed up. She fast-forwarded the tape, but there was nothing more of interest, until the picture broke up and was replaced by another shot of the cash register—the previous day's record.

"We can only keep those who leave evidence."

She listened, hard, but there were no sounds from the floor below.

Time to break the law. She wound the tape back and played with the controls. The tuner wasn't set to any channel, but that suited her. Carefully, she recorded static over the incriminating section of the tape. Then to compound the problem, she ejected the tape, and pressing the little latch on the side, opened up the protective door and exposed the bare tape.

No fingerprints. Carefully, she folded the tape lengthwise, and ran a crease down it with the edge of a pencil. From the first part of H's performance for about twelve feet, she made sure the tape wouldn't behave properly, no matter what was recorded on it. Then, she rewound the slack tape, with the crease intact and put it back in the machine. A tissue polished all the buttons and everywhere she could have touched it.

Tiptoeing back to the window, she whispered, "See you later H." She checked the street below and then let herself out, drifting swiftly down to ground level.

She was back to the truck before Jim and Helen returned.

"No luck," Helen reported. "Forester won't come up with the money."

Jenny was nearly bursting with the excitement of what she had done. The words spilled out.

"Did they show you the tape? I wonder if they really have it. Jim, you should go demand to see the tape."

He looked offended. "They wouldn't lie about it."

"But what if there wasn't a tape? Didn't they say that was their evidence?"

Helen looked at Jim. "Come on. Let's all go together. Maybe they will listen to Tink."

The sheriff was patient with them, and clearly offended that they wanted to see the tape. When Jim pulled out the business card of the lawyer that the show had on retainer and threatened to call him, he just laughed.

"Save your money. Come on up. I'll show you what we have on him."

When they walked up to the second floor. H stood up in his cell. Jenny cautiously put her finger to her lips. He nodded, barely.

The sheriff rewound the tape a little and then launched into his courtroom spiel as he recounted his arrival at the scene of the disturbance. He pressed play, and for a few seconds, they were treated to the view of the cash register, and then abruptly, the image broke up, and from the VCR came the distinctive buzz of a tape being eaten by the machine.

The sheriff shouted down the stairwell, "Donnelley! Get up here on the double!"

There was a brief, intense argument between the sheriff and the deputy, each blaming the other for the destroyed tape.

Jim waited for a pause in the debate before asking, "Then you don't have any evidence on H? Is that true?"

The sheriff did a slow burn, but he spoke levelly, "It appears that the tape has been damaged. That doesn't change the fact that your man was involved in that fight. I put those bandages on him myself."

"But is there any reason we can't pay the bail and take him back to our camp. We need him there."

There was a long silence. Then, "No. No reason."

After that, it was routine. Money changed hands, and paperwork was filled out. H walked out with them.

Jenny dropped back and tugged on his sleeve. He leaned down, and she whispered in his ear. "Never tell anyone." He nodded.

206

48

The magic books caught up with them the following week, while they were in Del Rio. From that moment on, Helen's spare time was spent at the table, pouring over the books and practicing the moves until she complained that her arms were ready to fall off.

Jenny kept working on the "Queen of Hearts" costume, but the money crunch kept the pace slow. Her brain churned with different ways to come up with more money, but in spite of her efforts to rescue H, she couldn't make the jump to more severe illegalities like second-story work. That left only a couple of moneymaking ideas for her to consider.

"We used to have a candy-apple concession," Jim said, when he came by to gripe about Helen's pre-occupation with her magic tricks. "I don't remember what happened to it."

"Was it the caramel, or the hard-red candy coating?" Jenny worked with her needle, regretting once again the loss of her mother's sewing machine. She had gotten out the needle and thread when Jim had arrived, but whatever Helen had told him had stuck. He made no more moves on her.

"The red ones."

She shook her head, "I don't know how to make that kind. Do you suppose Betty has a recipe?"

"Hmm. I'm sure Houston Popcorn sells the mix." He was distracted. "I get so tired of those tricks. They were cute at first, even when she made a mistake, but over and over and over..."

"She is just doing her bit to save Western."

That didn't change his distracted frown. "Somebody," he mumbled, "needs to save it."

She set down her needlework. "Jim, is it that bad?"

He looked up and after a pause, nodded. "Once the fair season is over, I don't expect the show to hold together. We will all be out of work soon enough."

Her heart beat faster and her head throbbed. What would she do without Western?

But she asked, "What will you do, without your job here?"

"That's what's been worrying me. Be a rigger or handler in some other show, maybe. Go look for a job somewhere."

Her mind was a whirl. "Would you take Helen with you?"

Before she could take the comment back, he shook his head. "Not if I can't support her." And before she could say anything else, he got up and left.

A bleak future, for herself, and for her friends, stretched ahead of her. The cloth and needle suddenly became worlds more important. She looked again at the work she had done. It had to be perfect, and she had to find some way to get more money.

A t a truck stop on the road back to the ranch, Jenny dashed into the store and picked up a picture postcard of a fisherman and a catfish the size of a railroad car. She had been thinking about it for days, and so the words and address she lettered on the back came swiftly. For a moment, the postcard to her father shook in her hand, and then resolved, she bought the stamp and dropped it in the mailbox before she could back out.

There! Now it all depends on if he can understand it.

T he next couple of weeks were an agony. The sewing stopped because there was nothing more she could do without more materials. Everyone was becoming annoyed at Helen. The tricks were becoming quite polished, but everyone had seen them too many times.

If it hadn't been for the arrival of Dennis's grand-nephew Rashid, it might have been a very gloomy camp. Jim's prediction for the break up of Western was shared to some extent by most of the old timers.

Rashid was seventeen, and dressed in the gangsta baggy pants, but it was plain that he was just a middle-class kid on a summer adventure. Supposedly, for some years Dennis had promised him that he could come work with him on the road. This was his first opportunity.

Dennis spent most of the time with the boy, teaching him everything he could about the Ferris wheel, and introducing him to everyone in the camp. Almost everyone respected Dennis, and for his sake, Rashid had a more open welcome to the camp than Jenny had seen.

Not that she minded. She already felt an integral part of Western, for as long as it survived, and she suspected that Rashid would never be more than a guest.

"Dis is my good frien' Tinkerbell," Dennis said.

Rashid held out his hand and she shook it solemnly.

"She gets to ride the wheel whenever she wants. Da wheel likes her." Rashid nodded, looking a little abashed by his Great-uncle.

"Tinkerbell? Like Disney?" he asked.

"Yes, like in the Peter Pan book." It was a subtle put-down, and he caught it. But he just grinned. "Zap me with pixie dust," he said, holding his hands out to his side.

She shook her head. "Too dangerous. Besides, you first have to find out what your favorite thing is."

He shrugged, and Dennis led him on to the next introduction.

Finally, she could bear the suspense no more, and she went to visit Cobb. One of the most distinctive vehicles in Western's caravan was Cobb's mechanic shop on wheels. About 40 feet long, it was a nearly complete auto-mechanics facility, with the pneumatic and hydraulic gear necessary to keep all the rolling stock in functioning order. Three times, in the weeks she had been there, the caravan had to stop while Cobb repaired a flat tire, or even once, a blown engine gasket. At the ranch, he regularly had some truck or another winched up on the ramp and partially disassembled.

On the back of the truck was a rack with three motorcycles, the legacy of an act that had faded away long before she had joined.

Cobb frowned when he saw her coming.

She smiled, "You said I could!"

"Yeah, but I don't like it. What if you get stranded?"

She shook her head, "It'll never happen. You said you tuned it yourself. What could possibly happen?"

He just snorted, and turned to unship one of the motorcycles.

Two hundred miles to the south, she pulled into a convenience store next to I-10 in Ozona. Her face was sunburned, and N-space was frantic to get loose from the saddlebag he had been riding in.

It was a mistake to bring him, she thought as he escaped and vanished around a corner. *I should do my business and hit the road instantly. What if I can't find him?*

She stood beside the motorcycle for a couple of minutes, with concern for the cat warring with the fear of what she would find out in the next few minutes.

I can't wait any longer. She went in and killed another few minutes buying a drink and draining it down to the crushed ice. The ride and been long and hot, and her flight suit had made it even hotter. She really needed an abbreviated suit, one for hot weather. But that would have to wait for money, like everything else.

She glanced at the motorcycle waiting for her. *Calm down. There is no way they could track me down.*

Not yet.

She approached the ATM machine cautiously, as if it could reach out and snatch her. She felt the edge of the card in her hand.

It is probably inactive. They think I am dead and shut the account down.

She looked around, but there was no one else who was waiting for the machine. She really had no reason to delay, except for the cat.

No. If I have to run, he would probably never notice I am gone. It's not like we have any relationship.

She swiped the card through the slot, and pressed the buttons. Her PIN number came automatically, a rude reminder that her former life hadn't vanished into the mists, in spite of everything that had happened to her.

$400. That was the maximum her account could handle, although she had never been that solvent. Beep. Beep. Beep-beep.

For three achingly long seconds, she held her breath, and then whir-whir-whir, the bills came spitting out. She grabbed them up gratefully.

Oh, Dad! You did understand!

That postcard had been a crazy, paranoid shot in the dark. It had a couple of innocuous sentences, "Having a nice time, wish you were here", and she had signed it, R. Kimball. The return address was fictitious, but the numbers had spelled out her bank account number.

With the name of the 'Fugitive', and knowing that he was a co-signer on her account, and that he had sent direct deposits to her bank several times in her first year at the university, she hoped he would put it altogether.

"More Transactions?" NO

A receipt spit out of the slot. She looked at the balance. $4617.34.

Five thousand dollars! Oh Dad, thank you!

But now the clock was ticking, she jammed the cash and the card, and especially the receipt into her pouch, and walked, carefully casually, out to the motorcycle.

N-space, where are you? I need to get out of here!

But there was no trace of the animal.

Every second built the tension. If this were a spy movie, a helicopter would already be in the air, and the local police would be talking on the phone right now.

She straddled the machine, and it started right up with a roar that sounded like it would wake the dead.

She looked. No cat.

Okay. It's your life, but you will miss the show.

She pulled out on the street, and it seemed like every eye in Ozona was on her. She wished for that helmet she lost high in the air after the lightning strike.

Don't look guilty. A couple of guys with skateboards paused to look at her. *That's it. I'm just too pretty to resist.* She sneered at herself.

Then, she slowed to a stop.

Up ahead, there was a streak of color. "N-space? What are you doing here?"

The cat paused, and turned his head towards her.

She twisted the throttle, and the engine revved.

There was a moment's indecision, but then he dashed up, and with a one-handed scoop, she tossed him into the saddlebag.

Seconds later, she was pushing the speed limit on the highway out of town.

49

Knock. Knock.
        "Hello?"
    "Helen, it's me. And guess what I've got."
    When the door opened, and Helen's eyes caught the glint of the afternoon sunlight on the shimmering bolt of cloth, Jenny couldn't contain herself. The both of them squealed for joy in chorus. Jim came out to see what the noise was about.

Two days of long hours went into the completion of Helen's Queen of Hearts costume. They previewed the act the night before they were to head out for a booking at Brady's 'World Champion Goat Cook-off'.
    Everyone was there at Betty's.
    Jim gave a hawker's introduction and when the Queen of Hearts stepped out through the curtain, there was a collective *ahh* of appreciation.
    Helen took only a second to get her bearings, and force herself into the regal posture of a life-long performer. Although the tricks were now familiar to all, and the patter of jokes and gestures of misdirection were old-hat to this crowd, she received a number of cheers and claps throughout the act. The applause was loud and sustained at the end, and Jenny beamed as Helen blushed at the outpouring of good will from her friends.
    When Forester stood up, most of the eyes went to him. He looked as sour as ever, but he said, "George, get a picture of her for the gate banner." To Helen, he said, "You're on the bill."
    The cheers were even louder.

The party lasted quite a while afterwards. Helen was thwarted from her attempt to go change out of the costume—all of the women wanted a look at how it was made, and all of the men just liked to have a look at her in it.

Jim stayed at her side the whole time. Jenny was forcibly reminded of her first day with the show, when Helen had hovered around Jim, making her claim. Jim obviously liked the looks of it on her, he had said so often enough, but it was being forced on him just how appealing Helen was to the other men.

"Excuse me, Tinkerbell," asked Lady Veronica, "but I can't tell you how impressed I am with what you have done with Helen's costume. It is quite striking."

"Thank you, but it was really just a design my brother Joe made."

"He is quite talented, but it was your hands that did the work."

Jenny sighed, "Before he died, designs like that came to him effortlessly. I miss him."

"I hadn't heard. I am sorry."

"It's okay. Days like this when people get to appreciate something he's done make it better, somehow."

Lady Veronica glanced across the lot, where her trailer was emblazoned by her picture in her gypsy fortune-teller costume. "I wonder, do you think you could help me improve my image a little, now that I've got Helen to compete with? Something with better materials, but not showing so much leg, of course, not at my age." She laughed.

Jenny smiled, "I would be glad to help, but I think I need to pace what I do, and I already have my next project planned."

"Well, I would appreciate whatever help you could spare."

Lady Veronica was only the first to come up to her with questions about costumes. The polished glamour that Helen showed caught a lot of people by surprise. For the first time, some of them were thinking about the differences between a casual midway carnival like they had always been, and the possibility of a small circus, with named acts, and star performers, and bigger crowds. It touched an ambition that was in all of them.

But Jenny gave the same answer. Her next project was already in the works. And sorry, no, she couldn't tell them what, not yet.

Brady, Texas was a comfortable town, down in a shallow bowl valley. At the center was a tall stone county courthouse, surrounded by the old buildings of a West Texas town. But Brady was a growing town as well, with an outer ring of modern stores and houses. Early in the morning, before the crowds started arriving, she borrowed Cobb's motorcycle and visited a couple of stores. When she returned, her saddlebag was bulging with cloth, and electrical components.

The summer-weight flight suit project was under way.

Helen was running hard, trying to do both of her jobs at once. The Queen of Hearts show was scheduled on the hour, and she was in and out of that costume all day long as she dashed over to keep her squadron of plastic ducks swimming around and around in the tub. Jenny took her lunch break to bring Helen a sausage wrap from Betty's.

"You need to get someone else to run the ducks. You can't keep this up."

"But I don't have anyone else to do it. I asked Rashid, but he took one look at it and turned me down."

"Not macho enough?"

"I guess."

"Still, you need to keep your energies for your act. Western needs you to be a hit. One good newspaper review and Forester could make us another couple of bookings."

Helen nodded. "I know. It's just ... what if I'm not good enough."

"Bah. I've seen the people going into the tent. You are selling tickets."

"But what if it's not enough?"

Jenny took her hand, "You just do your part. Nobody expects you to carry the whole show. Break away from this. Tell Forester to find a sucker if he has to. You have a talent, and you can't waste it. Make the Queen an act people will talk about."

On the last day of the Brady engagement, Jenny went by Betty's, and found her leaning up against her counter, reading a newspaper.

One hazard of cook-off events was that there was a lot of local competition for tastebuds. Betty's food pavilion, and some of the others were not doing well. Sometimes the appeal of barbecue goat was greater than a hamburger.

"Anything on the grill?" she asked.

Betty held up one finger and went back into her kitchen, but instead of food, she brought out another newspaper. She set it down flat on the counter, and circled something with a black marker.

It was the Personals section of the Classified Ads. Betty pushed it towards her.

"Joe's Sister: If you have drifted this far, contact the magician. ID:759388"

The magician? Mandrake?

Betty shoved another newspaper at her, and there she had another one circled, with the same wording except for different contact information. She glanced at the tops of the pages. One was the Brady newspaper, another one was from a town near the ranch, from last week.

Betty looked at her.

Jenny didn't know what to think. Even if it were Mandrake, she didn't want to announce herself. She had made her ATM withdrawals hundreds of miles apart, but even that still pointed to West Texas, and it wasn't a very populated area. She would have to be even more careful in the future.

Her eyes glanced down at the instructions on how to call the newspaper's voicemail system and key in the ID number to get more information. She itched to try it, but it would be much too dangerous.

"No, it's probably not me."

Betty raised one eyebrow. Betty seemed to know everything. Suspicion around camp was that she overheard all the conversations in her place. There were no secrets from the cook.

"There are lots of Joe's, and lots of sisters. But thanks for showing this to me."

She got her burger a couple of minutes later, and went back to her cotton-candy stand. She had a headache for most of the afternoon.

About an hour before closing, she shut down the stand and walked over to the Ferris wheel. Rashid was running it.

"Hello. Where's Dennis?"

He smiled at her, "He was tired and let me run 'da Wheel' by myself this evening."

"Well then, how is it going?"

He grimaced, "It's harder than it looks. Starting and stopping the wheel is one thing, but then you have to keep track of which people have had their turn, it can be a nightmare. I had an argument with one guy who claimed he didn't get enough time.

"Now, I've started a list, so I can tell which order I've loaded them, but Uncle kept it all in his head."

"Good move."

Rashid grinned, "Of course, I noticed that Uncle let couples run longer than the other people, but I can't handle that."

Jenny nodded, "I've suspected Dennis was a romantic. Your great-uncle is just good people."

"Do you want a ride tonight?"

She nodded, "I'd better. It's been a while. Will it mess up your list?"

"Oh no. I'll just leave your car number off, and that way it will never be your turn to unload. Just wave when you are done."

She settled in to the car and rested her cheek against the cool metal side, her hand at her belt control switch. As the wheel turned, she had the routine down so well, she didn't even think about it anymore.

In the air high above the midway, the lights and activity a familiar, comforting carpet below, she thought about where she was and where she needed to be.

I can't let Mandrake know where I am. I can't even tell my parents. The memory of the apartment in flames around her was too vivid. Privacy was dead in today's world. If she told anyone, even if they were trustworthy, the words would betray her. On paper, or in the wires, they were there for any high tech snoop to steal.

I'm a billion-dollar lab rat. Never forget that. People will kill to own me, or own my dead body.

She shivered, and her headache came back again. *Too much stress.* It was so nice to have friends, and it was so easy to forget why she had run away. *Western is my life now. I have to stay focused here.*

The crowd was thinning out below. Helen was probably worn out. She had finally given up on keeping the ducks running. She had taken the advice. The Queen of Hearts was more important to the show than one more game of chance.

I ought to take my own advice. I would make a great act, and draw in lots of customers, if I could just fly around with impunity. But real flying would likely attract too much attention.

She looked again at the midway below. Some of it was part of the traveling caravan, but there were a few permanent structures. Off in the distance, she could see someone lowering the big Texas flag, pulling down the cord looped through the pulley at the top of the flagpole.

Hmm. That's an idea.

"Cobb, can you make me something?"

"What would that be?" He set down his welding gear with a pop as the flame extinguished. He pushed his goggles back, and wiped the sweat off his forehead.

"You know everyone calls me Tinkerbell?"

He put his hand on his chest and said in mock shock, "You mean that's not your real name?"

"Be serious! But what I want is a pair of fairy wings, to go with a costume I am working on."

"Wings, huh? What kind? How realistic? What do you want them made of?"

She frowned in thought. "Not realistic. Just some kind of wire frame. I'll cover them with cloth myself. I had thought of just bending some wire coat hangers into shape, but I knew you could do so much better than that. What do you think?"

"How big? I can make something out of wire stock. Can you pay for materials?"

"Yes, I can pay."

They measured her shoulders, and sketched out a design on an old piece of cardboard.

The rest of the new costume came together easier than the original flight suit. For one thing, there was a lot less of it. She designed this one with arms and legs bare. She even toyed with a two-piece, but not only would it make the wiring a lot harder, but also considering who she wanted to entertain, a more modest white one-piece would be better.

But another factor made it easier—her growing experience. Nothing helped a craftwork skill better than practice.

It was two days into a booking in Victoria, down near the border, when she completed the new flightsuit.

Alone in her trailer, she suited up.

I would kill for a full-length mirror.

She ran her hand over the suit—white lace over white satin. She could barely feel the cabling below, and she was certain it wouldn't show. This design had eliminated almost all of the cable connectors. There was very little redundancy. This time, it wasn't a high-altitude suit. She could afford a little risk. There were two circuits, this time, and that would have to do. The battery pack was thin and disguised in an ornamental, lacy belt.

In white hose, and with the white lacy wings, she hoped she looked like Tinkerbell.

My hair is all wrong. Maybe I can get Helen to help me there.

But there was one thing she had to finish tonight.

Feeling ridiculous, she crept outside. N-space hissed, not liking her new incarnation.

"Be quiet."

There was no one visible, and it was a risk she had to take.

She slid the control on her belt, and she lifted off, drifting quickly up to twenty feet, before she brought herself back down.

It works, and I am a lot more stable than I thought I would be. All that practice flying made a big difference.

She dashed back inside.

Finish the harness, and I will be ready to make my debut.

Issue 9: Tinkerbell's Magic Flight

50

Forester was there, as he was every morning, to make change for the vendors and to handle special requests.

"What is it?"

"I have an act."

He sighed heavily. "You make the third since I added Helen. You have to understand that I won't approve anything that can't help the show. Jim mentioned that you were interested in adding candy apples. I can help you with that. I have catalogs from our suppliers."

She nodded. "I understand your problem, and believe me, if I didn't believe I could attract more people to the gate, I wouldn't be doing this."

"What kind of an act is it?"

"It is acrobatic. I don't really have a good name for it, but I think it would appeal to small children. I have a fairy costume, and I fly around on a wire."

"Equipment. You know we can't afford any equipment right now. All Helen needed was a table and time for her act in the tent."

"I already have the equipment. It will cost you nothing to let me try. If it's good enough, in your opinion, then we might need a pole to hang my rig on, but at least here, they already have a flagpole I can use."

"Safety. There are insurance issues with any kind of acrobatic act. We can't add anything to the policy right now."

"I'll sign a release."

"Even so, if you hurt yourself, we would be down a cotton-candy vendor."

"Ha! How long would it take to find someone else who wants to run off and join the circus?"

"The solid people are hard to find. I don't need another sucker trying to help. I need more people like you."

"You need a good act better."

"I don't know...."

"Let me try it out tomorrow, after Helen's act. If you don't think it's any good, that's the last you'll hear about it from me."

He thought a moment. "I'll need a name."

"Ahh. 'Fairy Flight'? 'Tinkerbell's Fairy Flight'?"

"'Tinkerbell's Magic Flight'."

"Good enough."

"Rigging?" he asked.

"No, I'll take care of everything."

Jenny started to work immediately.

"There's a special kids' show at 2:30 tomorrow", she said to her latest cotton-candy customer. She would tell everyone, and hope that the message spread. By the time she showed up at Betty's, that night, the benches were more crowded than usual.

"You going to give us a preview Tinkerbell?"

"No, George. I'm barely able to psych myself up for tomorrow."

"What kind of an act is going to be?" asked one of the handlers.

H surprised everyone by speaking. "A human fly."

She smiled. "No, not quite, but I do have wings."

"Tell us."

"Oh, just come to the show tomorrow, and you can tell me what kind it is."

A disgruntled voice said, "Soon everybody will have an act. We'll be shooting Rashid out of a cannon before the season is over."

She didn't sleep any that night. For one thing she had to wait until the camp got quiet before she could sneak out in her original flight suit and secure the cable spooler at the top of the flagpole.

For another, she was terrified.

What if someone saw her and reported her to her enemy?

What if she had a circuit failure in the new suit and fell?

What if the wind was too high for her to keep everything under control?

What if she lost control and crashed into some child?

And, what if the act was just plain bad, and people were disappointed in her?

She wore her new white costume under her street clothes while she sold her cotton candy in the morning, fretting all the while that she would get it dirty. Helen came by before her show and touched up her hairstyle, but then she had to run off to get ready for her own performance.

The last few minutes were unbearable, and she flipped the sign over to 'CLOSED' and walked around the long way to the little row of seats that had been set up near the flagpole. It was out in the open. They weren't going to charge entrance this first time, just in case it flopped badly.

She turned a corner, and there was George, hanging a new sign, "Tinkerbell's Magic Flight."

He smiled as she approached, "You'll do great."

She could only nod. There were twenty customers already, standing around. About a dozen members of the show were there as well.

She ducked into the nearby tent, and changed out of the street clothes, and attached her wings.

She touched the controls, and lifted off her feet, then set back down. Everything was ready.

This is really, really stupid.

Outside the tent, she heard Helen.

"Thank you all for coming to see the premier performance of what will be a spectacular act, by a very talented performer. Please join me in welcoming Tinkerbell!"

The applause was spotty, and she could barely move her feet. But they were waiting for her.

S he forced a smile and stepped out into the sunshine. Her wings almost snagged on the tent opening, but she kept going.

All those eyes! It was a physical pressure on her.

But then, one little girl, no more than two, peeked out from behind her mother's skirt, and smiled timidly at her.

She waved back, and the little face vanished again.

There were other children there, and from them, she felt genuinely welcomed.

"Thank you all for being here," she spoke down to the little faces. "My name is Tinkerbell."

She walked up to the pole, and waved a personal wave to several of the little ones in the front row while with her other hand, she found the cord she had hooked to the flagpole cable.

Snap. It fit easily into the hook on the back of her costume, centered between the wings.

"I have come to show you a little bit about how I fly."

With that, she jumped, hitting her belt switch.

H er jump took her out directly over the heads of the audience, and there was a gasp of amazement. She could feel the line start to pull.

The cord and reel were nothing more than a fishing jig that were sold practically everywhere. The spool was spring loaded, and would try to keep the line reeled back in, but the tension was weak enough that she could easily play it out.

With its pull, her climb changed into a wide sweeping arc that took her entirely around the pole. She adjusted her weight, sweeping down low over the crowd, and then climbing up again.

She could feel when the line wrapped around the pole, and kept the reel from doing its work, so she landed with a bounce and flew back around the other way.

The kids were delighted, laughing and clapping. The adults appeared stunned. Of course, that tiny fishing line couldn't hold her weight. Of course, something was very wrong with the slow speed she sailed through the sky. But of course, no one could really fly, so it had to be the line.

Jenny was counting on that reaction. Officer Davis couldn't believe she could fly, even when she told him so. He had rather believed in a cable that he couldn't even see. At least she was giving these people something to see.

She did a mid-air pirouette, then back the other way to untangle the line, finally adjusting her weight so she landed like a feather in front of the children.

"Tink-bell!" called out one little girl, and held out her arms to be picked up. She caught the mother's eye, and with a nod from her, Jenny took the little one into her arms.

"Fly! Fly!" She wiggled her little arms. Jenny, with her weight just barely enough to keep her on the ground against the pull of the reel, gave a little jump with the tips of her toes, and carried the joyous, squealing girl up about a dozen feet, and then drifted gently back down.

The mother looked relieved when Jenny handed the little girl back, but her worried look dissolved when her bundle of energy was in her face with excitement and joy.

"Me! Me!" There were others ready.

The next mother that was brave enough to turn over her child stepped up. At about four, he was a squirmy armful, and once in the air, he twisted from one side to the next, waving down at his parents, and nearly causing her to lose her balance. She would definitely have to put a weight limit on this.

The third was a serious little girl, excited, but with her eyes taking in everything. Up in the air, she craned her neck to look at the line connected to the fairy's back.

Jenny whispered, "I've got a secret to tell you."

"What?" she whispered back.

"I don't really need the string to fly. It's just there so your mommy won't worry."

The little face twisted in deep thought. "Like training wheels."

"That's right. But remember, it's a secret."

She nodded wisely.

On the way down, she spotted Forester in the crowd. He lifted his arm and pointed to his watch.

Is it time already?

She deposited her passenger, and then stepped back. Too many disappointed faces. She started rising slowly, straight up the flagpole.

"That's the show for now. Thank you for coming."

At the peak of the pole, she surreptitiously disconnected the reel and slipped it in her belt pouch. Holding on to the flagpole's cord loosely, she slid down, making a sweeping gesture with her free hand, until she touched down amid the applause.

She escaped her audience through the tent door, and collapsed in a heap on the chair, shaking like a leaf from the reaction.

Helen came in, almost running. "Tink, you were great! How did you do that?"

Jenny managed a smile. "How do you manage to do a performance every hour? I'm a nervous wreck after just one."

"You'll get used to it. But seriously ... it's all science stuff, right?" She looked a little uncertain.

Jenny nodded. "Science. One hundred percent science, with a little misdirection thrown in. It looks magical doesn't it."

"Yes! If I didn't know better..."

There was a voice at the door. "Are you decent in there?"

Jim entered, smiling. "Helen, you're on in two minutes."

She left, and Jenny asked, "How did it look?"

He just shook his head. "I've never seen anything like it. How do you move so slowly? I've seen other aerial acts, and this is very different."

"It's a secret, for now. Do you think Forester will approve it?"

He laughed, "He is out there right now, fending off a mob of parents with disappointed kids. Did you notice that the crowd more than tripled in size during your act? If he didn't let you go on again, he would get lynched." Forester came in a few seconds later.

"If I had known," he began gruffly, "that you were going to carry little kids up in the air, I would never have let you start this! Do you know how quickly a lawsuit would kill this show?"

She felt her heart sink like a stone.

"So, it's a no-go?"

He waved his hand. "No, I didn't say that. You have to go on again. But you've got Western between a rock and a hard place."

51

She didn't get back to the cotton-candy stand until after sunset. Forester, for all his gloom, was electric the way he swept through the camp. By the time they were done, a tent was moved closer to the flagpole, photos which Jenny had not noticed George taking were reviewed and approved, and a legal release form was drafted for parents to sign before Jenny could fly their kids.

Jenny had sweated over the photos, arguing hard to eliminate those that showed her face.

The costume looks good though. It was strange to see herself like that. *Not as sexy as the Queen of Hearts, but I do look cute. Tinkerbell is supposed to look cute.*

And she had three more performances, before they picked up and moved again. Part of the time spent was arguments among Forester, Jim Morgan, and several others that came and went over whether to charge a separate ticket for her show.

It was George, surprisingly, who came up with the compromise. Free admission to watch, mainly because it would be too hard to close off the area, with a special charge for making a photo of Tinkerbell and the child being carried.

Forester, who hated to leave a fee uncollected, reluctantly agreed. The front gate was most important. George, of course, was rubbing his hands with glee. He owned the camera and equipment.

When everything was settled, Jenny attempted to concentrate on her cotton candy stand, and try to figure out how to keep her fishing reel out of sight, even from the Western people. An imagined high-tech winch was one thing, a simple stamped metal fishing reel was another.

After closing, Betty's was filled with people asking questions, those that saw the performance, and those who didn't.

"I told you she was a scientist," maintained Helen.

"But that line is too thin to hold her weight."

Bill laughed, "She's lighter than she looks."

When she came back to the table with her food, all eyes were on her.

"Fess up," said Jim. "Tell us the secret."

She looked at the half-dozen at her table, and the others within easy earshot, and shook her head. "I can't say."

"It's Kevlar, isn't it," came one guess.

She put down her fork. They were going to keep it up all night, she was certain.

"Okay. I'll tell you a little, but please understand, this is a real secret. You have to keep it in-house."

There were nods, but she didn't believe a one of them.

"There was something invented in the lab where I worked. It is something new, something no one has heard of. Before we could proceed, my ... friend was killed, and the process was lost. The local cop suspected me, and that is one reason I left town. But even though there wasn't anything to report to the authorities, there was one sample left. I'm using it.

"But you have to understand, no one, not even the government, knows about this stuff. If I make too big of a splash here, they will come and take it away. I'm only doing this to help Western out of the hole, but it's a risk. If too many people know about this, the news will get out, and the act will be gone. I'll be gone. There won't be a flashy kid's show to pull in more gate.

"So, I'm just Tinkerbell hanging on a wire, just like Mary Martin doing Peter Pan on stage, it's nothing special. It's better that way. Understand."

There were some serious faces around her, as well as a couple of smirks from people too wise to buy such a story, but the conversation did shift away from the secret to more practical matters. The other performers were quick with advice on how to read a crowd, and there was speculation on whether Forester could wrangle a newspaper article out of it to use when trolling for new business.

The talk threatened to drag on into the morning hours, but Jenny complained of her headache and crept away to get some seriously needed sleep. She had an act to do tomorrow.

The next show was easier, although she still had problems keeping to her time limit. The kids were so eager to fly, and once the first mother allowed her pride and joy into the air, the others seemed willing. Jenny had to institute an age limit, only those two through four.

By the time she had finished her scheduled performances in Victoria, she had her act down pat. Acrobatics in the beginning to wow the crowd, and then pick out the cutest and best-behaved young ones in the special front row seats. That is where the ones with signed releases sat. Two more times, Jenny whispered a special secret to a child who looked at the world with honest questions and awe. It was her favorite moment of the act, and it was for one special person at a time.

She had the reel problem solved as well. Shortly before the act, she walked up to the flagpole in street clothes and ran the reel up to the top using the regular cords, leaving her hook secured down at waist level. At the finale, she retrieved the reel and came down the pole like she did the first time. It seemed to work.

After Victoria, they moved to Ballenger, where they set up next to an old railroad depot that had been converted into the courthouse.

Ballenger had a big cross on the hillside. When they rolled into town, and she spotted it for the first time, it reminded her of the church family she had grown up with.

Western Extravaganza Shows was like that. They weren't her real family, not in any genetic sense, but these quirky people had quickly come to mean more to her than almost anyone else in the world.

Helen is my sister, and Jim is my brother, and I love them dearly.

Somehow Betty found the newspaper article first. She posted the spread next to the food counter. When Jenny came in for late lunch, and a headache pill, a cluster of grinning faces were there to greet her.

"Okay, what is it this time?"

"You're famous. You'll be leaving us for Ringling Brothers any day now."

She shook her head. "Be serious. What is it?"

They showed it to her. The Victoria local paper had a full page spread on Western, and more than half the article was pictures, including her in the air, and a restrained glamour shot of Helen.

"Forester will love this." She looked up at Betty, "Can I get a copy of this? I can start a scrap book." They all laughed.

Her life became hectic in a hurry. Forester moved her up to three and then four performances per day. The cotton-candy stand was empty most of the time. After hours, she began work on costumes. Lady Veronica went with her on a morning run to the fabric store, in nearby Abilene, and they chose the iridescent blue-toned cloth she liked. The actual work took the better part of a week, partly because she was running tired.

I can't slack off, she thought, as the clock crept towards five in the morning. *If they think I have gotten a big head over this, they could all turn against me.*

When Lady Veronica took possession of her new costume, she was so pleased, she hired George to re-do the decorations on her trailer to match.

She had three more costume orders. It seemed the thing to do.

Helen came by shortly after she opened up the stand.

"What are you doing here?"

Jenny smiled through her morning headache. Her breakfast was starting to include a few little round pills from Betty's behind-the-counter aspirin stash. She was not getting nearly enough sleep.

"It's my job."

"I seem to recall you telling me to give up my ducks, don't I? Your reasons were good, but you don't seem ready to take your own advice. Don't get me wrong, but you are becoming a major attraction for the show, more than I am. If I had to concentrate on my act, for the good of everybody, then so do you."

"Oh, it's not that bad. You have an hourly show, and the costume changes alone made it necessary for you to give it up."

Helen crossed her arms. "Face it, Tink. You are running behind too. Go talk to Forester and have him take the stand back. He is paying you enough for the act, isn't he?"

She shrugged. They had discussed it the first day, but since they weren't charging a separate ticket for her performance, he had started paying her a flat fee per appearance. It wasn't much, but she didn't really have an idea what her act was worth. "I'm getting more than I had before, and Lady Veronica insisted in paying me for my work on her costume. I'm not hurting."

"That man!" Helen screwed up her face. "I'll see you later."

She stalked off.

J enny went back to the business of pre-packaging cotton candy.

I really don't have a head for business, do I? She smiled. Just a few dollars above abject poverty and she was already forgetting to count her change. With that bank balance she could still tap with her ATM card, and with just a few dollars more coming in to her pocket than going out, she could almost feel content.

But I should build up some cash. As soon as I get ahead of things, I should really put some thought into solving the dark matter problem. I'm not always going to have a Ferris wheel handy.

In a instant, a flash of images swirled through her head—the life that she was missing; with her family, with the work that she had chosen, with some man she could live out her life with, with children of her own—all the things she could not have until she solved her problem.

But I can't think about that now. I've got to finish up here and get ready for the show.

CC T inkerbell, wait up!"

Forester was almost running to catch up with her, as she headed to her trailer to change into her costume.

"Yes?"

"We need to talk about your act," he wheezed, catching a breath, "and how much you need to be making, so that you will be happy here."

"Well, I need to get ready for my act right now."

"Okay, yes. Fine. But we will talk after, okay?"

She looked puzzled, until she saw Helen, watching. *What did she say to him?*

"Okay, I'll come by your office sometime this afternoon."

He seemed content with that, and hurried off.

Jenny waved for Helen.

"Tell me."

Helen looked wide-eyed and innocent. "I just said that Jim had gotten a phone call from the Shriners about you."

"Really?"

"Well ... Jim had been making calls, looking for a possible job in case Western folded, but I sort of fibbed about them calling about you."

"Jim is leaving?"

"Not now," Helen beamed. "You and me, we've saved the show. That's what Jim says.

"Now you," she continued, "you have to make Forester cough up the cash. You saved his job, and he knows it."

Jenny laughed, "How about being my agent? I'm not sneaky enough."

52

"I know who you are," said the loud little boy in her arms, as they floated high above his parent's heads.

She whispered, "And who am I?"

He lowered his voice. "You're an angel! My friend 'Landa says, and she says her Momma tol' her."

"An angel? Are you sure I'm not a fairy?" She leaned to the side, and began the slow descent.

"Yep. An angel in disguise!" He was confident. Jenny landed, and handed him back to his mother. There was a flash as George took another picture.

"One more," she said to the parents on the front row. She held out her hand to a timid little dark-eyed girl, and her mother handed her over. Perhaps she was just overly sensitive, but it appeared the lady made a little curtsy bob as she took the girl. *What was that all about?*

This one was too shy to talk, and Jenny did her best to make her feel safe, not going as high as she did with some of the others. *I am favoring the girls. Somebody is going to call me on it sometime.*

She handed the girl back, coaxing a smile from her with one of her own. Then, she stood back, and did her pole-sliding climax.

As she touched down, and gave her closing remark about coming back, she saw a half-dozen of the mothers, mainly Hispanics, give that same sort of half-curtsy. It was no more than a bob of their head, but it was puzzling.

T heir next booking was Tucumcari, New Mexico and Jenny relished the long sleep on the trip.

Her first show gave a hint of the hot day to come, as the morning cool evaporated quickly.

The crowd was large for a morning show, and it soon became clear why—these kids had been prepared. A serious little four-year-old boy told her. The poster advertising Tinkerbell's Magic Flight had arrived last week. And did she know Wendy?

The first thing she did after the show was track down Jim.

"Can you get me a copy of the original Peter Pan book, in a hurry?"

He was in the middle of helping Cobb with something to do with the trucks, so he begged off. She nodded, understandingly.

I need to get that book, she fretted. *That was embarrassing.*

If two out of three little kids had questions the real Tinkerbell should know, she suspected there would be many more. It was lowering to realize she had picked up the whole of her Tinkerbell knowledge from Disney movies and Robin Williams. Maybe she should borrow a motorcycle and go looking for a bookstore herself. The next act was still two hours away.

"I'll go get it."

She looked up. H was standing a few feet away.

"Oh, would you? I am afraid of disappointing the kids. Do you know what I want? The real book, not the picture books."

He nodded. "I used to have a copy."

"Okay. Let me get you some money." She patted the sides of the white lace. "No pockets in this thing."

He held up his hand. "I've been paid. And I owe you."

It went against the grain to have him buy it for her. She suspected she already had more money than he did. But it came to her that he needed to do this favor for her. It was important to his self-respect.

She smiled. "Thank you. It's embarrassing to have little kids ask you questions you can't answer."

"Been there." He turned and headed towards the gate.

S he looked for H before the next show, but he wasn't around. Given his reputation, she hoped that the resources of the town hadn't distracted him.

The kids were easier to please this time. Her Disney version answers were fine with them. All except the littlest one, a little girl whose Spanish was just a little too fast and too mumbled for her to understand.

The audience had a high percentage of Hispanics, but although she looked for it, she saw none of the odd bowing she had seen before. So much for the theory that was some cultural thing she just hadn't seen before.

H arrived, almost running, sweaty in the heat, carrying a hardback book. "I'm sorry I'm late."

She took the book, a nicely bound copy of Barrie's classic.

"This is an expensive book. I didn't mean for you to spend that much! You have to let me pay you."

He pulled his hands back. "No. I had the money. They knew you were coming, and the lady at the store said they were almost sold out. A day care center had a special reading."

She looked at the smile on his face, and from the wrinkles, it looked as if it wasn't an expression he was used to.

"Thank you," she said, holding the book to her chest. He nodded, understanding that she really meant it.

The next day, H arrived at her cotton-candy stand, as she struggled to make as many sales as she could before her next show.

"Hello, H. Do you want a cotton-candy?"

He looked at the fluffy confections in the rack, as if he had never seen them before.

"No. I was just wondering, do you do costumes for men?"

She asked, and quickly found out that what he really wanted was a simple polo shirt, with the Western Extravaganza Shows emblem embroidered on it.

"I want to look like I belong here. I'm tired of being a bum."

The past couple of weeks flashed through her memory, and she suddenly realized he had been in camp almost the whole time. What had happened to his pattern of vanishing with his pay at every new town they visited?

She flipped the sign over to CLOSED, and said, "Come with me."

Forester listened carefully as she outlined her proposals. He nodded, and then turned to H.

"We can order some shirts. We used to have some like that. That was a good idea, H.

"But about the stand, I don't know. Can you handle something like that, dealing with people?"

"I think so. I don't know how to make the candy, though."

"I can teach you that," she said. "The rest is just being friendly with people and making change."

Forester considered it for a moment. "H, can you handle me double checking your money down to the penny, every day? You know why I have to do that."

He didn't bat an eye. "You would be stupid to do anything else. But I haven't had a drop in three weeks." He held out his hand and examined it for shakes.

"Then I'll give you a chance. Tink will get you started. She has an act in less than an hour, so go get out of here."

She read all night, and put down the book at last, thinking about Wendy, and Jane, and Margaret. She smiled in spite of a headache that was worse than normal.

Of course, I've gotten everything wrong. Tinker Bell's costume was made of leaves, too, like Peter's. And I should glow, especially during evening performances.

And how about her voice. How can I possibly sound like that?

At least, the children don't mind the mistakes.

She fell asleep quickly, not waking up until an hour before her show. Hurriedly, she rushed over to Betty's and downed some orange juice and a double-dose of aspirin.

During her show, when a little girl with dimples asked, "Can I have a thimble?" Jenny knew the night was well spent, and gave her a quick kiss on the cheek.

H seemed to handle the cotton-candy stand well enough. She watched from the sidelines as he took the orders, and made the candy. She noticed that he had to remind himself to smile, but other than that she had no worries.

"Betty. H has taken over the stand, and he will need some help with the supplies. I've told him what to do, but I know I made lots of mistakes, so take it easy on him."

She nodded, then pointed to Jenny's head.

"Oh, it's okay. I think I've just had a mild infection or something. Once I get up and about, it goes away."

Betty shook her head, and took down her order.

On the way back, a boy spotted her, and ran over.

"Hi! You're Tinkerbell, aren't you."

She smiled. He was a little taller than she was, but he was only nine or ten. "Yes. Did you see the show?"

"Oh, yes! And I wonder, can you take someone flying, that's not a little kid. I would do *anything* to go flying around like that. I mean, you really fly! Can you take me, please?"

"I am sorry," and she could see the eager expression on his face sag. "There really is a simple weight limit. You understand about the cable?"

He nodded. "But how about if I wore the harness? Would that work?"

She felt so bad. She had seen other, older children in the audience looking up at her, and tugging on their parent's sleeves.

"It doesn't seem fair, does it. But you have to understand that the rules are made by science, not people. Maybe, in a few years, someone will invent a better system—one that will let big people fly. But until then, you're just too big a man to fly."

"It isn't fair."

"I know, but remember," she touched him on the cheek, "there's only one boy who hasn't grown up."

He looked puzzled.

"Peter Pan," she explained with a smile.

He smiled briefly, and nodded.

By the time she had gone twenty feet, her eyes were filled with tears, and she was overcome with a wave of old hurt.

And Joe.

53

D ennis wandered into Betty's with a big grin on his face.
     "If yous plannin a week off at da ranch, ferget it. Da Boss booked us!"

There were a number of questions, and to Jenny, it was clear that he was most pleased at the location, Fredericksburg. That news just caused her to settle back on the hard wooden bench, and rub the back of her neck.

Neck aches, too. As if the headaches weren't bad enough. Is it the dark matter?

She had been regular in her Ferris wheel time, in spite of everything. She kept her weight stable, and with the flying time she was putting in on the act, it had been easy. But it could be some other side effect, an attack on her immune system, or something. It certainly felt like she was running mildly sick all the time.

And now this. Fredericksburg!

Not that she had anything against the town, she liked it.

That was the problem, the Old German town in the Hill Country was very popular with Austin residents. The great stone mountain near there, named Enchanted Rock, was a favorite with all the college students. Whether hang-gliding, or rock climbing, or just a hike to the top, all of her group were there regularly. The city itself was a charming place, with German restaurants and lots of places to shop.

Dennis was looking forward to another place.

"I'm gonna visit da Admiral Nimitz museum. Been plannin on it."

Someone asked, and he started talking about his time in the navy during da War. Jenny would have loved to stay and listen to him talk, but she had to get some sleep. They would be moving out first thing in the morning and she had to be ready.

When she stood, the world seemed to spin. She reached out and grabbed the edge of the table. For an instant, she though she was falling, but gratefully, she managed to stay upright. Almost everyone was focused on Dennis, and missed her involuntary acrobatics.

Betty was out from behind the counter, and heading towards her, but Jenny shook her head and waved her off. She forced a smile, and as steadily as she could manage, she left.

As he had for the past few weeks, H was on hand to load the trailers, and once again he loaded hers last, so that they would be the first to be unloaded. Only this time, the candy stand was his responsibility.

The headache was unbelievable. It was all she could do to just wave and smile when someone tried to talk to her. She felt like she was coming down with the flu. She kept her blanket with her, against the chills, and crawled into the truck cab, and went back to sleep.

The windmills on the top of the ridge overlooking Big Spring, Texas, giant three-bladed electrical power generators, drew her attention. *We must be here.*

The rest of the carnies were a whirlwind of activity around her, but she could barely keep track of where she was going and what she needed to do next.

The Ferris wheel was going together quickly in the large shopping center parking lot. The other stands and tents were appearing like magic, at least to her pain-befuddled brain.

I need to get ready. She looked around, and it was several minutes before she recognized her own trailer. N-space was sitting in the doorway when she opened it up, and the problem of how to get around him was deep and insoluable. She just stood there, holding the doorknob, until the cat got bored and wandered off.

Twice, she woke up, only partially dressed in her costume. *I can't let the kids down.* Finally, well after the portable fence was up and the ticket office open, she stepped out, and absently patted the belt pouch to confirm that she hadn't lost the spring-loaded reel.

At least she could walk. It felt like she should stumble and fall, but she didn't. She located the pole the handlers had erected, for those places like this one which didn't have a flagpole handy. She set that as her goal and made step-by-step progress.

No breakfast today, but I could use those pills.

She walked past a line of people on the other side of the fence, waiting to get in.

"Jenny!"

She heard the voice, but it was several steps later before she turned around to check.

It took a moment for the sea of faces to resolve.

And there was Mandrake. Shawn Breaker was beside him. They waved.

Hallucinations now. I've got the flu.

Pixie Dust

She took another couple of steps, then stopped.
Can't hold the kids with the flu. Can't ...
The world twisted, and spun, and went gray and featureless.

Issue 10: Clap for Tinkerbell

54

*G*et away from her. Jenny! Can you hear me? .... What's wrong with her? *Sleepwalking ....*

There was pressure on her shoulder. Jenny struggled to make sense of what was going on. Panic called to her, but its voice was faint and echoed as if deep in a well.

Get her away from the crowd....No, she's my friend! I won't let you take her away! She needs a doctor. Manny, help me. Look at this. What's happening? What's happening! WHAT'S HAPPENING!

*L*ook lady! See this? A doctor can't fix this, but I think I can! If you let me, *I can save her. She is going to die a painful, gruevesome death, today! Let me save her!*

Pixie Dust

*D*a Wheel likes her.... hours'n hours....

*M*y neck hurts. She was spinning through the air, out of control. She was flying out of the city, and her hands couldn't reach down to her controls. The windmills were spinning furiously, and she was heading towards them. She couldn't stop, and they cut her into pieces. Her head flew away into the sky.

*H*oney, just let me take care of it. You're sick, and it happens to the best of us. I'll get you cleaned up. Don't worry about it.

*I*t was dark, and cold, and she couldn't move. There were noises, familiar but muffled. Something was wrong with her head.

Suddenly, she slammed down on her head. Up was down, and she was being burried, upside down, smashed head first into something hard, partially cushioned.

Am I dead? Are they shoving me into the grave?

She had trouble breathing, and then she gasped in a gulp of air, fighting the pressure.

Then as abruptly as it started, the pressure went away. *I'm weightless,* she felt, even as the pressure of the seat below her belied the thought.

A few breaths later, it happened again, and she could only whimper as her head twisted of its own volition, aggravating the pain in her neck.

She tried to blink—to make the sight come, but there was nothing. *I'm blind, and paralyzed!*

The whimper grew into a feeble wail.

"Jenny!" The muffled voice was familiar, but she couldn't place it. The pressure vanished.

"Hello? Help me!"

"Jenny! You are okay. This is Shawn Breaker. Do you remember me?" She felt a touch, a hand on her shoulder. *Shawn? Was this another dream?*

"I'm blind! I can't see! I can't move."

"It's okay, Jenny! You are restrained. Relax. Your head is wrapped up in a bucket."

"What?" She couldn't understand. Her whole body ached, but especially her head and neck. She tried to move her arm. It didn't move, but she could feel the bindings.

"Untie me!" She gasped for air, breathing her own stale breath. "Get this off of me!"

The hands on her arms squeezed tighter. "It's okay Jenny! You are tied down for your safety. I am treating a buildup of dark matter in your head."

She stopped, her head full of puzzlement. How did he know? What was going on?

"Jenny, I have to turn the magnetism back on now. We are on the Ferris wheel. Do you understand?"

She didn't really, but the muffled noises were indeed the metallic creaks of the wheel in motion. But she tried to nod. Whatever was wrapped around her head didn't let that happen.

"Okay," she managed, weakly.

The pressure came again, and exhausted, the outside world went away.

"Huhh!" she gasped, when the pressure hit.

"Jenny?" it was Mandrake's voice, full of concern. "Jenny, are you awake again?"

"Manny?"

"Yes, Tink. It's me. Can you understand me?"

"The pressure. It hurts."

There was a gentle pat of his hand on hers. "It will be off in another few seconds." And it was.

"What's going on?"

"We are treating you. Do you remember what happened?"

She struggled to make sense of it all, and before she could put it all together, he said, "Time to flip the switch. Brace yourself."

The pressure hit, but warned, she was able to keep her neck straight, and it didn't hurt nearly as much. A few seconds later, it let up.

"We are on the Ferris wheel?"

"Right, and you've got your head in a bucket with wires wrapped around it. I'm running the switch. Shawn was doing it the first few hours."

"Shawn? I think I remember him, a little while ago. What went wrong? And how did you find me? How did Shawn find me?"

"Take it easy. I don't know the technical stuff. You'll have to ask him. But Shawn and I have been looking for you ever since your apartment complex burned down. I went to your place when I heard about the fire. He was wondering around the ashes too, and I recognized him from your description. We were both worried to death about you, so we teamed up. I hit the road and he hit the Internet."

"I can't move my arms."

"I know, little one. We had to take precautions. You were just a limp body, trying to fly away on us. We've got you trussed up seven ways from Sunday. I can't even unhook half the stuff, so please be patient."

"How much longer?"

"I dunno. Wait a second."

While she struggled with the cycle of pressure from the magnetism, she heard him switch on a radio.

"Shawn, are you listening?"

"I'm here," came the muffled little voice.

"Our patient is awake and talking, and just a little impatient with her restraints. She wants to know how much longer?"

"Good news! Give me the readings."

"About twenty-nine pounds, last turn."

"Roger. Give me a second."

Jenny asked. "What readings?"

Mandrake said, "We've got a fish scale on your bucket, where it is chained to the safety bar. When I...."

His explanation was interrupted. "Tell her another few hours. Jenny? Can you hear?"

Mandrake said. "She can hear you."

Jenny was going to ask some more questions, but a wave of weariness came over her, and she drifted off again.

"Jenny? It's about time for the changing of the guard. Can you hear me."

"Manny? Sorry. I didn't hear."

"Shawn is going to take over again. Dennis is stopping the wheel."

"Okay. What time is it?"

"Oh, it's morning. Seven-thirty. Your friend has been running the wheel all night for us."

There was the sensation of rocking as the wheel stopped.

"Dennis?" she called.

"'Lo miss. Are you doin okay?"

"I'm a lot better Dennis. The wheel is helping. Thank you."

"Glad ta help. Da Wheel an you always been friends."

"Shawn? What happened?" She understood part of what was going on, but in the dark and constantly having her world turned upside down was disorienting at the best of times.

"You had a dark matter build up in your skull. The pressure nearly killed you."

"I don't understand. I monitored my weight constantly. That shouldn't have happened."

He rapped the metal car. "This is the problem. You were using the Ferris wheel instead of free flight. Mandrake told me the rudiments of how you burned pixie dust when you flew. I can see how the Ferris wheel would do the same thing. It would have worked fine, except that your costume has your head bare."

"But I checked that. The field lines go through my head."

"In free flight they do. In air, the field lines make a nice fat torus, and the magnetism passed through the coils around your neck and keeps going for a bit before turning around and curving back to your feet. But the steel is ferromagnetic!"

"Oh!" She saw it at once.

"Right. The field lines in the steel car are drawn immediately from your neck to the metal, and all of them return via a much shorter path. Your head was getting no treatment at all. "

"And because I was weighing my total body, I didn't see the problem."

"Your white costume, because of the wider neckline, made it even worse. When you flew in it, you didn't get the full effect."

She would have nodded, if she could. In retrospect, it was so obvious. *How could I have been so stupid!*

"How did you figure out what the problem was?"

He laughed. "With Manny's briefing, it was pretty obvious. Your head had already gone negative. When you first saw us, you must have fainted, but you didn't fall down! By the time we got to you, you were totally limp, but your head was like a helium balloon, holding up most of your body. Even when we dragged you off to a motel room to get you out of sight, you wouldn't stay down in the bed, popping up like a jack-in-the-box.

"It was pretty obvious what the problem was, and when your friend Dennis came by to see how you were doing, and we realized you were using the wheel for hours on end, the rest became clear."

If it was so obvious, then why didn't I see it? He was irritatingly cheerful.

"Can you free my hands?" she said in frustration. "I can't talk without waving my hands."

He laughed again, and after a few tugs, she felt the restraints come free.

The first thing she did was put her hands up to feel her head. It was indeed encased in a bucket, one that appeared chained down to the safety bar of the Ferris wheel car.

"Your head is in a motorcycle helmet, with fifty turns of lamp cord wound around that. That whole assembly is stuffed into a plastic bucket, lined with towels for extra cushioning."

As he recited, she confirmed it all with her hands.

"I have some questions," he asked.

She sighed, "Yes, go ahead."

"I matched the battery polarity and the turns direction to the design of your costume. Is there a difference when you reverse the magnetic field? I didn't dare experiment."

"Not that I could detect. The effect appears related to the scalar, not the vector."

"Must be some higher order effect."

"Right." Jenny felt suddenly comfortable with the man. At least they spoke the same language, and understood the same jargon.

"Where do you work?" she asked. Could he have been at the university all along, and she had just never matched schedules?

"Taylor Devices. It's a hole-in-the-wall equipment manufacturer. One of a kind gadgets for local companies, usually. I've built industrial control stuff, custom radios, even toy robots for one customer with more money than sense."

"And one wire-wrapped bucket for my head. While I appreciate it, I would like to request a window in the next version."

"Ha, you're lucky I put air-holes in it. It was pretty intense around here when we weren't sure when your head would explode."

"Well, your design obviously worked. My mind is starting to work again. I haven't felt this clear in days."

"Cross your fingers that there was no permanent damage."

She was struck by how close to death she had come, and the conversation stalled. It was scary how it had snuck up on her. Somehow, she had always expected to see death coming, with time to get prepared.

I really need to contact my parents. It isn't fair to leave them hanging like this. At least tell them I am alive and well.

Oh God, how lost I am! She shifted in her seat, and felt the presence beside her. It was bitter, and paradoxically comforting, to know that she hadn't been able save herself. *I have friends.*

Thank you God, for them.

55

The regular cycle of pressure, the rhythm of the wheel, had gotten so predictable, than when it stopped, she was instantly awake.

"Shawn?"

"Umm. Oh, sorry!" He hit the switch. "I must've dozed off."

"No problem. How long have you been awake?"

"Let me see.... Looks like about 38 hours. I was already at work when Mandrake's call came, and then there was that hell-ride on Highway 87. Let me tell you that there is nothing that can keep you awake like riding high in an truck tractor at racing speeds through the Hill Country!"

"I thought Manny gave you a break on the wheel. Didn't you get some sleep then?"

"Well...I was examining the control box on your blue costume. It looked pretty charred."

"Yes. Didn't Manny tell you about that?" She recounted the lighting strike, and its aftermath.

"And you did that to get me off the hook with the police? Thank you. I knew Davis was aggravated about something when he let me go, but I didn't know why. All I knew was that they asked me a new round of questions, and then waved me goodbye."

He was slurring his words a bit, and Jenny knew that he was struggling to stay awake.

"Can't we stop the wheel for now?" she asked. "I need to get out of this bucket, and I am really parched." *And other things.*

He gave in after a little more argument, and waved for Dennis to unload them. She had to wait patiently while he unhooked the chains and wires that were connected to the bucket.

"Oh." The light of day was bright after staring at the inside of a bucket for hours. It took her a bit before her eyes regained the ability to focus.

The show was set up on a wide parking lot, and from the litter it was obvious that the first day had been a success, even without her act. They unloaded, and it was a tossup which of them were most unsteady. Dennis shook visibly, as he opened the door on their car, and gave her a kindly smile. Shawn moved slowly, and he was blinking his eyes, to try to keep them clear.

But Jenny, to her further embarrassment, couldn't make her legs work properly. Whether it was her upset balance and the stiffness from being so long restrained, or whether it was something more serious, she just could not keep herself standing.

Shawn tried to hold her arm for a couple of try's, and then gave up and picked her up and carried her.

"Wait, I just need to get my balance back." She twisted, trying to get free.

"It's no problem. I don't know if anyone has mentioned it to you, but you really don't weight very much." He started down the midway, and when she admitted to herself that she was too tired to fight, and maybe she really didn't mind having him hold her, she let herself relax against his arm.

"My trailer is over there."

He stopped. "Yes, I know, but Manny has taken a big room over at the Comfort Inn. That's where we took you after your collapse. It's your call, but your costumes and clothes are all moved over there, and it has a real bathroom."

She was miffed a little that her trailer had been raided, but it was that last that turned the tide. Her trailer was seriously lacking in the amenities.

The news that she was out of danger brought a flood of visitors. Helen met them before they got to the room, and the sight of the Queen of Hearts running down the sidewalk after a man carrying a woman and a bucket was enough to turn a few heads.

Helen sent Shawn off to Mandrake's truck with strict instructions to get some sleep, and then she locked the door and helped her get bathed and dressed in some clean dry clothes.

Helen was in charge, sending word back to cancel all her morning performances. Jenny tried to sleep, but soon gave it up as a lost cause. She was wobbly, but she shook off Helen's attempts to help. She had to see if she could walk.

"I think it's okay," she said as she settled down in a chair. "I may just need something to eat and drink." Mandrake, who arrived next, was sent off to acquire that.

Forester was clearly worried. "When will you be well? I've got a lot of angry parents knocking on my door. Tinkerbell's Magic Flight was a big part of the advertising."

Jenny had been thinking about that as well, from several angles. She said, "Just as soon as I can walk back to the pole under my own power. It's an acrobatic show, after all, and you don't want me do drop one of the kids."

He had to be satisfied with that. Helen made a few choice comments after he had left.

"Don't worry about it, Helen. If he weren't a hard old ... person, then Western would have folded long ago."

"Oh, I know. But one day, I would like to see him act like a human being."

George showed up a bit later, and then Cobb arrived about the same time as Lady Veronica.

Betty showed up with her breakfast, and indicated that Mandrake was minding the store for her.

All her guests were plainly pleased to see her recovering so fast, and just as plainly were puzzled as to what caused her collapse in the first place.

"Well..." she started, unsure of what people had seen.

Helen interrupted. "People, we have to keep a lid on this. Tinkerbell's doctor said that there was no chance at all that anyone else could be affected by her contamination, but if word gets out, the locals would close down the show in an instant. We have to keep this a family secret. Understand?"

After that round of visitors left, Jenny asked, "Helen, what do you know?"

Helen plopped down on the bed next to her. "Enough that my mind gets all scrunched up every time I think about it."

She looked Jenny in the eye. "You can fly, for real? That wire thing is all hokum?"

Jenny nodded. "For real; when I am in my costume and with fresh batteries. The wire just makes it easier for people to believe it's all a trick. If people really believed I could fly, then the government agents would come and I would vanish."

When Helen said, "Like in the spy movies."

"Right. Just like in the movies. So, the real question is—how many people know the truth? Am I going to have to run again?"

56

"What did he do to them!" Jenny felt a wave of dizziness, as she looked at her costumes spread out on the table. The white belt that went with the original blue flight suit was in a dozen pieces, with alligator clips and voltmeters and disconnected wires in a disorganized tangle. Her new white costume was a little better—fewer pieces because it was a simpler design.

Helen looked at the source of her upset. "Well, he seemed to know what he was doing. He would say 'Ah!' and 'Ah-ha!' every now and then."

Jenny picked up the edge of her white costume. "I'll never get this back together in time."

"In time for what?"

"My act! You heard Forester. I have to get back to work as soon as I can."

"But you're not well!"

Jenny sat down, and picked up the tangle of wires that was her new costume's controls. "Oh, it's not like I'm contagious. With some food in me, and a little time to get my balance back, I should be able to do it."

"Don't let Forester bully you into hurrying back."

Jenny shook her head. "It's not for him. It's for Western, and for those kids. Now let me be for a bit, while I try to figure this out."

When Mandrake showed up, she sent him to get Shawn. When Shawn arrived, she confronted him, holding a set of wires from her white costume.

"What is this?" she demanded, holding the new connector he had added to her circuit.

He blinked, still a little fuzzy from not enough sleep. "I was going to add…"

"Don't," she glared, "change my flight suits! My life depends on these things, and I can't afford to have surprises." A freefall with a burned out controller, with her re-wiring it as she dropped, was vivid in her memory.

He looked puzzled. After a moment, he said, "Okay. I am sorry. You were unconscious and…"

She waved her hand, cutting him off. "So what have you changed? How do I remove this?"

"It shouldn't be necessary. It's paralleled off the B-circuit. With nothing connected, there's no change from your original. Snip it off and tape the ends if it offends you."

It certainly did, but instead she turned to the blue suit's control box, or the pieces of it. "This is a disaster!"

He nodded. "I was rebuilding it. The switch contacts were carbonizing. Back EMF. I was going to replace the switches with make-before-break to a damper and with wetted contacts. I didn't have time to finish."

Jenny could feel her face getting hot. She was furious with the man, and it didn't help one bit that what he said made sense. It was her flight suit, no one else's!

Helen cleared her throat. "Tinkerbell? If you are doing okay here. I need to get back to the show. I have a performance in a few minutes."

Jenny waved, "Go!" But then, "Helen, I'm sorry. Thank you for taking care of me."

Helen nodded, and with a quick glance at Shawn, left.

He said, "I can put them back together. Nothing is damaged."

She was ready to tell him to keep his hands off her things, when there was a quick knock on the door, and Mandrake stuck his head in.

"Hi. You're up. Good. I've got a surprise for you."

He opened the door up wider, and ushered in her parents.

H er mother was across the room and they were in each other's arms. "Jen! I was so worried about you. Are you okay? He said you were sick. We got here as soon as we could."

Jenny was literally speechless as she absorbed the new turn of events. She just held tight, and soaked up her mother's love.

Her father was within reach and she touched his hand. He gripped back, and it was that moment when the tears started welling up, and she had to fight to keep her composure.

"How did you find me?"

Her father looked over at Mandrake. "He called us on the phone."

Mandrake looked a little sheepish, "Tink, when you were out of your head, you were calling for Momma and Daddy. Shawn did something on his laptop and came up with their phone numbers."

For an instant, she fought the impulse to blast away at him, the same way she had been berating Shawn. *No. That's not right.*

Instead, she nodded, "Thank you Manny."

She looked into the eyes of her parents. "I've been hiding, and I'm sorry I didn't try harder to get a message to you. I didn't feel like I could contact anyone."

"Jen," her father asked, "what is this all about?" He glanced a cautious eye at Mandrake. She recognized that look. It was the same one he had given Jase, back when she announced that she was going to stay on after graduation and study with him.

"I'll tell you everything, but it's a long story. Let me introduce you." She gestured Mandrake closer.

"This is my Uncle Manny. He has saved my life a couple of times now, isn't it? This is my father, Kenneth Quinn."

"I just helped."

Her father took his hand, "Uncle?"

Mandrake beamed, and exclaimed, "My long lost brother!" and took him in a bear hug.

Her mother laughed.

"And this is my mother, Amanda."

He took her offered hand, and with a twinkle in his eye, said, "Mandrake Samuelson. You have a very special daughter."

Shawn was introduced too, but he for the most part, didn't look up from his work on the table.

"Tell us," her mother said, "what this is all about."

"If I can." Her mind was churning. It wasn't a story that entirely made sense to her. How to explain it to her parents?

"Jenny, this one is done." Shawn held up the control belt for her white suit.

Okay.

She turned to Mandrake. "Go collect Helen when her show is over. Have her bring everyone who knows or suspects the whole secret here as soon as possible."

To her parents, she said, "I haven't told anyone the whole story, so I might as well do it all at once." She took the control belt and picked up the white costume. "You won't have to wait long."

J im and Helen, Cobb and Lady Veronica came in, making the room a bit crowded. Amanda Quinn blinked when the Queen of Hearts entered.

Jim said, "You wanted everyone, but Dennis is really exhausted, and no one can find H."

Jenny asked, "H is missing?"

He sighed, "Yes, and the cash from the stand."

"Oh." Her heart sank.

But everyone was settling in, filling the chairs and sitting on the beds. It was a mix of expressions, from the concerned puzzlement of her parents, to the self-assured Mandrake, who thought he knew all of it already, to the distracted Shawn who hadn't stopped working.

Where to start?

Her hand dropped to her belt.

"Something strange and unique has happened to me. There was an accident, when my professor and I tried to control something on the very edge of known physics. We failed. He is dead, and I..." she floated off the floor and hovered in mid-air, before eyes gone wide, "... and I have been contaminated with what Manny calls 'pixie dust'."

She told them everything. Even Shawn looked up from his work when she tried to put into everyday English the unknown mysteries of zero-point energy, and he nodded when she described Officer Davis.

Manny added a few words when she told about being hit by lightning.

But everyone was silent and attentive when she described the night of the fire.

"And you don't know who is after you?" asked her father.

She shook her head. "No, and believe me I have thought about everyone. Even Manny and Shawn were on my suspect list. I didn't know that many people, and I didn't think anyone hated me that much. But someone did.

"So I took my scraps of salvage...", she reached into her backpack and set them down on the edge of the table, "... and flew away into the night. After a time, I discovered Western, and the way I could keep the dark matter under control without exposing my secret."

Shawn reached over and picked up a torn scrap of yellow paper. She asked, "Yours?"

He nodded. "So you never read it?"

"Just these fragments. I puzzled for days trying to figure out who would address me as 'Ginny' with a 'G'."

"It was just a warning about Davis. Before they turned me loose, they tried to trick me into admitting I knew you. I didn't know your name, of course, so I didn't react to it. But when I was released, I did a search on the name. I found a 'Genevieve Quinn' in the university records. That gave me your address, and I tried to hide the note without being obvious to the police."

She sighed, "I wish I had known. So much of my paranoia about sinister government agents came from what I couldn't read from that yellow note."

She addressed the rest of them, "So you see, I had to hide. Someone tried to kill me—someone may still be trying to kill me, and the police are worse than useless.

"And the more people who know that I can fly—that there is a real anti-gravity—the more surely it will be that some government or some business will try to corner the market. And that makes me either dead, or a lab rat.

"I have to ask every one of you to keep this secret tight. My life is in your hands."

57

There were questions—a lot of questions.
Finally, as Jim got up to leave, she told him, "Tell Forester that I will be doing the next performance."

"Are you up to it?"

"I think so. And it is something I have to show my parents."

About an hour later, Jenny in her costume, and the quartet of her parents, Manny and Shawn started their walk over to the midway grounds. Jenny was pleased at her returning strength, and just a little self-conscious about walking the streets in her Tinkerbell outfit.

A car drove by, and there was a shout, and two little kids started clapping. That was just the first incident.

As they entered the gate, there were several children, and one mother in the ticket line who clapped. As they approached the pole, and Jenny stepped forward to install the reel, the clapping spread through the audience who had come to see her fly.

"Thank you, all of you."

She knew.

With one glance at her parents, she jumped into the sky.

After that performance, she realized that she was not back at full strength. *But all I need is some rest.*

She was only able to take one little one up into the air. It was a little more difficult to hold her and work the controls at the same time, so she finished the performance a little early.

The girl told her, "The lady said you were sick, and we had to clap to make you well. So I did."

"What lady?"

"The TV lady."

Jenny gave her a little squeeze. "Thank you, you saved me."

A little questioning of the crowd told the tale. A reporter on channel 9 had reported her falling sick, and had asked all the little children to clap to save Tinkerbell.

Jenny was touched. Everywhere she walked, she could hear little hands clapping—kind-hearted strangers wishing her well. She couldn't bring herself to retire back to the room. It seemed like there were hundreds of little children wanting to come and talk to her, and she in turn thanked them, every one, for the help that they had given her.

Forester caught up with her and beckoned her into the tent. Her quartet came in with her. Forester grimaced, but made no move to exclude them.

"Bad news. The insurance company has denied the request to include your act under the blanket coverage."

She sat down on the metal folding chair. "What does that mean?"

"Unless we can get your act covered, we will have to shut it down."

"But why?"

"No safety harness for the kids. That's what he wrote on the report."

Her father asked, "Can you appeal?"

Forester nodded, "I have to. Otherwise we have to shut down the act immediately."

"Can you rig a harness, Tink?" asked Mandrake.

She shook her head. *They would never approve a harness without an inspection. And that would include an inspection of the reel and line. A strong man could snap that in an instant. And there goes the illusion.*

"No. It would destroy the act."

"Well," said Forester, "think of something. We will only be able to keep operating for another couple of weeks before the final order comes through."

A fter Forester left, she headed back to the room to get a nap before the final performance.

Mandrake came by a little later.

"Shawn and I are going back to Austin. We'll catch up with you later, but we need to go back and rescue his car from where he left it beside the road."

She looked out the door, but he was not there. "Okay, I'm glad you showed up when you did, or I wouldn't have survived. I owe you my life, again."

Mandrake just grinned, "There's not enough magic in the world without you. I'm just glad to be able to help. But this time, it was Shawn who was the hero."

She nodded, "I know." It didn't help her annoyance at him, however.

Mandrake handed her a small radio. "Keep this with you. It is small enough to fit in your belt. It's only good for five miles, but Shawn and I both have radios set to the same channel. I'd feel better if you had it handy."

"Thank you." It was small. And there had been many times since the fire when she had wished mightily for some way to call him.

"One more thing, before you go?"

"Yes, Tink?"

"Who called you, and told you where I was?"

He frowned, and pursed his lips. "Hmm. Do you trust me?"

She reached around his middle, as far as she could, and hugged him. "Of course, Uncle Manny."

"Then, you'll just have to trust me on this one. I've been sworn to secrecy. I can't reveal who it is. But you don't have anything to worry about. Your secret is safe."

She was a little taken aback, but to be honest, she did trust Manny. "Okay. But tell me when you can. I have so many debts I owe, and this is one of them."

He grinned, "Don't worry. I have my own reasons on this one. By the way, the room is paid for through noon tomorrow, so just leave the keys on the table."

"Jen," said her father, "I'm heading back home. We left without even notifying the company, and I have some loose ends to take care of."

"But I'm staying," said her mother. "Someone has to do the babysitting."

Jenny reached out to her father and he took her into a hug. She was just getting used to the idea of having him here, and now he was going. "Do you have to leave?"

"I will be back." He glanced at his wife, and some message was exchanged.

"We've been planning this," she said. "When you vanished, we realized that nothing was as important as getting you back. We'll both be taking early retirement. If you're on the run, we can run with you."

Her father's hug meant more than anything right then. She sniffed and said, "Don't do anything foolish."

"Like running away to join the circus?" her father asked, with a smile. "No, nothing like that."

She took her mother to see the Queen of Hearts do her show, and as much as she was happy to see her mother's expressions of surprise as Helen pulled off each trick, she realized that the act had matured since she had seen it last. Helen was much better at it.

"Helen," she said afterwards, "my mother and I have the motel room for another night. Would you like to come spend the night there with us?"

The final performance of Tinkerbell's Magic Flight was almost up to her regular standards. She even managed to take three little ones for personal flights.

Almost as she touched down from the finale, a blond lady in a blazer stepped up, microphone in hand.

"Margaret Lakey, News West TV, channel 9." It was the lady who had asked the children to clap for her, and in spite of the *No! No!* running through Jenny's mind, she agreed to give a little interview and tape a thank you message to the Big Spring area children.

"Peter Pan has been my favorite book for years," the reporter confided.

Jenny smiled, "Was your mother's name Jane?"

The question caught her off guard, and amazingly, the professional talker blushed, and nodded. "But I'm still waiting for spring cleaning time."

Forester watched the whole process with a huge smile on his face. The shine of camera lights was the glitter of gold.

Issue 11: Costume Hero

58

The motel room was luxury accommodations, especially after her trailer. Jenny relaxed in the plush chair. Back to the lumpy mattress and cat hair tomorrow.

Helen changed out of her costume and sat down on the bed next to her mother.

"Back to normal. You looked a little shocked, when we first met, Mrs. Quinn."

"Call me Amanda. And no, those were your work clothes, I understand that. Believe me, after twenty years wearing a white lab smock every day, I was jealous.

"No, if anything, I was just surprised. You see, I thought I recognized you."

"Maybe you did," said Jenny.

"What?"

"Do you remember one of Joe's comic books? The one where the superhero with the long hair that shoots loops of energy fought the gang that was taking over the city?"

Her mother nodded, slowly. "Yes! And the bank teller..."

"... changed into the Queen of Hearts..." added Jenny.

"... and she caused all the ATM machines to spit out cash with her picture on it..."

"... until the superhero—Samson, that was his name—captured the Master Trump."

Her mother nodded, "And then ... oops." She put her fingers to her mouth. She said to Helen, "Well, let's just say that it was one of Joe's R-rated comics, and leave it at that."

Jenny smiled, glad that her mother liked Joe's stuff, too. They hadn't really talked much about it after his death. She had always wondered how her parents reacted to some of the racier bits of artwork her brother produced.

"And you made her costume, Jen?"

She nodded, "It took awhile. I have learned a lot about sewing since this happened."

"Well, show me your work! I'm glad you finally got interested."

In the morning, they checked out and moved all Jenny's stuff over to the trailer. Her mother, who had no luggage other than a large woven totesack and a change of clothes she had grabbed on the way out of the house when they had gotten the call from Mandrake, moved in with her. There was barely space for the two of them in the bed, but N-space had taken one look at the newcomer and escaped. Maybe he subscribed to the two's company, three's a crowd theory.

Jenny enjoyed the morning show, especially since she felt back to full strength. Her mother was there in the crowd, beaming.

When they went for lunch, Jenny introduced her to Betty, and several of the other regulars. It was just like when she had introduced her parents to all her friends at school.

The little boy was reaching up for her, with both arms held out, little fingers reaching. Jenny picked him up, and shifted him to her hip.

She had barely lifted off, when her eye noticed the mother, her head bowed. *What is this?*

She finished the performance, with more attention to the crowd than usual. After her final move, she was sure there were a half dozen of them. All Hispanic. All bowing to her.

I've got to get to the bottom of this. It isn't normal.

Mandrake showed up by noon. She half expected Shawn to be with him, but he was alone.

"You don't need to baby-sit me, you know."

"Oh, you can't deny me a vacation, now. I like the people here. I'll keep out of your hair."

"I'm not trying to run you off—it's just that I worry about causing you to lose your job. My parents are talking about early retirement, and now you, playing hooky!"

He shook his head, "Little Miss Independence, still! It's not your decision. It's mine. It's your parents'. Think it through, which is more rewarding, deep in your heart, to go to work day after day, or to help someone in trouble?

"Most people, parents especially, slave all their lives for their children, in that unrewarding daily grind. Is it any wonder they would leap at the chance for the special hardship, the grand gesture, the soul-satisfying leap of faith it takes to drop the predictable and *be there* for their loved one?

"No! Let people help you. Be there for them, when the time comes, but don't fill your head with debts that they don't require. It's all about love. They love you. You love them. Let it happen."

Lady Veronica said, "Could you come with me?" The way she said it hinted at something private.

Jenny called to her mother, sitting at the table chatting with the Snake man, "I'll be back in a few minutes."

She waved back.

They quickly walked over to Lady Veronica's trailer. Jenny was curious what was up, but the instant she climbed the steps and entered, it was obvious.

H was collapsed in a lounge chair, with a knitted cover draped over him. The air reeked of something pungent and alcoholic.

"He stumbled back here this morning, and Forester promptly fired him." She sighed. "Something about stealing the money from the candy stand."

"What happened?" Jenny asked, aching at the sight of him.

"You did."

Jenny looked up sharply.

She continued, nodding. "When you fell sick, he was frantic. He was at your side, and in the way, when those two men arrived to help you. Jim had to haul him away bodily when he was interfering with their work."

"Oh, H!" At the sound of her voice, he stirred in the chair.

Lady Veronica continued, "You were the one who stood up for him, when he was arrested, and he didn't know what to do when you were dying. So he took the cash and drank it up."

"But I didn't stop him from drinking. He did that on his own. He cleaned himself up, on his own."

The old performer gestured for her to sit down at the table. It was close quarters, but the living room was homey and comfortable.

"But he needed someone to believe in him. You were that someone. He has been mumbling, and when I can catch a phrase, it is about how you will think about him, now that he is drunk."

Jenny didn't know what to think. She had never had to deal with this before. "What do I do?"

Lady Veronica just shook her head.

Jenny reached over and felt his head. It was clammy, as if he were sweating the alcohol out.

"H? Can you hear me?"

An eye blinked open. He turned his head away. "Go 'way."

"H. Look at me." But he turned further.

Jenny was suddenly struck by his resemblance to her father. It wasn't in how he looked, or in the alcohol. If anything her father became even more strait-laced after Joe's death.

But her father had turned his face away and buried himself in silence at his loss. Even now, he hadn't come totally back.

"H. I am glad you are still here. I know you stopped drinking before, and I know you can do it again. And when you do, I will be there to argue for you. We ordered your shirt, you know. I'll make sure Forester listens, once you get yourself back together."

If he listened, he gave no sign. After a little while, Jenny and Lady Veronica went outside.

"What will he do?"

"Oh, I'll give him a place to stay, until he sobers up. After that ... who can say."

"That's good of you."

Lady Veronica dimpled. "Oh, not that good. I liked the way he cleaned up last time. If he plays his cards right, he could probably stay longer."

J enny went back to find her mother, and spotted Mandrake in Betty's, chatting away with the cook.

"Manny, you might talk to Forester. I suspect he's down a trucker."

He frowned. "Hmm. When would he need help? I have to get back to Waco in three days."

"Western is here tomorrow, to complete the weekend, and then Monday is moving day. The next booking is Fredericksburg."

"It might work. I'll track him down in a little bit," he looked back at Betty, "but right now I'm busy." She smiled.

59

S unday usually slacked off after the Saturday peak, but not this time. When Jenny walked to the pole for her first performance, it was like a sea of faces. And this time, the little bow was like a ripple through the crowd.

Whatever it is, is spreading.

She tried to put it out of her mind, and to do her performance with the lighthearted flair it deserved. When she landed at the front row, there were far more children than usual. While there were the usual cries of "Me! Me!", it felt like the mothers were more intent to push their children to the front of the pack.

It was intense, and intimidating. For the first time, she took a fourth, and then a fifth child up for a personal flight, even though it threw her way over her scheduled time. At least up close, the children were as full of wonder as ever.

H er mother's cell phone rang mid-afternoon. She picked it up and Jenny could tell it was her father. After she told her husband about what a wonderful time she was having, and how great all the show people were, she went quiet, and then handed over the phone.

"Jen?"

"Yes, Dad?"

"I think things have changed. You did a television interview recently?"

"Yes."

"Well, the local station sent it up to the network. I've seen it here in Amarillo on national news. It's just a human-interest piece, but they included a clip of you flying and even I can tell that something is wrong with the physics. Anyone with any science training can tell that there is more there than that little cable.

"You were worried about the government and big business before, and I thought it was nonsense when you first said it, but now I'm not so sure."

"Oh, Dad. I've blown it for sure, haven't I?"

"Maybe. Maybe not. But now we have to take some precautionary measures.

"Jen, I want you to hire me as your lawyer."

"What?"

"Hire me. In writing. Can you get to a fax machine?"

"Yes, Forester has one in his office, and he has a telephone line installed. But what's this all about."

Her father paused and his voice seemed to reach out and hold her. "Jen. You are my daughter, and there is nothing I wouldn't do for you, to protect you. But when it comes right down to it, you're an adult, and a father doesn't have any rights when you are of age. If you were hauled off to an army base somewhere, I would just be a noisy private citizen. But as your lawyer—" his voice took on an edge of steel "—as your lawyer, I can bring the whole legal system to your defense.

"If we do it right. And if we do it now. Can you get to the fax machine?"

His warning sobered her, but there was also warmth deep in her heart. Her father had not spoken with that kind of passion in years. She would do anything her Daddy said!

The document was simple, but it had the signatures. In addition, she wrote out the answers to some questions he had—mainly a time line of the original vacuum decay project, and who would be able to make a legal claim on the dark matter that it produced.

She sent it off, and then confirmed its arrival over the phone.

"Don't worry Jen. You could never have kept this secret anyway. At least we have time to make preparations."

If anything, the mid-afternoon show was even more packed that the one before. Jenny peeked out a fold in the tent door, looking over the people.

This isn't an audience. They aren't here to be amused and amazed. Look at the faces. They are too serious, too intense.

She almost didn't want to go out there.

She turned to George. "Could you do me a favor?"

He looked up from his camera. "Yes?"

"Could you be my spy? Listen out there. Something is going on with those people, and they aren't talking to me about it."

He nodded. "Looks like that to me too. Sure. I'll keep an ear out."

She took a deep breath, and walked out before the people.

She did another five-kid show, and people were pleading with her to take more of their precious children up when she ended the performance. The finale was more of a retreat against an onslaught. Jim and Cobb were there to bar the way when she retreated into the tent.

Their faces were firm and forbidding as they turned away a mother insistent that she hold her little girl.

Jenny knew her own face was pale.

I can't do this! Something has happened.

She changed into her normal clothes, and escaped to her trailer.

George arrived a little later.

"And?" she asked.

He was about to burst out laughing. "You won't believe it."

"Tell me."

He sat down on the steps. N-space appeared from nowhere and crawled into his lap. "Oh, there you are Brutus."

She refused to be distracted. "What won't I believe?"

He stroked the cat. "I listened, but most of what was going on was too fast for my Spanish. But, then, when the show was over, I saw two men in the back in a serious discussion.

"One was a priest, by the collar. Another was in a black suit and looked all the world like a preacher."

He looked up at her to see her reaction. "They were arguing whether you were an angel or a demon."

"What!"

"'Struth! In all seriousness too. The priest thought you were an angel, pretending to be a circus performer. The preacher was sure you were magic too, but since you didn't use the name of Jesus, you must be a demon."

Jenny felt herself collapse. Luckily the only place to collapse was on the bed. *I knew it.*

It was the cemetery caretaker. I'm sure of it. He called me an angel.

She was in a daze. She thanked George, and didn't even comment when N-space...Brutus, walked off with him.

For ten minutes, she just sat there, her mind churning. *It's not fair! I never claimed to be an angel! I wouldn't!*

The caretaker had told his family, maybe when the balloon incident hit the news, and then maybe someone had spotted her in the sky, and before long the stories connected. The story had spread among the Hispanic community in Austin and surrounding areas, and then, somehow, someone saw her act. *Never mind the cable, plain as day, attached to my back!*

And now, there was national publicity to compound the problem.

This would be great, if I wanted to start my own religion. She was angry, and bitter. She was just glad her mother wasn't here right now.

But what do I do? It would get out of hand. It had already gotten out of hand. Maybe it was just time to cut and run. She glanced at her bag.

There was cash in there. A lot more cash that she had the first time she had escaped. She still had her flight suit. Cleaned up and improved a little, she had to admit, by Shawn's attentions to it.

She closed the door to her trailer, and unloaded the bag, looking over her growing collection of possessions. Even in a nomadic life, it was surprising how quickly things multiplied.

She pawed through the pile, and paused over the scraps of paper from her previous life.

There were her scientific notes, which she had given precious little attention to.

And there were the scraps of yellow paper. A warning from Shawn that she had never been able to read.

And there was the page from her own Bible. Oh, how long ago it was that she paid attention to that.

She picked up the partial page, firm black ink on that thin paper that she always associated with Bibles.

It was the Jupiter and Mercury story, where Paul and Barnabas were hailed as gods after performing miracles. She read the words and a chill shook her as she stood. Her heart pounded.

She set the page down, and stared with unseeing eyes at the wall. *I know. I know what I have to do.*

She changed her clothes. Her wardrobe was sparse, and nothing was very fancy. But still, she had to make the effort.

The sink provided water to wash her face and comb her hair. What little she had in the way of a mirror told her that she looked simple, and plain, but clean.

She wrote out a little note and walked over to Forester's office and left it on his desk. *I won't be doing the evening show.*

60

It was a random walk. No other kind would do.

The show was set up on Fourth Street, a one-way artery that came from downtown to join the highway. Third Street went the other way.

She headed crossways, looking for a residential area, turning to the right and the left as the impulse hit her.

The church was crowded. Not only was it approaching the time of the evening service, but also there were nearly a dozen campers in its parking lot. The sign declared its affiliation, and below it was the single word. 'Bienvenidos', the common word of welcome to a bilingual church.

This is the one.

People recognized her as she approached, even dressed normally. Whether it was the look on her face, or just religious awe, no one spoke to her.

She walked into the foyer and picked up a flier from the pamphlet rack. Trying to be oblivious to the eyes watching her every move, she found a seat at the end of a pew towards the back and started to write.

The service began on time, and she was grateful that several of the songs were ones that she had known all her life. She sang as well as she could, dismayed that she couldn't seem to make her voice work right.

The service was bilingual, with a preacher and a translator that must have been doing it a long time, because it was smooth and not at all distracting. The sermon was on angels. For one disconcerting moment, the preacher locked eyes with her, and stalled in his presentation.

Go on. She willed him to continue. He suddenly shook off the paralysis and picked up the thread.

Jenny focused all her attention forward, even as her skin could feel the eyes on her.

After then sermon, came the invitation song.

Her heart pounded as the congregation rose and opened their songbooks.

She had to close her eyes, and take the first step purely on faith. She had to. Faith was all the strength she had left.

The walk down the isle to the first row was lost in suffocation. Now, every eye in the place was on her. The song faltered, but never died.

The preacher took her hand, and seated her.

In a clear whisper, he asked what she wanted.

"If I may," she held her written piece of paper, "I need to confess my sin."

He hesitated, but nodded. She had no will to read his face or to worry about what he thought about her. She needed every bit of it for what was to come.

The song ended, and the preacher stood.

"We have a petitioner who needs to unburden her heart. Please listen with the spirit to what she has to say." He nodded to her.

She was dizzy as she stood, and turned to the sea of faces. Not to perform, not this time. There was awe, on some, tears in the faces of others, puzzlement in many.

A motion caught her eye. A little hand waved to her. *From this morning—Mandy*. Her mother's face was unreadable.

There was no sound, not even a cough. They were all waiting on her.

She pulled up her paper. She had to read the words.

"My name is Genevieve Bell Quinn. I was born and was raised in Amarillo, Texas. I am like you." Her eyes came up to make contact with theirs. "I was raised by loving parents, and taken every Sunday to a church much like this one. I attended Sunday school, I read my Bible and I gave my life to Jesus.

"I have no excuse for the sin that I have done."

There was a whisper in the crowd. She couldn't listen. She had to continue.

"I am a performer, entertaining children in the Western Extravaganza Shows. I am sure you have seen its Ferris wheel and its lights downtown.

"For some time, I have suspected that something was not right. I wanted to ignore the problem, pretend that it had nothing to do with my actions. But it was my act that caused it.

"Some of my audience, perhaps some of you, have been giving me reverence that belongs to God. I can't let that go on.

"The first time a man called me an angel, I thought I should deny it, but I didn't try hard enough. It was easier to pretend, to play at fantasy.

"As a performer, fantasy is part of what I offer, and I had hoped to offer the light-hearted fantasy of 'Tinkerbell' the fairy of the Peter Pan book, just like in the Disney movie you probably have all seen. I thought that this fantasy was enough. I thought I could just ignore the whispers.

"But because I have ignored them, a simple child's entertainment has become something else.

"As I said, I have no excuse for my sin. I know the story of Paul and Barnabas, and how important it was to them to immediately and publicly deny that they were gods. I know of other stories in the Bible, where even real angels rejected, firmly, the reverence that people gave them.

"So I must say here, before you all:

"I am simply a girl, a person of flesh and blood, just like you. I entertain people for money, and for the smiles of the children. My acrobatics are amazing, I know that, but I confess to you that everything I do is just science. I have no power from God, and I certainly do not deserve the reverence due Him."

She looked over the crowd, unable to read their thoughts. She continued doggedly on.

"So tonight, before God and before you all, I wish to confess that I have not done enough! I plea for your prayers to forgive this lie that has misled some of you, and many others, and I plead for your leaders to write a letter to the other congregations of the area, to help me deny this lie, and to give God His due."

The preacher called for a church elder to pray for her, and before the bowed heads of them all, she felt the release.

After the service, she was immediately surrounded by loving smiles and encouraging words. If there were frowns in the crowd, as she suspected there were, these well-wishers shielded her. To the elder who had prayed, she offered them the money she had brought to defer the expenses of the letter. At first he turned it down.

"No, I have worked in a copy center and I know what these things cost. You must take it. It is the first step in my penance."

He nodded, and took the folded stack of bills, and then the speech she had written out. "I will see to it personally."

She nodded, "I know you will." In her mind, this kindly stranger was overlaid with the memory of Dr. Kantz, who had called her down for running in the church when she was five, and then taught her the joys of four part harmony singing when she was thirteen, and who had cried with her at Joe's funeral.

Then she saw her mother, and Jim and Helen in the crowd.

"I'm proud of you Jen." Her mother hugged her tight.

"You're braver than I am," said Helen. Then she whispered, with a grin. "I think Jim's nervous at being in a church."

When they finally made it back to the carnival, Jenny prepared herself for Forester's wrath, but he merely glared at her, and rushed off to deal with one more of the perpetual crises of the show.

Mandrake's rig was third in line as they headed out of Big Spring. Jim was driving the unused tractor, and Helen was driving Jim's pickup.

Jenny smiled when she spotted Betty up in Mandrake's cab.

Her mother rode with her, but without Helen, the card game didn't materialize. Instead the topic drifted off to costumes. Amanda Quinn was eager to find some way she could help, and Kelly started talking about how much she was jealous of the performers, and how she wished she had a costume, even though she was just running the darts and balloons.

"I've been to a restaurant where the waiters and waitresses all wore costumes," said Amanda. "We were served by Wonder Woman. They weren't performers, but it worked for them. Why don't you get a costume?"

"Fleschette," Jenny said. Her mother looked at her, "Right!"

"Who?" asked Kelly.

"Oh, one of my brother Joe's comic book characters. Think of a green costume with crossed bandoleers, except instead of bullets, you have belts across your chest with darts."

She frowned, "I'm not sure I can visualize it."

Amanda just waved her hand, "Then wait until tomorrow. Ken, my husband, will meet us at Fredericksburg and he will have Joe's things with him. Then you can see for yourself."

G illespie County Fairground at the outskirts of town was quite large and spread out, especially after Big Spring's shopping center parking lot. They parked and unloaded.

Jenny half expected H to appear and unload her trailer, but he was no-where to be seen, probably still hidden out with Lady Veronica.

Dennis was out and working hard, getting the Ferris wheel set up. The carnival was scheduled to open its doors at five and there was a lot of setup work to be done, especially the first day.

Jenny and her mother worked to get the cotton-candy stand up and running. It was strange to be coaching her mother, but in this, she was the expert.

"Do you think we could get some apples?"

Jenny asked, "What for?"

"Well, Betty gave me a sack with supplies, and there is this candy-apple powder. The instructions look simple enough, especially if I can find a cook-ing thermometer."

"Where?" She took the little bag and looked at instructions. "I asked for this a long time ago."

Then, she handed it back to her mother. "Well, I guess this is your job now.

A couple of hours before opening, an Itasca RV rolled into the area, and proceeded to pull into line with the others.

"It's Kenneth," said her mother.

"You have an RV?"

She nodded. "We were planning on tracking you down, and we didn't know how long it would take."

They shut down the cotton-candy machine and went out to meet him.

They had barely gone half the distance when Jim came running across the grounds, heading towards his truck.

"What's wrong?" called Cobb.

"Dennis!" he yelled, "Rashid just called. Dennis has collapsed in town. He may be dead."

61

Rashid jumped up from his seat when he saw them enter. Jim asked, "What's the news?"

It was clear that the boy was shaken. "Ah. They say it's a stroke." Jenny and her mother moved in to give him a hug.

Dennis had been walking through the Admiral Nimitz Museum, showing Rashid all the memorabilia from the War in the Pacific.

"He was showing me the picture of his ship, the one he was on. Pointed out the guns he worked on. Then he just made a noise and fell over sideways. I yelled, and the Park Ranger guy called 9-1-1."

It was not a long wait before the doctor came out.

"Mr. Johnson has suffered a stroke that is affecting the left side of his body. While he appears in otherwise excellent health for a man of his age, the recommendations limit what we can do for him."

Rashid asked, "Is he going to die?"

He didn't answer immediately. "The next three to five days are critical, but if I had to judge, I would say he has an excellent chance. Has his family been contacted?"

"I called my folks, but they're in Oklahoma City."

Amanda said, "We will make sure there is always someone to stay with him."

Jim nodded. "Everybody likes Dennis." He looked at the doctor. "Carnies are family. We will take care of him."

"Well, it is important that we monitor him for several days here in the hospital. With the size of the embolism, we have to be ready if there is any change."

Jim nodded. "I'm acting for our group. Let me give you my contact information."

As Jim went off to handle the details, Cobb tried to cheer up Rashid. He and Jenny's mother and father knew of others who had survived strokes.

Jenny kept her silence, because she knew all too well Sister Gladwell, an ancient little lady almost as short as she was. For several years, they had always exchanged greetings at church, as sisters of the bottom-shelf club.

She had a stroke, and Jenny barely had time for one visit in the hospital with her mother, and then she was gone.

And Dennis was worn out, staying up all night running his Ferris wheel for me. It is probably my fault he had this happen to him. In more ways that one, he had saved her life. One more name on that growing list of saviors. It was a pile of debt that she could never repay.

Rashid listened politely to their words for a bit, and then said, "He told me to take care of the Wheel."

Cobb nodded, "Then that's what you'll do—and I'll help. There is nothing that would do him more good than knowing you were in charge and keeping 'da Wheel' turning."

There was no shortage of volunteers to keep watch over Dennis, and Cobb took special responsibility to get Rashid back to the fairgrounds. He needed work to keep his mind off his worries.

Jenny added her name to the schedule, but it was important that the carnival keep running without missing a beat. The medical expenses would have to be paid somehow, and Western had been running too close to the red to provide health care insurance.

She gave her first performance, and her kids did much to lift her spirits. Becka asked, "Are you an angel?"

"No."

"Are you a fairy?"

"I'm a make-believe fairy. Do you play make-believe?"

Becka nodded.

"It's fun, isn't it?"

Becka didn't want to admit she was a little bit scared. "Yes."

Jenny touched down and handed Becka to her mother.

When she ducked into the tent, after the show, there was a man waiting. "Oh! Hello, Shawn." The sight of his smile, and that uncombed head of brown hair brought a grin to her face.

"Hello, Tinkerbell." He held a large bag.

"I guess I'm surprised to see you here. I thought I'd run you off."

"You'll have to try a lot harder than that. Fredericksburg is so close I can commute."

"Did you hear about Dennis?"

He hadn't. After she filled him in, he shook his head. "Mandrake and I should have swapped out running that wheel. I shouldn't have let him stay up all night."

Jenny shook her head. "'Da Wheel' was his baby. He would have insisted on doing it himself. It's not your fault."

"Still."

"I know."

They lapsed into silence for a moment. Then he straightened up and asked, "Did you cut off that connector I wired into your controller?"

"No."

He smiled. "Good. I felt bad about encroaching into your territory—but I had to do something to apologize, so ..." He pulled the bag around. "I feel like Santa Claus." He reached in.

She stepped closer. He pulled something out of the bag and presented it. "Your crown."

It was a tiara, silver and bejeweled. Her mouth came open. It was beautiful. And then she saw the wires.

"It's an additional coil, to extend the magnetic field from your neck through your head. It should keep the intensity level up, so that you won't get the disparity between the field in your body and that in your head."

He placed it on her head, and she was pleased at the nearly transparent connecting wires that she could conceal in her hair, and run down to the connector on her controller belt.

"Oh, Shawn, it's wonderful. I should've done this ages ago."

"You would have, eventually. Are you ready for number two?"

"Number two?"

"Jenny, I make gadgets for a living. You think I could stop with just one?"

Number two came out of the bag in its own wrapper. He removed the sleeve and took out a set of wings.

"This is from both Cobb and me. He'd been watching your show and wanted to make improvements. We talked, and ..." he grinned, "... things happened. He had some ideas, and I had the tools."

The mechanical fairy wings were the same general size as the ones she wore, but the instant she put her hands on them, she realized what he had done.

The original wings were a bronze outline with white lace stretched over them.

These new ones were lighter, much lighter. Shawn must have made the structural members out of aluminum or magnesium.

"And look at this." He grinned as he flipped a hidden switch, and the wings started slowly flapping.

"How pretty!"

"Try them on?"

Jenny nodded, and was pleased at how easily the new set fit into the harness. The slow motion of the wings was just enough to add life to the illusion.

She looked at Shawn, as he was drinking in her reactions. "I would never have gotten around to this. Thank you."

He gave a half bow. "Number three?"

"There's more?"

He nodded.

This one fit in his hand.

"It's a replacement for your reel. Your nylon line was going to snap eventually, and I had no faith that the spring wouldn't jam."

Shawn's version was freshly machined phosphor bronze, with a dial on the side to adjust the spring tension. "And this time, the line really is Kevlar."

She compared the two, her fishing reel and the new one. It was like day and night. She tried out the tension adjustment, and then with only a little regret, she stuffed the new reel in her belt.

"All done now?" she asked. It was a little like Christmas, only she didn't have anything to give him.

"Well... there is one more thing, but it isn't done yet." He moved in close and put his hands on her waist. Her heart raced as she let him lift her up onto the large trunk next to the tent wall.

"I'm going to take off your shoe," he said.

She nodded, feeling a warm tingle spread through her. She had no idea what he was up to, but she trusted him.

He pulled off the shoe, and massaged her foot. She melted in the sensation.

He grinned, and then reached into his bag. "This will be a little warm."

It was a jar with something in it like putty. He added a drop or two of some chemical and kneaded it in his hands. It was warm when he started molding it against the side of her foot. After about thirty seconds, he pulled out something with wires and molded it into the plastic as well.

Jenny watched every step, knowing what he was doing, but marveling at the skill and design. Shawn really was a gadget maker. She shouldn't have worried about what he had done to her suit. Why had she gotten so angry?

"Pivot your foot at the ankle." As she worked her foot, he adjusted the positioning of the wires. When he was satisfied with that, he checked the surface of the plastic with his finger and then put her shoe back on. "You should wear this for another hour, so the resin can set properly."

He ran another of those nearly invisible wires up her leg. She tingled at every touch. Then at her waist, with deft fingers and a pair of needle-nose pliers, he attached the wires to her controller.

"Okay, ready to try it out?"

She smiled, and let him help her down from the trunk.

"Adjust the power to just under the critical level." She reached for her knob and did as he said.

"Okay, now point your toes."

She did, and the new potentiometer at her ankle reacted, lifting her rapidly off the ground. Shawn grabbed her arm before she slammed up against the top of the tent. "Tilt your toes up."

Reacting to her foot, she settled back down.

"This is wonderful." She would no longer have to hold onto the kids with one hand, while adjusting the power with the other.

She took a step and pointed her toes, and with her wings gently flapping, she flew. *What freedom!*

She settled down slowly, controlling every inch effortlessly. She drifted close.

"I've got something for you, too," she said in a low voice.

"What's that?"

She grinned. "A thimble."

62

"Jen," said her father, "I am recommending that you incorporate."

"Why?" She settled into the bench seat behind the kitchen table in the RV.

He opened his briefcase, and double-checked his cell-phone.

"Part of the reason is that you have the potential to make a great deal of money, and the best way I know of to control that is with incorporation. Money protects itself. The legal system is set up specifically to make that happen. You, as the principal stockholder of a corporation, have much more protection than you would as a private individual."

"But, I don't really need to make money."

"Do you want control over your discovery?"

"Well, yes."

"Then you have to make money. Money and control are the same thing. Think of it this way—your control over something is only as good as the legal system thinks it is. Once your opponents start to call in heavy-duty lawyers, you must too. I am only one man and there are limits on what I can do. If this anti-gravity thing is as important as I think it is, then you will have opponents, and they will be ready to spend the money to take it away from you."

She nodded. "Okay, what do I have to do?"

He pulled out the papers.

"Daddy?"

"Yes, Jen?"

"I can let other people be stockholders, too, right?"

"Well, yes, within limits." He frowned. "You don't want to dilute your control too much, or it defeats the whole purpose."

"Good. I have a lot of debts that I owe."

Jenny located Shawn hanging around the Ferris wheel.

"Hi."

He smiled, "Hi back at you. Did the show go well?"

"Very well, especially with the better control I have. I always knew the belt control was distracting, and the toe pointing seems so natural."

"That's what I was hoping for. Are you still facing a problem with the insurance company?"

"Yes. That hasn't gone away. You haven't whipped up a child safety harness for me, have you?"

"Not yet, but I will if you want me to." He glanced over at Rashid, letting another set of people off the ride. "At the moment, I have been recruited to watch over him. There's a group of local kids that seems to delight in giving him a hard time."

"That's sad."

"Yes, but Rashid is taking the wheel duty very seriously. He's worried about Dennis."

"So am I. Any more news?"

He shook his head.

Jenny took a deep breath. "Shawn, could you come to a little meeting over at my parent's RV after my last show?"

"Sure. What's it about?"

"Something my father wants to do. He'll explain it."

He nodded.

In the early evening, when Jenny went back to her trailer to change into her costume, she noticed a lot of activity at the RV, and stopped in.

Her father was sitting in a chair, watching with a bemused expression on his face, as her mother was passing around a stack of Joe's comic books to several of the carnies.

"Oh, I like this one!" said Sheila Grant, who ran the ring-toss.

When Jen looked at what Kelly was reading, she wasn't surprised to see it was the one with Fleschette.

George was thumbing rapidly through several of the stories. "What's the copyright status of these?"

Kenneth Quinn said, "We own them. Joe, of course, never filed an application, but since he died intestate, they reverted to us, and should be good for another seventy some years. He would be happy to have people see them."

"And you would be willing to let me use these images for our posters?"

He nodded. "Within limits." He glanced at Jenny. "It's the least we can do."

Jenny felt a warm glow. Her father was really opening up. Perhaps he needed a challenge like this to shake him out of the crust that had grown up around him.

The people who came to see the angel were still in the crowd. *One announcement can't reverse a rumor months in the making.* Still, she was disturbed every time a head bobbed.

It was hard to deny something, when they didn't speak the words.

She picked up a little girl in a blue dress, with a yellow collar embroidered with a butterfly. "Hello? What's your name?"

"Tammy."

When she touched down, light as a feather now that she had such intimate control from Shawn's new addition, she smiled at the mother. "Tammy is just the kind of child I want when I get married."

There was only a fraction of a second's puzzlement before a mother's natural pride took over and she nodded in agreement that Tammy was the best little girl in the whole world.

Well, that's one more who doesn't believe I am an angel anymore. Talk to them. Let them know she was as human as they were.

On the way back to the RV, something in the parking lot caught her attention, but when she looked, there wasn't anything there but a trickle of cars leaving at the end of the day. She shook it off.

M andrake was the last of them to arrive. "I'll just stand," he said, when Amanda offered to make room for him at the table. "I think I've been sitting down for ten years straight."

Jim and Helen were as puzzled as the rest of them. Shawn, as usual, was making some kind of notes in a little notepad he always carried.

"My name is Kenneth Quinn, and I'm the one who called you here.

"You are all aware of Jen's story, and how there's some danger to her from some person or persons unknown. We are all taking care to keep an eye out for her, and if anyone tried anything, I know all of you would be ready to help.

"But as a lawyer, I am trained to look out for a different kind of threat, and I've talked Jen into forming a corporation, one that can better protect her discovery, and protect her in the bargain. Jen would be assigning the rights to her discovery over to the corporation.

"After much discussion, it is her intent to grant ten percent of the ownership to her parents, ten percent to Shawn Breaker, ten percent to Mandrake Samuelson, and ten percent to a trust fund, administered jointly by Helen McBride and Jim Morgan, for the benefit of the members of the Western Extravaganza Shows. The remaining sixty percent, a controlling interest, would remain with Genevieve Bell Quinn."

There was a long silence.

"Well," said Mandrake, "I for one don't need any share. I think Tinkerbell should keep seventy percent."

Shawn nodded, "I don't need anything either. I'm in this for the fun of it."

Kenneth held up his hands. "Okay, I understand. Frankly, I didn't expect anything different, not from the people Jen has put such trust in." He caught her eye. She nodded.

He continued, "However, she and I have already had a very long debate over this, and she is not one to give in. She credits you Mandrake, and you Shawn, with directly saving her life. It's a debt to her, one she feels powerless to repay any other way.

"Jim and Helen—Jen originally was set to hand out equal shares to dozens of people, many of them a part of Western. I talked her out of it. There's a chance that this will become more than just a gesture on her part. Possibly, a great deal of money could be made. The one thing I did not want was a mob of people, arguing about how to direct the course of Jen's discovery. She would surely be the loser in this, and I wouldn't let her do it.

"Her intent is that you two have the freedom to run this trust however you want, and to pay yourselves some fee as the administrators. She suggests, but does not dictate, that some kind of medical assistance for current and former members might be in order, as well as improvements in the show itself.

"All of this, of course, hinges on our ability to help Jen control this dark matter inside her, and to help her control the discovery's development. There is no money now, and no guarantee that there will ever be any money.

"But I have the papers here tonight to make this incorporation happen, and to set up the trust. I urge all of you to let Jen make this gesture, and to let me add this level of defense around my daughter.

"You have already shown her true friendship, and I believe her when she says she owes her life to you all. Whatever you decide, you have my personal thanks for what you have done for my Jen."

It took them over two hours to make their decisions, and to sign the papers, but as Jenny walked towards her trailer, she couldn't help but giggle.

I'm now a Chairman of the Board of a corporation. She shook her head. Her father was right. It sounded important, even though there was no more money than before, and she still had to get some rest for tomorrow's show.

Pixie Dust Enterprises. She liked the sound of it. Her father preferred something innocuous, and Jim liked Dark Matter, Incorporated, but Uncle Manny claimed that if they ever got around to making money, then Pixie Dust would be a whole lot easier to sell. After some discussion, he prevailed.

Jenny could have chosen any name she wanted, after all, she had 60% of the vote, but she had abstained early in the debate so that she wouldn't short circuit the ideas.

She rounded the Tilt-a-Whirl, and frowned at two men, huddled together between the row of RV's and the empty truck trailers that had hauled the smaller rides. They were shadowed from the parking lot's lights, and for a moment, she couldn't make out who they were.

It was George who spoke, in an angry, bitter voice. "It had to be those suckers. Even Rashid was having problems with them."

She stepped closer, and they glanced up at her approach. The other was H. He moved to the side, and then she realized that they were clustered around something on the ground. He was trying to block her view of it.

"What is it George?"

A glimmer of the streetlights reflected from his eye, and she realized he was crying, or as close to it as men got. He exhaled unevenly. "It's Brutus. Some local idiot knifed him."

"What?" She stepped quickly over, and her heart shriveled up as she saw the cat, laying on his side in a dark pool of blood. She reached down, but H stopped her hand.

"He's dead. Starting to cool. Let me clean it up."

"Yes, Tink." George said. "I'll bury him. He shared my trailer for about three years. I owe him at least that much."

She shook her hand loose and touched his flank. The life was gone out of him. N-space was gone.

She walked the rest of the way to her trailer without seeing much of anything. He was just a stray cat. He didn't even belong to her. He didn't even belong to George, and he had a better claim.

How can people be so cruel? She had heard others talking about the problems Rashid was having with some teenage boys, who couldn't handle the fact that Rashid was no older than they were, and in a responsible position. It was just young male dominance games, no different from young bucks or bulls or gorillas.

But that's no excuse to hurt a cat.

She reached for the door handle. *He won't jump out at me. Not any more.* Nor would she wake up with him sleeping on her chest.

The doorknob was loose. She turned it, and there was no resistance.

In spite of the darkness, the scratches on the frame were vivid. Her heart pounded.

She pulled the door open. The light switch was high, and she had to step up into the doorway to reach it.

Click. She could smell the gasoline.

It was hard to take the next step, but she had to. She stuck her head in and looked.

Oh, no. It was just like the apartment. Her clothes were scattered, stained with something. Her cabinet was opened, and everything was spilled out.

If the damage was less, it was only because she had fewer possessions, and some of those were still over at her parent's RV.

Wait. That's blood. The dark splashes marking her clothes were congealed, and red.

She reached for her belt, and pulled out the tiny radio.

"Shawn? Mandrake? Can you hear me?"

After a couple of seconds, "Yes! What is it?"

Almost on top of Shawn's response came Mandrake's. "What's up?"

"The both of you. Come over to my trailer, right now."

"On my way," said Mandrake. Shawn didn't take the time to answer.

She stared at the blood. N-space wasn't attacked by teenagers. This was her old enemy.

63

"Jen, it's time to get up," her mother said.

"I'm awake."

She hadn't gotten much sleep. Nor had half of the camp, she expected. The news spread fast, and everyone was up to inspect the trashed trailer, and to grow livid over the cat. It appeared N-space was known to a couple of the other carnies as well. N-space/Brutus/Tom was going to be missed.

And it was the agreement by all that he had died fighting. There would be many eyes out looking for anyone with cat scratches. If N-space hadn't attacked the intruder, the trailer would have gone up in flames, just like her apartment.

There wasn't much that was salvageable. She wrote off almost everything.

The exception was her original flight suit.

The intruder had ripped seams, opened and poked at the control belt, and had cut slashes across the ribbon cables. *This wasn't random violence.* She was sure of it. *He was examining it.*

Shawn claimed the suit, and took it with him when he left for the night. He seemed to think he could repair it. She didn't have the heart. If the white costume hadn't been over at the RV, she would have been lost, back to square one.

But I am going to give my show. I won't cut and run, not this time. She had to stand up for herself.

And this time, she had family and friends to back her up.

"How'se da boy doin'?" Dennis had to struggle with the words, and it hurt her to see him in distress. The stroke seemed to have turned the whole of his left side numb.

"Rashid is doing a good job. The Wheel keeps turning, and people are happy."

He nodded, and before long he drifted back to sleep. Lorene Cobb, who operated the inflatable moonwalk castle, had nothing much to talk about. Jenny sat in the high-backed chair and worried.

Dennis had family, and they were coming, but the doctor was still reluctant to declare his condition improved, or even stable. His future wasn't very bright. She had looked over the information on strokes in the hospital's booklets, and there wasn't any treatment that was likely to be used on anyone his age. In spite of the hundreds of thousands of people affected every year, it seemed that it was a disease without any huge federal research budgets. It was just something that people accepted, like old age.

God, Dennis is good. He has helped me, and others like me, all his life. The joy of his life is to see people happy. Help him come through this.

She thought about the conversation she had with Jim and Helen. If anything came from the dark matter, and there was money to be made like her father thought, then the trust fund's first priority was to see to it that Dennis, and other veterans of Western would have some kind of retirement care.

As for Dennis, she knew that his days of running 'da Wheel' were over. Unless his family had more money than she thought, he might be forced to sell it, just to cover the medical costs. Western itself might be in critical condition as well.

I need to spend more time solving the dark matter problem. So much depends on it now.

This morning, Forester indicated that he didn't feel that it would be worthwhile to repair the damage to the trailer. He was going to turn it over to a local consignment reseller for the few dollars it would bring.

I need to talk to Shawn when he gets back from Austin. He was the only one who could talk her language. *Maybe we can brainstorm.*

By the time the last show was done, Jenny had noticed one thing. She was never alone. *Daddy's work, I'd bet.* All through the day, no sooner did one friend leave, than another just happened to arrive.

But, at least, it gave her time to talk.

The whole show was well aware that she was being stalked, and people were ready to be there for her. She worried that it was spreading things too thin. With Dennis in the hospital, and the men watching over Rashid, and now with the need to keep watch over her too, it made the day-to-day work of running the show that much more difficult.

There was one bright spot on the horizon.

Joe's comics were being passed around, with clear warnings that each was a unique one-of-a-kind book, and that heads would roll if anything happened to them.

Characters were being claimed. George had put up a blackboard at his RV, and there was a growing list of which person would get which superhero. The talk was that each person in Western would eventually have a costume, and that the whole advertising portfolio would feature the pantheon that Joe had created.

George, when he came by, just by chance, was overflowing with ideas, on how to put it all together. Most of the books had already gone under his camera, and he was composing a banner with characters that Jenny had long ago resigned to dying a slow death in her mother's storage chest.

"You don't know what an asset this is!" he said. "Your brother was a great artist, and I can use his black and white drawings directly. If I had to do this with Superman and the Hulk, the licensing costs alone would bankrupt the show. Of course, it will take awhile to get all the costumes made, but your mother is almost as good a seamstress as you are, and she doesn't have a show to put on five times a day."

One thing they didn't talk about was the cat. The one time she started, he abruptly changed the subject. She didn't force it. Maybe it was best that George could jump into this other project, just like Rashid was dumped into his struggles with the Ferris wheel. Sometimes worry and grief had to be dealt with when the time was right.

Western has been a place of healing for me. I wouldn't trade my time here for anything.

K nock. Knock. Knock.
"Who is that?" grumbled her father. It was early, at least on a carnie's schedule.

It was Forester, looking harried, and just a little intimidated by Mr. Quinn.

"A television crew is coming by this afternoon. They want to interview Tinkerbell."

"I don't know," her father began.

"It's okay," Jenny put in, before Forester and her over-protective father got into another argument. "I've done it before and the sky hasn't fallen."

"Hasn't it?" he asked pointedly. "Your attacker probably found out where you were from the last interview."

"Then that just means that the damage is already done. Daddy, Western needs the public exposure. Especially now."

To Forester, she said, "Are they just interested in Tinkerbell, or would an appearance of the Queen of Hearts and George's new poster be possible?"

Forester grinned. "They just said they would be by this afternoon. They want to air on the six o'clock news."

Amanda Quinn appeared in her robe. "If that's so, then I know what I'll be doing today. The Fleschette costume is close to being finished."

Kenneth, ever the lawyer, said, "I still don't advise it."

Jenny gave him a hug. "It's settled then. Mom, I'll let Kelly know what to expect."

Forester turned to go. "I'll tell George."

T he morning's treasure was Heather. She eyed the crowd below as they went sailing in a large loop. Jenny was getting much better at using all of Shawn's control improvements to extend her arcs.

Heather craned her head to look at the cord attached to Tinkerbell's back. "Mamma said we could come back this afternoon. Can I fly again?"

"Do you like to fly?"

She nodded, eagerly.

"Me too. But there are a lot of other kids down there, and we have play fair, don't we?"

"I guess so."

Jenny gave her a little squeeze, to cheer her up.

"I've got a secret to tell you."

"What is it?" The cloud of disappointment disappeared.

"You see the string hooked to my back?"

"Yes?"

"I don't really need it. I really can fly, all by myself. The string is just to make the Mommies comfortable."

Her eyes got wider. "Can you teach me how?"

"Maybe some day. For now, we have to keep it a secret. Can you do that?"

She nodded solemnly.

"Okay, hang on now." Little hands tightened, and Jenny swooped down for a perfect landing.

64

"Jen, do you have a minute?"

"Yes, Dad?"

"I've got a reply from TEC. I think I can get legal clearance for you to prepare a final report for the Jason Williams grant."

"That's wonderful."

"Maybe not. They want publication of the paper, and a presentation at the university, with their funding acknowledgement, of course. They supply no more money, and they also want 80 percent of any patents arising out of the grant."

"That sounds high. Is that what Jase agreed to?"

"No, but I wasn't in a very good position to negotiate. If I drew attention to the money aspect, it just might put them on the scent."

"Wouldn't the fact that a lawyer was calling them be enough to do that?"

He smiled. She had seen that one before. He was pleased with himself. "Well, no. I was a concerned parent, with a daughter who was grieving for a dead professor she had been infatuated with."

"Dad! You didn't!"

He nodded. "Yes, I did. I was shameless, and it worked, too. They had already filed the grant as a total loss, and moved on. But the man in charge has a daughter too, and I pulled on the heart strings as hard as I dared."

Her face was getting hot. "Dad!"

He looked serious. "You would rather be stuck in legal limbo, with the very real chance that they would claim all of the discovery once you made your announcement?"

"Well, no—but it's embarrassing!"

"Was it a lie?"

Her thoughts skipped a beat. He had no right to ... Well. maybe he did.

"No," she said quietly, after a moment.

He squeezed her arm. "I know it's hard. Your mother told me when he died, how you reacted. But even before then, I suspected."

Her eyes were directed to the gravel beneath her feet.

"I have another confession," he said.

"What?"

"When you graduated, we were so proud of you. Then, when you introduced us to Professor Williams, and said you were going to stay and work with him, I could see it in your eyes and hear it in your voice, there was as much chemistry at work there as physics.

"But you were my daughter, and he was much too old for you. I wanted to put a stop to that any way I could.

"So I protested about the expense, and that was a mistake. That, more than anything, drove you away from us. I should never have tried to manipulate you like that, and I should have confessed my mistake much earlier.

"Will you forgive a stubborn old man?"

She nodded and snuggled into his hug. "I was foolish..." she began.

"Shush! You are a grown woman, and entitled to make your own mistakes. I overstepped, and it hurt all of us."

She sniffed. "Okay," she said, trying to get back on track before she started crying and ruining her face for the next show. "Is this agreement settled?"

He nodded. "We exchanged the faxes this morning. It's dangerous to give me a power of attorney. I'll use it!"

"So what do I need to do?"

"Two things: One, help me prepare the patent application for the original dark matter machine, and two, start work on your paper. You will be going back to school, for at least one day."

Her heart sank. *A paper. Do I have enough data for that? What will I say?*

But she said. "Okay. It will take some work."

"I know my daughter. You will do fine."

Kelly was all nerves. "What will I do?"

Amanda Quinn took a pin out of her mouth, and adjusted the wide green sash that contained all the darts. "You will just stand there, confidently—and look dangerous."

She waved her hands, "But I'm not dangerous."

Jenny said, "You'll do fine. Keep your head up and look straight at the interviewer. This isn't live, and if you make a mistake, they will just edit it out."

"She's right," said George, as he worked to fill in some spot color on his banner. "These human interest news things are just cheap entertainment for the TV station. We're all on the same side."

"But what will I do?"

Jenny thought a moment. "Do you remember when you came back from that date with the sucker from Del Rio?"

She grimaced, "Do I ever!"

George looked up, "That's it. You look ready to kill. Just think about that date, and wearing a costume covered with weapons will look perfectly natural."

Forester appeared in the doorway. "They're here. Are you ready?"

The TV crew introduced themselves, and Forester pushed George into the front as spokesman. Jenny thought it was a good choice. George was enthused by the new look that was sweeping over Western, and Forester still just looked like a tired old businessman in a rumpled suit.

They started with Helen, with the new banner as a backdrop. She wowed the male reporter with some tricks and her very professional patter. Kelly got through her brief introduction, and didn't stumble too much over her lines.

He turned to Jenny. "We will intro you with a clip from your performance and then cut to the interview. Okay?"

She nodded.

He picked up the microphone and changed to his on-air voice. "And this is Tinkerbell, already in her first season, the most talked about performer in the carnival circuit."

She gave a little bow, her wings slowly fluttering.

"Tinkerbell, while your show is spectacular, I have heard that you went to a church in Big Spring and declared that you weren't an angel. What prompted that decision?"

I was afraid of this.

She took a deep breath. "Thank you for asking. As a performer, it's important that I play the part and to please the audience with my fantasy, but it's also dangerous when the fantasy goes too far. I'm just an ordinary person, with a unique show that can confuse anyone. When I discovered that the rumors had crossed over into people's religious beliefs, I knew that I had to make a stand.

"I'm not an angel. I'm just a person happy to make little children's fantasies fly."

After they took some more shots and asked her a few more questions, they turned to George and asked about the costumes.

The reporter turned to Jenny's parents. "So this new look comes from you. I would like to get you on tape as well."

Kenneth Quinn shook his head. "I'm no performer. You don't want me."

"But I understand that these designs are from your son's work. I am sure the readers would love to know about him and how you came to be part of this carnival."

Amanda touched him on the arm. He looked down at her, and their eyes locked for just an instant.

He turned back to the reporter. "Well. Okay, I guess."

"My son Joe was a very talented artist, as I am sure you can see. When he was killed in a useless, senseless automobile accident, I retreated from the world and spent my days pushing papers in an office."

Jenny watched breathlessly as her parents faced the lights and the camera. They stood side by side, almost merged together, while her father spoke.

"There's nothing that shook me to the roots like losing my son. A father has hopes. When your boy does well, you're on the top of the world. When he makes mistakes, nothing can be more depressing.

"When he died, a big part of me died as well, and I became useless to my wife and my daughter."

"So as I look around today at the artistry and genius of my son, Joe Quinn, brought back to life by the hard work of these people, my wife, and especially, by my daughter Genevieve, I feel like I have come back to life myself." He looked past the camera, head up and unashamed of the glimmer in his eyes. He looked directly at her, and said. "Thank you for bringing Joe back to me."

They made arrangements for the cameraman to get to a good position before then next show started, in about an hour.

"You did good Kelly," said George.

All she could do was to hold out her hand and show him how much it was shaking.

Jenny watched quietly, as her parents communicated in some fashion she had never been able to understand. *Someday. Someday.*

Her mother squeezed his hand again, then turned to Kelly. "We need to get you out of that before the pins come loose."

Her father watched as Amanda took the girl in hand and headed towards the RV.

He is happy. I have never seen him look this happy.

"I thought I might find you here." Shawn came up beside her. "For a dangerous fugitive on the run, you sure spend a lot of time in front of the cameras."

"It couldn't be helped."

"Officer Davis is here."

"What!" She turned to check his face, in hopes he was just joking. There was no trace of levity.

"What's the matter?" asked her father.

Shawn told him.

"Then show him to me. I need to be able to recognize him." He turned to Jenny. "You go stay in the RV, and don't come out until I tell you!"

She nodded. The two men headed off into the crowd.

"Are you decent in there?"

Jenny unlocked the door for her father. It had been a tense ten minutes for her, trying to pretend that nothing was wrong while Kelly and her mother worked over her costume.

"Did you see him?"

He nodded. "I can't think he is here to arrest you. I may not practice criminal law, but I do know a few things. He has no jurisdiction here, and I see no signs that he has recruited a local policeman to come with him."

Shawn agreed. "He's just wandering around, looking like a tourist."

"Except," added her father, "that he is here alone, and doesn't look like he's interested in any of the attractions. I would feel a lot better if he had a date with him."

"Then what do I do? I have a show in less than an hour."

"I would suggest that you stay here until the last minute, then go do your performance. I will go tell the others what to look for. At the least, we can be ready to run interference if he does try anything."

She nodded, and he left.

Shawn took her hand. "Don't take this the wrong way, but I need to get out of here. The last time I had to deal with him, he was looking hard for a connection between the two of us, and to find me here would just feed whatever suspicions are running around in his brain. I'm pretty sure he hasn't caught sight of me yet, and I think we should keep it that way."

He started to let go of her hand, but she held on. "Stay a little bit. We need to talk, and I need some reassurance."

He didn't argue.

"So I am committed to writing a paper, but if I did it right now, there would be nothing more than bland observations. I really need some theory, some equation, which holds all the observations into a coherent whole. That's the only way I can really claim this discovery and make sure that Jase has his name on it."

Shawn listened to her talk about her professor with a sober expression on his face. She waved her hands as she tried to explain her problem.

"Simple facts do not make a discovery. Everybody sees rainbows. Newton split sunlight with a prism, wrote down the facts and his insight, and that linked his name with the discovery."

Shawn took a deep breath, and asked, "It's important to you that Williams gets credit?"

She nodded. "He died for it. I know that it'll probably weaken our claim on the dark matter, but I owe him this."

He nodded, straight faced. "Good for you. The world needs a little more loyalty. What can I do to help?"

He's a little jealous of Jase. She felt a little flutter in her stomach. *Think about that later.*

They talked a bit about the problem. So much of the original raw data was lost, either in the apartment fire, or out of reach in the file cabinets of the university.

"I'll have to do a number of experiments, and I hope I have enough time to do it all."

He nodded. "I can help with any equipment you need. Just tell me what you want." He glanced at his watch. "But, for now, I need to get out of Dodge, and your audience is probably gathering as we speak."

He took a look out the windows, and then gave her an encouraging grin, and slipped out the door. It felt like a bit of the oxygen went with him.

She was accompanied on all sides as she approached the flagpole, where the crowd was gathered. Her father and Mandrake were at either side, and her mother walked in front, trying to get people to open up and let her through.

A command performance, this time, she thought, as she could already see the television crew trying to make enough room for the cameraman to work.

People were turning towards her as she approached. She smiled and waved.

As the moving mass of people shifted, she caught a second's glimpse of Officer Davis, standing still, watching with all the others.

There were shouts, and for a moment, she thought that people were just cheering for her.

Then she heard it—the grinding shriek of metal under stress.

Everyone was suddenly looking, searching.

Off in the direction of the Ferris wheel, she could see a group of three teenage boys, running.

"The Wheel!" someone cried.

Every eye turned that way, and it was clear that something was wrong.

Up high, at the peak of the wheel, one of the cars was crooked, almost upside down. Above the shouts of the crowd, Jenny could hear one voice, the terrified shriek of a little girl.

Every sound but that one cry muted away. Every sight but the image of that car, and its two occupants vanished from her eye.

Jenny reached down to her belt control box, and jumped into the sky.

There was a wave of sound, as if a thousand voices came up and hit her in the chest. People could see her, but it didn't matter.

What mattered was control! Her jump, her lift, and the air on her wings—she had to stretch her glide as far as possible. She had to get to them.

Down below, she could see Rashid working furiously with the controls. He had stopped the wheel.

She rose swiftly, using the angle of her foot to carve an arc through the air directly to them.

Then suddenly, she was there, stopping herself with a hand on the steel.

The little girl was wailing, clinging tightly to her mother, who was struggling to hold onto the safety bar and hold onto her daughter for dear life.

"Hello, Heather."

Jenny moved hand over hand, weightlessly putting herself face to face with the mother and child.

"Help us!" cried the mother, her mouth almost unable to shape the words.

"I will get you down." Jenny tried to keep herself calm, although her own heart was trying to break out of her chest.

"I have to take you down one at a time, do you understand?"

The mother could only nod.

"Heather? Do you remember me?"

"Tinkerbell!"

Jenny tried to smile at her. "It looks like you will get your second ride after all. Are you ready?" She put her arm around the little one, and with only the briefest hesitation, reached for Jenny's neck.

Her mother still had a death grip on Heather's arm and only with an effort could she let go, and grab both hands tightly around the safety bar.

"I will be back for you as quickly as I can. Wrap your arm around the bar, and don't let go!" The lady, eyes wide in fear, nodded.

Jenny pushed off lightly and moved her foot.

Heather looked down, and then craned her neck to look for the string.

Jenny put her finger on Heather's nose and beeped it. "I told you, I can really, really fly. Didn't you believe me?"

"Yes. But Momma said you were joking."

They were drifting down rapidly. Jenny spotted her own mother fighting through the crowd.

"Well, you were right and she was wrong. But you've got to love Mommies. Would you like to see my Mommy?"

She nodded.

"Good, she's right here." Jenny touched down, and handed Heather to Amanda. "Now, I'll go get your Mommy."

There were hands clutching at the tips of her wings, but she didn't have time to do anything but shake free, and jump back up towards the Ferris wheel.

As she climbed, her mind was clicking, putting numbers in the equations. There was no way she could bring the mother, who was easily 120 pounds or more, and herself down to a soft landing. She had lift, but not that much.

The mother watched her approach, and tried to reach out for her.

"No! Wait. We aren't ready yet." The lady almost slipped, and she made a frantic grab back for the safety bar.

Jenny looked over the car, and saw what the problem was. Something like a crowbar was wedged in the works, locking the metal car in place, and not letting it swivel like all the others. She was coldly furious, remembering the boys who had fled the scene.

But there was no way she could free the car. Its weight had the crowbar locked into place.

And any moment, Heather's mother might lose her panic-inspired strength and slip.

Jenny reached for her belt to turn up the power, and then realized that the reel was still in her belt pouch.

That will help. Shawn said it was Kevlar. I hope he wasn't joking.

She slipped it out, and fastened the reel to the girder. A hard twist turned the spring tension all the way up, and then she snapped it into her wing harness. *It had better be enough.*

"Now I want you to hold on to me. I am not strong enough to hold you all by myself, but together we can make it down safely, okay?"

"Okay," she croaked.

Jenny talked her through it. "Move your left hand to here, and lock your right hand around your wrist. That's right. Over my shoulder, but not too high, because I have to keep my balance."

Jenny pointed her toe hard, and pushed off. They started to fall, and the lady gripped even tighter.

"Heather is down safely. She said you didn't believe I could fly."

"Ba...a." she tried to reply, but it was too much work.

Jenny kept an eye on the girders as they drifted by. Their arc was swinging them back towards the metal. Jenny reached out and pushed them off again.

The noise of the crowd was starting to penetrate, and suddenly, they were in the mob. Hands reached out to take the lady, even before they touched the ground. Free of her weight, Jenny worked her foot, and only tapped the ground before she was climbing back up.

"Hey, what about us?" called a stranded couple in one of the other cars.

Jenny was shaking with reaction, but she had enough strength to reply. "Just be patient. Your car is perfectly safe, and they will have the wheel in action in just a few minutes."

She drifted up the wheel, smiling and giving reassurances to all the passengers on that side. When she reached the top, she took a good hard look at the stuck car before she unfastened her reel and put it back in her pouch.

If I go back down, it will be all over for me. This would be the last time I would ever be alone.

Below was a solid carpet of faces, watching her every move. No more illusion. She could fly, and they knew it. The TV cameraman was hard at work.

She pushed off, and sailed down the other side of the wheel, giving reassurances to the people.

A few feet above the heads of the crowd, she called, "Rashid. There's a metal bar, jamming the car, but I don't think it will hit the supports. It is safe to turn the wheel."

He waved back, and turned to his controls.

Jenny made sure her wings were flapping gently, and then started a slow climb. She smiled and waved to the crowd.

"Tinkerbell!" People called her name, and she began a slow motion ballet over their heads, climbing all the time until she had cleared the height of the Ferris wheel.

Then she turned the power up and climbed quickly out of sight.

Issue 12: Credit

66

She waited until the ground below started to fade into the haze before she leveled off and drifted with the wind. The wings were nice, it gave her control she never had before in free flights, but they also kept her maximum speed low.

She pulled the little radio out.

"Hello—calling Manny or Shawn. Can anyone hear me?"

She released the push-to-talk switch, and listened. There was no sound, not even any static. She pushed again.

"Hello anybody! Can you hear me? I need help."

Silence.

The little display showed the right channel and codes, the ones Shawn had set up originally. It looked like it was working, but still no sound.

Come on! I need you.

She surveyed the horizon. There was the city below, and off in the distance, she could see the bare granite dome of Enchanted Rock pushing up above the green. Directly below was the winding path of the Pedernales River. The wind was pushing her no place in particular.

"Please help! Shawn. Mandrake. I need help."

Suddenly, a woman's voice, a stranger's voice, "T-t-t-ti-e-e-e-e..."

It was the worst case of stuttering that she had ever heard.

Oh! There was only one person likely to be in Mandrake's truck.

"Betty! Is that you?"

"Ye-Ye-Ye."

"Oh, thank God you heard me! Go get Mandrake and get him on the radio. He will know what to do."

"O. Ka-ka-kay."

It all became clear. That was how Mandrake and Shawn managed to show up right when she collapsed! Betty, who had been watching her fade day by day had contacted the newspaper personals.

So it is you who called them, and Mandrake has been protecting your secret, all this time. She felt a twist of pain in her chest as she realized the hurt Betty must have suffered to have choosen to be a mute.

"Hello, Tink?" It was Shawn, but the voice was weak and parts of the words dropped out. "Did you just call?"

"Yes! Shawn, I need a ground crew."

"What happened? Officer Davis?"

"No. I had to rescue someone, but Shawn, it was very, very public. I just flew away, once I was done."

"Okay. I had to stop the car and get out to pick up your signal. The radio is almost out of range. Which direction are you traveling?"

She checked the ground again. "It looks like I am heading east-southeast."

"Do you have your GPS?"

"No. Sorry. I wasn't planning this trip."

"No problem, I can find you with the radio signal strength and landmarks. I've done this kind of thing before."

"Can anyone overhear us? I suspect other people are looking for me. In this costume, I'm kind of hard to miss."

"No. The radios are digital and encrypted. Unless you know the codes, there won't be a peep, even on the same kind of radio. We can talk freely."

"Good."

A couple of minutes later, "Tinkerbell? Are you there?"

"Yes, Uncle Manny. I got a hold of another ground crew."

"That's good, because it's a madhouse here. I doubt I could get my rig out of the parking lot, and if I did, there would be five news crews following me. Honey, you made a bit of a splash."

"Sorry to leave you in the lurch, but I suspected something like that."

"We will be fine. Your father just put on his Important Lawyer voice, and is holding court. Everybody from Forester to Rashid is being interviewed. The police are all over the place, stringing yellow tape around the Ferris wheel. You did well to leave. I'll let your parents know you are okay, quietly."

"Thanks Manny. By the well, tell Betty I will keep her secret, and thank her for me for calling you when I got sick."

"She's listening now. She trusts you."

"Betty, thanks. And trust Mandrake. He is one of the best men I know."

"I. Kn-n-n-n-ow."

Shawn had the maps, Jenny the aerial view. Together they managed to locate her position and course, and targeted a deserted dirt road where it crossed Sandy Creek. She was closer, and was well able to cross-slip through the air to reach the spot. As soon as she touched down, she removed her wings and located a grove of trees to await his arrival out of sight.

It seemed forever, but she finally heard the rumble and saw the cloud of dust over the horizon.

She waited in her hiding spot, nervous as he slowed to a crawl and eased through the ford. The sound of rocks and gravel slipping testified to his progress and she stepped out onto the road as he came up onto dry land.

"You look good," he said as she opened the door and slipped her folded wings into the back seat.

"You look better," she said, sliding into the front seat with him.

He smiled, just looking at her for a moment, and then started unbuttoning his shirt.

"Ah...?"

"Here," he handed her the shirt. "You had better put this on over your costume. And take off the tiara. People will be looking for you and you would be hard to miss dressed as you are."

She tried to hide her flush, as she took his advice. She glanced at his chest. "Of course, now people will be looking at you." He was very attractive. The shirt smelled musky, but nice.

He laughed, and put the car in gear. "I will attract a lot less attention shirtless than you would have!"

She settled in for the long drive to Austin. Shawn was lavish in his praise for the rescue, and eager for all the details she could remember.

"Well, at least you have another career option—superhero!"

She shook her head, "No, I lack the one great attribute of a successful superhero—the ability to attract disaster wherever I go."

"I don't know about that. What about your apartment fire, and the second attempt at your trailer?"

Her smile faded a little. "That's not what I meant! I guess I mean I don't have the ability to be where my power would do some good. I am proud of myself. When the opportunity came, I acted, and then panicked later."

"What I am saying is that the opportunity never comes. This is the first time since the dark matter explosion that I could do a rescue, and it's not likely that it'll ever happen again."

"H doesn't count?"

She looked at his face, "You know about that?"

He shrugged. "When he fell off the wagon, he came by trying to find you and blubbered out the story of how you climbed up the wall of a two-story building and destroyed the tape. It was important to him, and he wasn't really in a condition to keep a secret."

She blushed. "Breaking the law isn't something I'm proud of."

"Still, it was a rescue. That makes two rescues in the span of a month. Surely your brother Joe could have spun that into one of his comic books, couldn't he?"

She pondered it for a moment. With the memory of Joe, quirky grin in place, looking over her shoulder. *Okay, I'm a superhero. I can live with that.* "Still, it's no way to make a living."

It took twice as long as normal to get to their destination, but using Shawn's well-worn maps, they traced a path along dirt roads and little-used two-lane blacktops clockwise around the Austin area and arrived in Pflugerville. In spite of their avoidance of populated areas, Jenny found herself gradually slumping lower and lower into the seat.

"We're here," he announced.

"Good. Very much longer and I would have crawled up under the dash."

"Stay put." He hopped out of the car, and she heard the metallic grate of a garage-door opening. He returned to the wheel and drove them in.

"Okay, you can get out now."

The room was empty to the framing. A pair of light fixtures hanging from the rafters were secured by little chains and plugged together with an extension cord. Shawn lowered the door partially, leaving a foot of air space open at the bottom.

He apologized. "For a self-storage building, it isn't bad. But I'm sorry it's the best I can do for a hide-out."

"Is this rented in your name?"

"No. We used it to store the hot-air balloon and pickup we used as the primary chase car. When the club disbanded, there was still a couple of month's rent already paid on it. The owner moved his stuff out, but if I keep the payments coming, there should be no problems."

"What happened to the balloon club?"

He looked uncomfortable. "Well, one of the members had his fifteen minutes of fame, and it made the others ... hesitant to meet with him."

"That's my fault. I'm sorry."

He shrugged it off. "I want to get my own balloon someday. I can wait.

"But for now, we need to make this place livable. You can't sleep on the bare concrete, and there are no bathroom facilities. Plus, it's hot now, and it's evening. By midafternoon tomorrow, this place will be an oven."

She must have looked disheartened, because he smiled and said, "Don't worry. I've done this before. When we worked on the pickup, we made some modifications. I already have the air-conditioner at my apartment, and the rest can be handled as well. I just have to make sure that I don't make anyone suspicious. And that means that I have to leave right now, before someone we know decides I'm a likely lead and starts following me around."

She felt her spirits sink. "Oh. I guess you do. I don't have to like it though."

He shook his head, "I suspect that before this is all done, you'll be grateful to get rid of me." He held out his hand. "My shirt? And make sure to keep the radio on at all times. Just in case, if I call you, don't answer unless I call you Genevieve."

She nodded, and took off the shirt. He gave her a last smile before leaving. Even so, she felt abandoned.

When the door closed, the place felt like a hot empty tomb. She wondered if the pharaohs felt as alone and scared as she did.

67

S hawn was back with a trailer-load of equipment, including a large wooden crate for her to hide in.

"I've paid another month's rent, and let the manager know that I will be using this place as a workshop for a while. He's happy—they surcharge for the electricity. I'll have to work with the doors open every now and then. Self-storage managers can get awfully nervous about people that keep things hidden. There's been everything from speed labs to toxic waste stored in these places. If I can let him sneak a peek every so often, we should be left alone."

She eyed the crate, and crawled inside. *Pretty luxurious for a homeless person. It helps sometimes to be small.*

Shawn worked a bit with the doors opened, unloading a small-sized refrigerator, a hand-pumped water sink much like she had used in her trailer, and a small portable toilet. She eyed the latter.

"Shawn?"

"Yes?"

"Close the doors and go for a walk."

He saw where she was looking, and nodded.

I t was amazing what air-conditioning and a little furniture did for the place. After Shawn detached a section of the corrugated metal roof and replaced it with a vent for the exhaust, they closed the doors and were finally able to relax.

"You have an apartment?"

"Yes, over in the Riverside area. I came to enroll in the university, and kept the place even after I dropped the idea of getting the degree."

"Why didn't you finish?"

He shrugged. "Money, mainly." He looked off into memory, "I never really intended to get a degree. My high-school grades back in Vancouver gave me a little scholarship, a couple of hundred dollars a year, but it did little more than buy a few books and give me some bragging rights in job interviews."

"You are Canadian, then?"

He shook his head. "I was born in L.A. We moved a lot, and when Dad died, the company pension was just barely enough for the family—I was child three of five. I just picked a school too far away for Mom to come visit, and then registered for the first semester. When I got a real job, there was no reason to continue."

She started to ask about his family, when the radio at her belt woke up.

"Hey kids, got your ears on?" It was weak, but recognizably Mandrake.

She reached for the radio, but Shawn shook his head and held out his hand. "Don't speak. I'll do the talking. Go hide."

He went to the garage door and opened it.

"Hello, Manny," he said.

The reply was a lot stronger once the metal door was out of the way. "Good to hear you! I've been talking into this little bitty thing for most of an hour. I suspect the batteries are suffering a bit."

"You sound fine now. Any news?"

There was a hesitation on the other end. "Are you sure this thing is encrypted?"

"Positive. Does it help your piece of mind that when my company bought them, they were over two grand apiece?"

"Ouch."

"That's why I only had these three. But go ahead and talk, no one can overhear you."

"If you say so. I've got at least two vehicles on my tail, and I've been alternating talking to friends on the CB and making calls into this thing because I'm sure they are listening.

"But anyway, I've got a message from Mr. Quinn."

"Go ahead." Shawn had the volume turned up, and he looked at her, peeking around the corner of the box. She could hear it well, and nodded.

"Okay." There was a rustle of paper. "'Jen, the TEC managed to put two and two together in record time. They smell money, and 80% isn't enough for them. There is a requirement in our arrangement that you write a paper and give a presentation. Well, they have advanced the deadline to the limit. We have two weeks to produce, or they will claim default. Get to work, I have confidence in you.'"

Shawn acknowledged the message, "But we have to keep this short. The signal itself can be revealing," he explained, "even if the words can't be detected."

Mandrake bade them good-luck, and continued on towards Waco.

Shawn looked worried. "With luck, we can keep communication going." He closed the door and Jenny stood up.

"I have work to do," she said. "Can you get me a computer?"

He nodded. "What else?"

Two weeks! That is not enough time.

"I need data. Lots of data, and most of it was burned up in the apartment fire."

The rest of the evening was spent on strategy. Jenny was to spend every waking moment preparing her paper. Shawn was to go back to his regular job and pretend to know nothing, but be her communications channel and supplier.

"All this will fall apart if someone links me to you and puts it in the newspaper. One hint of suspicion, and the storage building manager will be on the phone."

"I've thought of that," agreed Jenny, "and I have an idea."

Her presentation had to be as complete as possible. Once the announcement was released, every laboratory that hadn't been burned out on the cold-fusion fiasco would be trying to duplicate their results.

"I wish I had my notebooks," she said to the empty room.

But that wasn't possible. What wasn't ripped up and burned in the apartment was in the hands of the TEC. *No help there.*

I've been so cut off from the school—did Hausman manage to write a summation paper? Someone in his group is probably working hard on that task.

She folded over the notes she had been making on a yellow legal pad, and started to think about what her paper should look like.

First things first.

More important than the title, or even the abstract, she began the list of co-authors.

She smiled at the memory of that day, not too many years ago when she had been told the facts of life. Every scientist, good or bad, egoist or altruist, university or corporate, they all knew that that having your name on a published paper was the most important part of the job.

Credit was everything. If you published, you were able to work on the next thing. If not, you got another kind of job.

This is going to be a referenced paper. She knew that, but now, with pen on paper, she was just starting to feel it in her bones. One sure metric to determine if a paper is important or not is to see how many other papers make a reference to it. There were whole databases on the web that did nothing but track paper-to-paper references.

A lot of people would reference this one. She had to do everything right.

She listed Dr. Jason Williams first, and then her own name, and Ben Mitchell.

She raised her pen. *Who else?*

The credits on a paper didn't need to exactly match the people who did the work. Sometimes a name was added to pay off a favor, or traded for some other concession, or even for some totally unrelated reason. There was the famous example of the paper authored by Gamow and Alpher who added Hans Beth's name purely for esthetics, the Alpher, Beth, Gamow paper. *Alpha, Beta, Gamma. A, B, C.*

This is important, who should I add?

What about Hausman?

But had he helped? She reviewed her few meetings with him. *Well, yes, but only personally. He was never able to give me the access I needed.*

Let's see how Daddy's negotiations for a lecture hall goes. She had listed Hausman as the person for him to contact.

She was also tempted to include Shawn, even though he wasn't in the scholastic loop. *But it sounds like money was the barrier that kept him out. Maybe he will go back in the future.*

It was past midnight when the silence got to be too much for her. Her notes were rapidly filling yellow pages—she was surprised how detailed her memory was. She sketched the apparatus and listed equipment. She had spent so much time both before and after the accident sweating over everything, trying to understand what was important and what wasn't. Just like when she started duplicating Joe's costume designs, she blessed the way her memory worked.

If I had the parts, I could build another chamber from memory. I know I could.

Of course, who knew if it was enough to start generating the dark matter or not. Perhaps a single elusive particle of pixie dust was trapped when they sealed the chamber, and it bred there. So much was missing on the theory side. It would be a fatal flaw in her paper if she couldn't put the pieces together.

The air-conditioner kicked on again, stirring the stale air and making her realized how stiff she was getting, sitting on the wooden workbench.

I've got to tell Shawn to get me a good chair, when he gets back.

If he gets back.

She tried to shake off that thought. Shawn was reliable. She could trust him. She knew that.

But still…what if the police question him? What if he is being followed and has to avoid this place?

"Then he would call." She pulled the little radio from her belt and pushed the little mode switch to show her how much battery life she had left.

Everything was in order.

It's this cell. I might as well be a lab rat. At least they would have someone with me. A nice pleasant lady in a white coat to make sure I wouldn't do something foolish.

She lifted an eyebrow. *Something foolish. Now that's a thought.*

In the ceiling, she had talked Shawn into leaving an escape hatch for her. Foolish it was, but a minute later she was up on the roof. A nearby convenience store beckoned, and a Coke from an outside machine and a newspaper from a vending stand refreshed her body and mind. Reasonably confident she hadn't been seen, she made it back to her shelter with her treasures.

FLYING GIRL IN AERIAL RESCUE read the headline.

There were a half-dozen interlocked stories. It was amazing that they'd managed to cover so many bases in the short time from the actual event to the time the paper must have been printed, but it was clear the reporters were rushed, because so much was incomplete or simply wrong. One thing was clear. They knew who she was, and they were still looking for her.

68

"How is the paper coming?"

Shawn was far too cheerful, and she hadn't quite forgiven him for waking her up so early, although she felt invigorated by his arrival.

"I dunno." She rubbed her forehead. "I can write the history of the experiment easily enough, but without a theory, it is nothing more than a high school book report. And I don't have a theory."

"I thought you did." He unloaded a folding chair and handed her a fast-food breakfast in a sack. "The vacuum chamber caused dark matter to grow inside it. Put it in a magnetic field and it repels matter."

"No. No. That isn't a theory, that's just reporting. It isn't a theory unless I can tie the observed behavior to equations, and then predict new behavior from those equations."

"Oh," he shrugged. "I'm just a gadget man. I'm only interested in how it works. I couldn't care less how it fits into the whole grand scheme of physics."

She nodded. "Engineering versus theoretical physics. Mathematicians have their own pure vs. practical split. I have ... had a friend named Rae Bellamy who loves the equations for their own sake, and couldn't care less what you can do with them.

"But *I* need a good theory, more than just for this paper. If I can't do it, then I was wrong from the first day, and I should've turned myself in to the university and let more experienced people figure it out. It's pride, really. Something inside me knows I can solve this puzzle. I need to be the one. Jase would have expected it of me. I expect it of me."

He nodded, a somber expression on his face. After a moment, he brightened up and asked, "What do you need?"

She shrugged, "Data, and inspiration. There are two ways to tackle this. One is to come up with a brilliant theory, complete with its equation, and then collect the data to see if it matches the equation.

"The other, the one I have to use, is to collect the data first, and then find an equation that matches it. Hopefully, that equation would provide the necessary insight to make the theory clear.

"My big problem is that the data is messy. The only numbers I have are how my whole body reacts to the magnetic field. But every breath I take changes my body mass, and who knows what effect there is on the dark matter by being only molecular distances from ordinary matter.

"I have nightmares of being a lab rat. The only reasonable thing to do in that situation is to drop the rat into a blender and extract the pure dark matter, so real data can be taken."

She shivered. Months worth of running, and she was back at the beginning, with that first fear more real than ever. *Or maybe not ...*

Shawn asked, "So what can I do to help?"

She gave him a twisted grin, "I may have an idea, but it is messy, and you will really, really hate it."

When he went off to work, she went back to sleep. Her brain was far too fatigued from her late night worries to make any progress on the theoretical work she really needed. At least the plan they had hacked out gave her some new hope.

By the time the afternoon heat was fading, he showed back up. As she watched him unload the new portable toilet, and go to work, she marveled. *Give Shawn an idea, and he runs with it. No wonder he seems to be making a good living being a gadget man.*

The idea was simple. If dark matter was trapped inside her cells, then normal expiration and excretion should be shedding some of it all the time. All they had to do was trap it.

The execution was messy. Shawn was building a conical 'shower-stall' around the portable toilet, with something like the trap on a sink's drain inverted at the top. If the freed dark matter acted like an ultra-lightweight gas, then they should be able to trap it as it rose. With two portable toilets, he could take the used capture tank and treat it with more chemicals and ultrasonic agitation to free anything that might still be attached to regular matter.

"And I can process it through a 'magnetic still', to enhance the separation." He shook his head with a laugh. "My garage is going to stink to high heaven."

Jenny had a thought. "Shawn?"

"Yes."

"Did my father talk to you about patents?"

He nodded. "He wanted me to write out the details of that bucket over the head trick, so that he could file a patent on it. I told him it was nothing more what you had already designed for your flight suit."

"But Dad was right. I may be a physicist, but I'm also the daughter of a patent lawyer. Everything we do here is new territory, new discovery. You just talked about a magnetic still. That's certainly a patentable idea. So is this plastic teepee. It may slow us down, but we have to write this stuff up, and somehow get it to Daddy so that he can file it. The whole idea of this corporation is that we can use money to protect us. The only things that will bring in money are the dark matter itself, and the technology to use it. Patents are our only way to make money off of that technology."

Shawn did not show up the following day. They had talked about this eventuality, but it didn't make it any easier to take.

They pulled him in for questioning. I'm sure of it.

She had enough food in the refrigerator for several days, if she were cautious. *I need to stay cool, and work on my paper.... and keep an ear out for approaching police.*

But I miss him.

Every car that came though the self-storage facility sent her rushing to a quarter-inch crack high on the wall where she could see what was happening on the gravel driveway. It was hard to stay focused on her work.

She recharged the battery on her little radio, and rehearsed her escape plans. By midnight, she found herself opening the roof hatch again and making a run to buy another newspaper.

There was nothing about Shawn in the stories, although there was a considerable hunt going on for her. The university had given out the highlights of her work there, including the aborted experiment with Jase's vacuum chamber.

There was also the write up on her apartment fire. Much of it was a rehash of the coverage that occurred when it happened, but she had seen none of that. The fire had been found to be arson, and her disappearance was reported at the time.

Stories were still coming in from Fredericksburg. There was a whole section about the carnival and its people. She eagerly poured over the human-interest story about Dennis, his war service, and his life at the carnival. She never knew he was a certified war hero, with several saved lives to his credit when his ship was lost to a torpedo. Unfortunately, his medical prognosis was unchanged. At least his family had arrived to take care of him.

There was even a story about Joe, his comic book heroes, and how it was changing the carnival. The writer must have been a comic book fan as well, for the whole tone of the article was how superheroes saved Western. There were pictures, and in one of them, she saw her mother in the background, beaming with pride over her work.

She heard the footsteps and snapped awake. Someone was walking on the gravel outside the storage building.

It's morning. Just some other customer.

But the footsteps stopped, and it sounded like the person was just outside. She patted her belt, and prepared for a dash to the ceiling. If there was any noise from the lock, she would be gone by the time the door opened.

There was the sound of the metal door being brushed, and then abruptly, the crunchy steps of the person walking away.

She sat frozen, until the sound of her own heart beating was louder than the footsteps of the departed intruder. She tapped the controls and lifted herself up to the viewing crack.

Walking away in the distance was a man she could recognize, even from the back.

H! What is he doing here?

She looked down, and wedged under the door was a manila envelope.

The note was typed, from her father. "Jen, I have received a fax from Shawn Breaker. The police have questioned him, and he says that he is being followed everywhere he goes. He says to keep to the plan, whatever that means. The message was vague, probably because he suspects that my machine is bugged.

"We have set up a communications chain. You have a mind that would appreciate its deviousness, but I'll have to keep the details private until this is all over. Your friends are watching over you.

"I hope your paper is coming along well, because the date has been set. Your Dr. Hausman has come through with the approval for a university-sponsored presentation. It is next Wednesday, so you have about a week. It sounds like he has pulled quite a few strings for you, but he has to have a copy of the paper and any audio-visual needs at least a day in advance, and we are supposed to provide him with handout copies at least an hour before the 2 PM presentation time.

"It will be more like a press conference, rather than a scholarly meeting, and I know that is disappointing to you, but it has to be this way. When science and business get in bed together, there are a lot of unpleasant compromises to be made.

"Good luck, Jen. Your mother and I are very proud of you."

There was also a copy of Shawn's fax. It looked like it had been sent in a hurry. Her location wasn't mentioned, but somehow, he must have gotten that information to H.

She re-read the letter from her father.

Six days. Six days to invent a solid theory, with my only hope for data cut off.

At dusk, the next day, there was a tap-tap on the door, and then rapidly receding footsteps. She closed the window on the laptop reflexively, and looked down to see a slip of paper under the door.

I didn't even hear him approach. The writing was soaking up her attention. It was about the only thing keeping her from worrying.

She picked up the paper.

"Hi, Shorty. You might be interested in this:" it began, followed by a table of numbers.

The column headers were gauss numbers across the top, and quantity in "cc STPM", with values in gram-force.

Not my choice of units, but that's what computers are good at. What's STPM? Oh, 'Standard Temperature Pressure and Magnetism'. Yes it would have to be that. What kind of quantity measurement could you use for dark matter? Volume is as good as any right now.

She looked over the table and one thing jumped right out at her. *Shawn has separated dark matter, at least 3 cc's of it!*

A great weight lifted from her shoulders. She felt like she could fly without the controller. *A lab rat no more!*

If he were there, she would kiss him.

And I have DATA!

"Genevieve, Genevieve. Wondrous lady faire." It was Shawn's voice. She almost knocked the computer off the table reaching for the radio.

"Shawn?"

"In the flesh. Time to be a recluse."

"Gotcha."

She closed down the laptop and collected all her papers in a rush, stuffing them in the storage crate, and then crawling in after them.

He drove up a couple of minutes later. Casually, as if he were in no hurry, he opened the door and walked in. He gave her a wink in her hiding place and tidied up the floor, moving a few things around. After five minutes of that, he backed his truck into the storage building, and closed the door.

She was out and had her arms wrapped around his neck before he could fully get out from behind the wheel.

"You did it! You separated some pure dark matter."

His face inches from hers, he basked in her joy. He kissed her. With her co-operation, it stretched out a good twenty seconds, before they broke for air.

He held her, and she didn't mind in the least that her feet couldn't touch the ground.

"I've been busy," he said.

"I know. I got the messages, and the data. Thank you."

"I have more data. I didn't know exactly what you wanted, so I have run several different kinds."

"Anything, and everything, right now. I still have to put it all into some kind of theoretical framework."

He set her down, and reached into his pocket. He pulled out a glass test-tube, with a black rubber stopper. "Take a look."

Held to the light, she could see an interface layer inside, just like the layer you would expect if the test tube held oil and water, a boundary layer between two substances that didn't mix.

Only this was plainly clear gases, not liquids.

"Air at the bottom. Pixie dust above," he explained.

Then he let go of it.

She jerked to catch it, but it didn't fall.

"I put just the right amount in there, for neutral buoyancy."

The test tube floated, stopper down, wobbling from the motion it had when released. It drifted to the side, following the air currents from the air-conditioner.

"How much of this do you have?" she asked breathlessly.

"As much as you want. Take a look at this."

He had been busy. The new chart showed how fast the stuff grew based on magnetic intensity.

"I suspected this, based on your experience with the lightning," he said. "In a magnetic field, the dark matter repels normal matter. If it can move, it converts some of itself into energy, trying to get away, but if it cannot move, then it just grows."

Jenny nodded, "When I was hit by lightning, my own inertia kept me from moving fast enough, and my contamination increased."

"That's what I suspect. But now, look here." He pointed to the line on the chart where magnetism went to zero. "This is a real zero. I put it inside an adjustable coil and oriented it to counter the earth's residual magnetism."

"No growth at all."

"Right."

"Then I could stop it?"

He nodded. "Look at this. I had an idea for another gadget." He took a piece of paper and with a few clear lines, he sketched a bed inside a pair of adjustable hoops. "I could build this to automatically null out the Earth's magnetic field as you sleep. It would reduce your need to burn off the stuff, and if you were sick, there would be no need for drastic measures to keep it under control."

Her eyes started to mist. One after another, Shawn was evaporating her worst nightmares—turning them into impotent phantoms. He made her feel safe.

"Two things."

"Yes," he said.

"One. Patent this."

He nodded.

"Two." She looked into his eyes. "When you build it, make it a double bed."

"Just a couple more things before I go."

She frowned, "So soon. You just got here."

He sighed, turning back to the truck. "I have to! When they started following me, I made sure it was easy. I drove all over the place, but they didn't have any problems keeping track of me."

He pulled out a long box from the truck. "But today, I started out the same way, then went to a truck loading area over on Metric. I knew a shortcut out that isn't obvious, and the car following me was caught in the truck traffic heading out. I need to get away from here and show up from some other direction before they get too frantic and start calling out the helicopters. And I'm sure they won't get caught a second time, so this may be my last visit before the presentation."

He opened the box. "So I brought you everything." It was her original flight suit.

He showed her the re-engineered control box. "It has your same original triple redundant design, but I have added a damper setting, just in case you run into another lightning strike. The coils are also beefed up with a thicker gauge silver wire. And I added this."

The last was a white headband, wired into the control box just like the tiara on her fairy costume.

She held the suit up to the light. The slashes in the fabric were closed with crude stitches, but the wiring was flawless.

"Turn around and close your eyes." She had to try it out.

She changed in record time, behind the wooden crate. It felt so good to have it back on. And she liked the headband.

"Okay, you can look."

As he turned, she touched the controls, and felt the aggressive lift. She almost hit the ceiling as he called out, "Watch it! With the changed windings, you get a stronger field."

She touched back down. "Now you tell me."

On her toes, she danced over to the pickup and looked at her face in the rear-view mirror. Gleefully, she exclaimed, "I look positively Kryptonian."

"What?"

"Kryptonian." She glanced over at him. The expression of puzzlement on his face was genuine. "You didn't read comic books as a child did you?"

"Er. No. Not much."

She shook her head and smoothed her hair back under the headband. "If we're going to spend much time together, I'm going to have to fix some holes in your education."

He grinned. "I've saved the best for last."

She put her hand on her forehead, touching the band, and shook her head. "Have you slept since you were here last?"

He nodded. "Yes, but it wasn't by choice. You don't know how much fun I'm having. My brain is on fire. This is a gadget man's paradise. A whole new technology that makes new marvels with every stray thought."

He pulled another box out of the truck. He looked at her sheepishly. "I feel guilty about this one. It is your discovery, after all." He opened it up and took the apparatus out.

"I just couldn't help myself. It was right there in the numbers. It's the dream of every tinkerer like me." He looked at her with a timid grin and turned a switch.

The little flywheel started spinning, and a standard sized lightbulb started glowing, brightening even as the flywheel increased in speed.

Jenny looked at the simple wiring, the position of the coils and the magnet. "A dark matter power generator!"

"More than that," he tapped the little control circuit. "It is tuned to match power output to dark matter growth.

"A perpetual motion machine." He took in a deep breath. His eyes glowed.

Jenny reached out and took his hand. "Unlimited energy. Is it scalable?" she whispered.

He nodded. "Why not? Do you see any show stoppers?"

She could only shake her head. It had been one of the driving concepts behind the whole zero-point energy experiment. She knew she was getting free energy when she flew.

But seeing the little generator, something any high school student could construct—it made it all real.

"Everything changes here," she said. "You have remade the world."

He gave her a nervous grin. "We have changed it."

She nodded, absently. Flying was one thing. That had potential. But free unlimited energy!

"We're putting some powerful companies out of business."

"And creating whole new ones," he said.

"Governments will fall."

He nodded. "Oil will be worth its weight in plastic and chemicals, but we won't go to war for it any more."

She shivered. "How many people have already figured this out? Our lives would be a cheap price to pay to protect the status-quo."

He sighed. "I know. Until you go public, to be seen is to paint a target on your back."

69

She changed the scale on the graph and told the spreadsheet to recalculate. Slowly, in steps, the experimental data was tracked with her new equation.

Still not close enough. She glanced at the date and time at the top of the screen. *Less than two days. I should be practicing my speech, not still trying to find an equation that works.*

Shawn had not returned, and she missed having him to talk to. Communication via H was erratic, but she had at least heard from her folks again, and her idea to leave a message to be picked up had worked. She needed a suit, something formal for the presentation, and her mother could pick one out.

I need to print a draft of this in just a few hours. H should be here shortly after sunset, and I have to have something for Dr. Hausman.

NOTES ON VACUUM DEGENERACY AND GENERATION OF A NEW KIND OF MATTER. It wasn't a bad paper, especially for an initial discovery. With the experimental data in place, and a sample of the dark matter for proof, it would be respectable enough. She referred to the dark matter as "Williams's matter" twice. That should be enough to make it stick.

It just wasn't good enough for her.

She sighed, and reprinted it. Better to have a copy in hand than to delay until the last minute, and make H stand there in plain sight waiting for her.

The crunchy footsteps in the gravel had gotten very familiar. H had a distinctive pace. She reached down to the envelope she had left for him. When he grabbed for it, she held on.

"Tink?" he whispered.

"H, do you have a car?"

"Yes."

"There is a little food store just two blocks to the west. Be there at nine PM."

"Okay."

She released the envelope. He walked away.

This is stupid of me. Now is not the time she should be going out in public. *But I have to solve this puzzle!*

The Physics-Math-Astronomy library was in a medium sized glass tower, looking a little aged, even though it was one of the more modern buildings on the campus. She had spent untold hours there in its little study rooms. It was an ideal place to work out theories, with the riches of the shelves right at hand.

She walked into the entrance alone. Dressed from head to toe in baggy clothes and an oversized ball cap with the brim obscuring a casual look at her face, she didn't look at all out of place among the other students. H stayed out in the car. With his weathered and rough appearance, he would attract curious eyes immediately.

She held her papers under her arm and took the stairway up to the study rooms. Her guess that there would be available rooms this time of year was proving true. She chose a smaller one and arranged her stuff so that her back was to passers-by.

Printouts of her charts and data tables had to be enough to give her the right equation. She desperately needed inspiration. She checked the wall clock. H would come in looking for her in three hours. That was her deadline.

The clock was creeping towards midnight, and the stack of books on her table was getting vulgar. She had always been a stickler for re-shelving the books she used, but just this once, she didn't have time. Hausman already had the unsatisfactory paper, and this was her last chance.

What was that? She looked out the doorway. That was the third time in the last thirty minutes that she had felt like she was being watched, but when she checked, there was no one there.

Just a guilty conscience.

There was also a growing stack of canned Cokes, and the caffeine buzz was making her jittery. *I shouldn't even worry about trying to get some sleep tonight. It'll be impossible in any case.*

But in spite of everything, the campus library felt comfortable. It was a second home, where she spent her hours, and talked with her friends. It was a place where she had turned so many book-stale concepts into parts of her own mind—a place where ideas became real.

The article she was reading made a reference to an Israeli journal, and she put her pencil between the pages for a bookmark and went to the stacks to find the reference.

She found it quickly enough, and started walking back, thumbing through the bound collection of magazines to locate the page.

She looked up, and saw someone in her work-area.

Rae! The dark figure was bent over her papers, glancing through the tables of data and the charts. Jenny quickly moved back out of sight, her journal forgotten.

I should have never come here. Too many people know me. And what would Rae do? Rae had to know who it was. Did she read the papers?

The memory of her shredded apartment flashed back. She had talked herself out of believing Rae had done it. It had never seemed her style. *But do I know anyone anymore?* She had never believed she had an enemy in the world either.

She peeked again. Rae was gone.

Cautiously, she edged out of her hiding, but there was no one in the corridor. She stepped quietly back to her stack of papers. They were disarrayed, but nothing seemed shredded, or damaged.

Then she saw the writing. Scribbled above one of her charts was an equation, and Rae Bellamy's own monogram, an R with three rays emanating from it.

What is this? She sat down, and looked at the notation. *A series expansion. Only Rae could do this. If you are right, I hope you don't mind your name on a physics paper.* Jenny was intensely jealous of her friend's ability to glance at the numbers and immediately recognize the structure beneath. Knowing just a little of the academic credentials the mathematician had already accumulated, she had little doubt that it was correct.

Wait a minute! I think I recognize this.

Her mind went into overdrive. *Late 1980's. Indian. What was his name?*

Heedless of attracting attention now, she jumped up and ran back toward the stacks. *Was it in Nature? No.* She opened one bound copy of Physical Review, and immediately discarded it. She at least had a visual memory of seeing the page. She grabbed another.

On her fifth try, she found it, and ran back to her table, and slapped Rae's formula against the opened pages of the journal.

Rasheemee's formulation.

Among all the other attempts, this Indian theoretical physicist from New Delhi had put together an equation that ought to have been a unified field theory, in string theory terms, combining the various electromagnetic, strong, weak and gravitational fields into one coherent whole. Unfortunately, like so many of these attempts, parts of the equation wouldn't behave.

Attempts had been made to make the odd-factors in the expansion re-normalize away, leaving the even-factors, which seemed to accurately describe reality. But those attempts had all failed, making the theory flawed and useless.

My dark matter is described by the odd-terms. She could feel the puzzle pieces click into place, as she checked one term against the other.

Yes! That is exactly why it reacts to magnetism, it rotates the field vector out of one of the tight dimensions, into 3-space.

And there, that factor is negative. It is a repulsive force!

She glanced at the clock. Nearly twenty minutes had gone by, and she hadn't even noticed. She had to wrench her attention back to her surroundings.

I've got to get out of here.

She grabbed her papers, and the precious journal, and went bounding down the stairway, pausing only at the copy machine to duplicate the critical article before stuffing it into the re-shelve slot.

H was already walking up the sidewalk as she raced out. He looked alarmed, but she just waved for him to go.

I have to re-write the whole paper. But it is worth it! It is worth it!

J enny hated the spell-checker. It just could not handle technical jargon, and insisted on trying to make precisely worded, perfectly balanced sentences into juvenile nonsense. She corrected the last barbarism, and sent it, once again, to the printer. *Why is it that I can only see this kind on problem on paper! It would be so much easier if I could find it earlier.*

The radio came on.

"Jen honey, are you there?" It was her mother.

She grabbed for it, and almost pressed the talk button, when she froze.

"Oh, I almost forgot—Genevieve."

"Hi. You had me worried there for a second, Mother."

"Silly spy stuff."

"It's not silly to me. You have a seriously paranoid daughter."

"Well, it should be all over today, right?"

"I certainly hope so. Are you my ride?"

"Part way. If this map is correct I am almost there."

J enny looked at the clock on the laptop again, and mentally called it quits. *That is the final draft. If there are problems, then they will have to wait.*

Her mother had a little trouble with the door, and Jenny risked being seen to help her get it open and her car inside.

"Mother, you're a godsend," she said, when the first thing out of the car was a stack of towels and soaps. With all the other things that could go wrong, one of her top worries had been that she would stink from her too long solitary confinement and that some reporter would focus on that particularly unpleasant piece of information.

A thorough sponge bath, and then she let her mother help her into her flight-suit.

"What did you get me?" she asked, as her mother brought out a large garment box.

"I hope it is okay."

She pushed back the crinkly wrapping paper, and let out an "Ahh."

"I chose white. I hope that works."

Jenny held up the white-on-white pantsuit, and said, "It's perfect." She had been visualizing herself it a black suit, but who said she had to look that conservative!

As usual, her mother had chosen the perfect size. It fit over her flight suit and the pleated design hid the bulges from the flight suit quite well. As she looked herself over in the mirror, she fitted the headband in place. Even that worked.

I will look great on camera.

Jenny chuckled as she listened to her mother tell about the day's activities. They had no fewer than seven cars driving around Austin, after they had joined up. Anyone trying to follow them would have a hard time of it. What is more, when her father noticed Shawn's name as a co-author on the draft of the paper, he had immediately started the rumor that Shawn, not she, was going to be giving the presentation.

It was still four hours before the press conference, and her mother drove her to a location near Town Lake, where she was handed the keys to a rental car.

"You are supposed to wait until the last minute, and then drive to the point nearest Hausman's office. If you can find a parking space, fine, but spend no time on it, just double-park and abandon the car. Get inside as quickly as possible and Hausman supposedly knows a tunnel that connects his building with the conference center.

"By that time," her mother said, waving the printout of the paper, "I should have the copies made of this and already in Hausman's hands. If you get stopped, then Shawn will make the speech. If he gets stopped, then your father will do it. After that, it will be me, even though I don't have a thing to wear."

Jenny smiled, because her mother always looked nice, and she was already dressed up for the occasion.

"I would hate to have that happen," she said. "I've been practicing my opening line for days now."

The only problem left was where to hide. She couldn't be late, and driving around or waiting at a park would just insure that police would notice her.

But she knew the campus area, and there was a comic book store just three blocks to the north in the Speedway residential area. The man behind the counter looked up as she entered, but turned back to the book he was reading.

She felt her belt. *Batteries, GPS, cash, radio.* Things could still go very wrong. She drove with her eyes hunting in all directions, waiting to be spotted.

There! It was a faculty parking spot, but it would be less noticeable than leaving the car double-parked.

She had to grit her teeth and force herself to move slowly, casually. *Don't move like a fugitive.*

She carried her folder of papers under her arm. Making the presentation with the laptop for slides would have been nice, but she had decided to skip it. All she had for graphics were her charts, and she knew she could make transparencies of those with the machines she had seen in Hausman's office. Keep the technology simple.

"There you are!" Hausman was waiting in the outer office. "I was afraid you wouldn't make it."

She smiled. "A friendly face. It's good to see you, Doctor."

"Come on, let's get you out of sight." He held the door and ushered her in. "This cloak and dagger stuff is hard on my nerves."

They walked into his inner office. "I need to make transparencies."

"Fine. Right this way." He led her to the machines. "I just want to say that I was touched to see my name on the list of contributors to this seminal paper. It wasn't necessary."

She shook her head. "Your help was critical, and I'm sure that you gave important help to Jase as well. It was proper to have you listed."

She quickly made the copies. "Did you get to see the revised paper? My mother was supposed to deliver it."

"Yes, I did. Excellent work. Really excellent. Your credit is assured. And I met your mother. We decided that she should get to the reserved seats though the regular entrance to throw off suspicion."

"Oh." Jenny had hoped that she would be able to walk with her, for moral support. "Has Shawn Breaker shown up?"

He shook his head. "Your alternate, right? No, I haven't seen him." He glanced at his watch. "The tunnel route is private, but it's not direct. We need to be moving. With something like this, we can't afford to keep the audience waiting."

He gestured towards the door.

She sighed, then nodded. *Alone it is. I hope Davis hasn't arrested him.*

They walked down the deserted corridor, and then took a stairway down to a basement level.

"I noticed in your paper that you said very little about the flying, but that rescue at the circus certainly speaks volumes. Were you contaminated by the dark matter?"

"Yes. It's been a constant battle to keep it under control. I still have to fly regularly to burn off excess, so that I won't lose my weight totally."

He nodded solemnly, "It must've been a hard time. I am sorry for that."

The tunnel passages had several branches, and Jenny quickly lost her sense of direction. She expected Hausman knew the routes blindfolded. He had been a professor here for decades.

Abruptly, he started walking a little faster, and she increased her pace to keep up.

"It's times like this that you really feel the religion of science, the ritual presentations, and the listing of names," he said. "It makes you feel at one with all the old masters."

She nodded, she felt it herself, but to be honest, she was feeling her stage fright grow more intense with each step.

"The fight for credit has stained quite a few illustrious careers." He gave her a quick smile. "It has been refreshing to see you work so selflessly." He shook his head, and frowned at some private thought.

"Jase certainly deserved the credit for his work. I had to complete this, for his sake."

He nodded. "A great scientist deserves his credit. It is a positive crime against humanity, and against all science, to see a man's life long work vanish through a cruel twist of fate."

He put his hand on an unmarked door. He looked down at her. "I am sorry for everything that has happened to you. You deserve more than fate has decreed, but there are more important issues at stake here. A great scientist shouldn't have to be relegated to the scrap heap by every new discovery. Jase didn't understand that. My work is too important. Too many people depend on me. I have to protect them."

There were flickers of tears in his eyes. "I am truly, very, very sorry about this."

She didn't stop to shout what was screaming in her head, *You killed Jase!* She turned instantly to run, to get away, before he killed her.

He turned the doorknob. Behind the door, there was a heavy click. She reached for her controls, but there was no escape.

The magnetic pulse was intense. She was slapped instantly against the concrete ceiling of the tunnel. The harsh actinic light of the discharging capacitors across the switch was the last thing she saw before everything went black.

70

A gunshot echoed through the tunnel. It shook her into a dull awareness. Her head was one sharp ache.

"Stop right there! You are under arrest."

"Officer! I am so glad you are here. There has been a terrible accident. I'm afraid this young girl has killed herself."

There was the sound of handcuffs clicking shut.

"No! You don't understand! She was just..."

Davis barked, "Shut up, and listen! 'You have the right to remain silent...'"

Another wave of pain came over her, and she whimpered.

"Look! She is alive?" There was a note of incredulity in Hausman's voice. "You, wait right here."

Strong hands turned her over. Officer Davis directed his flashlight into her eyes. "You may have a concussion. Stay where you are."

Jenny felt the gritty surface beneath her hand. "No. I have to get up. I will get dirty."

"Stay put."

She pushed up. It was easy. "I have to go. I have to give a paper."

She looked at Hausman, his forearm bleeding, sitting against the wall. "You killed Jase."

He glared at her, hatred oozing out with his blood. But he said nothing.

She turned to Officer Davis, "He killed Jase."

"A jury will decide that. Right now, the both of you need medical attention. Stay put. My radio doesn't work down here, but there was a phone just a little ways back."

She shook her head. "No, I have to get to the presentation."

He put his hand on her arm. "Forget it. You are staying right here!"

"You will take your hand off of her!" The sharp words echoed down the corridor. Shawn walked towards them, holding a pipe in his hand. Blood matted the side of his face.

Officer Davis turned his gun towards Shawn. "You will put that down, right now, no argument."

Shawn looked at the gun, and then at his hand, and nodded. The pipe rang the tunnel with echoes.

But he repeated, just as stridently. "You will take your hand off of her, right now!"

Davis looked at him evenly, then nodded, and released his grip.

Shawn walked unevenly to her side, and she gratefully reached for his arms.

"Watch the blood," he warned. She nodded.

"We have to get to the presentation," she said.

"Okay."

"No you don't! You two will stay put until I say different."

Shawn looked over at the policeman, still holding his gun.

"That man," he pointed at Hausman, "hit me over the head with the intent to kill. I will swear it in court. He is your murderer."

Davis nodded. "I believe you are right. But both you and she are material witnesses, and there are some serious questions you both have to answer."

Shawn forced himself a little taller. "*You* don't understand. We must be at the presentation hall in five minutes! If we don't make it, then you will be investigating our deaths before too long. Do you even have an idea what is at stake here?"

Davis inclined his head. "Maybe I do."

"Then you just might have a hint how much money will be lost by important people if she makes her speech. If he," he pointed at Hausman, "would stoop to triple murder just to protect his academic empire, what makes you think people with real money at stake would do any different.

"When Jenny talks, the secret is out, and we are safe."

Davis looked sullen. "Crimes have been committed, and I do have the right to hold you."

Shawn almost shouted, "Oh be smart! You know as well as I do that you can only hold the people who leave you evidence."

Davis blinked.

Shawn continued. "You have nothing on us, and everything we did was to protect ourselves. We can prove that to a court, and more importantly, we can prove it to the media."

He nodded down to the girl in his protective embrace. "Do you even have an idea who this is?

"Jenny Quinn is going to be the most famous scientist in the entire world, for some time to come. School children will write reports about her life for centuries. She is going to be the most famous media celebrity of the year—she already is, you know that.

"And you, Officer Davis, just saved her life! We know it, and we aren't afraid to say so."

Jenny battled her ringing headache enough to nod. "Yes."

Shawn continued, "So be smart! You've got the bad guy. You're the hero. Let us go do what we have to do!"

Davis sighed, and waved them on, his gun still in his hand. He turned his full attention back to the man on the ground.

Shawn started leading her back the way they came.

"I ... I don't know the way." She felt lost, in more ways than one.

"I'll get you there. I saw a map."

They were slightly late, and Jenny had her head clear quite a bit on the walk over. Shawn ducked into a restroom to clean off the blood on his head.

Jenny touched the back of her head, and winced at the little blood clot there. Shawn's improvements in her flight suit had saved her life. The controls had been in the dampening position when Hausman's boobytrapped door had closed the switch. The super intense magnetic field was intended to throw her against the ceiling with enough force to crush her skull. He would have come out on the stage and report her untimely accident, however he had thought to spin it, and turn the center of attention from her to him.

But the silver wired coils surrounding her body were set to short themselves out. It was a classic magnetic shield. Hausman's pulse had enveloped the wiring in her suit, and that wiring had put up a strong reverse magnetic field in resistance. She had certainly been slammed against the ceiling, but it had not been fatal. Not like it had been when Hausman had used the same trick to kill his old friend Jason Williams.

Jase, why did you have to confide in the one man who would kill to protect his branch of academia from your discovery?

For Hausman would certainly lose everything. Decades of big money had been spent chasing plasma confinement fusion power. He had seen the potential of something like Shawn's little perpetual motion machine, churning out free power, radiation-free power, for all time. His life's work had been turned to dust.

"Pixie dust."

The man at the edge of the stage turned to face her, "Are you ... yes you are! I recognize you. Where is Hausman?"

"He will be late."

"Uh. Okay. There is some disturbance in the back, but we should be able to start any minute. Do you have any cue for the video? "

"Video?"

"Yes, the clip where you are measuring the gap under the chamber. Fascinating stuff."

The camcorder tapes Jase had made that first day! Hausman had them all along.

"Uh, no, I will just have to say 'start the video.' Can you present these transparencies for me?"

He smiled, "Can do."

She glanced back, and Shawn was waiting in the wings. He nodded and gave her an encouraging smile.

Okay. She took a deep breath. *You've done your homework. It's show time.*

She stepped up to the podium, but most of the audience had their attention focused on an argument going on at the rear entrance. One group was trying to keep another group out.

That's Daddy! He was in his power suit, working with a like-dressed group at his side. The group trying to come in looked military. At least a couple of them were in uniform, but she couldn't tell the details from that distance.

The military are going to shut me up, or at least try. It was one of her more common worries.

"Well not today!"

She grabbed the podium microphone and unclipped it from the boom, and reached for her belt.

"EXCUSE ME!" her voice echoed strongly out over the crowd, and every eye turned toward her.

She was floating ten feet above the stage, and jaws dropped.

As television cameras and lights turned from the fight at the rear to center on her, she said calmly, "I have strong sentimental reasons for giving this presentation here, at the university, where I have been trained, and where I have been given such wonderful support—but if there is such strong objection, I could certainly take this outside..."

There was a united shout, and angry voices were turned towards the combatants at the back.

"Come on, speak!" "Speak." Encouragement then turned towards her, and she eased herself down to the podium, and nodded to the man with the transparencies, and took a deep breath.

"I thank God I have been given this chance to be here today. I want to tell you of new science, and a new type of matter, revealed by the ground breaking work of the late Dr. Jason Williams."

She didn't remember, afterwards, exactly what she said. It was recorded, and she marveled at how smoothly it sounded, but she blamed her concussion for the gaps.

There were problems, of course. Early in the presentation a number of people were disturbed by the differences between the paper on the screen and the advance handout that they had received.

Hausman's work. He had re-written her draft paper, and his paper clearly gave himself primary credit for William's work. He was listed as primary author, and while she was credited, only the three of them were on the author list. With both Jase and her dead, he would have been in complete control of the discovery.

Shawn quickly located the copies her mother had made, and distributed them among the audience.

When she went to the video, more of Hausman's work was evident. Clips of his smiling face were edited into the tape Jase and she had made that fateful day, giving the impression he had been there in the middle of everything.

She tried not to think about that, as the old familiar voice of her mentor played out the speakers. Jase excitedly described the lifting of the vacuum chamber, and the progression of the dark matter.

Speak well, Jase. This is your discovery.

She had tears in her eyes when the clip ended, and the lights turned back to her.

"I think... I think you will all agree," she said, "that this discovery of Williams' Matter is a pivotal event in modern physics."

There was a murmur of agreement in the audience.

It was probably just the concussion, but just for an instant, she thought she saw him in the audience, giving her a thumbs-up salute and a smile, but she blinked, and the illusion was gone.

As she finished, Shawn was up by her side. He knew which way she should move, to avoid the mob, and she was grateful for his lead.

Her father pushed through the collection of professors, reporters, and other lawyers. "You did great!" He had to shout to be heard over the noise.

"Sorry about the confusion at the beginning. Luckily, TEC realized that if the military managed to serve their gag order, then their money was gone as well. They sent me a troop of lawyers to bar the door." Another man grabbed Mr. Quinn and pulled close to say something in his ear. He waved reassuringly at her, and then headed off with the other man.

Shawn pointed towards one wall. Her mother, plainly overwhelmed by all the people, had found shelter next to a multimedia cabinet. Jenny paused.

"We can't stop here," Shawn said. "Stick with me."

"I will." Jenny waved to her mother and got a smile and a wave back.

They made it to the side hallway, and as they approached the exterior door, Shawn put a hand on her shoulder. "There are more reporters out there. Are you up to it?"

She nodded. "If you stay with me."

"I'll be with you forever." He opened his mouth, as if to say more, but he looked uncertain.

She felt her heartbeat pick up.

He gave her a timid grin, and started to say something a second time, and failed.

"Does your head still hurt?" It was the only thing she could think of to say. Other than a concussion, there was only one thing she could think of that would turn him incoherent like that. And she wanted it to be true.

He finally shook his head, "No. I'm fine. It's just ... now that you are famous. Do you think you could...."

She put her palm across his mouth to stop the words.

"There is a problem." In three short, severe sentences, she told him of her medical worries. She could not risk sex. She could not risk a child while her body was still contaminated with the dark matter.

He listened, and nodded. As she lowered her hand, he smiled, "We will work it out!"

Epilog

It took three years.

"Ladies and Gentlemen," the minister concluded. "It is my great honor to present Mrs. Genevieve and Mr. Shawn Breaker."

The auditorium erupted with the applause and congratulations of three thousand people.

Shawn, her husband, held her hand tightly, and the ultra-white of her wedding costume and the absolute black of his made a striking contrast.

He whispered, "Are you ready?"

She nodded, and together, they lifted off of the stage. The crowd noise rose to a still higher pitch. As, still hand in hand, they began their slow exit processional, a flight over the heads of their friends, families, and well wishers.

"Good luck, Jen," called her father, her mother tightly at his side. She waved.

It feels different, she thought, now that the pixie dust was contained in her flight suit, instead of in her body. *It is better this way.* In the third row, she spotted Dr. Merrel, and blew him a kiss. The last three full-body scans under the NMR showed no sign of sprinkle clusters. *It is a good thing to be the first person to be cured of Tinkerbell's Syndrome.*

There were more relatives in the crowd than she had imagined she had. With the money they had these days, it was nothing to fly everyone here. She gave Shawn's hand a squeeze. She could still rib him about his lower position than her on the Fortune list. The university had finally settled, unable to turn down the offer of 4% of Pixie Dust Enterprises, Inc. The TEC, with it's 7% share was expanding like mad, and would probably be the world's leading energy producer by the end of the year. They were consuming almost all of pixie dust made. *And every generator they build has to pay us royalties.*

TEC and the university had been furious when they realized that their claims only covered the original vacuum chamber process, one that had yet to produce a single sprinkle of pixie dust. The real money came from the corporation's patents, and the pixie dust being bred in their plants. They only had one competitor, an aggressive group that had tracked every step of the time she had been contaminated and bought every bathroom she had visited while in hiding, scavenging every trace of pixie dust she had left behind.

But even they have to pay the patent fees.

Out of the wings, four brightly costumed figures rose, carrying congratulatory banners. She waved at the Western Circuses performers. She had heard they were in negotiations with Ringling Brothers. Western was in good shape, the only live entertainers with enough cash to buy flight suits.

There they are! She waved down at Helen and Jim and little Abbe cuddled between them.

And there is Dennis! She directed Shawn's attention to the distinguished old man, standing proudly, with the help of his prototype no-weight medical harness hidden under his suit, waving at them with his good hand. They waved back. H, standing at his side, looked strong and proud in his Western livery.

Mandrake was there with Betty, of course. No one knew what he was doing with his money. The couple still drove everywhere in that truck of his, and had successfully resisted the trappings of wealth.

She turned her head from side to side, trying to wave at everyone.

So many people in headbands. People magazine had credited her with the fashion trend of headbands in formal wear, but she still wasn't used to seeing it on other people.

They reached the end of the auditorium, and on cue, the large windows started opening.

"Let's go."

She nodded, and they rose, climbing through the opening into the sunlight.

If the crowd in the auditorium was packed, the crowd outside was unbounded. She immediately got a bright spotlight in the eye. The news crews had been restricted inside, just a handful, and existing-light cameras only. Out here, it seemed the national media had the locals outnumbered three to one.

There was an orchestrated squeal of female voices off to the left.

She shook her head. "Your fan club is at it again." Not that she could blame them. It wasn't often that one of the richest men in the world was as young and good looking as Shawn.

But you can't have him.

"Oh, no. They got to my car," he said.

She looked, and yes indeed there were long banners secured to his pride and joy.

Shawn started the little impellers on his belt. She started hers, and they turned towards the car's mooring mast.

The hand-buffed cherry-red speedster, open topped and capable of a top speed of 200 miles per hour in open air was known to everyone who subscribed to Popular Mechanics, Popular Science, Motor Trend or any of the other boys-with-toys magazines. Jenny thought it was a little silly when Shawn had first sketched out the little sports flyer, after all, she would have preferred a personal space ship.

But after six months of sunset flights with Shawn, where they could duck into the nearest cloud when they really needed some privacy, she loved the thing.

Just not quite as much as he did.

"Wait a second," she said, before he could start to rip off the ornaments. "Let them alone until we get some distance. It's just our friends."

"If you say so," he grumbled.

They settled into the seats, fastened their belts and turned off their suits.

"Now wave to your public."

He grunted, and pushed the button that released the tether's magnetic tip and reeled it in. They started waving to the crowd fifty feet below, as Shawn pulled away, accelerating and climbing. It wasn't a minute later that the banners began pulling free from where they were taped.

Jenny relaxed in her seat. "Are we there yet?"

He patted her hand, then leaned forward to glare at the console.

"Problem?" she asked.

"Eyes."

She sighed, and looked back where the city was starting to lose distinctness in the haze. There were two dark spots, rapidly growing in size. She looked at Shawn, "Are you going to dodge them?"

He grinned. "Nope."

She looked back again, and the spherical aerial camera platforms were already close enough to make out the colors of their respective news organizations. "This is too much. I wish you had never invented them."

He nodded, but opened the little keypad on the dash, and typed in a command.

Suddenly, like a double crack of thunder, they were both gone.

"What happened? Did they blow up?"

Shawn closed the keypad with a satisfied snap. "Nope. But isn't it amazing that they both had catastrophic power supply overloads at exactly the same instant. I don't think they will reach outer space, but at the rate they left, I am not sure."

"Shawn Breaker, did you leave a trap door in their system software?" She tried to sound stern, but she had a problem with the edges of her mouth.

He put his hand on his chest, "Me? I'm a model of public decency. Didn't you read my write-up in Time?

"But anyway, we are here."

"Saved by the bell."

He steered the speeder around the peaks of some lower cumulus clouds and there it was—a castle in the air, four stories tall, complete with turrets and a drawbridge and portcullis. The only thing it lacked was ground underneath.

Shawn put the speeder down on the landing pad before the gate, and locked the mooring cable.

Jenny stepped out and walked to the railing to look out over the clouds and the ground far below.

"Where will we be tomorrow?" she asked lazily.

"Wherever the winds take us." He moved up beside her, and took her into his arms. "Wherever the winds take us."

THE END

Small Towns, Big Ideas

Six titles, and more are coming. This series that appeals to age 12 and up by Henry Melton is available now. Starting in the here and now, these tales follow the trials of high school aged heros that take that extra step into the fantastic when something unexpected drops into their lives. Many of the classic science fiction ideas like teleportation, alien contact and time travel are explored in a way totally accessible to many readers who "don't read that kind of stuff" as well as being an exciting adventure for those who do.

Henry Melton is often on the road with his wife Mary Ann, a nature photographer. From the Redwood forests to Death Valley to the Great Lakes to Delaware swamps to the African bush, scenes out the windshield become locales for his fiction work. He is frequently captivated by the places he visits, and that has inspired his latest series of novels; Small Towns, Big Ideas. Check his website, HenryMelton. com for current location, his stories, a blog of his activities, and scheduled appearances. Henry's short fiction has been published in many magazines and anthologies, most frequently in Analog. Catacomb, published in Dragon magazine, is considered a classic

Falling Bakward

by Henry Melton
ISBN 978-0-9802253-6-5

Jerry Ingram wanted to be special, more than just a sixth-generation farmer in South Dakota and spent hours after school digging at the mystery spot in the back fields, searching for Indian artifacts. With Sheriff Musgrave always picking on his family and Dad always worried about money, an important discovery would be a great lift. But those bones he found weren't Indian, and when a cave-in drove him into the metal craft buried since the last ice age he found a portal to the world of the Bak, and discovered that the gentle, zebra-striped giants had been waiting for his family for thousands of years!

✌

"...just about everyone in Jerry's family has secrets...the story flows well and is easy to follow. The Bak are an engaging race, and the Kree are suitably terrifying. I can almost see this as a '50s monster movie, but with much better characterization. Lots of thrills, plenty of suspense, and widescreen action... If you're looking for YA science fiction in the sense-of-wonder vein, check out Falling Bakward." Bill Crider, author of the Sheriff Dan Rhodes series, among many other things. 3/15/09

"His writing style is much like that of Robert A. Heinlein and Isaac Asimov when they were writing what was known at the time as Juvenile Fiction...a satisfying read for adults as well... It was quite awhile before I put it down again and then only reluctantly. " Elizabeth J. Baldwin, author of Horses 3/10/09

Lighter Than Air

by Henry Melton

ISBN 978-0-9802253-1-0

Winner of the 2009 Eleanor Cameron / Golden Duck Award

It could be the best prank in the history of Munising High School's unofficial Prank Day. Working for a next door neighbor inventor had left Jon Kish with unlimited quantities of lighter-than-air foam, perfect for building...say, a full-sized flying saucer! High school honor demanded it. Plus with the family stress of his mother's surgery, he needed something to keep his mind occupied. But little sister Cherry had her own schemes in play, and events more serious than high school pranks or Mother's cancer were about to focus the world's attention on this little northern town.

❧

"Lighter Than Air is a good read for the whole family that teenagers will love from start to finish! Ample scientific facts are scattered throughout the story, thus enriching the plot and feeding the mind. It is entertaining and exciting to read" Liana Metal, Midwest Book Review 12/2008

"Melton weaves a tale of secrets and suspense, science and pranks, emotion and intrigue...the tedium of the scientific jargon is minimalized by Melton's exquisite ability to tell a story...the scene where Jon and his friend and co-conspirator, Larry, unleash their UFO on an unsuspecting Halloween Festival crowd is priceless. The scary part of the story, though, is not how the characters deal with the issue of death, but that of Internet predators...I found the possibility all too real, and you might as well." Benjamin Potter, October 13, 2008

Extreme Makeover

by Henry Melton

ISBN 978-0-9802253-2-7

Lightning brought a towering redwood crashing down around her, and something dripped on her skin. After that, high school senior Deena Brooke struggled to make sense of the impossible changes to her body. She was grateful for the interest Luther Jennings had in her puzzling insights and quirky urges, until she discovered that he was hiding a deadly secret of his own. Alien nanobots had invaded her body, an unseen influence that was changing her into something else! And was Luther helping her or dragging her into some criminal scam of his own?

❧

"I've recently read the #1 best-selling YA novel, and Henry's is much better written. It's also better paced and has a better story and better-realized characters. Trust me." Bill Crider, Author of the Sheriff Dan Rhodes series and others. 10/08/08

"The plot is quite tight and believable, and so are the characters. They are 'real' kids with their own family problems who try to solve the riddle of Deena's sudden change. It is a very exciting story from the very first page to the last one." Liana Metal, Midwest Book Review September 2008

"Once in awhile you read something that is really fun. If you pick up a Henry Melton book that's what you'll find...this is a superb example of young adult science fiction." Benjamin Potter, August 11, 2008

Roswell or Bust

by Henry Melton

ISBN 978-0-9802253-0-3

Teenager Joe Ferris was raised to help guests -- he was third generation in his family's motel business -- but once he connected with mute Judith, they were off on an epic thousand mile road trip through the Southwest, all to help the most unique guests of all -- the Roswell aliens stranded far from home since 1947. With the Men in Black hot on their trail, and discovering that the aliens had more tricks up their sleeves than their captors had ever discovered, Joe and Judith have to wonder just who is taking whom on the ride of their lives!

ᙣ

"Reading Roswell or Bust will give let you enjoy Science Fiction, even if you haven't been a big fan in the past, and will clue you into why Melton was chosen for an award from the SF community in his first outing as a novelist. It's a great escape (and not only for the aliens who've been kept captive for many decades) Benjamin Potter, April 7, 2008

"The plot is tight... A strange talkie, a mysterious courier and a couple of spies are all involved in this exciting story that will entertain kids of that age... It caters to all the family." Liana Metal, Midwest Book Review July 2008

"...whimsically amusing. The story inside is a wonderful read...His characters are real, complete with the small concerns and everyday trials... adventures are zany and compelling, keeping the reader enthralled to the end when the book can be closed with satisfaction." Ethan Rose, coauthor of Rowan of the Wood

Emperor Dad

by Henry Melton

ISBN 978-0-9802253-4-1

Winner of the 2008 Darrell Award for Best Novel.

His dad was up to something, but it wasn't until James Hill saw the theft of the British Crown Jewels live on CNN and the bizarre claims of this new Emperor of the Earth, did he realize Dad might have invented teleportation in the shed in the back yard. Bob Hill had a plan to protect the world from his disruptive invention, but when the police forces of the world move in on him, no one knew James had hacked the family computer and had taken the power of teleportation himself. Now only he could save his family, and the world.

એ

"It follows in the best tradition of other juvenile SF/action adventure novels in that it follows a young man trying to solve the usual problems that confront any young man (the search for self-identity, relationships with girls, family, and society) at the same time as he must solve the larger problems that surround him (such as whether his father is a mysterious shadowy figure branded as a global terrorist, and what to do when FBI agents show up at the door)... great job of balancing suspense and humor...no real belly laughs, but there were quite a lot of chuckles." Chris Meadows, Teleread January 7th, 2009

"It's a fast-moving SF adventure that's a lot of fun ... Cool cover." Bill Crider -- August 1, 2007

"I had a blast reading this book! With every page turned, you don't want it to end." J. Stock August 16, 2007

Golden Girl

by Henry Melton
ISBN 978-0-9802253-5-8

Debra Barr was barely out of bed when she found herself thrust into a pivotal role in the future of the human race. Plucked out of her bedroom in small town Oquawka, Illinois to a future Earth destroyed and poisoned by a major asteroid impact, the future scientists explained how she could walk a few steps differently, and with YouTube, save the planet. But everything they told her was wrong. Instead of returning to her bedroom, she appeared two hundred years in the past, in the wilderness on the banks of the Mississippi River and it was up to her to discover the rules of time travel without killing herself or anyone else in the process. Bouncing through time, only one thing was certain, anything she decided to do could mean life or death for her family and friends and the route she chose would likely cost her everything. Unfortunately, the more she discovered, the more she suspected that everyone was lying to her.

❦

Not Your Usual Time Travel Story

"Stories that give serious consideration to the issues of paradox and causality in time travel are few and far between. But Henry Melton's latest young-adult book, Golden Girl, is one that treats time travel the right way. It starts from an interesting premise, adds a unique time travel mechanic, and puts a teen-aged girl at the center of an interesting dilemma—with nothing less than the survival of the entire human race at stake!

One of the things I have always enjoyed about Henry Melton's books is that they feature intelligent, self-reliant teens who are by and large able to solve their own problems. There is nothing juvenile in how these young-adult novels are put together. Henry Melton is a master storyteller, and I will be anxiously awaiting his next work."

Chris Meadows TeleRead